Transcendental Tales
from
Isaac Asimov's
SCIENCE·FICTION·MAGAZINE

Transcendental Tales
from
Isaac Asimov's

SCIENCE·FICTION·MAGAZINE

edited by Gardner Dozois
foreword by Charles Ardai
design by Patrick Smith

**THE
DONNING COMPANY**
PUBLISHERS
NORFOLK/VIRGINIA BEACH

Copyright © 1989 by Davis Publications, Inc.

The Donning Company/Publishers
5659 Virginia Beach Boulevard
Norfolk, Virginia 23502

Library of Congress Cataloging-in-Publication Data

Transcendental Tales from Isaac Asimov's science fiction magazine /
   edited by Gardner Dozois ; foreword by Charles Ardai.
        p.   cm.
      1. Science fiction, American.   I. Dozois, Gardner R.   II. Isaac
Asimov's science fiction magazine.
PS648.S3T7   1989
813'.0876208—dc20   89-1494
                                                                 CIP
ISBN 0-89865-762-8 : $7.95

Printed in the United States of America

Table of Contents

Acknowledgements

The Editor would like to thank Cynthia Manson, who had the idea for this book in the first place; Charles Ardai, who believed in this project from the start, and contributed much invaluable research and indefatigable work, as well as writing the Foreword; Sheila Williams, who provided vital help in selecting stories, and who often played a part in the decision-making process involved in the buying of them in the first place; Rachel Darias, for help with the Foreword; Florence B. Eichin, for clearing the permissions; Susan Casper, for help with much of the thankless scut-work involved in the production of an anthology; and Stanley Hainer and Jean Campbell, who know a good project when they see one.

Foreword

Some of the oldest questions of all remain unanswered: What are we? Who are we? What is the true nature of our world, and what (if anything) lies beyond our understanding of existence? Are there powers and perceptions we cannot reach, levels of reality we do not understand?

In the past, people were persecuted for asking such questions: Galileo, for instance, was silenced for asking whether it mightn't be the case that the Earth moves around the sun, and not the other way around. Galileo was right, those who tried to silence him were wrong; but right or wrong, no one should be persecuted for seeking knowledge, for trying to find the answers to those old questions.

Today, people are free to seek new answers, rather than merely to accept the answers which have already been found. New answers are not always better than old ones, but asked questions are always better than unasked ones—and even an answer we don't completely understand is better than no answer at all. The realm of the possible, after all, is infinite.

And possibilities are what science fiction is all about. For the past ten years, Isaac Asimov's Science Fiction Magazine has been exploring these uncharted realms in fascinating, sensitive, and moving short fiction. In this collection, you will find stories by authors who have opened their minds to the entire spectrum of possibility and impossibility. For a woman seeking reunion with a deceased love, for instance, there is no choice but to go beyond the boundaries of ordinary reality; this is the story Lisa Goldstein tells in "Death Is Different." Orson Scott Card, in one of his most controversial stories, creates a new messiah whose mission is to give North America back to the Indians, in "America." Howard Waldrop brings an Egyptian pharaoh back to life in the person of a child unaware of the ancient heritage he carries within him, in "He-We-Await." Marc Laidlaw searches for a balance between the mystic and the mundane, in "Shalamari." Transcendental experiences, new perspectives on the mind, contact with spirit beings who might either protect or destroy, visions of life before birth and after death, a man who fights with ghosts, another who goes to visit God . . . you'll find them all here, realms of infinite possibility, explored by some of the most intensely curious minds of our age.

Most of all, you will find questions: What is? What can be? What is really out there? Most importantly, what unexplored possibilities are in us?

As for the answers the authors uncover . . . well, an answer can be valid or invalid, right or wrong, debatable, questionable, unprovable, credible or incredible—but the point is, you can't know which until you've asked the question. Wrong answers are everywhere; there's no such thing as a wrong question.

This anthology asks the questions.

—Charles Ardai

Charles Ardai is an anthologist and a mystery writer, author of FROM ZAIRE TO ETERNITY. He lives in New York City.

BAD MEDICINE

by Jack Dann

"Bad Medicine" was purchased by Shawna McCarthy, and appeared in the October 1984 issue of IAsfm, with an illustration by Robert McMahon. It went on to be a finalist for that year's World Fantasy Award, as well as for that year's Nebula Award. Taut and scary, the story explores the Old Ways and unknown forces which still exist everywhere on the periphery of our brightly-lit and tidily-rational modern world.

Jack Dann is one of the most respected writer/editors of his generation. His books include the critically-acclaimed novel The Man Who Melted, *as well as* Junction, Starhiker, *and a collection of his short fiction,* Timetipping. *As an anthologist, he edited the well-known anthology* Wandering Stars; *his other anthologies include* More Wandering Stars, Immortal, Faster Than Light *(co-edited with George Zebrowski), and several fantasy anthologies co-edited with Gardner Dozois. His most recent book is the acclaimed Vietnam War anthology* In The Field Of Fire, *co-edited with Jeanne Van Buren Dann. Upcoming is a new novel,* The Burning Cathedral.

Stephen was trapped in the sweaty darkness and eagles were devouring him, tearing off pieces of flesh and flapping their wings, blasting him with waves of wet searing air.

He woke up coughing, pushing his way out of the dream

and into the secure and familiar darkness of his bedroom. His wife Helen stirred beside him, then turned over, pushing her rump against him. He looked over at the digital clock on the nightstand: it was five-thirty in the morning.

He sat up in bed. He had a long drive ahead of him, and he was nervous about going. That was why he had slept fitfully during the night. It was a relief to be awake, to be *going.* The morning darkness made everything seem unreal now that he was sitting up in bed, already removed from the security of everything he knew and loved. He felt like a ghost in his own house.

Who the hell would have thought that he, of all people, would be getting into this kind of stuff? Into religion, and Indian religion at that . . . as if his own wouldn't do. Christ, being a Jew was hard *enough.* Well, he thought, if I hadn't met John, then it probably would have been something else. He was looking for *something* . . . some kind of meaning, something that rang true. An authentic religious experience. He'd smoked the pipe with John, who rented the furnished room under Stephen's real estate office, smoked it out of curiosity, or perhaps just to do something he could talk about. But when he smoked that pipe in the woods with John, he felt . . . something, something that breathed power and truth. It was as if Stephen could somehow *feel* everything the earth felt . . . he couldn't verbalize it. He still couldn't say if he really believed. But he was *willing* to believe.

He smiled to himself. He was a realtor turned mystic.

"Steve?" Helen mumbled, then, as if finding her voice, she said, "What are you doing up at this hour?"

"I told you, I'm going with John to that guy's vision-quest ceremony."

"Oh, Jesus . . . why don't you just take us to the Temple? The kids would like that. It *is* Saturday."

"We've been over this a million times," Stephen said. "I know how you feel, but this is something I want to do. Please try to understand. Think of it as a passing phase, male menopause, something like that."

She reached toward him, but he was too geared up to make love. His mind was on the ceremonies, on the vision-quest and the sweat-lodge. Some guy was going to sit naked on top of a hill without eating or drinking for four days . . . just to have a vision. Screaming for a vision, they called it. And he, Stephen, was going to sit in a sweat-lodge . . . if he could survive it.

He wished he could just make love to Helen and make everything right. But he *couldn't*. He just couldn't turn himself on and off.

She drew away from him; he knew she was hurt and angry. "First it was all that Zen-Buddhism business at the college," she said, "and then that pseudo-Jungian philosopher, that self-styled, guru, what was his name?"

Stephen winced, and shook his head. "I don't remember . . . . "

"And then there was the Transcendental Meditation kick, and that goddamn EST, which you dragged *me* into. Christ, that was the worst. They wouldn't even let you go to the bathroom during those stupid meetings. And now it's something else. Do you really believe in all this Indian business?"

"I don't know *what* I believe in."

"And I don't know why I converted . . . you don't seem to want to have anything to do with your own religion."

"We did it for the family," Stephen said lamely. Helen had always been a religious woman; she *knew* that God existed. Perhaps He'd made Himself known to her in the operating room, amidst all the cancer and broken bones and smashed skulls. She was an operating-room nurse. She had told him that it didn't matter whether she was Christian or Jewish. God was God. But Stephen shouldn't have asked her to convert. Now he had a responsibility to her which he couldn't live up to. He was a hypocrite . . . and now Helen had nothing. She wasn't comfortable in the synagogue without him; it was a foreign place to her.

"I did it for you," she said softly. She always looked the best to Stephen in the morning, her thick long black hair framing her childlike face. "I don't know what you think you can find with those Indians. I think you're getting into something dangerous. You're not an Indian."

"Just bear with me a little bit longer," Stephen said. "I feel I have to do this." He kissed her and stood up. "Go back to sleep, I'll be back tonight and we'll talk about it."

"I'll be here," Helen said, yawning. She'd been on call all last night and had only slept for a few hours. "I do love you . . . I hope you find whatever it is you're looking for . . . ."

John was waiting for him on the metal steps which led up to Stephen's real estate office. He was wearing a woolen shirt over a torn white tee-shirt, faded dungarees, worn boots, and a vest with lines of bright beads worked in geometrical patterns. He was in his early sixties, and he wore his coarse white hair long in the Indian fashion. His face was craggy and deeply-lined. That face looked as cracked and baked as the earth itself, as if it were some undecipherable roadmap of the man's past. On his lap he held a soft white and blue rolled-up blanket. Inside the blanket, protected, was his ancient pipe and an eagle's wing.

The morning light was gray, and the air was still full of the night's dampness.

John stood up when he saw Stephen, but he paused, looking at the sky as if something was written there that he couldn't read. Then he got into the car and said, "I stopped being *wrong* today." Stephen looked perplexed. "You know," John continued, and then he raised his hand to his mouth as if he were drinking from an invisible bottle. "Gonna lay off the booze. Gonna stay straight . . . I figure I owe it to Sam, the guy we're going to see, to help him out with his ceremony."

Stephen got onto Route Seventeen easily; there was hardly any traffic at this time of the morning, especially on a Saturday. Those who were going to the Catskills for the week-end had already left last night or would be leaving later today. The light fog and slanting morning sunshine gave the mountains a dreamlike appearance, as if they'd been painted by Maxfield Parrish.

John kept his window open, even though there was a chill to the air. The breeze made Stephen uncomfortable, but he didn't say anything to John. John seemed to be looking for something, for he kept leaning forward to look upwards out of the windshield. "What are you looking for?" Stephen asked.

"Eagles."

"What?" Stephen asked.

"When I became a medicine man," John explained, "I was given the gift of eagles."

"I didn't know you were a medicine man."

"A sweat-lodge man can also be a medicine man . . . and vice versa. But I'm a good sweat-lodge man; that's probably why Sam wants me to help him out with his sweat."

"You never talked about being a medicine man," Stephen said. He wasn't going to give John the chance to change the subject so easily.

"I haven't been a medicine man for a while. Booze and medicine don't mix."

"What did you do when you were a medicine man?" Stephen asked.

"Same things I do now, mostly . . . except for the drinking. I used to help people out."

"How do you mean?"

"Just help out."

"Like a doctor or a minister?"

John laughed at that. "Maybe like both."

"What do the eagles have to do with it?" Stephen asked.

"They're my medicine."

"You're talking in circles."

John chuckled, then said, "I always went on binges. My downfall was always the booze and the broads, but then I'd pray my ass off and try to be right again and sooner or later the eagles would come back, I'd look up and there'd always be one or two just circling around, way the hell up, and, man, those eagles would keep me on the straight path, keep me good, until I just couldn't stay being right and I'd go and get messed up and leave all my responsibilities behind, and I'd lose the eagles again. I haven't had them for a couple of years now, since I've been on the booze. And I've been paying for *that,* you'd better believe it. Now I'm right again, I think maybe they'll come back."

"I still don't understand," Stephen said. "Are you telling me that wherever you go, there are eagles flying around . . . even in the city?"

"I've seen them in the city . . . once. It was my first time in New York, and I was scared shitless of all those cars and concrete and people. One of the people I was with . . . we went to do some politics and ceremonies . . . pointed up to

13

the sky, and sure as shit there was an eagle making a circle. I wasn't afraid to be in that city anymore . . . I mean I was no more afraid than the next guy."

"No disrespect," Stephen said, "but I'll believe it when I see it."

"Maybe when we do the sweat . . . maybe one will fly into the sweat lodge and bite your pecker off," John said. "Then would you believe?"

Stephen laughed. "Yes, *then* I'd believe."

They reached the outskirts of Binghamton in the early afternoon. It was a clear sunny day, dry with the softest touch of fall. Stephen turned onto a rough road flanked by white cement gas stations, and they drove uphill, over a bridge that overlooked an automobile graveyard, and followed the turns as the road narrowed.

"I've been here before," John said, "so I'll remember the house."

"Is it your friends house?" Stephen asked.

"Sam's parents own it. It's a farm, and Sam is sort of living there now."

"How do you come to know him?"

"Sam came to learn some things from me when I was living in South Dakota," John said. "He was hoping to become a medicine man."

"Is he?"

"Never quite came around that way. Like most of us, he got sidetracked. Fell in with some kinds of people."

"What do you mean?" Stephen asked, slowing down for a turn. There were trees thick on both sides of the road. This was good country, gnarly and wild, and, although close to the city, thinly populated.

"He got medicine things mixed up with human things," John said. "All the people he was with were blaming everything on bad medicine instead of on themselves. When anything had happened, they thought that somebody had done something to them."

"What do you mean?" Stephen asked nervously, remembering what Helen had said to him this morning . . . that they were dangerous. Maybe he *was* getting in over his head.

"They blamed everything on sorcery."

14

"Sorcery? Do *you* believe in that?" Stephen was a non-believer, but just the idea that magic could be real, that there was more than just getting up in the morning and going to bed at night, excited him.

"Sorcery's real," John said flatly, quietly. "Medicine is just there, it can be used in good ways or bad ways. But I think that Sam just got himself messed up. He came out west for a sun dance, and stayed with me for almost a year. He started to become a pretty good sweat-lodge man, but he wanted to go too fast, he wasn't ready to be a healer, and I thought he should work and learn from someone younger for a while. So I sent him to Virginia, where a Sioux guy I know lives . . . Joseph Whiteshirt. He's a young medicine man with a good talent. Anyway, Sam needed to study in a different place. Different places have different medicine, different powers. Well . . . he ended up screwing the guy's wife and almost got himself a knife in the belly for that. Was a lot of bad blood between Sam and Whiteshirt . . . maybe some bad medicine, too. Anyway, Whiteshirt blamed me for what happened with Sam and his wife. He thought I put Sam up to it or something. Everybody got sick . . . I guess I was responsible. When they needed help, I was drinking and didn't have any power to help anybody, including myself. But that's no excuse . . . ."

"So where's this Whiteshirt now?" Stephen asked. Christ, he *was* getting into something over his head.

"He's at Sam's . . . so is his wife, they got back together."

"What?"

"There's still a lot of bad blood," John said, "but Whiteshirt has to help Sam out on his vision-quest whether he likes Sam or not . . . if he's a real medicine man. Maybe doing some ceremonies together will help them all out."

"What about you?" Stephen asked. He was nervous about this whole thing now, but he couldn't back out. He knew it was foolish, but it was a matter of male pride. Helen would have laughed at the idea of him still being macho, here in the quiche-eating eighties, but there it was.

"Maybe it'll help me out, too," John said, smiling faintly. "But then again maybe the ceremonies won't change Sam and Whiteshirt and the other people mixed up in this, maybe their hearts will stay hard. You sure you still want

15

to go along? If you're nervous, you can drop me at the house. I'll get back. No trouble.

"I came to do a sweat and Im going to do it," Stephen said.

John laughed. "Don't worry, I won't let you die in there .... You'd better start slowing down now," he said as Stephen came to another sharp curve in the road.

On Stephen's side of the car were hayfields stretching back to smooth, fir-covered hills. The fields were still green, but beginning to brown. An old cannibalized mowing machine was rusting in the middle of one of the fields. On the other side of the road, on John's side, were a few modern, expensive houses owned by executives who worked in town, but they were outnumbered by farms and the ever present country shacks, their front yards littered with old car hulks and ancient appliances, their porches filled with mildewed mattresses and torn couches and broken cabinets.

"There's the house," John said, pointing. It was red clapboard, set about fifty feet from the road. Behind it on higher ground was a dilapidated red barn and several storage sheds. The sheds were unpainted, and one was caving in.

Stephen pulled into the driveway, behind a green Ford truck, which had a poster in the rear-view window proclaiming that it was an Official Indian Car. On the back of the truck was painted AKWESASNE in large block letters.

"What does that mean?" Stephen asked.

"It's a Mowhak reservation, not far from here," John said. "It got invaded, you might say, by white folk . . . poachers, and the Indian people had it out with the state police. Sam was there, so was Whiteshirt. But there ain't no more poachers."

"What about you?" Stephen asked.

"I was home getting blind." Then, after a beat, John said, "There might be people here who are really against me . . . do you still want to come?"

"Christ, I'm already *here*." Stephen hoped he would not regret it.

"Anyway, you don't believe in any of that superstitious nonsense like we were talking about, do you?" John asked, grinning, his demeanor suddenly changed, as if he had just put on a mask, or taken one off.

"You're crazy," Stephen said. Yet he felt a chill run down the back of his neck . . . or perhaps it was just sweat.

They crossed the road and cut across a field, passing the rusting mowing machine. On the western edge of the field was woodland. They walked through the woods, which opened up into a clearing. A man in his late twenties with jet-black shoulder-length hair waved at them as they approached him.

Stephen knew it was too late to turn back now.

"Steve, this is Sam Starts-to-Dance," John said.

He doesn't *look* like an Indian, Stephen thought as he shook hands with Sam. Sam's features were fine and thin, almost nordic; but he wore a beaded shirt and a headband . . . and he did have that black hair.

"I'm glad you came," Sam said to John, as they all walked over the stones of a dry riverbed onto a well-worn path that wound up a gentle incline. "I didn't think you were going to make it."

"I told you I'd be here," John said flatly.

"We got the sweat-lodge ready," Sam said, "and the women went and got the meat; they're preparing it now. Are you going to take flesh?"

"Didn't Whiteshirt take flesh?" John asked. He stopped walking just before they reached the crest of the hill.

"He said he thought it was proper for you to do that."

John nodded. "That's good . . . how are things going? Still bad blood?"

"Whiteshirt's doing what he's supposed to," Sam said. "He's helping me to do this thing. But it feels very bad between us. Most of the people that were with him in Virginia have left. He's got new people, too many Wannabees."

"What's that?" Stephen asked.

But John laughed. "A Wannabee is a white who wants to be an Indian." Stephen felt his face grow hot. "Don't worry about that," John said.

"Anyway," Sam said, "I hear that there's some bad stuff going down there at Whiteshirt's place."

"Is he back together with Janet?" John asked.

"Yeah, she's here with him. She's taking care of the other women."

"Well . . . that's good."

"She did a lot of sweats, and vision-quested, and the spirits told her to stay with Whiteshirt and help him out. That's what she says. But it's over between us. Even though she says she doesn't love Whiteshirt, what we did was wrong. It was my fault, and you were right, it was a human thing."

"Happens," John said. "Maybe it can be put behind all of you."

"But I still think something's going on."

"Bad blood doesn't mean there has to be bad medicine," John said.

Sam didn't say anything; he looked down at the ground. Then he said, "Janet told me some things . . . that Whiteshirt blames you for what happened. He thinks you sent me to him to bring him trouble."

"Why would he think that?" John asked.

"He says the spirits told him that you were using bad medicine on him because you'd lost your power . . . because you'd stopped being a medicine man. He thinks *you're* a witch." After an awkward pause, Sam said. "I think Whiteshirt's jealous of you."

"Why?"

"Because most people come to see you when they have problems, even when you're drinking . . . most traditional Indian people don't have much respect for Whiteshirt. They call him a white man's medicine man."

"Maybe we'll talk about that," John said, "or pray about it."

"I think you should be very careful, anyway," Sam said. "Whiteshirt's changed. He's not the man you used to know."

"I'll think right about him until I see otherwise."

"I'm glad you're here," Sam said. "It's going to be right for me now, I can *feel* it."

"Well, we're soon going to find out," John said; and then he turned to Stephen and asked, "You know how Sam got his name?" John had put on another one of his masks and switched moods. "He touched a rock in the sweat-lodge once and jumped around so much that he got a new name."

"It certainly beats being called Sam Smith," Sam said, and then he went on ahead to let everyone know John was here and going to take flesh.

"Sam likes you, I can tell," John said.

"How can you tell that?" Stephen asked, distracted. He was uneasy about all this. Sam and John talked about magic as if it were a given. They didn't even question it!"

"You think he'd talk like that if he didn't?" John asked. "You can feel right about Sam."

"What's this taking flesh business?" Stephen asked. If it's what I think it is, then I *will* have to leave, he told himself. It was almost a relief to think about leaving . . . to have a valid excuse.

"You got that bad face on again," John said. "You don't have to come along on this, I told you. If you're worried and—"

"Just tell me about this flesh business. What do you do, cut somebody up?" Although he'd committed himself to trying to find God or *something* inside the burning steam of the sweat-lodge, Stephen would not stand by and watch someone get mutilated.

"It's a ceremony," John said. "It's a kind of prayer, a gift . . . the only thing we really have to give of our own is our flesh. That's the only thing that's really ours. So everyone who wants to make a gift for Sam, that he should have a good vision-quest and find what he's looking for, everyone gives a little of himself. I usually take flesh off the arm, with a needle. I don't carve out steaks, if that's what you think."

"Are you going to do this to yourself, too?"

"I might have Whiteshirt take my flesh after Sam's vision-quest is over . . . if everything is okay. But not now, people might think I was following my ego and not my heart. After the vision-quest is a good time to do that; also, there'll be lots of food, Indian food . . . a good time. You'll see . . . maybe I'll even take flesh from *you*."

"The hell you will!" Stephen said, and they walked down the hill toward the ceremonial grounds below. Stephen glanced up at the sky; there were certainly enough birds flapping around up there. Maybe some of those *were* John's eagles, swooping around, waiting for John to get to be a medicine man again.

Maybe they weren't either.

John introduced Stephen to several people, one of whom was white: a young guy with shoulder-length dirty-blond hair who was wearing a headband, faded dungarees, and a teeshirt. He asked Stephen if he wanted to smoke his pipe. Stephen politely declined and sat down under a large oak to watch John take flesh from the men and women standing around him.

Although he felt awkward and out of his depth, Stephen could not help but be awed by this place. It seemed to be completely secluded, a grotto. The sun filtered through trees, giving the place a dusty, soft quality, and the blanket of leaves on the ground made Stephen feel somehow secure here . . . and it *seemed* quiet, even though children were running around, shouting, playing games, and men and women and adolescents were all busy doing something: attending the large fire, which would heat the rocks for the sweat-lodge; tearing pieces of cloth; carrying stones and blankets; or just sitting around talking in huddled groups, passing pipes back and forth.

But sitting under that tree, feeling the cool dampness of the ground, smelling grass and sage and the burning of the fire, Stephen felt as he had when he smoked the pipe with John.

He watched John as he talked to a young woman wearing a sleeveless flower-patterned blouse. She had curly reddish hair and looked Mexican. She held John's pipe in both hands upon her lap and stared at it. Her mouth moved. She must be praying, Stephen thought. Then John began making lines down her arm with a razorblade. He gave her a yellow piece of cloth to hold in her palm, and with a needle began to remove tiny pieces of her flesh. She didn't flinch as John cut her, and Stephen noticed that she had scar-lines from previous cuttings . . . neat little indentations, pieces of flesh removed. They made Stephen think of tatoos.

To Stephen's right, about thirty feet away from him, was the sweat-lodge, a small squat, round frame of willow shoots covered with old blankets. A dark skinned woman with wiry hair pulled back from her face was piling up blankets and tarpaulins beside the lodge. About ten feet east of the sweat-lodge several men were attending a large, crackling fire, which had been prepared in a special way under the supervision of a scowling heavy-set man. Rocks for the sweat-lodge had been placed on the fire, and the heavy-set man squinted at them, as if he was reading the entrails of some sacred beast.

"These rocks should be just about ready now," one of the men shouted to John, who nodded.

Stephen just looked at the sweat-lodge nervously and wondered how the hell anybody was going to fit in there. It was so *small.*

The woman who had been piling up the blankets said something to the heavy-set man and walked over to Stephen. She couldn't have been more than five feet tall; she had a dark, flat face, high cheekbones, dark large almond eyes, and a thin mouth. She was missing a tooth, but there was a feral beauty about her; it was as if she, like John, had come from the earth. She carried a different map etched across her face, but the lines were there, even though she looked to be only in her mid-thirties. There were laugh lines and worry-lines on that face, which looked like it had never been touched by make-up. There was also a smell to her, the smell of the fire mixed with perspiration, a perfume like grass and mud, sweet and sour. "You came with John, didn't you?" she asked.

"Yes . . . although I feel like a fish out of water."

She chuckled. "I'm Janet, Joe Whiteshirt's woman. This is a good place, been some good ceremonies here, good feelings, before . . . before a lot of things turned sour and people's hearts became hard to each other. But John is a good man . . . and so was . . . is Joe. Maybe Sam's vision-quest will bring them close again. I know Sam told you about . . . us. He liked you."

"That's what John told me," Stephen said, "but you couldn't prove anything by me. He hasn't said anything to me—he was talking to John."

"Before a vision-quest is a quiet time, you're not supposed to talk much or mingle around. A vision-quest is dangerous. Sam's getting ready. Sometimes people who go up on the hill don't come back . . . people have been known to just disappear."

"Do you *believe* that?"

"Yes," Janet said, "I do."

More bullshit, Stephen thought with a sudden flash of renewed skepticism, but he kept his mouth shut about that. "Why do they do it, then?" he asked almost embarrassedly.

"We go to have a vision, sometimes find a name . . . the spirits give us things there . . . medicine. You find out who your spirits are, where you came from. Hasn't John told you *anything* about this?"

"A little," Stephen said. "I guess I never felt right about asking."

"I can see why he likes you. I once heard John tell Joe that we're like trees, all of us. But when you look at a tree you only see the trunk and branches and leaves, but deep down in the roots is where we take our life from, that's where the dreams and visions are . . . that's where our life *comes* from. That's why we vision-quest . . . to go back to the roots . . . and don't you worry while you're in the sweat, no matter how hot it gets," she said, changing the subject. She gave him a sprig of sage, pressed it into his hand. "Use this in the sweat-lodge, it'll help you breathe easier. You breathe through it like this"—and she showed him—"so you won't feel the heat so bad. It really helps."

"Thanks," Stephen said, feeling awkward.

"Everyone will take care of you," Janet continued. "No matter what's between John and Joe, neither one will let any harm come to you." But she averted her eyes from his when she said that, as if she wanted to believe it, but somehow couldn't.

"Which one is your husband?" Stephen asked. He was on edge—soon he would be in the sweat-lodge with them all, helpless.

"The big one, tending the rocks on the fire."

Stephen looked towards the fire and saw Whiteshirt, the same heavyset man he had seen before. Whiteshirt had a large belly and huge arms. His black hair was long, and for an instant, when their eyes met, Stephen felt a chill feather up his spine. The man seemed to look right through him.

"Those rocks have to be hot for the sweat-lodge; they glow like coals," Janet said.

Then there was a loud crack, and something hit the tree just above Stephen. Stephen and Janet jumped away from the tree.

"It's those damn river rocks," Janet said apologetically. "They explode sometimes like that. The next time, if there is a next time, we're going to bring our own rocks."

But Stephen had the uneasy feeling that Whiteshirt had somehow *willed* that rock to explode ... as surely and as certainly as if he had fired a warning shot from a pistol.

The women brought out bowls of raw heart and raw liver. Everyone took a piece, even the children. When it was Stephen's turn, John said, "Eat just a little. It's good for you, give you strength." Then John bit down on a large piece of raw liver.

Stephen ate a piece of the chewy, slippery meat quickly, not knowing whether he was eating heart or liver, hoping he wouldn't gag. God knows what kind of germs are crawling around on this meat, he thought. He wondered if he'd get sick on it, or develop worms ....

It was time to go into the sweat. The willow-stick skeleton of the lodge had been covered with old blankets and large tarpaulins.

John and Stephen took off their clothes behind a tree and left them in a pile. Stephen hadn't brought a towel or blanket for himself, but John got one for him. They walked around the sweat-lodge, careful not to walk between the altar and the lodge. The altar was a mound of dirt set back from the opening of the sweat-lodge; the ceremonial pipes were propped against it. John told Stephen to wait, that Janet—who was keeping the door, as he called it—would tell him when to enter. Then John crawled in through the low, narrow opening, and said, "*Pila miya,* thank you." Whiteshirt crawled in after him, but not before giving Stephen a look of pure hatred, as if he hated Stephen just because he was with John. But the others would no doubt interpret it as simply Whiteshirt's dislike for honkies. Two young whites and two Indians, who looked like brothers, followed Whiteshirt into the sweat-lodge.

Stephen stood back, feeling anxious and also foolish wrapped in a blanket and holding the sprig of sage that Janet had given him. He didn't want to sweat ... not with Whiteshirt in there.

Sam walked over to Stephen and said, "Come on, your

23

turn next." Then he smiled and said, "Don't worry, it'll be a good sweat, good ceremony. Jim and George, they're brothers, they know some old songs, and John, he's one of the best sweat-lodge men around. He says you and he are a lot alike." Sam laughed. "Both fucked up."

Stephen forced a smile and crawled into the sweat-lodge, trying not to crawl on his blanket and trying to keep it around his waist. Sage and sweetgrass had been scattered over the earthen floor, and their smell was overpowering. He already felt claustrophobic, even though the door of the lodge was still open, letting in some light. But he felt locked in—the blankets and tarpaulins and willow sticks of the sweat-lodge might as well have been made of steel. He could hear the women standing and chatting outside. They would listen to the prayers and watch for the eagles to dive out of the sky into the top of the sweat-lodge.

"Did John ever tell you about his eagles?" Sam asked Stephen in a whisper. He was sitting on John's right. "Those eagles can really be something. We've had them right here inside the sweat-lodge . . ."

What the hell am I *doing* here? Stephen asked himself as he grunted something back to Sam. He sat back against one of the willows, but the sweat-lodge was so small that he couldn't sit up straight. He looked at John, who looked back at him, but didn't say a word; then he looked at Whiteshirt, who was gazing into the pit in the center of the sweat-lodge, where the rocks would be placed. Everyone sat with his legs crossed, but even then, toes were almost touching the pit. Stephen would have to watch himself, lest he burn his feet.

There was a tension in here, palpable, growing stronger. Stephen felt a pressure on his eyes, and he looked up. He caught Whiteshirt glowering at him. Whiteshirt averted his eyes and stared once again into the pit.

But Stephen was certain that Whiteshirt was going to make trouble . . . for all of them. He felt the hair on the back of his neck rise. It was too late to get out now.

"Okay," John said, "let me have a small rock," and Janet handed in a glowing coal on the end of a shovel. John used a forked stick to push it into the hole. He asked for his pipe, which he purified over the coal. He sprinkled sweetgrass on the rock, and the sweetgrass sparkled like fireflies.

John passed the pipe around, and everyone made a prayer. Stephen just asked that he get out of here alive. Then John asked for more rocks, and Janet brought in a shovelful. John took a large rock and placed it in the center of the hole with his stick, and said *"Ho Tunkashila,"* which everyone repeated ... everyone except Whiteshirt, who seemed to be praying on his own, as if *he* had to purify the lodge himself, as if *John* was making them impure. But John ignored Whiteshirt and scraped the rocks from the shovel. Stephen could feel the heat already, and then John said, "Okay, close the door," and everything was darkness, except for the reddish glowing rocks. Every bit of light was blotted out, for the women outside stamped down the blankets whenever the men saw any light.

"Aha," John said, "we thank the rock people, the rock nation, for these good rocks which are sacred, we pray they will not break and kill us in the darkness. It is from your sacred breath, the breath of life, that we inhale, that our people will live. Oh, rocks, you have no eyes, no ears, and you cannot walk, yet you are life itself, alive as we are."

Then John explained the ceremony. He talked about how the *Inipi,* the sweat-bath, was probably the oldest ceremony in Indian religion. "The steam brings friends and families and even enemies together. It heals. It is the strongest medicine. The sweat is a way to make ourselves pure, and it gives us much of our power. No matter what the ceremony—sundance or vision-quest—we do this first. It binds us. Even though Sam here is going to vision-quest alone on the hill, we all sweat with him now. We pray together and suffer together. We'll help him now, and he'll remember when he's alone on the hill tonight facing the dreams and spirits." Everyone agreed, and there was much yeaing in the darkness. Only Whiteshirt was silent.

John prayed to the Grandfathers and the Four Directions. He prayed to *Wakan-Tanka,* he prayed for the two-leggeds and four-leggeds and wingeds and everything else on the earth, but he also seemed to be talking to God as if He were a presence in the sweat-lodge. He prayed for everyone in the sweat-lodge, for Stephen who he said was walking a different path, yet they were all walking together ...

whatever the hell that meant, Stephen thought.

But in the blackness, you couldn't tell if you were cramped in a small space, or whether you were somehow suspended in eternity. Stephen felt as if everything was being pushed up right against him, yet paradoxically, he had no sense of breadth or width or height here. He felt dizzy. He could hear the others beside him ... he could smell them. It was already getting too hot. It was difficult to breathe. He stared at the glowing rocks, and heard the water swishing in the bucket as John stirred with the dipper ... and he *felt* Whiteshirt's glowering presence, even though he couldn't see him in the dark. He felt that same pressure against his eyes and knew that Whiteshirt was watching him.

It was then that Stephen realized how frightened he was.

John prayed, but Whiteshirt was praying louder, trying to drown him out.

John poured a dipperful of water onto the rocks.

It was as if a gun had been fired. Suddenly, Stephen couldn't breathe. He was screaming, bending forward to get away from the searing steam. Everyone was shouting, *"Hi-ye, Pilamaya,* thank you, thank you," and Stephen found himself shouting, too, but he didn't know what he was saying.

He had to get out of here. He was going to die. He pressed the sage to his mouth, but it was still like breathing fire. He didn't know where he was; it was as if part of his mind knew, but another part was soaring, taking him miles into darkness, from where he might not return.

Another retort, as more water was poured on the rocks. This time, though, it didn't seem so bad. Stephen heard the brothers singing. The melody was strange and harsh and ancient; through what seemed to be a hole in Stephen's consciousness, he could hear John's prayers for them all.

"If anybody has to eliminate, that's okay," John said. "This is a place to get purified, to get out all the evil, to get all the garbage picked up from the world outside out of your system."

Stephen started coughing. He couldn't get his breath, but he heard Whiteshirt say, 'The evil's right here, *inside* the sweat-lodge."

"Well, if it is, then we'll just have to burn it right out," John said in an even, cutting voice.

George laughed at that. "Don't worry, John . . . if you get burned, I'll take over the ceremony for you."

After a pause, John said, "We came here to pray, remember? And to sweat." Then he poured water on the rocks.

Stephen felt the pain as a searing wave. He pressed his blanket to his face, trying to breathe, trying to find respite from the rising heat. After a few seconds, he could breathe again. He removed the blanket from his face and stared into the darkness. He could swear that he could see something flickering in the blackness. John would have called them spirits.

Sam handed Stephen a bucket to cool him off, and automatically Stephen ran his hands through his hair. It was hot to the touch, as if on fire. He splashed water on his face. I'm not going to last, he thought. John had told them all that if anyone had to get out to say, "All my relatives," and the door would be opened for them.

Stephen would try a little longer.

More rocks were brought in, glowing red, and Stephen burned in the darkness. But he thought he was beginning to understand something about this ceremony, that if he was going to pray—and he really wasn't sure if there *was* anyone or anything to pray to—he had to do it like this. Prayers had to be somehow *earned.* You had to go through the pain and sit with your ass in the mud like an animal.

He felt the mud beneath him. He was part of the earth. He was connected.

As the steam exploded again, Stephen thought of Helen and his children, and he started crying for them, for the pain he had caused them . . . and he hallucinated that he was not drenched in sweat, but in blood.

John told everyone not to wrap their towels and blankets around themselves, but to let the steam sink into their bodies. "The pain is good," he said as he ladled more water on the rocks. Stephen heard the hiss of steam and felt the hot blast burn over him.

"The pain is only good if it comes from the spirits," Whiteshirt said loudly, belligerently. "Only the spirits can burn away bad medicine . . . only *they* can drive a witch out of the sweat-lodge . . ."

John began to pray, as if nothing had been said, as if nothing had gone sour. "Oh, Grandfather, *Wakan-Tanka,* we're sending you a voice. Please hear us . . . pity us for we are weak. Give us the strength and wisdom so that our hearts may soften."

Whiteshirt began praying, too. But he was praying as if he was fighting. He was mocking. He was accusing. He was trying to drown out John.

But John didn't raise his voice.

The tension was electrifying the steaming, boiling darkness.

Then John decreed that the first round was over and called for the door to be opened. Janet, who looked distraught, pulled the blankets and tarpaulins away from the sweat-lodge . . . letting in the blessed light and air and a cool, chilling breeze.

John explained that this was gong to be a "hot" round. He also told everyone that this was going to be a "spirit round," and that anyone could ask the spirits for help, or ask them to answer questions, but they'd better be sure they really wanted an answer.

Then Whiteshirt said, "Just as long as it's really the spirits that's doing the talking."

John ignored the remark, as he had the others, and called for the "door" to be closed. Once again the women draped the blankets and tarpaulins over the lodge and it was pitch-dark inside.

Maybe John hadn't ignored Whiteshirt's remark, after all, for he ladled enough water onto the rocks to melt iron. Stephen buried himself in his blanket to escape the burning steam, and everyone shouted thanks.

Stephen gagged and coughed. For an instant, everything went blank. Then Stephen found himself praying and crying for his family, for every family, for everyone. He was praying and crying *because* of the heat and the pain. He believed in the spirits flickering all around him, and yet at the same time he disbelieved. Part of his mind seemed to shrink back, and he was left with the part that believed what was happening to him. He was in the center, he was praying for his own, for himself, for his family . . . and for the trees and the rocks and birds and animals and every other goddamn thing in the world. Words were *things.* They could *do* things. They could help or harm. Magic was real.

And praying was something that was as practical as cooking food.

Then he caught himself . . . he was thinking crazy.

His lungs were raw, but he wasn't coughing. He saw things in the darkness; maybe they were words or spirits or just something like the patterns you see behind your eyes when you press them hard with your palms.

One part of him saw the trails of spirits. Another part dismissed them. He was fighting with himself, believing and disbelieving, and just trying to breathe . . . to stay alive so he could get out and know that he had done it.

The spirits flickered in the dark and left trails like particles in a cloud chamber.

John poured more water onto the rocks, and everyone screamed with pain. Time seemed to slow down for Stephen, contracting hours and events into instants. In these flashing beads of time were buried hours of mistakes and cruelty, all the memories of his life. He screamed out against himself, for everything wrong he had done, for his failures as a man, as a father and a son and a husband, and he saw blood . . . he was breathing it . . . he was tasting it . . . it was the very steam itself . . . it was the rocks, which were of the same stuff, coagulated.

Then the questions began.

Everyone had a question for the spirits, and John seemed to be talking, but it wasn't quite his voice. It was somehow shrill, and it certainly wasn't John's personality. He was laughing at almost everything; he was cutting, witty, nasty. But always laughing . . . and Stephen began to believe that it really *wasn't* John who was speaking. He heard different voices, yet he didn't hear what the spirits were telling the individual people in the sweat-lodge. The words seemed mostly garbled, except for a phrase or sentence here or there. John had told him that usually happened . . . that you only heard what you were meant to hear . . . what was important for *you.* This was a private place, even with the others sitting and groaning and sweating beside you.

But when it came to Stephen's turn, he didn't ask the spirits any questions. Once the spirits gave you an answer, you had to follow what they told you to do, and Stephen wasn't taking any chances. John, however, asked for him. He seemed to appear in the middle of those spirit voices, and he asked that Stephen be helped to find himself with his family. The spirits thought that was funnier than hell, and it gave Stephen a chill to hear those laughing voices and see those flickerings in the dark. He wondered what had happened to John. He felt naked and alone. Vulnerable.

Did John just disappear? Or was he just talking funny . . . of course, *that* was it.

It was . . . and it wasn't. Something else seemed strange in Stephen's mind. Even if the flickerings and the voices were phoney, he found that he somehow didn't care. It was real even if it wasn't. That felt true, but it didn't make a bit of sense. Still . . .

Then it was Whiteshirt's turn. Stephen had blanked everyone else out, just as John had told him to do. But he was going to listen now. He supposed everyone else felt the same way because the tension returned to the darkness like a storm.

It was then that Stephen saw the coal move in the pit.

Whiteshirt picked up the glowing coal, hot as it was, and put it in his mouth. It illuminated his face in red, as if that face was hanging in the darkness, disconnected. It was as if Whiteshirt had become a spirit himself . . . or maybe the spirits were *inside* him. Whiteshirt turned toward John and grinned; the coal was clenched between his teeth, its glow illuminated the hatred and frustration and sickness on his face. Whiteshirt was making a funny keening noise as if the spirits were speaking through him.

It's a trick! Stephen thought. It's got to be . . .

Then the coal moved toward John, as if Whiteshirt were embracing him. John screamed, an animal scream of pure agony, and the smell of burning flesh pervaded the sweat-lodge.

"Open the door, for Christ's sake," Sam shouted. "All my relatives. Goddammit, open the door!"

The women pulled down the blankets and tarpaulins from the willow framework of the sweat-lodge. The light was blinding. Everyone was silent, stunned. John had fallen forward. Blood oozed from large ugly gashes in his back. It wasn't the glowing coal that had burned and cracked John's flesh; the coal was just a symbol of Whiteshirt's power. It was the heat that had torn him open . . . the heat contained in Whiteshirt's burning heart.

John groaned and sat up, shaking his head as if warding off something invisible. Whiteshirt stared at him in hard satisfaction. He didn't say a word, but his wife, Janet, applied sage moistened with her spittle to the gashes in John's back. John finched every time she touched him.

"You were wrong to do this thing," she said to her husband.

"I didn't do it," Whiteshirt said flatly. "It was the spirits."

"You were *wrong,* Janet said again, and Stephen could see in her face how much she hated this man . . . or perhaps the intensity of her hatred was fueled by love and guilt.

This can't go on," Sam said. "I'll vision-quest another time. I need to pray about all this . . . let's forget it all for now."

"No," John said, a quaver in his voice, "we're going to do the last round . . . and you're going to keep your promise to the spirits and make your vision-quest. Today. But first there's something between Joe Whiteshirt and me that has to be finished. Everybody, get out of the sweat-lodge. We're going to let the spirits decide about this bad thing that has come between us."

"The spirits *already* decided," Whiteshirt said. "They made their mark on your back. Do you want them to burn you again?

"That was *you,* Joe," John said. "So you *are* using medicine to get what you want. But you won't get it. Nobody will follow you . . . you're a witch, not a medicine man." John spoke in low, even tones, as if he were simply reciting facts. But he was trembling, exposing his rage and humiliation . . . and perhaps his fear.

"This time you'll die," Whiteshirt said. "That will be proof enough."

"We'll see . . ."

"You're not going to do this thing," Janet said to Whiteshirt, but it was already as good as done because the men were leaving the sweat-lodge.

"What's going *on?*" Stephen asked John, but John wouldn't answer him. He just nodded his head, indicating that Stephen should get out with the others.

When everyone was out, John said, "Close it up." The blankets and tarps were thrown back on the lodge, and one of the men handed in a shovelful of glowing rocks. Janet had refused to act as keeper of the door.

John asked for another shovelful ... enough for *two* rounds.

"More rocks aren't going to help you," Whiteshirt said.

John didn't answer. He was praying in Sioux.

Stephen tried to approach Sam and Janet and ask them to try and stop John and Whiteshirt from sweating. Sam just shook his head, and Janet gently told him not to interfere in matters he didn't understand. So Stephen went back to the sweat-lodge and stood with the others. An older woman in a cotton print housedress stood beside him. Every once in a while, she would nervously look up at the sky, as if watching for eagles ... waiting. Even the children were quiet. Everyone was listening, waiting to hear what was going to happen inside the sweat-lodge. There was a communal sense that what was about to happen was out of human control. The next few minutes would, indeed, be decided by the spirits.

"Close the door," John said, and the keeper of the door closed the last opening of the sweat-lodge with a tarp.

Stephen could hear John stirring the water with the aluminum ladle. Then there was a hissing of steam as John poured some water on the rocks. Both men prayed in Sioux. Once again Whiteshirt prayed louder than John, drowning him out. But then he switched to English. He called John a witch ... a spy for the white world. He blamed John for what had happened between Sam and Janet. He blamed John for sending Sam with a disease ... bad medicine, a disease that had afflicted everyone at Whiteshirt's camp. But now the spirits were gong to put things to right. He called them down from the heavens to destroy his enemy.

Whiteshirt worked himself into a frenzy.

When Whiteshirt paused to catch his breath, John said,

"Okay, we *will* let the spirits decide. We'll make this a short round." Then there was an ear-splitting cracking sound like an explosion inside the sweat-lodge. Everyone outside jumped back. John must have thrown most of the bucket onto those rocks. And right after that there was another explosion.

"You bastard," Whiteshirt screamed, "You're going to die for this."

But now John was praying . . . it was his turn to scream for the spirits. "Oh, Grandfather, *Wakan-Tanka, Tunkashila,* send down the eagle to guard the sacred pipe and the life of the People. Send *Wakinyan-Tanka,* the great thunderbird to scourge out the evil." He intoned, "Send us the one that has wings, but no shape. Send us the one that has an eye of lightning. Send us the one that has no head, yet has a beak filled with the teeth of the wolf. Send us the winged one to devour whatever is bad inside us, just as it devours its own young."

Stephen listened, his hands resting on the outside of the sweat-lodge. He heard a flapping noise like the working of wings. It sounded as if there was a huge bellows inside the sweat-lodge. The noise grew louder. Something was beating against the inside of the sweat-lodge. Stephen could hear and *feel* it slapping against the blankets and tarpaulins. It was as if a great bird was trapped in there with John and Whiteshirt, and it was thrashing its wings, beating to get out of the darkness . . . to find the cold blue of the upper air.

But that's impossible, Stephen thought, even as he felt the sweat-lodge shake.

There was scuffling inside . . . and screaming.

Then there was sudden silence.

Stephen pressed the side of his face against the rough canvas of the sweat-lodge to hear better, but all he could hear was his own heart beating in his throat . . . a tiny trapped eagle.

"Open the door," John said in a voice that was hardly more than a whisper. "It's over . . . . "

They quickly pulled the tarpaulins and blankets away from the willow frame of the sweat-lodge . . . and found John sitting by himself. He blinked in the bright sunlight.

His pipe rested on his lap. He didn't seem to notice that he was sitting stark naked, his blanket underneath him. He looked pale and drawn, as if he had just sweated away part of his life. The dead coal that had been in Whiteshirt's mouth lay in the dirt before him. It was all that was left of Whiteshirt.

Whiteshirt had disappeared . . . .

"Do you believe in the eagles now?" John asked Stephen.

Stephen could only shrug. It was all some sort of a trick, he told himself, even though the hairs on the back of his neck were still standing up. Whiteshirt couldn't have just disappeared . . . he had to have sneaked away somehow.

John smiled weakly. "Next time, maybe the eagles *will* bite your pecker off." Then he raised his head and gazed into the sky. He was still smiling.

Stephen looked uneasily upward at the eagles circling high overhead, and he thought about Helen and his children and the blood he had tasted inside the sweat-lodge. There wouldn't be a next time, he told himself. He was certain of that. He was ready to go home.

Perhaps John understood because he started laughing like a spirit. ●

OF SPACE-TIME AND THE RIVER

by Gregory Benford

"Of Space-Time And The River" was purchased by Gardner Dozois and appeared in the February 1986 issue of IAsfm, *with an evocative cover by Terry Lee (his first for us) and a striking interior illustration by Gary Freeman. It became one of the year's most popular stories — hardly surprising, as Benford is one of the modern giants of the field. His 1980 novel* Timescape *won the Nebula Award, the John W. Campbell Memorial Award, the British Science Fiction Association Award, and the Australian Ditmar Award, and is widely considered to be one of the classic novels of the last two decades. His other novels include* The Stars In Shroud, In Ocean Of Night, Against Infinity, Artifact, *and* Across The Sea Of Suns. *His most recent novels are the bestselling* Great Sky River *and* Tides Of Light. *Benford is a professor of physics at the University of California, Irvine.*

Here he takes us to the shadow of the Pyramids for an encounter with a race of enigmatic aliens who are strongly fascinated with Egypt's ancient past . . .

Dec. 5, Monday, 2048

We took a limo to Los Angeles for the 9 AM flight, LAX to Cairo.

On the boost up we went over 1.4 G, contra-reg, and a

35

lot of passengers complained, especially the poor things in their clank-shank rigs, the ones that keep you walking even after the hip replacements fail.

Joanna slept through it all, seasoned traveler, and I occupied myself with musing about finally seeing the ancient Egypt I'd dreamed about as a kid, back to the turn of the century.

If thou be'st born to strange sights,
Things invisible to see,
Ride ten thousand days and nights,
Till age snow white hairs on thee.

I've got the snow powdering at the temples and steadily expanding waistline, so I guess John Donne applies. Good to see I can still summon up lines I first read as a teenager. There are some rewards to being a Prof. of Comp. Lit. at UC Irvine, even if you do have to scrimp to afford a trip like this.

The tour agency said the Quarthex hadn't interfered with tourism at all—in fact, you hardly noticed them, they deliberately blended in so well. How a seven-foot insectoid thing with gleaming russet skin can look like an Egyptian I don't know, but what the hell, Joanna said, let's go anyway.

I hope she's right. I mean, it's been fourteen years since the Quarthex landed, opened the first diplomatic interstellar relations, and then chose Egypt as the only place on Earth where they cared to carry out what they called their "cultural studies." I guess we'll get a look at that, too. The Quarthex keep to themselves, veiling their multi-layered deals behind diplomatic dodges.

As if six hours of travel wasn't numbing enough, including the orbital delay because of an unannounced Chinese launch, we both watched a holoD about one of those new biotech guys, called *Straight From The Hearts.* An unending string of single-entendre jokes. In our stupefied state it was just about right.

As we descended over Cairo it was clear and about 15°C. We stumbled off the plane, sandy-eyed from riding ten thousand days and nights in a whistling aluminum box.

The airport was scuffy, instant third world hubbub, confusion and filth. One departure lounge was filled exclusively with turbaned men. Heavy security everywhere. No

Quarthex around. Maybe they do blend in.

Our bus across Cairo passed a decayed aqueduct, about which milled men in caftans, women in black, animals eating garbage. People, packed into the most unlikely living spots, carrying out peddler's business in dusty spots between buildings, traffic alternately frenetic or frozen.

We crawled across Cairo to Giza, the pyramids abruptly looming out of the twilight. The hotel, Mena House, was the hunting lodge-cum palace of 19th century kings. Elegant.

Buffet supper was good. Sleep came like a weight.

Dec. 6

Keeping this journal is fun. Joanna says it's good therapy for me, might even get me back into the habit of writing again. She says every Comp. Lit. type is a frustrated author and I should just spew my bile into this diary. So be it:

Thou, when thou return'st, wilt tell me

All strange wonders that befell thee.

World, you have been warned.

Set off south today—to Memphis, the ancient capital lost when its walls were breached in a war and subsequent floods claimed it.

The famous fallen Rameses statue. It looks powerful still, even lying down. Makes you feel like a pigmy tip-toeing around a giant, *a la* Gulliver.

Saqqara, principal necropolis of Memphis, survives three km. away in the desert. First Dynasty tombs, including the first pyramid, made of steps, five levels high. New Kingdom graffiti inside are now history themselves, from our perspective.

On to the Great Pyramid!—by camel! The drivers proved even more harassing than legend warned. We entered the Khefren pyramid, slightly shorter than that of his father, Cheops. All the 80 known pyramids were found stripped. These passages have a constricted vacancy to them, empty now for longer than they were filled. Their silent mass is unnerving.

Professor Alvarez from UC Berkeley tried to find hidden rooms here by placing cosmic ray detectors in the lower known rooms, and looking for slight increases in flux at certain angles, but there seem to be none. There are seismic and even radio measurements of the dry sands in the Giza region, looking for echoes of buried tombs, but no big finds so far. Plenty of echoes from ruins of ordinary houses, etc. though.

No serious jet lag today, but we nod off when we can. Handy, having the hotel a few hundred yards from the pyramids.

I tried to get Joanna to leave her wrist comm at home. Since her breakdown she can't take news of daily disasters very well. (Who can, really?) She's pretty steady now, but this trip should be as calm as possible, her doctor told me.

So of course she turns on the comm and it's full of hysterical stuff about another border clash between the Empire of Israel and the Arab Muhammad Soviet. Smart rockets vs. smart defenses. A draw. Some things never change.

I turned it off immediately. Her hands shook for hours afterwards. I brushed it off.

Still, it's different when you're a few hundred miles from the lines. Hope we're safe here.

Dec. 7

Into Cairo itself, the Egyptian museum. The Tut Ankh Amen exhibit—huge treasuries, opulent jewels, a sheer wondrous plentitude. There are endless cases of beautiful alabaster bowls, gold-laminate boxes, testifying to thousands of years of productivity.

I wandered down a musty marble corridor and then, coming out of a gloomy side passage, there was the first Quarthex I'd ever seen. Big, clacking and clicking as it thrust forward in that six-legged gait. It ignored me, of course—they nearly always lurch by humans as though they can't see us. Or else that distant, distracted gaze means they're ruminating over strange, alien ideas. Who knows why they're intensely studying ancient Egyptian ways, and ignoring the rest of us? This one was cradling a stone urn, a meter high at least. It carried the black granite in three akimbo arms, hardly seeming to notice the weight. I caught a whiff of acrid pungency, the fluid that lubricates their joints. Then it was gone.

We left and visited the oldest Coptic church in Egypt,

supposedly where Moses hid out when he was on the lam out of town. Looks it. The old section of Cairo is crowded, decayed, people laboring in every nook with minimal tools, much standing around watching as others work. The only sign of really efficient labor was a gang of men and women hauling long, cigar-shaped yellow things on wagons. Something the Quarthex wanted placed outside the city, our guide said.

In the evening we went to the Sound & Light show at the Sphinx—excellent. There is even a version in the Quarthex language, those funny sputtering, barking sounds.

Arabs say, "Man fears time; time fears the pyramids." You get that feeling here.

Afterward, we ate in the hotel's Indian restaurant; quite fine.

Dec. 8

Cairo is a city being trampled to death.

It's grown by a factor of fourteen in population since the revolution in 1952, and shows it. The old Victorian homes which once lined stately streets of willowy trees are now crowded by modern slab concrete apartment houses. The aged buildings are kept going, not from a sense of history, but because no matter how rundown they get, somebody needs them.

The desert's grit invades everywhere. Plants in the court-yards have a weary, resigned look. Civilization hasn't been very good for the old ways.

Maybe that's why the Quarthex seem to dislike anything built since the time of the Romans. I saw one running some kind of machine, a black contraption that floated two meters off the ground. It was laying some kind of cable in the ground, right along the bank of the Nile. Every time it met a building it just slammed through, smashing everything to frags. Guess the Quarthex have squared all this with the Egyptian gov't, because there were police all around, making sure nobody got in the way. Odd.

But not unpredictable, when you think about it. The Quarthex have those levitation devices which everybody would love to get the secret of. (Ending sentence with preposition! Horrors! But this is vacation, dammit.) They've been playing coy for years, letting out a trickle of technology, with the Egyptians holding the patents. That must be what's holding the Egyptian economy together, in the face of their unrelenting population crunch. The Quarthex started out as guests here, studying the ruins and so on, but now it's obvious that they have free run of the place. They *own* it.

Still, the Quarthex haven't given away the crucial devices which would enable us to find out how they do it—or so my colleagues in the physics department tell me. It vexes them that this alien race can master space time so completely, manipulating gravity itself, and we can't get the knack of it.

We visited the famous alabaster mosque. It perches on a hill called The Citadel. Elegant, cool aloofly dominating the city. The Old Bazaar nearby is a warren, so much like the movie sets one's seen that it has an unreal, Arabian Nights quality. We bought spices. The calls to worship from the mosques reach you everywhere, even in the most secluded back rooms where Joanna was haggling over jewelry.

It's impossible to get anything really ancient, the swarthy little merchants said. The Quarthex have bought them up, trading gold for anything that might be from the time of the Pharaohs. There have been a lot of fakes over the last few centuries, some really good ones, so the Quarthex have just bought anything that might be real. No wonder the Egyptians like them, let them chew up their houses if they want. Gold speaks louder than the past.

We boarded our cruise ship, the venerable *Nile Concorde.* Lunch was excellent, Italian. We explored Cairo in mid afternoon, through markets of incredible dirt and disarray. Calf brains displayed without a hint of refrigeration or protection, flies swarming, etc. Fun, especially if you can keep from breathing for five minutes or more.

We stopped in the Shepheard Hotel, the site of many Brit spy novels (Maugham especially). It has an excellent bar— Nubians, Saudis, etc. putting away decidedly non-Islamic gins and beers. A Quarthex was sitting in a special chair at the back, talking through a voicebox to a Saudi. I couldn't tell what they were saying, but the Saudi had a gleam in his eye. Driving a bargain, I'd say.

Great atmosphere in the bar, though. A cloth banner over the bar proclaims,
Unborn tomorrow and dead yesterday,
why fret about them if today be sweet.
Indeed, yes, ummm—bartender!

Dec. 9, Friday, Moslem holy day

We left Cairo at 11 P.M. last night, the city gliding past our stateroom windows, lovelier in misty radiance than in dusty day. We cruised all day. Buffet breakfast & lunch, solid Eastern and Mediterranean stuff, passable red wine.

A hundred meters away, the past presses at us, going about its business as if the pharaohs were still calling the tune. Primitive pumping irrigation, donkeys doing the work, women cleaning gray clothes in the Nile. Desert ramparts to the east, at spots sending sand fingers—no longer swept away by the annual flood—across the fields to the shore itself. Moslem tombs of stone and mud brick coast by as we lounge on the top deck, peering at the madly waving children through our binoculars, across a chasm of time.

There are about fifty aboard a ship with capacity of a hundred, so there is plenty of room and service as we sweep serenely on, music flooding the deck, cutting between slabs of antiquity; not quite decadent, just intelligently sybaritic. (Why so few tourists? Guide says people are maybe afraid of the Quarthex. Joanna gets jittery around them, but I don't know whether that's her old fears surfacing again).

The spindly, ethereal minarets are often the only grace note in the mud-brick villages, like a lovely idea trying to rise out of brown, mottled chaos. Animal power is used everywhere possible. Still, the villages are quiet at night. The flip side of this peacefulness must be boredom. That explains a lot of history and its rabid faiths, unfortunately.

Dec. 10

Civilization thins steadily as we steam upriver. The mud-brick villages typically have no electricity; there is ample power from Aswan, but the power lines and stations are too expensive. One would think that, with the Quarthex gold, they could do better now.

Our guide says the Quarthex have been very hard-nosed—no pun intended—about such improvements. They will not let the earnings from their patents be used to modernize Egypt. Feeding the poor, cleaning the Nile, rebuilding monuments—all fine (in fact, they pay handsomely for restoring projects). But better electricity—no. A flat no.

We landed at a scruffy town and took a bus into the western desert. Only a kilometer from the flat floodplain, the Sahara is utterly barren and forbidding. We visited a Ptolemaic city of the dead. One tomb has a mummy of a girl who drowned trying to cross the Nile and see her love, the hieroglyphics say. Nearby are catacombs of mummified baboons and ibises, symbols of wisdom.

A tunnel begins here, pointing SE toward Akhenaton's capital city. The German discoverers in the last century followed it for 40 kilometers—all cut through limestone, a gigantic task—before turning back because of bad air.

What was it for? Nobody knows. Dry, spooky atmosphere. Urns of dessicated mummies, undisturbed. To duck down a side corridor is to step into mystery.

I left the tour group and ambled over a low hill—to take a leak, actually. To the west was sand, sand, sand. I was standing there, doing my bit to hold off the dryness, when I saw one of those big black contraptions come slipping over the far horizon. Chuffing, chugging and laying what looked like pipe—a funny kind of pipe, all silvery, with blue facets running through it. The glittering shifted, changing to yellows and reds while I watched.

A Quarthex riding atop it, of course. It ran due south, roughly parallel to the Nile. When I got back and told Joanna about it she looked at the map and we couldn't figure what would be out there of interest to anybody, even a Quarthex. No ruins around, nothing. Funny.

Dec. 11

Beni Hassan, a nearly deserted site near the Nile. A steep walk up the escarpment of the eastern desert, after crossing the rich flood plain by donkey. The rock tombs have fine drawings and some statues—still left because they were cut directly from the mountain, and have thick wedges securing them to it. Guess the ancients would steal anything not nailed down. One thing about the Quarthex, the guide says—they take nothing. They seem genuinely interested in restoring, not in carting artifacts back home to their neck of the galactic spiral arm.

Upriver, we landfall beside a vast dust plain, which we crossed in a cart pulled by a tractor. The mud brick palaces of Akhenaton have vanished, except for a bit of Nefertiti's palace, where the famous bust of her was found. The royal tombs in the mountain above are defaced—big chucks pulled out of the walls by the priests who undercut his monotheist revolution, after his death.

The wall carvings are very realistic and warm; the women even have nipples. The tunnel from yesterday probably runs under here, perhaps connecting with the passageways we see deep in the king's grave shafts. Again, nobody explored them thoroughly. There are narrow sections, possibly warrens for snakes or scorpions, maybe even traps.

While Joanna and I are ambling around, taking a few snaps of the carvings, I hear a rustle. Joanna has the flashlight and we peer over a ledge, down a straight shaft. At the bottom something is moving, something damned big.

It takes a minute to see that the reddish shell isn't a sarcophagus at all, but the back of a Quarthex. It's planting sucker-like things to the walls, threading cables through them. I can see more of the stuff further back in the shadows.

The Quarthex looks up, into our flashlight beam, and scuttles away. Exploring the tunnels? But why did it move away so fast? What's to hide?

Dec. 12

Cruise all day and watch the shore slide by.

Joanna is right; I needed this vacation a great deal. I can see that, rereading this journal—it gets looser as I go along.

As do I. When I consider how my life is spent, ere half my days, in this dark world and wide ...

The pell-mell of university life dulls my sense of wonder, of simple pleasures simply taken. The Nile has a flowing, infinite quality, free of time. I can *feel* what it was like to live here, part of a great celestial clock that brought the perpetually turning sun and moon, the perennial rhythm of the flood. Aswan has interrupted the ebb and flow of the waters, but the steady force of the *Nile* rolls on.

Heaven smiles, and faiths and empires gleam.

Like wrecks of a dissolving dream.

The peacefulness permeates everything. Last night, making love to Joanna, was the best ever. Magnifique!

(And I know you're reading this, Joanna—I saw you sneak it out of the suitcase yesterday! Well, it *was* the best—quite a tribute, after all these years. And there's tomorrow and tomorrow . . .)

He who bends to himself a joy

Does the winged life destroy;

But he who kisses the joy as it flies

Lives in eternity's sunrise.

Perhaps next term I shall request the Romantic Poets course. Or even write some of my own . . .

Three Quarthex flew overhead today, carrying what look like ancient rams-head statues. The guide says statues were moved around a lot by the Arabs, and of course the archaeologists. The Quarthex have negotiated permission to take many of them back to their rightful places, if known.

Dec. 13

Landfall at Abydos—a limestone temple miraculously preserved, with its thick roof intact. Clusters of scruffy mud huts surround it, but do not diminish its obdurate rectangular severity.

The famous list of pharaohs, chiseled in a side corridor, is impressive in its sweep of time. Each little entry was a lordly pharaoh, and there are a whole wall jammed full. Egypt lasted longer than any comparable society, and the mass of names on that wall is even more impressive, since the temple builders did not even give it the importance of a central location.

The list omits Hatchepsut, a mere woman, and Akhenaton the scandalous monotheist. Rameses II had all carvings here cut deeply, particularly on the immense columns, to forestall defacement—a possibility he was much aware of, since he was busily doing it to his ancestors' temples. He chiseled away earlier work, adding his own cartouches, apparently thinking he could fool the gods themselves into believing he had built them all himself. Ah, immortality.

Had an earthquake today. Shades of California!

We were on the ship, Joanna was dutifully padding back and forth on the main deck to work off the opulent lunch. We saw the palms waving ashore, and damned if there wasn't a small shock wave in the water, going east to west, and then a kind of low grumbling from the east. Guide says he's never seen anything like it.

And tonight, sheets of ruby light rising up from both east and west. Looked like an aurora, only the wrong directions. The rippling aura changed colors as it rose, then met overhead, burst into gold, and died. I'd swear I heard a high, keening note sound as the burnt-gold line flared and faded, flared and faded, spanning the sky.

Not many people on deck, though, so it didn't cause much comment. Joanna's theory is, it was a rocket exhaust.

An engineer says it looks like something to do with magnetic fields. I'm no scientist, but it seems to me whatever the Quarthex want to do, they can. Lords of space/time, they called themselves in the diplomatic ceremonies. The United Nations representatives wrote that off as hyperbole, but the Quarthex may mean it.

Dec. 14

Dendera. A vast temple, much less well known than Karnak, but quite as impressive. Quarthex there, digging at the foundations. Guide says they're looking for some secret passageways, maybe. The Egyptian gov't is letting them do what they damn well please.

On the way back to the ship, we pass a whole mass of people, hundreds, all dressed in costumes. I thought it was some sort of pageant or tourist foolery, but the guide frowned, saying he didn't know what to make of it. The mob was chanting something even the guide couldn't make out. He said the rough-cut cloth was typical of the old ways, made on crude spinning wheels. The procession was ragged, but seemed headed for the temple. They looked drunk to me.

The guide tells me that the ancients had a theology based on the Nile. This country is essentially ten kilometers wide and seven hundred kilometers long, a narrow band of liveable earth pressed between two deadly deserts. So they

believed the gods must have intended that, and the Nile
was the center of the whole damned world.

The sun came from the east, meaning that's where things
began. Ending—dying—happened in the west, where the
sun went. Thus they buried their dead on the west side of
the Nile, even 7000 years ago. At night, the sun swung below
and lit the underworld, where everybody went finally. Kind
of comforting, thinking of the sun doing duty like that for
the dead. Only the virtuous dead. though. If you didn't
follow these rules ...

Some are born to sweet delight,
Some are born to endless night.

Their world was neatly bisected by the great river,
and they loved clean divisions. They invented the 24 hour
day but, loving symmetry, split it in half. Each of the 12
daylight hours was longer in summer than in winter—
and, for night, vice versa. They built an entire nation-
state, an immortal hand or eye, framing such fearful
symmetry.

On to Karnak itself, mooring at Luxor. The middle and
late pharaohs couldn't afford the labor investment for
pyramids, so they contented themselves with additions to
the huge sprawl at Karnak.

I wonder how long it will be before someone rich notices
that for a few million or so he could build a tomb bigger
than the Great Pyramid. It would only take a million or so
limestone blocks—or much better, granite—and could be
better isolated and protected. If you can't conquer a conti-
nent or scribble a symphony, then pile up a great stack of
stones.

L'eternité,
ne fut jamais perdue.

The light show this night at Karnak was spooky at times,
and beautiful, with booming voices coming right out of the
stones. Saw a Quarthex in the crowd. It stared straight
ahead, not noticing anybody but not bumping into any
humans, either.

It looked enthralled. The beady eyes, all four, scanned
the shifting blues and burnt-oranges that played along the
rising-columns, the tumbled great statues. Its lubricating
fluids made shiny reflections as it articulated forward,

clacking in the dry night air. Somehow it was almost rever-
ential. Rearing above the crowd, unmoving for long moments, it seemed more like the giant frozen figures in stone
than like the mere mortals who swarmed around it, keeping
a respectful distance, muttering to themselves.

Unnerving, somehow, to see
... a subtler Sphinx renew
Riddles of death Thebes never knew.

Dec. 15

A big day. The Valleys of the Queens, the Nobles, and
finally of the Kings. Whew!

All are dry washes (wadis), obviously easy to guard and
isolate. Nonetheless, all of the 62 known tombs except Tut's
were rifled, probably within a few centuries of burial.

It must've been an inside job.

There is speculation that the robbing became a needed
part of the economy, recycling the wealth, and providing
gaudy displays for the next pharaoh to show off at *his*
funeral, all the better to keep impressing the peasants. Just
another part of the socio-economic machine, folks.

Later priests collected the pharaoh mummies and hid
them in a cave nearby, realizing they couldn't protect the
tombs. Preservation of Tuthmosis III is excellent. His hook-
nosed mummy has been returned to its tomb—a big, deep
thing, larger than our apartment, several floors in all,
connected by ramps, with side treasuries, galleries, etc. The
inscription above reads *You shall live again forever.*

All picked clean, of course, except for the sarcophagus,
too heavy to carry away. The pyramids had portcullises,
deadfalls, pitfalls, and rolling stones to crush the unwary
robber, but there are few here. Still, it's a little creepy to
think of all those ancient engineers, planning to commit
murder in the future, long after they themselves are gone,
all to protect the past.

Death, be not proud.

An afternoon of shopping in the bazaar. The old Victorian hotel on the river is atmospheric, but has few guests.
Food continues good. No dysentery, either. We both took
the EZ-Di bacteria before we left, so it's living down in our
tracts, festering away, lying in wait for any ugly foreign bug.

Comforting.

Dec. 16

Cruise on. We stop at Kom Ombo, a temple to the crocodile god, Sebek, built to placate the crocs who swarmed in
the river nearby. (The Nile is cleared of them now, unfortunately; they would've added some zest to the cruise ...)
A small room contains 98 mummified crocs, stacked like
cordwood.

Cruised some more. a few km. south, there were gangs
of Egyptians working beside the river. Hauling blocks of
granite down to the water, rolling them on logs. I stood on
the deck, trying to figure out why they were using ropes and
simple pulleys, and no powered machinery.

Then I saw a Quarthex near the top of the rise, where the
blocks were being sawed out of the rock face. It reared up
over the men, gesturing with those jerky arms, eyes glittering. It called out something in a half-way human voice, only
in a language I didn't know. The guide came over, frowning,
but he couldn't understand it, either.

The laborers were pulling ropes across ruts in the stone,
feeding sand and water into the gap, cutting out blocks by
sheer brute abrasion. It must take weeks to extract one at
that rate! Further along, others drove wooden planks down
into the deep groves, hammering them with crude wooden
mallets. Then they poured water over the planks, and we
could hear the stone pop open as the wood expanded, far
down in the cut.

That's the way the ancients did it, the guide said kind
of quietly. The Quarthex towered above the human teams,
that jangling, harsh voice booming out over the water, each
syllable lingering until the next joined it, blending in the
dry air, hollow and ringing and remorseless.

note added later

Stopped at Edfu, a well-preserved temple, buried 100
feet deep by Moslem garbage until the late 19th century.
The best aspect of river cruising is pulling along a site, viewing it from the angles the river affords, and then stepping
from your stateroom directly into antiquity, with nothing
to intervene and break the mood.

Trouble is, this time a man in front of us goes off a way to photograph the ship, and suddenly something is rushing at him out of the weeds and the crew is yelling—it's a crocodile! The guy drops his camera and bolts.

The croc looks at all of us, snorts, and waddles back into the Nile. The guide is upset, maybe even more than the fellow who almost got turned into a free lunch. Who would reintroduce crocs into the Nile?

Dec. 17

Aswan. A clean, delightful town. The big dam just south of town is impressive, with its monument to Soviet excellence, etc. A hollow joke, considering how poor the USSR is today. They could use a loan from Egypt!

The unforeseen side effects, though—rising water table bringing more insects, rotting away the carvings in the temples, rapid silting up inside the dam itself, etc.—are getting important. They plan to dig a canal and drain a lot of the incoming new silt into the desert, make a huge farming valley with it, but I don't see how they can drain enough water to carry the dirt, and still leave much behind in the original dam.

The guide says they're having trouble with it.

We then fly south, to Abu Sembel. Lake Nasser, which claimed the original site of the huge monuments, is hundreds of miles long. They enlarged it again in 2008.

In the times of the pharaohs, the land below these waters had villages, great quarries for the construction of monuments, trade routes south to the Nubian kingdoms. Now it's all underwater.

They did save the enormous temples to Rameses II—built to impress aggressive Nubians with his might and majesty—and to his queen, Nefertari. The colossal statues of Rameses II seem personifications of his egomania. Inside, carvings show him performing *all* the valiant tasks in the great battle with the Hittites—slaying, taking prisoners, then presenting them to himself, who is in turn advised by the gods—which include himself! All this, for a battle which was in fact an iffy draw. Both temples have been lifted about a hundred feet and set back inside a wholly artificial hill, supported inside by the largest concrete dome in the world. Amazing.

"Look upon my works, ye Mighty, and despair!"
Except that when Shelley wrote *Ozymandias,* he'd never
seen Rameses II's image so well preserved.

Leaving the site, eating the sand blown into our faces by
a sudden gust of wind, I caught sight of a Quarthex. It was
burrowing into the sand, using a silvery tool that spat ruby-
colored light. Beside it, floating on a platform, where some
of those funny pipe-like things I'd seen days before. Only
this time men and women were helping it, lugging stuff
around to put into the holes the Quarthex dug.

The people looked dazed, like they were sleep-walking
or something. I waved a greeting, but nobody even looked
up. Except the Quarthex. They're expressionless, of course.
Still, those glittering popeyes peered at me for a long moment, with the little feelers near its mouth twitching with
a kind of anxious energy.

I looked away. I couldn't help but feel a little spooked
by it. I mean, it wasn't looking at us in a friendly way.
Maybe it didn't want me yelling at its work gang.

Then we flew back to Aswan, above the impossibly narrow ribbon of green that snakes through absolute bitter
desolation.

Dec. 18

I'm writing this at twilight, before the light gives out. We
got up this morning and were walking into town when the
whole damn ground started to rock. Mud huts slamming
down, waves on the Nile, everything.

Got back to the ship but nobody knew what was going
on. Not much on that radio. Cairo came in clear, saying
there'd been a quake all right, all along the Nile.

Funny thing was, the captain couldn't raise any other
radio station. Just Cairo. Nothing else in the whole Middle
East.

Some other passengers think there's a war on. Maybe so,
but the Egyptian army doesn't know about it. They're
standing around, all along the quay, fondling their A-K 47s,
looking just as puzzled as we are.

More rumblings and shakings in the afternoon. And now that the light's about gone, I can see big sheets of light in the sky. Only it seems to me the constellations aren't right.

Joanna took some of her pills. She's trying to fend off the jitters and I do what I can. I hate the empty, hollow look that comes into her eyes.

We've got to get the hell out of here.

Dec. 19

I might as well write this down, there's nothing else to do.

When we got up this morning the sun was there all right, but the moon hadn't gone down. And it didn't all day.

Sure, they can both be in the sky at the same time. But all day? Joanna is worried, not because of the moon, but because all the airline flights have been cancelled. We were supposed to go back to Cairo today.

More earthquakes. Really bad this time.

At noon, all of a sudden, there were Quarthex everywhere. In the air, swarming in from the east and west. Some splashed down in the Nile—and didn't come up. Others zoomed overhead, heading south toward the dam.

Nobody's been brave enough to leave the ship—including me. Hell, I just want to go home. Joanna's staying in the cabin.

About an hour later, a swarthy man in a ragged gray suit comes running along the quay and says the dam's gone. Just *gone*. The Quarthex formed little knots above it, and there was a lot of purple flashing light and big crackling noises, and then the dam just disappeared.

But the water hasn't come pouring down on us here. The man says it ran *back the other way.* South.

I looked over the rail. The Nile was flowing north.

Late this afternoon, five of the crew went into town. By this time there were fingers of orange and gold zapping across the sky all the time, making weird designs. The clouds would come rolling in from the north, and these radiant beams would hit them, and they'd *split* the clouds, just like that. With a spray of ivory light.

And Quarthex, buzzing everywhere. There's a kind of high sheen, up above the clouds, like a metal boundary or something, but you can see through it.

Quarthex keep zipping up to it, sometimes coming right up out of the Nile itself, just splashing out, then zooming up until they're little dwindling dots. They spin around up there, as if they're inspecting it, and then they drop like bricks, and splash down in the Nile again. Like frantic bees, Joanna said, and her voice trembled.

A technical type on board, an engineer from Rockwell, says he thinks the Quarthex are putting on one hell of a light show. Just a weird alien stunt, he thinks.

While I was writing this, the five crewmen returned from Aswan. They'd gone to the big hotels there, and then to police headquarters. They heard the TV from Cairo went out two days ago. All air flights have been grounded because of the Quarthex buzzing around and the odd lights and so on.

Or at least, that's the official line. The Captain says his cousin told him that several flights *did* take off two days back, and they hit something up there. Maybe that blue metallic sheen?

Anyway, one crashed. The others landed, even though damaged.

The authorities are keeping it quiet. They're not just keeping us tourists in the dark—they're playing mum with everybody.

I hope the engineer is right. Joanna is fretting and we hardly ate anything for dinner, just picked at the cold lamb. Maybe tomorrow will settle things.

Dec. 20

It did. When we woke, we went up on deck and watched the Earth rise.

It was coming up from the western mountains, blue-white clouds and patches of green and brown, but mostly tawny desert. We're looking west, across the Sahara. I'm writing this while everybody else is running around like a chicken with his head cut off. I'm sitting on deck, listening to shouts and wild traffic and even some gunshots coming from ashore.

I can see further east now—either we're turning, or we're rising fast and can see with a better perspective.

Where central Egypt was, there's a big, raw, dark hole.

The black must be the limestone underlying the desert. They've scraped off a rim of sandy margin enclosing the Nile valley, including us—and left the rest. And somehow, they're lifting it free of Earth.

No Quarthex flying around now. Nothing visible except that metallic blue smear of light high up in the air.

And beyond it—Earth, rising.

Dec. 22

I skipped a day.

There was no time to even think yesterday. After I wrote the last entry, a crowd of Egyptians came down the quay, shuffling silently along, like the ones we saw back at Abu Simbel. Only there were thousands.

And leading them was a Quarthex. It carried a big disc thing that made a humming sound. When the Quarthex lifted it, the pitch changed.

It made my eyes water, my skull ache. Like a hand squeezing my head, blurring the air.

Around me, everybody was writhing on the deck, moaning. Joanna, too.

By the time the Quarthex reached our ship I was the only one standing. Those yellow-shot, jittery eyes peered at me, giving nothing away. Then the angular head turned and went on. Pied piper, leading long trains of Egyptians.

Some of our friends from the ship joined at the end of the lines. Rigid, glassy-eyed faces. I shouted but nobody, not a single person in that procession, even looked up.

Joanna struggled to go with them. I threw her down and held her until the damned eerie parade was long past.

Now the ship's deserted. We've stayed aboard, out of pure fear.

Whatever the Quarthex did affects all but a few percent of those within range. A few crew stayed aboard, dazed but okay. Scared, hard to talk to.

Fewer at dinner.

The next morning, nobody.

We had to scavenge for food. The crew must've taken what was left aboard. I ventured into the market street nearby, but everything was closed up. Deserted. Only a few days ago we were buying caftans and alabaster sphinxes and beaten-bronze trinkets in the gaudy shops, and now it was stone cold dead. Not a sound, not a stray cat.

I went around to the back of what I remembered was a filthy corner cafe. I'd turned up my nose at it while we were shopping, certain there was a sure case of dysentery waiting inside ... but now I was glad to find some days-old fruits and vegetables in a cabinet.

Coming back, I nearly ran into a bunch of Egyptian men who were marching through the streets. Spooks.

They had the look of police, but were dressed up like Mardi Gras—loincloths, big leather belts, bangles and beads, hair stiffened with wax. They carried sharp spears.

Good thing I was jumpy, or they'd have run right into me. I heard them coming and ducked into a grubby alley. They were systematically combing the area, searching the miserable apartments above the market. The honcho barked orders in a language I didn't understand—harsh, guttural, not like Egyptian.

I slipped away. Barely.

We kept out of sight after that. Stayed below deck and waited for nightfall.

Not that the darkness made us feel any better. There were fires ashore. Not in Aswan itself—the town was utterly black. Instead, orange dots sprinkled the distant hillsides. They were all over the scrub desert, just before the ramparts of the real desert that stretches—or did stretch—to east and west.

Now, I guess, there's only a few dozen miles of desert, before you reach—what?

I can't discuss this with Joanna. She has that haunted expression, from the time before her breakdown. She is drawn and silent. Stays in the room.

We ate our goddamn vegetables. Now we go to bed.

Dec. 23

There were more of those patrols of Mardi Gras spooks today. They came along the quay, looking at the tour ships moored there, but for some reason they didn't come aboard.

We're alone on the ship. All the crew, the other tourists—all gone.

But that's not the big news. Around noon, when we were getting really hungry and I was mustering my courage to go back to the market street, I heard a roaring.

Understand, I hadn't heard an airplane in days. And those were jets. This buzzing, I suddenly realized, is a rocket or something, and it's in trouble.

I go out on the deck, checking first to see if the patrols are lurking around, and the roaring is louder. It's a plane with stubby little wings, coming along low over the water, burping and hacking and finally going dead quiet.

It nosed over and came in for a big splash. I thought the pilot was a goner, but the thing rode steady in the water for a while and the cockpit folded back and out jumps a man.

I yelled at him and he waved and swam for the ship. The plane sank.

He caught a line below and climbed up. An American, no less. But what he had to say was even more surprising.

He wasn't just some sky jockey from Cairo. He was an astronaut.

He was part of a rescue mission, sent up to try to stop the Quarthex. The others he'd lost contact with, although it looked like they'd all been drawn down toward the floating island that Egypt has become.

We're suspended about two Earth radii out, in a slowly widening orbit. There's a shield over us, keeping the air in and everything—cosmic rays, communications, space-ships—out.

The Quarthex somehow ripped off a layer of Egypt and are lifting it free of Earth, escaping with it. Nobody had ever guessed they had such power. Nobody Earthside knows what to do about it. The Quarthex who were outside Egypt at the time just lifted off in their ships and rendezvoused with this floating platform.

Ralph Blanchard is his name, and his mission was to fly under the slab of Egypt, in a fast orbital craft. He was supposed to see how they'd ripped the land free. A lot of it had fallen away.

There are an array of silvery pods under the soil, he says, and they must be enormous anti-grav units. The same kind that make the Quarthex ships fly, and that we've been trying to get the secret of.

The pods are about a mile apart, making a grid. But between them, there are lots of Quarthex. They're building stuff, tilling soil and so on—upside down! The gravity works opposite on the underside. That must be the way the whole thing is kept together—compressing it with artificial gravity from both sides. God knows what makes the shield above.

But the really strange thing is the Nile. There's one on the underside, too.

It starts at the underside of Alexandria, where *our* Nile meets—met—the Mediterranean. It then flows back, all the way along the underside, running through a Nile valley of its own. Then it turns up and around the edge of the slab, and comes over the lip of it a few hundred miles upstream of here.

The Quarthex have drained the region beyond the Aswan dam. Now the Nile flows in its old course. The big temples of Rameses II are perched on a hill high above the river, and Ralph was sure he saw Quarthex working on the site, taking it apart.

He thinks they're going to put it back where it was, before the dam was built in the 1960s.

Ralph was supposed to return to Orbital City with his data. He came in close for a final pass and hit the shield they have, the one that keeps the air in. His ship was damaged.

He'd been issued to suborbital craft, able to do reentries, in case he could penetrate the airspace. That saved him. There were other guys who hit the shield and cracked through, guys with conventional deep-space shuttle tugs and the like, and they fell like bricks.

We've talked all this over but no one has a good theory of what is going on. The best we can do is stay away from the patrols.

Meanwhile, Joanna scavenged through obscure bins of the ship, and turned up an entire case of Skivaa, a cheap Egyptian beer. So after I finished this ritual entry—who knows, this might be in a history book someday, and as a good academic I should keep it up—I'll go share it out in one grand bust with Ralph and Joanna. It'll do her good.

She's been rocky. As well,
   Malt does more than Milton can
   To justify God's ways to man.

Dec. 24

This little diary was all I managed to take with us when the spooks came. I had it in my pocket.

I keep going over what happened. There was nothing I could do, I'm sure of that, and yet . . .

We stayed below decks, getting damned hungry again but afraid to go out. There was chanting from the distance. Getting louder. Then footsteps aboard. We retreated to the small cabins aft, third class:

The sounds got nearer. Ralph thought we should stand and fight but I'd seen those spears and hell, I'm a middle-aged man, no match for those maniacs.

Joanna got scared. It was like her breakdown. No, worse. The jitters built until her whole body seemed to vibrate, fingers digging into her hair like claws, eyes squeezed tight, face compressed as if to shut out the world.

There was nothing I could do with her, she wouldn't keep quiet. She ran out of the cabin we were hiding in, just rushed down the corridor screaming at them.

Ralph said we should use her diversion to get away and I said I'd stay, help her, but then I saw them grab her and hold her, not rough. It didn't seem as if they were going to do anything, just take her away.

My fear got the better of me then. It's hard to write this. Part of me says I should've stayed, defended her—but it was hopeless. You can't live up to your ideal self. The world of literature shows people summoning up courage, but there's a thin line between that and stupidity. Or so I tell myself.

The spooks hadn't see us yet, so we slipped overboard, keeping quiet.

We went off the loading ramp on the river side, away from shore. Ralph paddled around to see the quay and came back looking worried. There were spooks swarming all over.

We had to move. The only way to go was across the river. This shaky handwriting is from sheer, flat out fatigue.

I swam what seemed like forever. The water wasn't bad, pretty warm, but the current kept pushing us off course. Lucky thing the Nile is pretty narrow there, and there are rocky little stubs sticking out. I grabbed onto those and rested.

Nobody saw us, or at least they didn't do anything about it.

We got ashore looking like drowned rats. There's a big hill there, covered with ancient rock-cut tombs. I thought of taking shelter in one of them and started up the hill, my legs wobbly under me, and then we saw a mob up there.

And a Quarthex, a big one with a shiny shell, It wore something over its head, too. Supposedly Quarthex don't wear clothes, but this one had a funny rig on. A big bird head, with a long narrow beak and flinty black eyes.

There was madness all around us. Long lines of people carrying burdens, chanting. Quarthex riding on those lifter units of theirs. All beneath the piercing, biting sun.

We hid for a while. I found that this diary, in its zippered leather case, made it through the river without a leak. I started writing this entry. Joanna said once that I'd retreated into books as defense, in adolescence. She was full of psychoanalytical explanations—it was a hobby. She kept thinking that if she could figure herself out, then things would be all right. Well, maybe I did use words and books and a quiet, orderly life as a place to hide. So what? It was better than this "real" world around me right now.

I thought of Joanna and what might be happening to her. The Quarthex can—

New Entry
I was writing when the Quarthex came closer. I thought we were finished, but they didn't see us. Those huge heads turned all the time, the glittering black eyes scanning. Then they moved away. The chanting was a relentless, singsong drone that gradually faded.

We got away from there, fast

I'm writing this short break. Then we'll move on.

No place to go but the goddman desert.

Dec. 25

Christmas.

I keep thinking about fat turkey stuffed with spicy dressing, crisp cranberries, a dry white wine, thick gravy—

No point in that. We found some food today in an abandoned construction site, bread at least a week old and some dried-up fruit. That was all.

Ralph kept pushing me on west. He wants to see over the edge, how they hold this thing together.

I'm not that damn interested, but I don't know where else to go. Just running on blind fear. My professional instincts—like keeping this journal. It helps keep me sane. Assuming I still am.

Ralph says putting this down might have scientific value. If I can even get it to anybody outside. So I keep on. Words, words, words. Much cleaner than this gritty, surreal world.

We saw people marching in the distance, dressed in loincloths again. It suddenly struck me that I'd seen that clothing before—in those marvelous wall paintings, in the tombs of the Valley of Kings. It's ancient dress.

Ralph thinks he understands what's happening. There was an all frequencies broadcast from the Quarthex when they tore off this wedge we're on. Nobody understood much—it was in that odd semi-speech of theirs, all the words blurred and placed wrong, scrambled up. Something about their mission or destiny or whatever being to enhance the best in each world. About how they'd made a deal with the Egyptians to bring forth the unrealized promise of their majestic past and so on. And that meant isolation, so the fruits of ages could flower.

Ha. The world's great age begins anew, maybe—but Percy Bysshe Shelley never meant it like this.

Not that I care a lot about motivations right now. I spent the day thinking of Joanna, still feeling guilty. And hiking west in the heat and dust, hiding from gangs of glassy-eyed workers when we had to.

We reached the edge at sunset. It hadn't occurred to me, but it's obvious—for there to be days and nights at all means they're spinning the slab we're on.

Compressing it, holding in the air, adding just the right rotation. Masters—of space/time and the river, yes.

The ground started to slope away. Not like going downhill, because there was nothing pulling you down the face of it. I mean, we *felt* like we were walking on level ground. But overhead the sky moved as we walked.

We caught up with the sunset. The sun dropped for a while in late afternoon, then it started rising again. Pretty soon it was right overhead, high noon.

And we could see Earth, too, farther away than yesterday. Looking cool and blue.

We came to a wall of glistening metal tubes, silvery and rippling with a frosty blue glow. I started to get woozy as we approached. Something happened to gravity—it pulled your stomach as if you were spinning around. Finally we couldn't get any closer. I stopped, nauseated. Ralph kept on. I watched him try to walk toward the metal barrier, which by then looked like luminous icebergs suspended above barren desert.

He tried to walk a straight line, he said later. I could see him veer, his legs rubbery, and it looked as though he rippled and distended, stretching horizontally while some force compressed him vertically, an egg man, a plastic body swaying in tides of gravity.

Then he started stumbling, falling. He cried out—a horrible, warped sound, like paper tearing for a long, long time. He fled. The sand clawed at him as he ran, strands grasping at his feet, trailing long streamers of glittering, luminous sand—but it couldn't hold him. Ralph staggered away, gasping, his eyes huge and white and terrified.

We turned back.

But coming away, I saw a band of men and women marching woodenly along toward the wall. They were old, most of them, and diseased. Some had been hurt—you could see the wounds.

They were heading straight for the lip. Silent, inexorable.

Ralph and I followed them for a while. As they approached, they started walking up off the sand—right into the air.

And over the tubes.

Just flying.

We decided to head south. Maybe the lip is different there. Ralph says the plan he'd heard, after the generals had studied the fast survey mission results, was to try to open the shield at the ground, where the Nile spills over. Then they'd get people out by boating them along the river.

Could they be doing that, now? We hear roaring sounds in the sky sometimes. Explosions. Ralph is ironic about it all, says he wonders when the Quarthex will get tired of intruders and go back to the source—*all* the way back.

I don't know. I'm tired and worn down.

Could there be a way out? Sounds impossible, but it's all we've got.

Head south, to the Nile's edge.

We're hiding in a cave tonight. It's bitterly cold out here in the desert, and a sunburn is no help.

I'm hungry as hell. Some Christmas.

We were supposed to be back in Laguna Beach by now.

God knows where Joanna is.

Dec. 26

I got away. Barely.

The Quarthex work in teams now. They've gridded off the desert and work across it systematically in those floating platforms. There are big tubes like cannon mounted on each end and a Quarthex scans it over the sands.

Ralph and I crept up to the mouth of the cave we were in and watched them comb the area. They worked out from the Nile. When a muzzle turned toward us I felt an impact like a warm, moist wave smacking into my face, for all the world like being in the ocean. It drove me to my knees. I reeled away. Threw myself further back into the cramped cave.

It all dropped away then, as if the wave had pinned me to the ocean floor and filled my lungs with a sluggish liquid.

And in an instant was gone. I rolled over, gasping, and saw Ralph staggering into the sunlight, heading for the Quarthex platform. The projector was leveled at him so that it no longer struck the cave mouth. So I'd been released from its grip.

I watched them lower a rope ladder. Ralph dutifully climbed up. I wanted to shout to him, try to break the hold that thing had over him, but once again the better part of valor and all that—I just watched. They carried him away.

I waited until twilight to move. Not having anybody to

talk to makes it harder to control my fear.

God, I'm hungry. Couldn't find a scrap to eat.

When I took out this diary I looked at the leather case and remembered stories of people getting so starved they'd eat their shoes. Suitably boiled and salted, of course, with a tangy sauce.

Another day or two and the idea might not seem so funny. I've got to keep moving.

Dec. 27

Hard to write.

They got me this morning.

It grabs your mind. Like before. Squeezing in your head.

But after a while it is better. Feels good. But a buzzing all the time, you can't think.

Picked me up while I was crossing an arroyo. Didn't have any idea they were around. A platform.

Took me to some others. All Egyptians. Been caught like me.

Marched us to the Nile.

Plenty to eat.

Rested at noon.

Brought Joanna to me. She is all right. Lovely in the long draping dress the Quarthex gave her.

All around are the bird-headed ones. Ibis, I remember, the bird of the Nile. And dog-headed ones. Lion-headed ones.

Gods of the old times. The Quarthex are the gods of the old time. Of the great empire.

We are the people.

Sometimes I can think, like now. They sent me away from the work gang on an errand. I am old, not strong. They are kind—give me easy jobs.

So I came to here. Where I hid this diary. Before they took my old uncomfortable clothes I put this little book into a crevice in the rock. Pen too.

Now writing helps. Mind clears some.

I saw Ralph, then lost track of him. I worked hard after the noontime. Sun felt good. I lifted pots, carried them where the foreman said.

The Quarthex-god with ibis head is building a fresh temple. Made from the stones of Aswan. It will be cool and deep, many pillars.

They took my dirty clothes. Gave me fresh loincloth, headband, sandals. Good ones. Better than my old clothes.

It is hard to remember how things were before I came here. Before I knew the river. Its flow. How it divides the world.

I will rest before I try to read what I have written in here before. The words are hard.

days later

I come back but can read only a little.

Joanna says You should not. The ibis will not like if I do.

I remember I liked those words on paper, in my days before. I earned my food with them. Now they are empty. Must not have been true.

I do not need them any more.

Ralph and his science. It was all words too.

later

Days since I find this again. I do the good work, I eat, Joanna is there in the night. Many things. I do not want to do this reading.

But today another thing howled overhead. It passed over the desert like a screaming black bird, the falcon, and then fell, flames, big roar.

I remembered Ralph.

This book I remembered, came for it.

The ibis-god speaks to us each sunset. Of how the glory of our lives is here again. We are one people once more again yes after a long long time of being lost.

What the red sunset means. The place where the dead are buried in the western desert. To be taken in death close to the edge, so the dead will walk their last steps in this world, to the lip and over, to the netherworld.

There the lion-god will preserve them. Make them live again.

The Quarthex-gods have discovered how to revive the dead of any beings. They spread this among the stars.

But only to those who understand. Who deserve. Who bow to the great symmetry of life.

One face light, one face dark.

The sun lights the netherworld when for us it is night. There the dead feast and mate and laugh and live forever.

Ralph saw that. The happy land below. It shares the sun.

I saw Ralph today. He came to the river to see the falcon thing cry from the clouds. We all did.

It fell into the river and was swallowed and will be taken to the netherworld where it flows over the edge of the world.

Ralph was sorry when the falcon fell. He said it was a mistake to send it to bother us. That someone from the old dead time had sent it.

Ralph works in the quarry. Carving the limestone. He looks good, the sun has lain on him and made him strong and brown.

I started to talk of the time we met but he frowned.

That was before we understood, he says. Shook his head. So I should not speak of it I know.

The gods know of time and the river. They know.

I tire now.

again

Joanna sick. I try help but no way to stop the bleeding from her.

In old time I would try to stop the stuff of life from leaving her. I would feel sorrow.

I do not now. I am calm.

Ibis-god prepares her. Words hard and good over her.

She will journey tonight. Walk the last trek. Over the edge of the sky and to the netherland.

It is what the temple carving says. She will live again forever.

Forever waits.

I come here to find this book to enter this. I remember sometimes how it was.

I did not know joy then. Joanna did not.

We lived but to no point. Just come-go-come-again.

Now I know what comes. The western death. The rising life.

The Quarthex-gods are right. I should forget that life. To hold on is to die. To flow forward is to life.

Today I saw the pharaoh. He came in radiant chariot,

black horses before, bronze sword in hand. The sun was high above him. No shadow he cast.

Big and with red skin the pharaoh rode down the avenue of the kings. We the one people cheered.

His great head was mighty in the sun and his many arms waved in salute to his one people. He is so great the horses groan and sweat to pull him. His hard gleaming body is all armor for he will always be on guard against our enemies.

Like those who fall from the sky. Everyday now more come down, dying fireballs to smash in the desert. All fools. Black rotting bodies. None will rise to walk west. They are only burned prey of the pharaoh.

Pharoh rode three times on the avenue. We threw ourselves down to attract a glance. His huge glaring eyes regarded us and we cried out, our faces wet with joy.

He will speak for us in the netherworld. Sing to the undergods.

Make our westward walking path smooth.

I fall before him.

I bury this now. No more write in it.

This kind of writing is not for the world now. It comes from the old dead time when I knew nothing and thought everything.

I go to my eternity on the river. ●

DEATHBINDER

by Alexander Jablokov

"Deathbinder" was purchased by Gardner Dozois and appeared in the February 1988 issue of IAsfm, with a powerful illustration by Nicholas Jainschigg. With only a handful of elegant, cooly-pyrotechnic stories, like the one that follows, Jablokov has established himself as a headliner with the magazine's readers, and is regarded as one of the most promising new writers in SF. He lives in Somerville, Massachusetts, and is currently working as co-editor of a projected anthology of "Future Boston" stories being put together by the Cambridge Writer's Workshop. He has just completed work on his first novel.

Shakespeare said, "but in that sleep of death, who knows what dreams may come?" In the chilling story that follows, Jablokov shows us what dreams may come—and it's a revelation you'll never forget.

The El station platform was empty, and the winter Chicago Sunday afternoon had turned into night. Stanley Paterson paused at the turnstile and rubbed his nose doubtfully. The overhead lamps cast circular pools of light on the gouged surface of the platform, but this made Stanley feel obvious, rather than safe. He hunched his shoulders inside his wool topcoat, puffed out his cheeks, and shuffled along the platform, looking down the tracks in the direction of the expected train. His mind was still full of the financial affairs of a medium-sized Des Moines metals trading company which was slated for acquisition. It was a big project, worth working weekends for, so, aside from the inside of his condominium, the inside of his office, and the inside of various El trains, he no longer knew what anything looked like. Winter had somehow arrived without an intervening autumn. He'd been to Oak St. Beach once, near the end of the summer, he remembered. Or had that been last year?

The wind blew dried leaves past him; delicately curved, ribbed, and textured leaves. He felt himself among them, heavy and gross, and thought about going on a diet. It was tough when you worked as hard as he did, he thought, excusing himself. It was hell on your eating habits. Today he'd eaten—what? He couldn't remember. The coat slapped his legs. The skin by his nose was oily, there was an itch under his right shoulder blade, and he was hungry. He wondered what he could put in the microwave when he got home. What did he have left in the freezer? Chinese? Chicken Kiev? Hell, he'd see when he got there. High above him floated the lighted windows of the city, rank upon rank, like cherubim.

The turnstile clattered. Stanley tried to tell himself that it was ridiculous to feel afraid, even in the dark, alone on the platform, but succeeded only in feeling afraid and ridiculous, both. He leaned forward, looking again for the train, trying to pull it into the station by the force of his gaze, but the tracks remained empty. He glanced towards the turnstile. A man stood there, a shadow. He didn't look like a big man, and his race was not obvious, but he wore a hat, which looked like leather. Respectable people did not wear hats, Stanley felt. Particularly not leather ones. It looked too silly. The man turned, and with slow, confident steps, walked towards Stanley.

Stanley thought about running, but didn't. It would have made him feel like a fool. He rocked back on his heels, hands in his pockets, and ignored the other. He tried to project an air of quiet authority. The platform on the other side of the tracks was completely empty.

He never saw it, but he felt the knife press, sharp, against his side, just above the right kidney. There was, somehow, no doubt whatsoever about what it was.

"Your money."

"Excuse me? I—"

"Your money."

The knife cut through the expensive fabric of his coat and grazed his flesh. Stanley felt a surge of annoyance at the wanton damage. Spontaneously, unthinkingly, like a tripped mousetrap, Stanley cried out and hit the man in the face with a balled fist, remembering only at the last second not to put his thumb inside his fingers. It was like striking out in sleep, but he did not awaken, as he usually did, sweat-soaked and tangled in sheets. Instead, the dark cold night remained around him, and as the man stumbled back, Stanley grappled with him, and tried to get his hands around his throat. He really was a small man, much smaller than he had expected, and he couldn't remember why he had been so frightened of him. The knife blade twisted, and Stanley felt it penetrate flesh. A scream cut the night. There was suddenly a warm glow in Stanley's belly, which spread up through his chest. He felt dizzy, and flung his suddenly weightless assailant across the platform, seeing him whirl tiny, tiny away, joining the leaves in their dance, then vanishing back through the turnstile, which clattered again. Blackness loomed overhead like a tidal wave and blotted out the lights of the windows. The dark heaviness knocked Stanley down on to the platform, and he heard a wailing sound, like sirens, or a baby crying. He rested on the platform, which had become as soft as a woman's breast. It was late, he was tired, and the train did not seem to want to come, so he decided to take a well-deserved nap.

The scream of the nurse, who had come in to check Margaret's pulse, but found, when she pulled back the blankets, that her patient had turned into a mass of giant black bats which burst up from the rumpled sheets to fill the bedroom with the fleshy beating of their wings, became the shrill ring of the telephone. Matthew Harmon woke up with a shock, jerked the cord until the phone fell on the bed, and cradled the receiver under his ear.

"Dr. Harmon," the voice on the phone said. A simple, flat

statement, as if someone had decided to call in the middle of the night to wake him up and reassure him about his identity. Harmon felt a surge of irritation, and knew he was once again alive. He reached up and turned on the bedside lamp, which cast a pool of light over the bed. He did not look at the other half of the bed, but he could hear Margaret's labored breathing there. She muttered something like "Phone, Matt ... phone," then choked, as if having a heart seizure. There were no bats, at least.

"Yes?" he said. "What is it?" His throat hurt again, and his voice was husky.

A pause. "I was asked to make this call. Against my better judgement ... it's information I don't think you should have. But," a deep sigh, "it seems that we have one of what you call ... abandoned souls. That is what you call them, isn't it?" Another pause, longer than the first. "This is stupid. I wonder why I called you."

"That makes two of us." The voice on the line was contemptuous, but uncomfortably so, ill at ease despite its advantage of identity and wakefulness. It was a familiar voice, from somewhere in the past, one of so many familiar voices, voices of medical students, interns, residents, nurses, fellow doctors, researchers, all ranged through over forty years of memory, some respectful, some exasperated, some angry. He ran his hand over his scalp and thought about that tone of defensive contempt. "Orphaned. Not abandoned. Though that will do just as well." Given the subject of the call, it had to be someone at an Intensive Care unit, probably at a city hospital. Possibly connected with a trauma center. That narrowed things ... got it. "Masterman," he said. "Eugene Colin Masterman. Johns Hopkins Medical School, class of '75. You're at Pres St. Luke's now. I hope that you are finally clear on the difference between afferent and efferent nerves. I remember you had trouble with the distinction, back in my neuroanatomy class at Hopkins. Just remember: SAME, sensory afferent, motor efferent. It's not hard. But, as you said, you didn't decide to call me. Leibig, chief of your ICU, told you to. How is Karl?"

Dr. Leibig is well," Masterman said sulkily. "Aside from the inevitable effects of age. He has a renal dysfunction, and seems to have developed a vestibular disorder which keeps him off his feet. He will be retiring next year."

"A pity," Harmon said. "A good man. And three years younger than I am, as I'm sure I don't have to remind you. Well, Eugene, why don't you tell me the story?" Masterman, he recalled, hated being called Eugene.

Masterman gave it to him, chapter and verse, in offensively superfluous detail. Patient's name: Paterson, Stanley Andrew. Patient's social security number. Patient's place of employment, a management consulting firm in the Loop. Locations of stab wounds, fractures, lacerations. Patient's blood type and rejection spectrum. Units of blood transfused, in the ambulance, in the Emergency Room, in the ICU, divided into whole blood and plasma. Names of the ambulance crew. Name of admitting doctor. Name of duty nurse. All surname first, then first name and middle initial.

"Who was his first grade teacher?" Harmon said.

"What—Dr. Harmon, I did not want to make this call, understand that. I did so at the specific request of Dr. Leibig."

"Who also wonders if I am crazy. But he did it for old time's sake, bless him. Eugene, if, as it seems, you are not enjoying this call, perhaps you should make an effort to be more ... pithy."

"Paterson suffered a cardiac arrest at, let's see, 1:08 AM. We attempted to restart several times with a defibrillator, but were finally forced to open the chest and apply a pacemaker. We have also attached a ventilator. His condition is now stable."

"Life is not stable," Harmon said, but thought, "The stupid bastards." Would they never learn? Didn't they understand the consequences? *Doctors.* Clever technicians who thought themselves scientists. "Brain waves?"

"Well ... minimal."

"Minimal, Eugene? Where did he die?"

"He isn't dead. We have him on life support."

"Don't play games with me! Where was he murdered?"

"At the Adams St. El station, at Adams and Wabash. The northbound platform." He paused, then the words spilled out. "Listen, Harmon, you can't go on doing this, talking about ghosts and goblins and all sorts of idiocy about the spirits of the unburied dead. This isn't the Middle Ages, for crissakes. We're doctors, we know better, we've learned. We *know* how things work now. Have you forgotten everything? You can't just let people under your care die to protect their souls. That's crazy, absolute lunacy. I don't know how I let Leibig talk me into this, he knows you're crazy too, and the patient's *not* dead, he's alive, and if I have anything to say about it he'll stay that way, and I won't pull the plug because of some idiotic theory you have about ghosts. And I do so know the difference between afferent and efferent. Afferent nerves—"

"Never mind, Dr. Masterman," Harmon said wearily. "At this hour, I'm not sure I remember myself. Get back to your patients. Thank you for your call." He hung the receiver up gently.

After a moment to gather his strength, he pulled his legs out from under the comforter and forced them down to the cold floor. As they had grown thinner, the hair on them, now white, seemed to have grown thicker. He pulled the silk pajamas down so that he could not see his shins. The virtues of youth, he thought, too often become the sins of age. He had once been slim, and was now skinny. His nose, once aquiline, was a beak, and his high, noble forehead had extended itself clear over the top of his head.

These late night phone calls always made him think of Margaret, as she had been. He remembered her, before their marriage, as a young redhead in a no-nonsense gray suit with a ridiculous floppy bow tie, and later, in one of his shirts, much too long for her and tight in the chest, as she raised her arms in mock dismay at the number of his books she was expected to fit into their tiny apartment, and finally, as a prematurely old woman gasping her life out in the bed next to him. None of it had been her fault, but it had been she who had suffered.

He dialed the phone. It was answered on the first ring. "Sphinx and Eye of Truth Bookstore, Dexter Warhoff, Owner and Sole Proprietor. We're closed now, really, but we open at—"

"Dexter," Harmon said. "Sorry to bother you. It looks like we have another one."

"Professor!" Dexter said with delight. "No bother at all. I was just playing with some stuff out of the Kabbalah. Kind of fun, but nothing that won't wait. Where is this one? Oh, never mind, let it be a surprise. Usual place, in an hour? I'll call him and get him ready. Oh boy."

Harmon restrained a sigh. He could picture Dexter, plump and bulging in a shirt of plum or burgundy, with his bright blue eyes and greasy hair, behind the front desk at the Sphinx and Eye of Truth Bookstore, where he spent most of his waking hours, of which he apparently had many, scribbling in a paperback copy of *The Prophecies of Nostradamus* with a pencil stub or, as tonight, rearranging Hebrew letters to make anagrams of the Name of God.

The store itself was a neat little place on the Near North Side, with colorful throw pillows on the floor and the scent of jasmine incense in the air. It carried books on every imaginable topic relating to the occult and the supernatural, from Madame Blavatsky to Ancient Astronauts, from Edgar Cayce to the Loch Ness Monster, from Tarot cards to ESP. It had been almost impossible for Harmon to go there, but go there he did, finally, after exhausting every other resource, to accept a cup of camomile tea from Dexter's dirty-fingernailed hands and learn what he reluctantly came to understand to be the truth.

"Yes, Dexter. St. Mary's, as usual."

"Right. See ya."

Harmon hung up. He'd searched and searched, down every avenue, but he was well and truly stuck. When it came to the precise and ticklish business of the exorcism and binding of the spirits of the uneasy dead, there was no better assistant alive than Dexter Warhoff.

A train finally pulled into the station. It was lit up golden from inside, like a lantern. The doors slid open, puffing warm air. Stanley thought about getting up and going into the train. He could get home that way. But he remembered how uncomfortable the seats were on the train, and what a long, cold walk he had from the station to his condo, so he just remained where he was, where the ground was soft and warm. After waiting for a long moment, the train shut its doors and whooshed off, up along the shining metal tracks as they arched into the sky, to vanish among the stars and the windows of the apartment buildings, which now floated free in the darkness, like balloons let loose by children.

Once he was alone again, Stanley found himself standing, not knowing how he had come to be so. The wind from Lake Michigan had cleared the sky, and a half moon lit the towers of the city. The city was alive; he could hear the soughing of its breath, the thrumming of its heart, and the murmuration of its countless vessels. Without thinking about it, he swung over the railing and slid down the girders of the El station to the waiting earth. The city spread out before him, Stanley Paterson ambled abroad.

After some time, the wind carried to him the aroma of roasting lamb, with cumin and garlic. He turned into it, like a salmon swimming upstream, and soon stood among the cracked plaster columns and fishing nets of a Greek restaurant. A blue flame burst up in the dimness, and Stanley moved towards it. A waiter in a white sailor's shirt served a man and a woman saganaki, fried kasseri cheese flamed with brandy.

Stanley could taste the tartness of the cheese and the tang of the brandy as they both ate, and feel the crunch of the outside and the yielding softness of the inside. He could taste the wine too, the bitterly resinous heaviness of retsina.

They looked at each other. She was young, wearing a cotton dress with a bold, colorful pattern, and made a face at the taste of the wine. The man, who had ordered it, was older, in gray tweed, and grinned back at her. Stanley hovered over the two of them like a freezing man over a fire. However, as he drew close, something changed between them. They had been friends for a long time, at the law office where they both worked, but this was their first romantic evening together. She had finally made the suggestion, and now, as she looked at him, instead of thoughts of romance, her mind wandered to the coy calculations already becoming old to her, of getting to his apartment, giggling, of excusing herself at just the right moment to insert her diaphragm, of her mock exuberant gesture of tossing her panties over the foot of the bed at the moment he finally succeeded in getting her completely undressed, of how to act innocent while letting him know that she wasn't. The older man's shoulders stiffened, and he wished, too late, that he had resisted her, resisted the urge to turn her from a friend into yet another prematurely sophisticated young woman, wished that he could stop for a moment to think and breathe, in the midst of his headlong pursuit of the Other. The saganaki grew cold as they examined, silently, the plastic grapes that dangled in the arbor above their heads. Stanley moved back, and found himself on the street again.

Music came to him from somewhere far above. He slid up the smooth walls of an apartment building until he reached it. The glass of the window pushed against his face like the yielding surface of a soap bubble, and, then, suddenly, he was inside.

A woman with a mass of curly gray hair and an improbably long neck sat at the grand piano, her head cocked at the sheet music as she played, while a younger woman with lustrous black hair and kohl-darkened eyes sat straight-backed on a stool with an oboe. The music, Stanley knew, though he had never heard it before, was Schumann's *Romances for Oboe and Piano,* and they played it with the ease of long mutual familiarity. Their only audience was a fuzzy cat of uncertain breed who sat on a footstool and stared into the fire in the fireplace.

Stanley felt the notes dance through him, and sensed the blissful self-forgetfulness of the musicians. He wanted desperately to share in it, and moved to join them. The oboist suddenly thought about the fact that, no matter how well she played, and how much she practiced, she would never play well enough to perform with the Chicago Symphony, or any orchestra, ever, and the love of her life would always remain a hobby, a pastime. The pianist's throat constricted, and suddenly she feared the complexity of the instrument before her, knowing that she was inadequate to the task, as she was to all tasks of any importance, that no one would ever approve of her, and that she was old. The instruments went completely out of sync, as if the performers were in separate rooms with soundproof walls between them, and the music crashed into cacophony. The cat stood up, bristling, stared right at Stanley, and hissed. The pianist tapped one note over and over with her forefinger. The oboist started to cut another reed, even though she had two already cut. Stanley passed back out through the window.

He left the residential towers and wandered the streets of three-story brownstone apartment buildings. He felt warm, soapy water on his skin, and drifted through the wide crack under an ill-fitting door.

The bathroom was warm and steamy, heated by the glow of a gas burner in one wall. A plump woman in a flower print dress, with short dark hair, washed a child in that most marvelous of bathing devices, a large, freestanding claw-foot bathtub. The little girl in the tub had just had her hair washed, and it was slicked to her head like a mannikin's. She stared intently down into the soapy water like a cat catching fish.

"Point to your mouth, Sally. Your mouth." Sally obediently put her finger in her mouth. "Point to your nose." She put her finger in her nose. "Very good, Sally. Can you point to your ear? Your ear, Sally." After a moment's thought, the little girl put her finger in her ear. "Where is your chin?" Sally, tiring of the game, and having decided which she liked best, stuck her finger back up her nose and stared at her mother. Her mother laughed, delighted at this mutiny. "Silly goose." She poured water over the girl's head. Sally closed her eyes and made a "brrr" noise with her lips. "Time to get out, Sally." The little girl stood up, and her mother pulled the plug. Sally waved as the water and soap bubbles swirled down the drain and said, "Ba-*bye,* Ba-*bye.*" Her mother pulled her from the tub and wrapped her in a huge towel, in which she vanished completely.

The feel of the terry cloth on his skin, and the warm, strawberry scent of the mother covered Stanley like a benediction. He stretched forward, as the mother rubbed her daughter's hair with the towel until it stood out in all directions. The mother's happiness vanished, and she felt herself trapped, compelled, every moment of her life now given over to the care of a selfish and capricious creature, no time to even think about getting any work done on the one poem she'd been working on since she left high school to get married, her life predetermined now until she grew old and was left alone. She rubbed too vigorously with the towel and Sally, smothered and manipulated by forces she could not control, or even understand, began to shriek. "Quiet, Sally.

Quiet, *damn it.*"

Stanley remembered the platform. What was he doing in here? He had a train to catch, he had to get home. He could not even imagine how he had managed to stray. He turned and hurried off to the El station.

The two of them walked down the street together, Harmon with a long, measured stride, and Dexter with the peculiar mincing waddle he was compelled to use because of the width of his thighs. Harmon wore a long thick over-coat and a karakul hat, but the cold still struck deep into his bones. He wore a scarf to protect his throat, which was always the most sensitive. He remembered a time, surely not that long ago, when he had enjoyed the winter, when it had made him feel alive. He and Margaret had spent weekends in Wisconsin, cross-country skiing, and making grotesque snowmen. No longer. Dexter wore a red wind-breaker that made him look like a tomato, and a Minnesota Vikings cap with horns on it. As he walked, he juggled little beanbags in an elaborate fountain. He had a number of sim-ilar skills—such as rolling a silver dollar across the back of his knuckles, like George Raft, and making origami an-imals—all of which annoyed Harmon because he had never learned to do things like that. He thought about the image the two of them presented, and snorted, amused at himself for feeling embarrassed.

"Father Toomey looked a little bummed out," Dexter said. "I think we woke him up."

"Dexter, it's three-thirty in the morning. Not everyone sits up all night reading books on the Kabbalah."

"Yeah, I guess. Anyway, he cheered up after we talked about the horoscope reading I'm doing for him. There's a lot of real interesting stuff in it."

"An ordained Catholic priest is having you do his *horo-scope?*"

Dexter looked surprised. "Sure. Why not?"

Why not indeed? Harmon hefted his ancient black leath-er bag. The instruments it contained had been blessed by Father Toomey, and sprinkled with holy water from the font at St. Mary's. Harmon, in the precisely rigorous theo-logical way that devout atheists have, doubted the efficacy of a blessing from a priest so far sunk in superstition that he had his horoscope done, and performed holy offices for a purpose so blatantly demonic, but he had to admit that it always seemed to do the job. When he handed the sleepy, slightly inebriated priest the speculum, the wand, the silver nails, the censer, the compass, and the rest of the instruments of his new trade, they were nothing but dead metal, but when he took them in his hands after the blessing, they vibrated with suppressed energy. The touch of such half-living things was odious to him, essential though they were. It disturbed him that such things worked. As quickly as he could, he wrapped them in their coverings of virgin lamb hide, inscribed with Latin prayers and Babylonian symbols, and placed them, in correct order, into his bag. That bag had once held his stethoscope, patella reflex hammer, thermometer, hypodermics, laryngoscope, and the rest of his medical instruments, and though he had not touched any of them in years, it had pained him to remove them so that the bag could be used for its new purpose.

"You know, Professor, the other day I was reading an interesting book about the gods of ancient Atlantis—"

"Oh, Dexter," Harmon said irritably. "You don't really believe all these things, do you?"

Dexter grinned at him, yellow-toothed. "Why not? You believe in *ghosts,* don't you?"

Dexter's one unanswerable argument. "I believe in them, Dexter, only because I am forced to, not because I like it. That's the difference between us. It would be terrible to *like* the idea that ghosts exist."

"Boy, did you fight it," Dexter said with a chuckle. "You sat with me for an hour, talking about Mary Baker Eddy. Then you shut up. I asked you what was wrong. 'A ghost,' you said. 'I've got to get rid of a ghost.' Took you three cups of tea to say that. You don't even like camomile tea, do you?"

"It served."

"It sure did. You remember that first time, don't you? I'll never forget it. We hardly knew what we were doing, like two kids playing with dynamite. I had pretended I knew more about it than I did, you know."

"I know." They often talked about the first ghost. They

never talked about the second.

"I thought I could handle it, but it almost swallowed me and you had to save my ass. Quite a talent you have there. Strongest I've ever heard of. You should be proud."

"I feel precisely as proud as I would if I discovered that I had an innate genius for chicken stealing."

Dexter laughed, head thrown back. He had a lot of fillings in his back teeth. "Gee, that's pretty funny. But anyway, this Kabbalah stuff is real interesting . . . . "

Harmon suffered himself to be subjected to a rambling, overly-detailed lecture on medieval Jewish mysticism, until, much too soon, they were at the El station.

Dexter craned his head back and looked up at the dark girders of the station, his face suddenly serious. "I feel him up there. He's a heavy one. Strong. He didn't live enough, when he had the chance. Those are always the worst. Too many trapped desires. Good luck to you. Oh . . . wait. They lock these things when the trains stop running, and we're not exactly authorized." He reached into his pocket and pulled out a little black pouch, which, when opened, revealed a line of shiny lock-picking tools.

"I used to pick locks at school," Dexter said. "Just for fun. I never stole anything. Figuring out the locks was the good part. Schools don't have very good locks. Most students just break in the windows." He walked up to the heavy metal mesh door at the base of the stairs, and had it opened about as quickly as he could have with a key. He signed, disappointed. "The CTA doesn't either. I don't even know why they bother. Well, now it's time. Good luck." They paused and he shook Harmon's hand, as he always did, with a simple solemnity.

Nothing to say, Harmon turned and stared up towards the El station.

They *were* always the worst. "The people who want to live forever are always the ones who can't find anything to do on a rainy Sunday afternoon," as Dr. Kaltenbrunner, the head of Radiology at Mt. Tabor Hospital, had once said. Dr. K was never bored, and certainly never boring, enjoyed seventeenth-century English poetry, and died of an aneurism three months before Harmon encountered his first ghost. Died and stayed dead. Harmon always thought he could have used his help. Thomas Browne and John Donne would have understood ghosts better than Harmon could, which was funny, because there hadn't *been* enough ghosts in the seventeenth century to be worth worrying about.

Some doctors managed to stay away from ER duty, and it was mostly the young ones—who needed to be taught, by having their noses rubbed in it, about the mixture of fragility and resilience that is the human body—who took the duty there, particularly at night. In his time, Harmon had seen a seventy-year-old lady some anonymous madman had pushed in front of an onrushing El train recover and live, with only a limp in her left leg to show for it, and a DePaul University linebacker DOA from a fractured skull caused by a fall in the shower in the men's locker room.

As Harmon climbed the clattering metal stairs up to the deserted El platform, he remembered the first one. It was always that way with him. He was never able to see the Duomo of Florence without remembering the first time he and Margaret had seen it, from the window of their pensione. There were some words he could not read without remembering the classroom in which he learned them, and whether it had been sunny that day. It meant there were some things he never lost, that he always had Margaret with him in Florence. And it meant that he could never deal with a ghost without remembering the terror of the first one.

He had been working night duty, late, when they brought in a bloody stretcher. It had been quiet for about an hour, in that strange irregular rhythm that Emergency Rooms have, crowded most of the time, but sometimes almost empty. A pedestrian had been hit by a truck while crossing the street. There was a lot of bleeding, mostly internal, and a torn lung filled with blood, a hemothorax. His breathing was audible, a slow dragging gurgle, the sound a straw makes sucking at the bottom of a glass of Coke when the glass is almost empty. Harmon managed to stop much of the bleeding, but by that time the man was in shock. Then the heart went into ventricular fibrillation. Harmon put the paddles on and defibrillated it. When the heart stopped altogether, he put the patient on a pacemaker and an external ventilator. The autopsy subsequently showed substantial damage to the brainstem, as well as complete kidney failure. Every measure Harmon took, as it turned out, was useless, but he managed to keep the patient alive an extra hour, before everything stopped at once, in the ICU.

A day or so later, the nurse on duty came to him with a problem. Rosemary was a redhead, cute, and reminded him of Margaret when she was young, so he was a little fonder of her than he should have been, particularly since Margaret had been sick. The nurse wasn't flirting now, however. She was frightened. She kept hearing someone drinking out of a straw, she said, in a corner of the ER, only there wasn't anyone there. She was afraid she was losing her mind, which can happen to you after too many gunshot wounds, suicides, and drug overdoses. Harmon told her, in what he told himself was a fatherly way, that it was probably something like air in the pipes, which he called an "embolism," a medical usage which delighted her. She teased him about it.

Harmon remembered being vaguely pleased about that, while he searched around and listened. He didn't hear anything. It was late, and he finally climbed up on a gurney and went to sleep, as some of the other doctors did when things weren't busy. He'd never done it before, and why he did it was something he could not remember, though everything about the incident, from the freckles around Rosemary's nose to the scheduling roster for that night's medical staff, was abnormally clear in his mind, the way memories of things that happened only yesterday never were. When he woke up, he heard it. A slow dragging gurgle. He listened with his eyes closed, heart pounding. Then it stopped.

"Hey, have you seen my car?" a voice said. "It's a blue car, a Cutlass, though I guess it's too dark here to see the color. I know I parked it near here, but I just can't find it."

Harmon slowly opened his eyes. Standing in front of him was a fat man in a business suit, holding a briefcase. He wasn't bloody, and his face was not pasty white, but Harmon recognized him. It was the man who had died the night before.

"Look, I have to get home to Berwyn. My wife will be going nuts. She expected me home hours ago. Have you seen the damn car? It's a Cutlass, blue. Not a good car, God knows, and it needs work, but I gotta get home."

Harmon had met the wife, when she identified the body. She had, indeed, expected him hours ago.

"Jeez, I don't know what I could have done with it."

Harmon was a logical man, and a practical man, and he hadn't until that moment realized that those two character-istics could be in conflict. What he saw before him was un-dubitably a ghost, and as a practical man he had to accept that. He also knew, as a logical man, that ghosts did not, indeed could not, exist. This neat conundrum, however, did not occur to him until somewhat later, because the next time the dead man said, "Do you think you could help me find my car? I gotta get home." he launched himself from the gurney, smashing it back into the wall, bolted from the ER, and did not stop running until he was sitting at the desk in his little office on the fifth floor, shaking desperately and trying not to scream.

The El platform was windswept and utterly empty. Harmon walked slowly across its torn asphalt until he came to the spot where it had happened. The police had cleaned up the blood, and erased the chalk outline, that curious symbol of the vanished soul used by police photographers as a record of the body, so morning commuters would not be unpleasantly surprised by the cold official evidence of violent death. He didn't have to see it. He could feel it, like standing in the autopsy room and knowing that someone had left the door to the cold room where the bodies were kept open because you could feel the cold formaldehyde-and-decay scented air seeping along the floor.

He didn't know why he had this particular sense, or abili-ty, or whatever. To himself he compared it to someone with perfect pitch and rhythm who nevertheless dislikes music, someone who could play Bach's *Goldberg Variations* through perfectly after hearing the piece only once, and yet hate every single note. It was a vicious curse. He set his black bag down, opened it, and began to remove his instruments.

To start, Harmon had, cautiously, cautiously, sounded out his colleagues on the subject of ghosts. He'd read too many books where seemingly reasonable men lost all of their social graces when confronted by the inexplicable and started jabbering and making ridiculous accusations, frightening and embarrassing their friends. So, in a theoretical manner, he asked about ghosts. To his surprise, instead of being suspicious, people either calmly said they didn't believe in them, or, the majority, had one or more anecdotes about things like the ghost of a child in an old house dropping a ball down the stairs or a hitchhiking girl in a white dress who would only appear to men driving alone and then would vanish from the car. Others had stories about candles being snuffed out in perfectly still rooms, or dreams about dying relatives, or any number of irrelevant mystical experiences. No one, when pressed, would admit to having actually seen anything like a real, demonstrably dead man walking and talking and looking for a blue Cutlass. A man who persisted, week after week, in trying to get Harmon to help him find the damn thing. Harmon transferred from the E.R. Rosemary thought it was something personal, because she'd asked him to her house for dinner, and they rarely spoke after that.

He told Margaret, however, as much of it as he could. It gave her something to think about, as she lay there in bed and gasped, waiting for the end. She wondered, of course, if the strain of her illness had not made her husband lose what few marbles he had left, as she put it, but she only said this because both of them knew Harmon was coolly sane. It interested her that some people could hear ghosts, but that Harmon could see them and talk to them. She, like Dexter, used the word "gift."

In good scholar's style, Harmon did research, in the dusty, abandoned stacks of the witchcraft and folklore sections of Northwestern, the University of Chicago, and the University of Illinois, Circle Campus. He even had a friend let him into the private collections of the Field Museum of Natural History. He learned about lemures, the Roman spirits of the dead, about the hauntings of abandoned pavilions by sardonic Chinese ghosts, and about the Amityville Horror. It was all just . . . literature. Stories. Tales to tell at midnight. Not a single one of them had the ring of truth to it, and Harmon was by this time intimately familiar with the true behavior of ghosts.

Everyone was very good to him about Margaret, and about what he did to himself as a result, though no one understood the real reason for it. It got to be too much, in the apartment, in the hospital, and he finally started to say things that concerned people. They didn't think he was crazy, just "under stress," that ubiquitous modern disease, which excuses almost anything. Then, someone at the Field Museum mentioned, with the air of an ordinarily respectable man selling someone some particularly vile pornography, that Dexter Warhoff, of the Sphinx and Eye of Truth Bookstore, might have some materials not available in the museum collection. It was rumored that Dexter possessed a bizarrely variant scroll of the Egyptian *Book of the Dead,* as well as several Mayan codexes not collected in the *Popul Vuh* or the *Dresden Codex,* though no one was quite sure. Harmon had come to the conclusion that using ordinary reason in his new circumstances was using Occam's Razor while shaving in a fun house mirror. Common sense was a normally useful instrument turned dangerous in the wrong situation. So he went to Dexter's store, drank his sour tea, and talked with him. Dexter scratched his head with elaborate thoughtfulness, then took Harmon upstairs, where he lived, to a mess with a kitchen full of dirty dishes, and brought him into a room piled with newspaper clippings, elaborately color coded, in five different languages, as well as sheets of articles transcribed from newspapers in forty languages more.

"You poor guy," Dexter said sadly. "That's a terrible way to find out about what's hidden. I can see that it was terrible. But I must say, I've been wondering about a few things. You've got the key there, I think, with this life support stuff. Look at this." He showed Harmon a French translation of a photocopied Russian *samizdat* document from the Crimea. It described ghosts haunting a medical center at an exclusive Yalta sanatorium. The tone was slightly metaphorical, but, for the first time, Harmon read things that confirmed his own experience. Dexter showed him an article from the house newspaper of a medical center in Bombay, an excerpt from the unpublished reminiscences of a surgeon in Denmark, and a study of night terrors in senile dementia cases in a Yorkshire nursing home, from *Lancet.* The accounts were similar. "There's almost nothing before the 1930s, very few up to about 1960, and a fair number from the 70s and 80s."

"Life support," Harmon said, when he was done reading. "Artificial life support is responsible."

"Now, Professor, let's not jump to conclusions . . . . " But Harmon could see that Dexter agreed with him and, for some strange reason, that pleased him.

"When the body is kept alive by artificial means, for however long, when it should be dead and starting to rot, the soul, which normally is swept away somewhere—heaven, hell, oblivion, the Elysian Fields, it doesn't matter—is held back in this world, tied to its still-breathing body. And, being held back, it falls in love with life again." Harmon found himself saying it again, alone on the platform. It had seemed immediately obvious to him, though it was not really an "explanation" of the sort a scientist would require. It was, however, more than sufficient for a doctor of medicine, whose standards are different. A doctor only cares about what works, without much attention to why.

None of his colleagues had understood, though. He had gotten a little cranky on the subject, ultimately, he had to admit that, but he felt like someone in the eighteenth century campaigning against blood letting. He had always known that doctors were, by and large, merely skilled fools, so he quickly stopped, but not before acquiring a certain reputation.

He drew his chalk circle on the rough surface of the platform, using the brass compass. Using a knife with a triangular blade, he scraped some material from within the circle. No matter how well the police had cleaned, it would contain some substance, most likely the membranes of red blood cells that had belonged to the dead man. He melted beeswax over a small alcohol lamp whose flame kept going out, then mixed in the scraped up blood. He dropped a linen wick into a mold of cold worked bronze and poured the wax in. While he waited for the candle to harden, he arranged the speculum, the silver nails, and the brass hammer so that he could reach them quickly. It was strange that most of the techniques they used had their roots in earlier centuries, when ghosts were the extremely rare results of accidental comas or overdoses of toxic drugs. People had had more time then to worry about such things, and some of their methods were surprisingly effective, though Dexter and Harmon had refined them. He set the candle in the center of the circle, lit it, and called Stanley Paterson's name.

The train still had not come. What was wrong? Why had there been no notification by the CTA? Stanley stood on the platform and shivered, wondering why he had wandered away, and why he had come back. Where was the damn train? Beneath his feet he could see a circle of chalk, and a half-melted candle, but he didn't think about them. Had he daydreamed right past the train, with those thoughts of musicians and mothers? Had the trains stopped for the night?

There was a rumble, and lights appeared down the tracks. They blinded him, for he had been long in darkness, and he stumbled forward with his eyes shut. He felt around for a seat. It seemed like he'd been waiting forever.

"It's a cold night, isn't it Stanley?" a man's voice said, close by.

"Wha—?" Stanley jerked his head around and examined the brightly lit train car. It was empty. Then he saw that the man was sitting ne?t to him, a tall old man with sad brown eyes. He was wearing a furry hat. "What are you talking about? How do you know my name?" Not waiting for an answer, he turned and pressed his nose against the glass of the window. A form lay there on the platform, sprawled on its back. It wore a long black overcoat. A large pool of blood, black in the lights of the station, had gathered near it, looking like the mouth of a pit.

"Stanley," the man said, his voice patient. "You have to understand a few things. I don't suppose it's strictly necessary, but it makes me feel less . . . cruel."

The train pulled into the next station. Out on the platform lay a dead man with a black coat. Three white-clad men burst onto the platform and ran towards it with a stretcher. The train pulled out of the station. "I don't care how you feel," Stanley said.

The man snorted, "I deserve that, I suppose. But you

must understand, the dead cannot mix with the living. It just cannot be. We had a dead man in our Emergency Room once. He wouldn't go away. He tried to be part of everything. A ward birthday party turned gloomy because he tried to join it, and the patient whose birthday it was sickened and died within the week. He tried to participate in the close professional friendship of a pair of nurses, built up over long years of night duty and family pain, and they had fights, serious fights, and stopped ever speaking to each other. The gardener, whose joy in his plants he tried to share, grew to hate the roses he took care of, and in the spring they bloomed late and sickly. I've always liked roses. Life is hell with ghosts around, Stanley. Believe me, I know all about it" He had put the roses last, he noticed, as if they were more important than people. How much like a doctor he still was . . . .

Stanley watched as the white-clad men strapped the man in the black coat into the stretcher and rushed off, one of them holding an IV bottle over his head. The trained pulled out of the station. "I—you don't understand, you don't understand at all." Stanley found himself shaken with sobs. How could he explain? As a child he'd wanted to play a musical instrument, like his sister, who played the piano, or even Frank, his next door neighbor, who played the trumpet in the school band. He'd tried the piano, the saxophone, the cello. None had lasted longer than two years, and he never practiced, despite his mother's entreaties. As an adult he'd tried the recorder, the guitar, and failed again. Yet, this very night, he'd felt what it was like to play Schumann on a piano and an oboe, and feel the music growing out of the intersection of spirit and instrument. He'd felt what it was like to be alive. "I know what to *do* now, don't you see. I realize what I was doing wrong, how I was wasting everything. Now I know!"

"So now, at last, you know." The man shook his head sadly, and held a flat, polished bronze mirror in front of Stanley's face. Stanley looked into the speculum, but saw nothing but roiled darkness, like an endless hole to nowhere. He felt weak. "Lie down, Mr. Paterson," Harmon said softly. "You don't look at all well. You should lie down."

Somehow they had come to be standing on the same

damn platform again, as if the train had gone absolutely nowhere at all. The unnatural blankness of the mirror had indeed made him feel dizzy, so Stanley lay down. The platform was hard and cold on his back now. Nothing made sense anymore. He watched the stars spin overhead. Or was it just the lights of the apartment buildings?

"You can't leave me here," he said. "Not just when I've figured it out."

"Shut up," Harmon said, savagely. "It's too late." He drove a long silver nail into Stanley's right wrist. Stanley felt it go in, cold, but it didn't hurt. "You're dead." He drove another nail through Stanley's foot, tinking on the head with a little hammer. "That first one, in the ER. He almost killed *us,* he was so strong. But we bound him, finally, once we'd figured out what to do. If I went back there now, I would hear him, talking to himself, as if he'd just woken up from a nap and was still sleepy. I hear you everywhere, where I have bound you, on street corners, in hallways, in alleys. In beds." Harmon found himself crying, tears wetting his cheeks, as if he were the one Stanley Paterson was supposed to be feeling sorry for. Stanley Paterson, who would have only the understanding that he was dead, not alive, to keep him for all eternity. "Don't worry, Stanley. Life is hateful."

"No!" Stanley cried. "I want to live!" He reached up with his free hand and grabbed Harmon by the throat.

Harmon felt like he was being buried alive, but not buried in clean earth. He was being buried, instead, in the churned-over, corrupted earth of an ancient cemetery, full of human teeth and writhing worms. It pushed, damp and greasy, against his face. The smell was unbearable. Darkness swelled before him, and he almost let go.

The darkness drained away, and the platform reappeared. Dexter stood over him, his tongue sticking out slightly between his lips. He held the speculum over Stanley's face, forcing him back. Dexter's clothes flapped, and he leaned forward, as if into a heavy, foul wind. "Quick, Professor," he choked. "He's a strong one, like I said." Harmon tapped the fourth nail into Stanley's left wrist.

"I want to live!" Stanley said, quieter now.

Harmon said nothing. Dexter held the fifth nail for him,

and he drove it through Stanley's chest. "There. Now you will remain still." He rested back on his heels, breathing heavily. How like a doctor, he thought. He could eliminate the symptom, but not cure the disease. Those ghosts, no longer disturbing the living, would lie where he had nailed them until Judgement Day. And there was nothing he could do to help them. He sat there for a long time, until he felt Dexter's hand on his shoulder. He looked up into that kindly, ugly face, then back at the platform, where five silver dots glittered in the overhead lights.

"That was a bad one, Professor."

"They're all bad."

"It's worse if they never lived before they died. They want it then, all the more." Dexter packed the instruments away. Then he rubbed the tension out of Harmon's back, taking the feel of death up into himself. Dexter, with his credulous beliefs in anything and everything, absurd in his Minnesota Vikings cap with the horns. Without him, Harmon could not have kept moving for even a day.

Harmon thought about going home. Margaret would be there, as she always was, on the side of the bed where the blankets were flat and undisturbed. He hadn't acted in time, when she had her final, fatal heart attack. He had waited, and doubted his own conclusions, and let them put her on life support for three days, in the cardiac ICU, before he decided it was hopeless, and let them pull the plug on her. By then, of course, it had been much too late. He should simply have let her die there, next to him. But how could he have done that? Whenever he changed the sheets, he could see the rounded heads of the five silver nails driven into the mattress, to keep her fixed where she died.

She had loved life, but she had wanted to stay with him . . . always. So he had laid down on the bed with her and felt her cold embrace. For a doctor with a good knowledge of anatomy his suicide attempt had been shockingly bad. Slitting your own throat is rarely successful. It's too imprecise. They had found him, and healed him, reconstructing his throat. Modern medicine could do miracles. When he was well enough, though still bandaged, he went and found Dexter. They took care of the man in the ER, and then Margaret. She had cried and pleaded when the nails went in. But she had loved life, so it wasn't as hard as it could have been, though Harmon could not imagine how it could have been any harder.

When he came back, she would ask him, sleepily, how it had gone. She always sounded like she was about to fall asleep, but she never did. She never would.

"Let's go," Dexter said. "It'll be good to get back to bed. I gotta open the store in three hours. Jeez."

"Yes, Dexter," Harmon said, "It will be good to get to bed." ●

AMERICA

by *Orson Scott Card*

"America" was purchased by Gardner Dozois, and appeared in the January 1987 issue of IAsfm, *with an evocative interior illustration by Janet Aulisio. Card is one of the most popular authors to appear in* IAsfm, *and one of the most popular young writers in science fiction. His novels* Ender's Game *and* Speaker For The Dead *won both the Nebula and the Hugo Award in two consecutive years. His "Hatrack River," an* IAsfm *story, won the World Fantasy Award in 1987, and another* IAsfm *story, "Eye For Eye," won last year's Hugo Award. His other novels include* Hot Sleep, A Planet Called Treason, Songmaster, *and* Hart's Hope. *His most recent books are the novels in the "seventh son" series—including* Seventh Son, Red Prophet, *and* Prentis Alvin—*and the collection* Cardography.

In the story that follows, he spins an engrossing tale of a young boy's obsession with a mysterious Indian woman, and the stunning consequences for the whole world that unfold from it.

Sam Monson and Anamari Boagente had two encounters in their lives, forty years apart. The first encounter lasted for several weeks in the high Amazon jungle, the village of Agualinda. The second was for only an hour near the ruins of the Glen Canyon Dam, on the border between Navaho country and the State of Deseret.

When they met for the first time, Sam was a scrawny teenager from Utah and Anamari was a middle-aged spinster Indian from Brazil. When they met the second time, he was governor of Deseret, the last European state in America, and she was, to some people's way of thinking, the mother of God. It never occurred to anyone that they had ever met before, except me. I saw it plain as day, and pestered Sam until he told me the whole story. Now Sam is dead, and she's long gone, and I'm the only one who knows the truth. I thought for a long time that I'd take this story untold to my grave, but I see now that I can't do that. The way I see it, I won't be allowed to die until I write this down. All my real work was done long since, so why else am I alive? I figure the land has kept me breathing so I can tell the story of its victory, and it has kept *you* alive so you can hear it. Gods are like that. It isn't enough for them to run everything. They want to be famous, too.

Agualinda, Amazonas

Passengers were nothing to her. Anamari only cared about helicopters when they brought medical supplies. This chopper carried a precious packet of benaxidene; Anamari barely noticed the skinny, awkward boy who sat by the crates, looking hostile. Another Yanqui who doesn't want to be stuck out in the jungle. Nothing new about that. Norteamericanos were almost invisible to Anamari by now. They came and went.

It was the Brazilian government people she had to worry about, the petty bureaucrats suffering through years of virtual exile in Manaus, working out their frustrations by being petty tyrants over the helpless Indians. No, I'm sorry we don't have any more penicillin, no more syringes, what did you do with the AIDS vaccine we gave you three years ago? Do you think we're made of money here? Let them come to town if they want to get well. There's a hospital in São Paulo de Olivença, send them there, we're not going to turn you into a second hospital out there in the middle of nowhere, not for a village of a hundred filthy Baniwas, it's not as if you're a doctor, you're just an old withered up Indian woman yourself, you never graduated from the medical schools, we can't spare medicines for you. It made them feel so important, to decide whether or not an Indian child would live or die. As often as not they passed sentence of death by refusing to send supplies. It made them feel powerful as God.

Anamari knew better than to protest or argue—it would only make the bureaucrat likelier to kill again in the future. But sometimes, when the need was great and the medicine was common, Anamari would go to the Yanqui geologists and ask if they had this or that. Sometimes they did. What she knew about Yanquis was that if they had some extra, they would share, but if they didn't, they wouldn't lift a finger to get any. They were not tyrants like the Brazilian bureaucrats. They just didn't give a damn. They were there to make money.

That was what Anamari saw when she looked at the sullen light-haired boy in the helicopter—another Norteamericano, just like all the other Norteamericanos, only younger.

She had the benaxidene, and so she immediately began spreading word that all the Baniwas should come for injections. It was a disease that had been introduced during the war between Guyana and Venezuela two years ago; as usual, most of the victims were not citizens of either country, just the Indios of the jungle, waking up one morning with their joints stiffening, hardening until no movement was possible. Benaxidene was the antidote, but you had to have it every few months or your joints would stiffen up again. As usual, the bureaucrats had diverted a shipment and there were a dozen Baniwas bedridden in the village. As usual, one or two of the Indians would be too far gone for the cure; one or two of their joints would be stiff for the rest of their lives. As usual, Anamari said little as she gave the injections, and the Baniwas said less to her.

It was not until the next day that Anamari had time to notice the young Yanqui boy wandering around the village. He was wearing rumpled white clothing, already somewhat soiled with the greens and browns of life along the rivers of the Amazon jungle. He showed no sign of being interested in anything, but an hour into her rounds, checking on the results of yesterday's benaxidene treatments, she became aware that he was following her.

She turned around in the doorway of the government-built hovel and faced him. 'O que é?" she demanded. What do you want?

To her surprise, he answered in halting Portuguese. Most of these Yanquis never bothered to learn the language at all, expecting her and everybody else to speak English. "Posso ajudar?" he asked. Can I help?

"Não," she said. "Mas pode olhar." You can watch.

He looked at her in bafflement.

She repeated her sentence slowly, enunciating clearly. "Pode olhar."

"Eu?" Me?

"Você, sim. And I can speak English."

"I don't want to speak English."

"Tanto faz," she said. Makes no difference.

He followed her into the hut. It was a little girl, lying naked in her own feces. She had palsy from a bout with meningitis years ago, when she was an infant, and Anamari figured that the girl would probably be one of the ones for whom the benaxidene came too late. That's how things usually worked—the weak suffer most. But no, her joints were flexing again, and the girl smiled at them, that heartbreakingly happy smile that made palsy victims so beautiful at times.

So. Some luck after all, the benaxidene had been in time for her. Anamari took the lid off the clay waterjar that stood on the one table in the room, and dipped one of her clean rags in it. She used it to wipe the girl, then lifted her frail, atrophied body and pulled the soiled sheet out from under her. On impulse, she handed the sheet to the boy.

"Leva fora," she said. And, when he didn't understand, "Take it outside.'

He did not hesitate to take it, which surprised her. "Do you want me to wash it?"

"You could shake off the worst of it," she said. "Out over the garden in back. I'll wash it later."

He came back in, carrying the wadded-up sheet, just as she was leaving. "All done here," she said. "We'll stop by my house to start that soaking. I'll carry it now."

He didn't hand it to her. "I've got it," he said. "Aren't you going to give her a clean sheet?"

"There are only four sheets in the village," she said. "Two of them are on my bed. She won't mind lying on the mat. I'm the only one in the village who cares about linens. I'm also the only one who cares about this girl."

"She likes you," he said.

"She smiles like that at everybody."

"So maybe she likes everybody."

Anamari grunted and led the way to her house. It was two government hovels pushed together. The one served as her clinic, the other as her home. Out back she had two metal washtubs. She handed one of them to the Yanqui boy, pointed at the rainwater tank, and told him to fill it. He did. It made her furious.

"What do you want!" she demanded.

"Nothing," he said.

"Why do you keep hanging around!"

"I thought I was helping." His voice was full of injured pride.

"I don't need your help." She forgot that she had meant to leave the sheet to soak. She began rubbing it on the washboard.

"Then why did you ask me to . . . "

She did not answer him, and he did not complete the question.

After a long time he said, "You were trying to get rid of me, weren't you?"

"What do you want here?" she said. "Don't I have enough to do, without a Norteamericano *boy* to look after?"

Anger flashed in his eyes, but he did not answer until the anger was gone. "If you're tired of scrubbing, I can take over."

She reached out and took his hand, examined it for a moment. "Soft hands," she said. "Lady hands. You'd scrape your knuckles on the washboard and bleed all over the sheet."

Ashamed, he put his hands in his pockets. A parrot flew past him, dazzling green and red; he turned in surprise to look at it. It landed on the rainwater tank. "Those sell for a thousand dollars in the States," he said.

Of course the Yanqui boy evaluates everything by price. "Here they're free," she said. "The Baniwas eat them. And wear the feathers."

He looked around at the other huts, the scraggly gardens. "The people are very poor here," he said. "The jungle life must be hard."

"Do you think so?" she snapped. "The jungle is very kind to these people. It has plenty of them to eat, all year. The Indians of the Amazon did not know they were poor until Europeans came and made them buy pants, which they couldn't afford, and build houses, which they couldn't keep up, and plant gardens. Plant gardens! In the midst of this magnificent Eden. The jungle life was good. The Europeans made them poor."

"Europeans?" asked the boy.

"Brazilians. They're all Europeans. Even the black ones have turned European. Brazil is just another European country, speaking a European language. Just like you Norteamericanos. You're Europeans too."

"I was born in America," he said. "So were my parents and grandparents and great-grandparents."

"But your bis-bis-avós, they came on a boat."

"That was a long time ago," he said.

"A long time!" She laughed. "I am a pure Indian. For ten thousand generations I belong to this land. You are a stranger here. A fourth-generation stranger."

"But I am a stranger who isn't afraid to touch a dirty sheet," he said. He was grinning defiantly.

That was when she started to like him. "How old are you?" she asked.

"Fifteen," he said.

"Your father's a geologist?"

"No. He heads up the drilling team. They're going to sink a test well here. He doesn't think they'll find anything, though."

"They will find plenty of oil," she said.

"How do you know?"

"Because I dreamed it," she said. "Bulldozers cutting down the trees, making an airstrip, and planes coming and going. They'd never do that, unless they found oil. Lots of oil."

She waited for him to make fun of the idea of dreaming true dreams. But he didn't. He just looked at her.

So she was the one who broke the silence. "You came to this village to kill time while your father is away from you, on the job, right?"

"No," he said. "I came here because he hasn't started to work yet. The choppers start bringing in equipment tomorrow."

"You would rather be away from your father?"

He looked away. "I'd rather see him in hell."

"This is hell," she said, and the boy laughed. "Why did you come here with him?"

"Because I'm only fifteen years old, and he has custody of me this summer."

"Custody," she said. "Like a criminal."

"He's the criminal," he said bitterly.

"And his crime?"

He waited a moment, as if deciding whether to answer. When he spoke, he spoke quietly and looked away. Ashamed. Of his father's crime. "Adultery," he said. The word hung in the air. The boy turned back and looked her in the face again. His face was tinged with red.

Europeans have such transparent skin, she thought. All their emotions show through. She guessed the whole story from his word—a beloved mother betrayed, and now he had to spend the summer with her betrayer. "Is that a *crime?*"

He shrugged. "Maybe not to Catholics."

"You're Protestant?"

He shook his head. "Mormon. But I'm a heretic."

She laughed. "You're a heretic, and your father is an adulterer."

He didn't like her laughter. "And you're a virgin," he said. His words seemed calculated to hurt her.

She stopped scrubbing, stood there looking at her hands. "Also a crime?" she murmured.

"I had a dream last night," he said. "In my dream your name was Anna Marie, but when I tried to call you that, I couldn't. I could only call you by another name."

"What name?" she asked.

"What does it matter? It was only a dream." He was

taunting her. He knew she trusted in dreams.

"You dreamed of me, and in the dream my name was Anamari?"

"It's true, isn't it. That *is* your name, isn't it?" He didn't have to add the other half of the question: You *are* a virgin, aren't you?

She lifted the sheet from the water, wrung it out and tossed it to him. He caught it, vile water spattering his face. He grimaced. She poured the washwater onto the dirt. It spattered mud all over his trousers. He did not step back. Then she carried the tub to the water tank and began to fill it with clean water. "Time to rinse," she said.

"You dreamed about an airstrip," he said. "And I dreamed about you."

"In your dreams you better start to mind your own business," she said.

"I didn't ask for it, you know," he said. "But I followed the dream out to this village, and you turned out to be a dreamer, too."

"That doesn't mean you're going to end up with your pinto between my legs, so you can forget it," she said.

He looked genuinely horrified. "Geez, what are you talking about! That would be fornication! Plus you've got to be old enough to be my mother!"

"I'm forty-two, she said. "If it's any of your business."

"You're *older* than my mother," he said. "I couldn't possibly think of you sexually. I'm sorry if I gave that impression."

She giggled. "You are a very funny boy, Yanqui. First you say I'm a virgin—"

"That was in the dream," he said.

"And then you tell me I'm older than your mother and too ugly to think of me sexually."

He looked ashen with shame. "I'm sorry, I was just trying to make sure you knew that I would never—"

"You're trying to tell me that you're a good boy."

"Yes,' he said.

She giggled again. "You probably don't even play with yourself," she said.

His face went red. He struggled to find something to say. Then he threw the wet sheet back at her and walked furiously away. She laughed and laughed. She liked this boy very much.

The next morning he came back and helped her in the clinic all day. His name was Sam Monson, and he was the first European she ever knew who dreamed true dreams. She had thought only Indios could do that. Whatever god it was that gave her dreams to her, perhaps it was the same god giving dreams to Sam. Perhaps that god brought them together here in the jungle. Perhaps it was that god who would lead the drill to oil, so that Sam's father would have to keep him here long enough to accomplish whatever the god had in mind.

It annoyed her that the god had mentioned she was a virgin. That was nobody's business but her own.

Life in the jungle was better than Sam ever expected. Back in Utah, when Mother first told him that he had to go to the Amazon with the old bastard, he had feared the worst. Hacking through thick viney jungles with a machete, crossing rivers of piranha in tick-infeste? dugouts, and always sweat and mosquitos and thick, heavy air. Instead the American oilmen lived in a pretty decent camp, with a generator for electric light. Even though it rained all the time and when it didn't it was so hot you wished it would, it wasn't constant danger as he had feared, and he never had to hack through jungle at all. There were paths, sometimes almost roads, and the thick, vivid green of the jungle was more beautiful than he had ever imagined. He had not realized that the American West was such a desert. Even California, where the old bastard lived when he wasn't traveling to drill wells, even those wooded hills and mountains were grey compared to the jungle green.

The Indians were quiet little people, not headhunters. Instead of avoiding them, like the adult Americans did, Sam found that he could be with them, come to know them, even help them by working with Anamari. The old bastard could sit around and drink his beer with the guys—adultery *and* beer, as if one contemptible sin of the flesh weren't enough —but Sam was actually doing some good here. If there was anything Sam could do to prove he was the opposite of his father, he would do it; and because his father was a weak, carnal, earthy man with no self-control, then Sam had to be a strong, spiritual, intellectual man who did not let any passions of the body rule him. Watching his father succumb to alcohol, remembering how his father could not even last a month away from Mother without having to get some whore into his bed, Sam was proud of his self-discipline. He ruled his body; his body did not rule him.

He was also proud to have passed Anamari's test on the first day. What did he care if human excrement touched his body? He was not afraid to breathe the hot stink of suffering, he was not afraid of the innocent dirt of a crippled child. Didn't Jesus touch lepers? Dirt of the body did not disgust him. Only dirt of the soul.

Which was why his dreams of Anamari troubled him. During the day they were friends. They talked about important ideas, and she told him stories of the Indians of the Amazon, and about her education as a teacher in São Paulo. She listened when he talked about history and religion and evolution and all the theories and ideas that danced in his head. Even Mother never had time for that, always taking care of the younger kids or doing her endless jobs for the church. Anamari treated him like his ideas mattered.

But at night, when he dreamed, it was something else entirely. In those dreams he kept seeing her naked, and the voice kept calling her "Virgem America." What her virginity had to do with America he had no idea—even true dreams didn't always make sense—but he knew this much: when he dreamed of Anamari naked, she was always reaching out to him, and he was filled with such strong passions that more than once he awoke from the dream to find himself throbbing with imaginary pleasure, like Onan in the Bible, Judah's son, who spilled his seed upon the ground and was struck dead for it.

Sam lay awake for a long time each time this happened, trembling, fearful. Not because he thought God would strike him down—he knew that if God hadn't struck his father dead for adultery, Sam was certainly in no danger because of an erotic dream. He was afraid because he knew that in these dreams he revealed himself to be exactly as lustful and evil as his father. He did not want to feel any sexual desire for Anamari. She was old and lean and tough, and he was afraid of her, but most of all Sam didn't want to desire her because he was not like his father, he would never have sexual intercourse with a woman who was not his wife.

Yet when he walked into the village of Agualinda, he felt eager to see her again, and when he found her—the village was small, it never took long—he could not erase from his mind the vivid memory of how she looked in his dreams, reaching out to him, her breasts loose and jostling, her slim hips rolling toward him—and he would bite his cheek for the pain of it, to distract him from desire.

It was because he was living with Father; the old bastard's goatishness was rubbing off on him, that's all. So he spent as little time with his father as possible, going home only to sleep at night.

The harder he worked at the jobs Anamari gave him to do, the easier it was to keep himself from remember his dream of her kneeling over him, touching him, sliding along his body. Hoe the weeds out of the corn until your back is on fire with pain! Wash the Baniwa hunter's wound and re-place the bandage! Sterilize the instruments in the alcohol! Above all, do not, even accidentally, let any part of your body brush against hers; pull away when she is near you, turn away so you don't feel her warm breath as she leans over your shoulder, start a bright conversation whenever there is a silence filled only with the sound of insects and the sight of a bead of sweat slowly etching its way from her neck down her chest to disappear between her breasts where she only tied her shirt instead of buttoning it.

How could she possibly be a virgin, after the way she acted in his dreams?

"Where do you think the dreams come from?" she asked.

He blushed, even though she could not have guessed what he was thinking. Could she?

"The dreams," she said. "Why do you think we have dreams that come true?"

It was nearly dark. "I have to get home," he said. She was holding his hand. When had she taken his hand like that, and why?

"I have the strangest dream," she said. "I dream of a huge snake, covered with bright green and red feathers."

"Not all the dreams come true," he said.

"I hope not," she answered. "Because this snake comes out of—I give birth to this snake."

"Quetzal," he said.

"What does that mean?"

"The feathered serpent god of the Aztecs. Or maybe the Mayas. Mexican, anyway. I have to go home."

"But what does it mean?"

"It's almost dark," he said.

"Stay and talk to me!" she demanded. "I have room, you can stay the night."

But Sam had to get back. Much as he hated staying with his father, he dared not spend a night in this place. Even her invitation aroused him. He would never last a night in the same house with her. The dream would be too strong for him. So he left her and headed back along the path through the jungle. All during the walk he couldn't get Anamari out of his mind. It was, as if the plants were sending him the vision of her, so his desire was even stronger than when he was with her.

The leaves gradually turned from green to black in the seeping dark. The hot darkness did not frighten him; it seemed to invite him to step away from the path into the shadows, where he would find the moist relief, the cool release of all his tension. He stayed on the path, and hurried faster.

He came at last to the oilmen's town. The generator was loud, but the insects were louder, swarming around the huge area light, casting shadows of their demonic dance. He and his father shared a large one-room house on the far edge of the compound. The oil company provided much nicer hovels than the Brazilian government.

A few man called out to greet him. He waved, even answered once or twice, but hurried on. His groin felt so hot and tight with desire that he was sure that only the shadows and his quick stride kept everyone from seeing. It was maddening: the more he thought of trying to calm himself, the more visions of Anamari slipped in and out of his waking mind, almost to the point of hallucination. His body would not relax. He was almost running when he burst into the house.

Inside, Father was washing his dinner plate. He glanced up, but Sam was already past him. "I'll heat up your dinner."

Sam flopped down on his bed. "Not hungry."

"Why are you so late?" asked his father.

"We got to talking."

"It's dangerous in the jungle at night. You think it's safe because nothing bad ever happens to you in the daytime, but it's dangerous."

"Sure, Dad. I know." Sam got up, turned his back to take off his pants. Maddeningly, he was still aroused; he didn't want his father to see.

But with the unerring instinct of prying parents, the old bastard must have sensed that Sam was hiding something. When Sam was buck naked, Father walked around and *looked,* just as if he never heard of privacy. Sam blushed in spite of himself. His father's eyes went small and hard. I hope I don't ever look like that, thought Sam. I hope my face doesn't get that ugly suspicious expression on it. I'd rather die than look like that.

"Well, put on your pajamas," Father said. "I don't want to look at that forever."

Sam pulled on his sleeping shorts.

"What's going on over there?" asked Father.

"Nothing," said Sam.

"You must do *something* all day."

"I told you, I help her. She runs a clinic, and she also tends a garden. She's got no electricity, so it takes a lot of work."

"I've done a lot of work in my time, Sam, but I don't come home like *that.*"

"No, you always stopped and got it off with some whore along the way."

The old bastard whipped out his hand and slapped Sam across the face. It stung, and the surprise of it wrung tears from Sam before he had time to decide not to cry.

"I never slept with a whore in my life," said the old bastard.

"You only slept with one woman who wasn't," said Sam.

Father slapped him again, only this time Sam was ready, and he bore the slap stoically, almost without flinching.

"I had one affair," said Father.

"You got caught once," said Sam. "There were dozens of women."

Father laughed derisively. "What did you do, hire a detective? There was only the one."

But Sam knew better. He had dreamed these women for years. Laughing, lascivious women. It wasn't until he was twelve years old that he found out enough about sex to know what it all meant. By then he had long since learned that any dream he had more than once was true. So when he had a dream of Father with one of the laughing women, he woke up, holding the dream in his memory. He thought through it from beginning to end, remembering all the details he could. The name of the motel. The room number. It was midnight, but Father was in California, so it was an hour earlier. Sam got out of bed and walked quietly into the kitchen, and dialed directory assistance. There was such a motel. He wrote down the number. Then Mother was there, asking him what he was doing.

"This is the number of the Seaview Motor Inn," he said. "Call this number and ask for room twenty-one twelve and then ask for Dad."

Mother looked at him strangely, like she was about to scream or cry or hit him or throw up. "Your father is at the Hilton," she said.

But he just looked right back at her and said, "No matter who answers the phone, ask for Dad."

So she did. A woman answered, and Mom asked for Dad by name, and he was there. "I wonder how we can afford to pay for two motel rooms on the same night," Mom said coldly. "Or are you splitting the cost with your friend?" Then she hung up the phone and burst into tears.

She cried all night as she packed up everything the old bastard owned. By the time Dad got home two days later, all his things were in storage. Mom moved fast when she made up her mind. Dad found himself divorced and excommunicated all in the same week, not two months later.

Mother never asked Sam how he knew where Dad was that night. Never even hinted at wanting to know. Dad never asked him how Mom knew to call that number, either. An amazing lack of curiosity, Sam thought sometimes. Perhaps they just took it as fate. For a while it was secret, then it stopped being secret, and it didn't matter how the change happened. But one thing Sam knew for sure—the woman at the Seaview Motor Inn was not the first woman, and the Seaview was not the first motel. Dad had been an adulterer for years, and it was ridiculous for him to lie about it now.

But there was no point in arguing with him, especially when he was in the mood to slap Sam around.

"I don't like the idea of you spending so much time with an older woman," said Father.

"She's the closest thing to a doctor these people have. She needs my help and I'm going to keep helping her," said Sam.

"Don't talk to me like that, little boy."

"You don't know anything about this, so just mind your own business."

Another slap. "You're going to get tired of this before I do, Sammy."

"I love it when you slap me, Dad. It confirms my moral superiority."

Another slap, this time so hard that Sam stumbled under the blow, and he tasted blood inside his mouth. "How hard next time, Dad?" he said. "You going to knock me down? Kick me around a little? Show me who's boss?"

"You've been asking for a beating ever since we got here."

"I've been asking to be left alone."

"I know women, Sam. You have no business getting involved with an older woman like that."

"I help her wash a little girl who has bowel movements in bed, Father. I empty pails of vomit. I wash clothes and help patch leaking roofs and while I'm doing all these things we talk. Just talk. I don't imagine you have much experience with that, Dad. You probably never talk at all with the women *you* know, at least not after the price is set."

It was going to be the biggest slap of all, enough to knock him down, enough to bruise his face and black his eye. But the old bastard held it in. Didn't hit him. Just stood there, breathing hard, his face red, his eyes tight and piggish.

"You're not as pure as you think," the old bastard finally whispered. "You've got every desire you despise in me."

"I don't despise you for *desire,*" said Sam.

"The guys on the crew have been talking about you and

this Indian bitch, Sammy. You may not like it, but I'm your father and it's my job to warn you. These Indian women are easy, and they'll give you a disease."

"The guys on the crew," said Sam. "What do they know about Indian women? They're all fags or jerk-offs."

"I hope someday you say that where they can hear you, Sam. And I hope when it happens I'm not there to stop what they do to you."

"I would never *be* around men like that, Daddy, if the court hadn't given you shared custody. A no-fault divorce. What a joke."

More than anything else, those words stung the old bastard. Hurt him enough to shut him up. He walked out of the house and didn't come back until Sam was long since asleep.

Asleep and dreaming.

Anamari knew what was on Sam's mind, and to her surprise she found it vaguely flattering. She had never known the shy affection of a boy. When she was a teenager, she was the one Indian girl in the schools in São Paulo. Indians were so rare in the Europeanized parts of Brazil that she might have seemed exotic, but in those days she was still so frightened. The city was sterile, all concrete and harsh light, not at all like the deep soft meadows and woods of Xingu Park. Her tribe, the Kuikuru, were much more Europeanized than the jungle Indians—she had seen cars all her life, and spoke Portuguese before she went to school. But the city made her hungry for the land, the cobblestones hurt her feet, and these intense, competitive children made her afraid. Worst of all, true dreams stopped in the city. She hardly knew who she was; if she was not a true dreamer. So if any boy desired her then, she would not have known it. She would have rebuffed him inadvertently. And then the time for such things had passed. Until now.

"Last night I dreamed of a great bird, flying west, away from land. Only its right wing was twice as large as its left wing. It had great bleeding wounds along the edges of its wings, and the right wing was the sickest of all, rotting in the air, the feathers dropping off."

"Very pretty dream," said Sam. Then he translated, to

105

keep in practice. "Que sonho lindo."

"Ah, but what does it mean?"

"What happened next?"

"I was riding on the bird. I was very small, and I held a small snake in my hands—"

"The feathered snake."

"Yes. And I turned it loose, and it went and ate up all the corruption, and the bird was clean. And that's all. You've got a bubble in that syringe. The idea is to inject medicine, not air. What does the dream mean?"

"What, do you think I'm a Joseph? A Daniel?"

"How about a Sam?"

"Actually, your dream is easy. Piece of cake."

"What?"

"Piece of cake. Easy as pie. That's how the cookie crumbles. Man shall not live by bread alone. All I can think of are bakery sayings. I must be hungry."

"Tell me the dream or I'll poke this needle into your eye."

"That's what I like about you Indians. Always you have torture on your mind."

She planted her feet against him and knocked him off his stool onto the packed dirt floor. A beetle skittered away. Sam held up the syringe he had been working with; it was undamaged. He got up, set it aside. "The bird," he said, "is North and South America. Like wings, flying west. Only the right wing is bigger." He sketched out a rough map with his toe on the floor.

"That's the shape, maybe," she said. "It could be."

"And the corruption—show me where it was."

With her toe, she smeared the map here, there.

"It's obvious," said Sam.

"Yes," she said. "Once you think of it as a map. The corruption is all the Europeanized land. And the only healthy places are where the Indians still live."

"Indians or? half-Indians," said Sam. "All your dreams are about the same thing, Anamari. Removing the Europeans from North and South America. Let's face it. You're an Indian chauvinist. You give birth to the resurrection god of the Aztecs, and then you sent it out to destroy the Europeans."

"But why do I dream this?"

"Because you hate Europeans."

"No," she said. "That isn't true."

"Sure it is."

"I don't hate *you*."

"Because you know me. I'm not a European anymore, I'm a person. Obviously you've got to keep that from happening anymore, so you can keep your bigotry alive."

"You're making fun of me, Sam."

He shook his head. "No, I'm not. These are true dreams, Anamari. They tell you your destiny."

She giggled. "If I give birth to a feathered snake, I'll know the dream was true."

"To drive the Europeans out of America."

"No," she said. "I don't care what the dream says. I won't do that. Besides, what about the dream of the flowering weed?"

"Little weed in the garden, almost dead, and then you water it and it grows larger and larger and more beautiful—"

"And something else," she said. "At the very end of the dream, all the other flowers in the garden have changed. To be just like the flowering weed." She reached out and rested her hand on his arm. "Tell me *that* dream."

His arm became still, lifeless under her hand. "Black is beautiful," he said.

"What does *that* mean?"

"In America. The U.S., I mean. For the longest time, the blacks, the former slaves, they were ashamed to be black. The whiter you were, the more status you had—the more honor. But when they had their revolution in the sixties—"

"You don't remember the sixties, little boy."

"Heck, I barely remember the seventies. But I read books. One of the big changes, and it made a huge difference, was that slogan. Black is beautiful. The blacker the better. They said it over and over. Be proud of blackness, not ashamed of it. And in just a few years, they turned the whole status system upside down."

She nodded. "The weed came into flower."

"So. All through Latin America, Indians are very low status. If you want a Bolivian to pull a knife on you, just call him an Indian. Everybody who possibly can, pretends to be of pure Spanish blood. Pure-blooded Indians are slaughtered wherever there's the slightest excuse. Only in Mexico is it a little bit different."

"What you tell me from my dreams, Sam, this is no small job to do. I'm one middle-aged Indian woman, living in the jungle. I'm supposed to tell all the Indians of America to be proud? When they're the poorest of the poor and the lowest of the low?"

"When you give them a name, you create them. Benjamin Franklin did it, when he coined the name *American* for the people of the English colonies. They weren't New Yorkers or Virginians, they were Americans. Same thing for you. It isn't Latin Americans against Norteamericanos. It's Indians and Europeans. Somos todos indios. We're all Indians. Think that would work as a slogan?"

"Me. A revolutionary."

"Nós somos os americanos. Vai fora, Europa! America p'ra americanos! All kinds of slogans."

"I'd have to translate them into Spanish."

"Indios moram na India. Americanos moram na America. America nossa! No, better still: Nossa America! Nuestra America! It translates. Our America."

"You're a very fine slogan maker."

He shivered as she traced her finger along his shoulder and down the sensitive skin of his chest. She made a circle on his nipple and it shriveled and hardened, as if he were cold.

"Why are you silent now?" She laid her hand flat on his abdomen, just above his shorts, just below his naval. "You never tell me your own dreams," she said. "But I know what they are."

He blushed.

"See? Your skin tells me, even when your mouth says nothing. I have dreamed these dreams all my life, and they troubled me, all the time, but now you tell me what they mean, a white-skinned dream-teller, you tell me that I must go among the Indians and make them proud, make them strong, so that everyone with a drop of Indian blood will call himself an Indian, and Europeans will lie and claim native ancestors, until America is all Indian. You tell me that

I will give birth to the new Quetzalcoatl, and he will unify and heal the land of its sickness. But what you never tell me is this: Who will be the father of my feathered snake?"

Abruptly he got up and walked stiffly away. To the door, keeping his back to her, so she couldn't see how alert his body was. But she knew.

"I'm fifteen," said Sam, finally.

"And I'm very old. The land is older. Twenty million years. What does it care of the quarter-century between us?"

"I should never have come to this place."

"You never had a choice," she said. "My people have always known the god of the land. Once there was a perfect balance in this place. All the people loved the land and tended it. Like the garden of Eden. And the land fed them. It gave them maize and bananas. They took only what they needed to eat, and they did not kill animals for sport or humans for hate. But then the Incas turned away from the land and worshipped gold and the bright golden sun. The Aztecs soaked the ground in the blood of their human sacrifices. The Pueblos cut down the forests of Utah and Arizona and turned them into red-rock deserts. The Iroquois tortured their enemies and filled the forests with their screams of agony. We found tobacco and coca and peyote and coffee and forgot the dreams the land gave us in our sleep. And so the land rejected us. The land called to Columbus and told him lies and seduced him and he never had a chance, did he? Never had a choice. The land brought the Europeans to punish us. Disease and slavery and warfare killed most of us, and the rest of us tried to pretend we were Europeans rather than endure any more of the punishment. The land was our jealous lover, and it hated us for a while."

"Some Catholic you are," said Sam. "I don't believe in your Indian gods."

"Say *Deus* or *Cristo* instead of *the land* and the story is the same," she said. "But now the Europeans are worse than we Indians ever were. The land is suffering from a thousand different poisons, and you threaten to kill all of life with your weapons of war. We Indians have been punished enough, and now it's our turn to have the land again. The land chose Columbus exactly five centuries ago. Now you

109

and I dream our dreams, the way he dreamed."

"That's a good story," Sam said, still looking out the door. It sounded so close to what the old prophets in the Book of Mormon said would happen to America; close, but dangerously different. As if there were no hope for the Europeans anymore. As if their chance had already been lost, as if no repentance would be allowed. They would not be able to pass the land on to the next generation. Someone else would inherit. It made him sick at heart, to realize what the white man had lost, had thrown away, had torn up and destroyed.

"But what should I do with my story?" she asked. He could hear her coming closer, walking up behind him. He could almost feel her breath on his shoulder. "How can I fulfill it?"

By yourself. Or at least without me. "Tell it to the Indians. You can cross all these borders in a thousand different places, and you speak Portuguese and Spanish and Arawak and Carib, and you'll be able to tell your story in Quechua, too, no doubt, crossing back and forth between Brazil and Colombia and Bolivia and Peru and Venezuela, all close together here, until every Indian knows about you and calls you by the name you were given in my dream."

"Tell me my name."

"Virgem America. See? The land or god or whatever it is wants you to be a virgin."

She giggled. "Nossa senhora," she said. "Don't you see? I'm the new Virgin *Mother*. It wants me to be a *mother;* all the old legends of the Holy Mother will transfer to me; they'll call me virgin no matter what the truth is. How the priests will hate me. How they'll try to kill my son. But he will live and become Quetzalcoatl, and he will restore America to the true Americans. That is the meaning of my dreams. My dreams and yours."

"Not me," he said. "Not for any dream or any god." He turned to face her. His fist was pressed against his groin, as if to crush out all rebellion there. "My body doesn't rule me," he said. "Nobody controls me but myself."

"That's very sick," she said cheerfully. "All because you hate your father. Forget that hate, and love me instead."

His face became a mask of anguish, and then he turned

and fled.

He even thought of castrating himself, that's the kind of madness that drove him through the jungle. He could hear the bulldozers carving out the airstrip, the screams of falling timbers, the calls of birds and cries of animals displaced. It was the terror of the tortured land, and it maddened him even more as he ran between thick walls of green. The rig was sucking oil like heartblood from the forest floor. The ground was wan and trembling under his feet. And when he got home he was grateful to lift his feet off the ground and lie on his mattress, clutching his pillow, panting or perhaps sobbing from the exertion of his run.

He slept, soaking his pillow in afternoon sweat, and in his sleep the voice of the land came to him like whispered lullabies. I did not choose you, said the land. I cannot speak except to those who hear me, and because it is in your nature to hear and listen, I spoke to you and led you here to save me, save me, save me. Do you know the desert they will make of me. Encased in burning dust or layers of ice, either way I'll be dead. My whole purpose is to thrust life upward out of my soils, and feel the press of living feet, and hear the songs of the birds and the low music of the animals, growling, lowing, chittering, whatever voice they choose. That's what I ask of you, the dance of life, just once to make the man whose mother will teach him to be Quetzalcoatl and save me, save me, save me.

He heard that whisper and he dreamed a dream. In his dream he got up and walked back to Agualinda, not along the path, but through the deep jungle itself. A longer way, but the leaves touched his face, the spiders climbed on him, the tree lizards tangled in his hair, the monkeys dunged him and pinched him and jabbered in his ear, the snakes entwined around his feet; he waded streams and fish caressed his naked ankles, and all the way they sang to him, songs that celebrants might sing at the wedding of a king. Somehow, in the way of dreams, he lost his clothing without removing it, so that he emerged from the jungle naked, and walked through Agualinda as the sun was setting, all the Baniwas peering at him from their doorways, making clicking noises with their teeth.

He awoke in darkness. He heard his father breathing. He must have slept through the afternoon. What a dream, what a dream. He was exhausted.

He moved, thinking of getting up to use the toilet. Only then did he realize that he was not alone on the bed, and it was not his bed. She stirred and nestled against him and he cried out in fear and anger.

It startled her awake, "What is it?" she asked.

"It was a dream," he insisted. "All a dream."

"Ah yes," she said, "it was. But last night, Sam, we dreamed the same dream." She giggled. "All night long."

In his sleep. It happened in his sleep. And it did not fade like common dreams, the memory was clear, pouring himself into her again and again, her fingers gripping him, her breath against his cheek, whispering the same thing, over and over: "Aceito, aceito-te, aceito." Not love, no, not when he came with the land controlling him, she did not love him, she merely accepted the burden he placed within her. Before tonight she had been a virgin, and so had he. Now she was even purer than before, Virgem America, but his purity was hopelessly, irredeemably gone, wasted, poured out into this old woman who had haunted his dreams. "I hate you," he said. "What you stole from me."

He got up, looking for his clothing, ashamed that she was watching him.

"No one can blame you," she said. "The land married us, gave us to each other. There's no sin in that."

"Yeah," he said.

"One time. Now I am whole. Now I can begin."

And now I'm finished.

"I didn't mean to rob you," she said. "I didn't know you were dreaming."

"I thought I was dreaming," he said, "but I loved the dream. I dreamed I was fornicating and it made me glad." He spoke the words with all the poison in his heart. "Where are my clothes?"

"You arrived without them," she said. "It was my first hint that you wanted me."

There was a moon outside. Not yet dawn. "I did what you wanted," he said. "Now can I go home?"

"Do what you want," she said. "I didn't plan this."

"I know. I wasn't talking to you. And when he spoke of home, he didn't mean the shack where his father would be snoring and the air would stink of beer.

"When you woke me, I was dreaming," she said.

"I don't want to hear it."

"I have him now," she said, "a boy inside me. A lovely boy. But you will never see him in all your life, I think."

"Will you tell him? Who I am?"

She giggled. "Tell Quetzalcoatl that his father is a European? A man who blushes? A man who burns in the sun? No, I won't tell him. Unless someday he becomes cruel, and wants to punish the Europeans even after they are defeated. Then I will tell him that the first European he must punish is himself. Here, write your name. On this paper write your name, and give me your fingerprint, and write the date."

"I don't know what day it is."

"October twelfth," she said.

"It's August."

"Write October twelfth," she said. "I'm in the legend business now."

"August twenty-fourth," he murmured, but he wrote the date she asked for.

"The helicopter comes in the morning," she said.

"Good-bye," he said. He started for the door.

Her hands caught at him, held his arm, pulled him back. She embraced him, this time not in a dream, cool bodies together in the doorway of the house. The geis was off him now, or else he was worn out; her body had no power over his anymore.

"I did love you," she murmured. "It was not just the god that brought you."

Suddenly he felt very young, even younger than fifteen, and he broke away from her and walked quickly away through the sleeping village. He did not try to retrace his wandering route through the jungle; he stayed on the moonlit path and soon was at his father's hut. The old bastard woke up as Sam came in.

"I knew it'd happen," Father said.

Sam rummaged for underwear and pulled it on.

"There's no man born who can keep his zipper up when

a woman wants it." Father laughed. A laugh of malice and triumph. "You're no better than I am, boy."

Sam walked to where his father sat on the bed and imagined hitting him across the face. Once, twice, three times.

"Go ahead, boy, hit me. It won't make you a virgin again."

"I'm not like you," Sam whispered.

"No?" asked Father. "For you it's a sacrament or something? As my daddy used to say, it don't matter who squeezes the toothpaste, boy, it all squirts out the same."

"Then your daddy must have been as dumb a jackass as mine." Sam went back to the closet they shared, began packing his clothes and books into one big suitcase. "I'm going out with the chopper today. Mom will wire me the money to come home from Manaus."

"She doesn't have to. I'll give you a check."

"I don't want your money. I just want my passport."

"It's in the top drawer." Father laughed again. "At least I always wore my clothes home."

In a few minutes Sam had finished packing. He picked up the bag, started for the door.

"Son," said Father, and because his voice was quiet, not derisive, Sam stopped and listened. "Son," he said, "once is once. It doesn't mean you're evil, it doesn't mean you're weak. It just means you're human." He was breathing deeply. Sam hadn't heard him so emotional in a long time. "You aren't a thing like me, son," he said. "That should make you glad."

Years later Sam would think of all kinds of things he should have said. Forgiveness. Apology. Affection. Something. But he said nothing, just left and went out to the clearing and waited for the helicopter. Father didn't try to say good-bye. The chopper pilot came, unloaded, left the chopper to talk to some people. He must have talked to Father because when he came back he handed Sam a check. Plenty to fly home, and stay in good places during the layovers, and buy some new clothes that didn't have jungle stains on them. The check was the last thing Sam had from his father. Before he came home from that rig, the Venezuelans bought a hardy and virulent strain of syphilis on the black market, one that could be passed by casual contact, and released it in Guyana. Sam's father was one of the first million to die, so fast that he didn't even write.

Page, Arizona

The State of Deseret had only sixteen helicopters, all desperately needed for surveying, spraying, and medical emergencies. So Governor Sam Monson rarely risked them on government business. This time, though, he had no choice. He was only fifty-five, and in good shape, so maybe he could have made the climb down into Glen Canyon and back up the other side. But Carpenter wouldn't have made it, not in a wheel-chair, and Carpenter had a right to be here. He had a right to see what the red-rock Navaho desert had become.

Deciduous forest, as far as the eye could see.

They stood on the bluff where the old town of Page had once been, before the dam was blown up. The Navahos hadn't tried to reforest here. It was their standard practice. They left all the old European towns unplanted, like pink scars in the green of the forest. Still, the Navahos weren't stupid. They had come to the last stronghold of European science, the University of Deseret at Zarahemla, to find out how to use the heavy rainfalls to give them something better than perpetual floods and erosion. It was Carpenter who gave them the plan for these forests, just as it was Carpenter whose program had turned the old Utah deserts into the richest farmland in America. The Navahos filled their forests with bison, deer, and bears. The Mormons raised crops enough to feed five times their population. That was the European mindset, still in place: enough is never enough. Plant more, grow more, you'll need it tomorrow.

"They say he has two hundred thousand soldiers," said Carpenter's computer voice. Carpenter *could* speak, Sam had heard, but he never did. Preferred the synthesized voice. "They could be all right down there, and we'd never see them."

"They're much farther south and east. Strung out from Phoenix to Santa Fe, so they aren't too much of a burden on the Navahos."

"Do you think they'll buy supplies from us? Or send an army in to take them?"

"Neither," said Sam. "We'll give our surplus grain as a

gift."

"He rules all of Latin America and he needs *gifts* from a little remnant of the U.S. in the Rockies?"

"We'll give it as a gift, and be grateful if he takes it that way."

"How else might he take it?"

"As tribute. As taxes. As ransom. The land is his now, not ours."

"We made the desert live, Sam. That makes it ours."

"There they are."

They watched in silence as four horses walked slowly from the edge of the woods, out onto the open ground of an ancient gas station. They bore a litter between them, and were led by two—not Indians—Americans. Sam had schooled himself long ago to use the word *American* to refer only to what had once been known as Indians, and to call himself and his own people Europeans. But in his heart he had never forgiven them for stealing his identity, even though he remembered very clearly where and when that change began.

It took fifteen minutes for the horses to bring the litter to him, but Sam made no move to meet them, no sign that he was in a hurry. That was also the American way now, to take time, never to hurry, never to rush. Let the Europeans wear their watches. Americans told time by the sun and stars.

Finally the litter stopped, and the men opened the litter door and helped her out. She was smaller than before, and her face was tightly wrinkled, her hair steel-white.

She gave no sign that she knew him, though he said his name. The Americans introduced her as Nuestra Señora. Our Lady. Never speaking her most sacred name: Virgem America.

The negotiations were delicate but simple. Sam had authority to speak for Deseret, and she obviously had authority to speak for her son. The grain was refused as a gift, but accepted as taxes from a federated state. Deseret would be allowed to keep its own government, and the borders negotiated between the Navahos and the Mormons eleven years before were allowed to stand.

Sam went further. He praised Quetzalcoatl for coming

to pacify the chaotic lands that had been ruined by the Europeans. He gave her maps that his scouts had prepared, showing strongholds of the prairie raiders, decommissioned nuclear missiles, and the few places where stable governments had been formed. He offered, and she accepted, a hundred experienced scouts to travel with Quetzalcoatl at Deseret's expense, and promised that when he chose the site of his North American capital, Deseret would provide architects and engineers and builders to teach his American workmen how to build the place themselves.

She was generous in return. She granted all citizens of Deseret conditional status as adopted Americans, and she promised that Quetzalcoatl's armies would stick to the roads through the northwest Texas panhandle, where the grasslands of the newest New Lands project were still so fragile that an army could destroy five years of labor just by marching through. Carpenter printed out two copies of the agreement in English and Spanish, and Sam and Virgem America signed both.

Only then, when their official work was done, did the old woman look up into Sam's eyes and smile. "Are you still a heretic, Sam?"

"No," he said. "I grew up. Are you still a virgin?"

She giggled, and even though it was an old lady's broken voice, he remembered the laughter he had heard so often in the village of Agualinda, and his heart ached for the boy he was then, and the girl she was. He remembered thinking then that forty-two was old.

"Yes, I'm still a virgin," she said. "God gave me my child. God sent me an angel, to put the child in my womb. I thought you would have heard the story by now."

"I heard it," he said.

She leaned closer to him, her voice a whisper. "Do you dream, these days?"

"Many dreams. But the only ones that come true are the ones I dream in daylight."

"Ah," she sighed. "My sleep is also silent."

She seemed distant, sad, distracted. Sam also; then, as if by conscious decision, he brightened, smiled, spoke cheerfully, "I have grandchildren now."

"And a wife you love," she said, reflecting his brightening

mood. "I have grandchildren, too." Then she became wistful again. "But no husband. Just memories of an angel."

"Will I see Quetzalcoatl?"

"No," she said, very quickly. A decision she had long since made and would not reconsider. "It would not be good for you to meet face to face, or stand side by side. Quetzalcoatl also asks that in the next election, you refuse to be a candidate."

"Have I displeased him?" asked Sam.

"He asks this at my advice," she said. "It is better, now that his face will be seen in this land, that your face stay behind closed doors."

Sam nodded. "Tell me," he said. "Does he look like the angel?"

"He is as beautiful," she said. "But not as pure."

They embraced each other and wept. Only for a moment. Then her men lifted her back into her litter, and Sam returned with Carpenter to the helicopter. They never met again.

In retirement, I came to visit Sam, full of questions lingering from his meeting with Virgem America. "You knew each other," I insisted. "You had met before." He told me all this story then.

That was thirty years ago. She is dead now, he is dead, and I am old, my fingers slapping these keys with all the grace of wooden blocks. But I write this sitting in the shade of a tree on the brow of a hill, looking out across woodlands and orchards, fields and rivers and roads, where once the land was rock and grit and sagebrush. This is what America wanted, what it bent our lives to accomplish. Even if we took twisted roads and got lost or injured on the way, even if we came limping to this place, it is a good place, it is worth the journey, it is the promised, the promising land. ●

SHALAMARI
by Marc Laidlaw

"Shalamari" was purchased by Gardner Dozols and appeared in the December 1987 issue of IAsfm, *with an interior illustration by J. K. Potter. A moody story, full of dark bells and sullen music, "Shalamari" takes us deep into the Himalayas, to one of the most remote locales on the face of the Earth, for an eerie tale of reincarnation, karma, and the unstoppably-spinning Wheel of Fate.*

Marc Laidlaw is a young writer who has recently moved to Long Island from San Francisco. His short work has appeared in most of the major SF magazines, and his first novel, Dad's Nuke, *was published to good critical response. His most recent novel,* The Neon Lotus, *is set in 23rd century Tibet—an area of the world that obviously fascinates him.*

Pemba set out at dawn from the ancient fortress city, while the snow melt ran at its lowest ebb through the ravines and irrigation canals. Behind him, in the dark second story of his clay-walled house, he left his wife Sonma in the care of his younger brother, who might also have been the father of the child that now tore at her vitals, as if in a demonic fury to free itself. Her screams had followed him through the narrow streets of the city, louder than the wind above the walls. He could not forget the last sight of fear in his brother Taktser's eyes, as he huddled protectively over the woman to whom both of them were wed. "I won't let her die, Pemba," Taktser had said. "You fetch the Lama of Dzorling and I will keep her alive until you return. Somehow I'll do it."

The city gate opened at dawn. Pemba was there at the head of the crowd, risking his life in the stampede of yaks that were driven out each morning to find what nourishment they could on the Plain of Winds and the surrounding slopes. It was quiet beyond the wall, the light filtered and grey in a gentle snowfall; the winds for which the plain had been named would not rise until noon, when they would bear down the passes from Nepal into Tebet, using the rocky barrens of Kricheb as their accustomed corridor. He stalked ahead, leaning into the snow, thankful that he'd finished weaving himself a new set of grass soles for his boots. With every plait of the fibers he had invoked the protection of those spirits that watched over travelers; this was certain defense against frostbite but would also keep him from losing his way. He had been to Dzorling, the monastery of the curled stones, only once before, and that many years ago in clear weather. As he passed alongside the canals, between fields plowed in spiral patterns but still unsown with barley, he began to pray that he would keep to the proper path.

An old man when Pemba had saved his life, the Lama of Dzorling must by now be ancient. It would be a grueling journey for him, through the snows and over rough ground, to save a child and its mother. Clearly if the Lama saved the child, and if it were a boy, it should be brought up for the monastic life. But Pemba and Taktser desperately needed a son to take over the household before age made them decrepit. Oh, let this be a boy, and then let Somma bear them a second son to enter the monastery, and beyond that a daughter or two, and more sons. Fine! But first, no matter the child's sex, let it live. Let both Sonma and the child live. He prayed that his heart would not be broken like ice in the spring thaw.

By midmorning, the snows of the night had evaporated and the sun was burning his black hair. The wind began to rise. The noon sun found him above the plains, following a little-used track between high cliffs of soft green stone. A recent landslide obliged him to clamber above the path, but the inauspiciousness of this obstacle was countered by his discovery of a shalamar in the midst of the slide. It was a black stone in the shape of a spiral, perfectly formed, with the lines of small chambers scoring its sides. He tucked it into the inner pocket of his chuba, knowing that he must be near Dzorling.

He became so accustomed to the twists and turns of the path, and to the desolation of the fantastically colored cliffs towering around him, that when he finally reached the monastic dwelling he almost passed through them without noticing, so intent was he on watching where to place his feet on the narrow and rocky trail. He was called from his concentration by a low, chilling howl—the sound of a god keening its loneliness to the deep blue sky. He looked up, in fear that a monstrous shadow would blot out the turquoise bowl of heaven and the golden coin of the sun. And there he saw Dzorling.

The faces of the cliffs on both sides were scored by the mouths of caves, high and inaccessible as the aeries of birds. But from one of these black holes emerged the silver tip of an immense trumpet whose bellowing echoed back and forth between the crushing walls of stone. Now an ominous drumming began, as if to summon dragons from the sky. Bells began to ring, sustaining ghostly notes right up to the edge of silence. Pemba covered his head and sank down on the trail, moaning. He knew these sounds from festivals— they were meant to chase demons from Kricheb, not to attract them. But it was one thing to hear such sounds in the fortress, surrounded by friends. Here in this desolate realm, the sound filled him with terror. He thought it meant that death had come to Sonma, and now sought him as well.

When the last peal of trumpeting had died out, and the bells had finally faded, Pemba heard a brief sharp cry. Peering out from between his hands he saw the shorn head of a young monk looking down at him.

"Who are you?"

"My name is Pemba. I've come from the capital to see the Lama of Dzorling. Please tell him that my wife is dying."

"The Lama is in meditation," the youth replied. "He won't be out for a year."

"He promised to help me if I needed him. You must tell him—"

"He has not spoken for many years."

"I'm the boy who found him with his feet frozen in a stream and carried him back to Dzorling."

"That won't matter to him. He has loftier concerns. He is learning to inhabit an infinite number of bodies in which to work compassionate acts throughout the universe of sentient suffering beings."

"Surely he can spare one body to visit my wife. I beg you . . ."

"I can't disturb him! There are other lamas in the mountains. Find one who's not so important and doesn't have a million bodies to tend."

Pemba, in rage and despair, began to shriek at the young monk. "What kind of fool are you? How did you get to be a monk?"

The boy scowled at him. "It was my father's idea. Do you think I like living in a hole like this, making tea for an old man who won't say a word, fetching nettles for his meals, getting up at dawn to blow that blasted kangling? How would you like to do tens of thousands of full prostrations on a cold rock floor and say mantras until you're hoarse, and read in dim light until you're half blind, and stay up all night visualizing tutelary spirits—*aieee!*"

The young monk disappeared into the cave. Pemba heard breaking crockery and watched patterns of dust sifting out into the air. After a moment the monk reappeared, his scalp smudged with ash, tears in his eyes.

"You'd better come up," he said. "Wait right there."

Several minutes later, the young monk appeared at a bend in the trail. He was a short fellow, skinny but muscular—no doubt from his many prostrations. Upon seeing Pemba, he bowed deeply with his hands cupped before his face, and stuck out his tongue in respect. Then he turned, beckoning for Pemba to follow him. They reached a heavy wooden door hidden back in a tumble of rocks at the face of the cliff. They entered and the young monk barred it from within. They scaled ladder after ladder, rising through a series of caves, some windowless, some overlooking the path. In a few of the rooms, monks sat with eyes half shut, lips moving as they fed polished rosaries through their fingers. The meagerest of fires burned in several chambers, and the walls were hung with tankas—religious paintings whose detail he could scarcely discern in the dimness.

Finally they came into a massive temple room, its floor made of smooth wooden beams from days long past, when Kricheb had been a forested region. There was a huge wooden altar at the far end of the room; above it, in the place of honor, were row upon row of huge cloth-wrapped bundles: books. Immense golden images lined the walls, most of them covered the dust.

"Fortunately," the young monk said, "the Lama's seclusion ended precisely when you arrived. I seem to have lost track of the time."

Pembra looked for the Lama, but the chamber was empty except for the two of them. A hundred monks would have been needed to make the place seem at all occupied. It was a huge natural cave, the walls embedded with spiral shalamari like the one in his pocket.

"Wait here," he was told. The monk disappeared between two gemflecked statues of Buddha. The monastery, like all Kricheb, had outlasted its wealth; it was no longer a religious center for the Himalayas. At the time of his first visit, Dzorling had seemed an active and thriving place, but perhaps that had been in the festival season, when the itinerant monks came in from their pilgrimages to build offerings, sculpt tormas from barley flour, and receive empowerments and instruction from visiting spiritual teachers. He had almost wished, in those days, that he had been part of the order, for he had envied the monks their hierarchy, the pageantry, the service they did for the infinity of suffering beings. Now he saw the other aspect of their existence: solitude, empty caves, the loneliness of the true ascetic. He thought of his warm two-story house in the fortress city, and the warmer flesh of his wife. Sonma ... he began to weep for her, staring through a narrow window at the sandstone wall across the way.

Pemba," said a windy, carvernous voice.

He turned and saw an old man coming toward him, in an orange robe draped with faded yellow scarves. Quickly Pemba fumbled in the pocket of his chuba for the fresh white silk kata he had brought, and bending low he offered the fine scarf to the Lama of Dzorling. The Lama took the kata and draped it around Pemba's own neck and shoulders, bidding him rise.

He did not look any older than he had in Pemba's boyhood, not at first. But as Pemba looked more closely, he began to see that the Lama of Dzorling was only a man, and like any man time had done its work on him. His hair was a thick gray mat, uncombed and unclipped for years. He put a gentle hand on Pemba's shoulder and walked with him to the window, which was fringed by the last remnants of some old brown paper that had probably never kept drafts out of the temple.

"You've come all the way from the fortress to see me? Your wife is ill?"

Pemba could hardly speak at first. He recalled Taktser's great hope for his expedition. How could Sonma still be alive, except by his brother's will? He began to speak of his fears.

Sonma had lost two children, both of them at inauspicious times. The first had slipped out amid much blood, no more than five months along, during a terrible earthquake that had threatened to turn Pemba's house and the fortress walls to rubble; later it was found that a river had changed its course during the tremor, sweeping away a great deal of excellent farmland and drowning the region's most prized chörten, a brightly painted shrine maintained for centuries on the main road. The second child was much closer to term when she lost it. He recalled the night when it had died. He and Sonma had gone up onto the roof where a thicket of branches formed a windbreak, and while they were looking out over the sea of rooftops she had pointed out a star falling from the violet sky toward the sea of eroded, snow-smoothed peaks that surrounded the Plain of Winds. With a gasp she had clutched her belly and turned such a look of sadness toward him that he'd known two things at once: that it had been his child and not Taktser's, but that now something fearful had happened—not only to the child, he felt, but to Kricheb. It was stillborn a week later, but for a week she carried the corpse within her, the small death staring blankly out through her eyes. On the day of its birth, the first army of Khampa soldiers had reached the Plain of Winds and demanded grazing rights for their ponies;

they were members of Chushi Gangdruk, the Tibetan resistance, and since that date they had lingered in Kricheb, making it the home for their assaults on the Red Chinese, a handful of miles to the north.

"And now the third child has come. I fear it will kill her. She complains that it tears at her heart; she believes it has teeth already and is gnawing at her liver. She has nightmares, horrible dreams that wake the house. She says it is not a child she carries, but a demon."

The Lama thought deeply on this. "She is close to term?"

"By her reckoning, she is past due. She dates the night of conception to an evil dream. We cannot convince her otherwise. Could a demon have come to her in a dream and caused her to conceive?"

"Tell me what you remember of that night."

"Nothing," Pemba said. "Neither my brother nor I remember a thing." He hesitated before admitting his worst fear. "I have wondered if the demon might have entered one of us as we slept, and caused us to lie with her in a nightmare, then entered through our seed."

The Lama nodded. "That is the usual method."

"No!"

"What I fear most is the conjunction of disasters with your wife's miscarriages. Earthquake, invasion, and what next? In my seclusion, I've seen far too many signs that I should stir and return to the world. I do not know what I can do for your wife, but if I can give some comfort, I will pray for her."

"It is said in the city that you studied medicine in Tibet."

The Lama's lips tightened, then he took a deep breath and seemed to stand taller. "That was long ago, but I have forgotten even the prayers to the Medicine Buddha. Do you know, when I graduated from the college I could identify all the herbs of the field by touch alone—even blindfolded? That is the skill a physician must posses in order to treat wisely. I cannot remember when last I took a pulse. I have let my techniques lapse."

"You must remember something."

"I remember my mistakes," he said. "I swore never to act as physician again; I could not trust myself. You see, I caused a death—not merely allowed it, but caused it with my needles. I pierced the points that could either preserve a man's heart or stop its beating. There was no foreknowing which of these would happen. In the instant I used my knowledge thus, I broke my vows to preserve life. I have been repairing them ever since."

"But surely you had a good reason—"

"Consequences, not reasons, are what follow one. Walled up in a cave, detached from my past, I have never been so crowded by consequences. My past gathers around me like a flock of jabbering ghosts. Can you not hear them calling now?"

"I hear only the wind."

"Then you are fortunate. To me, these caves are full of voices."

"Doctor, you must try."

There are doctors in the city."

"None trained as you have been. None who use the needles."

The Lama started as through Pemba had thrown a pail of melted snow over him. his eyes were bright, clearer than before, with an angry intensity. "You came to test my vow."

"Which vow? To put away your needles, or to preserve life?"

The Lama shook his head. "All I may be able to do is kill both your wife and child."

Pemba bowed his head and felt the wind rushing up against him from behind. He imagined what it would be like to plunge through the caves, down the trail and through the tortured barrens back to the fortified city, there to see his brother's face and Sonma at the end of her life, there to say, "I could not persuade him to come." But before he began to plead, the Lama touched him lightly.

"I must accept this challenge. For your sake and for that of Kricheb. If your wife loses this child, who knows what disaster may come."

Relief was a physical sensation, a weakening. He wished he could drop to the ground and let his exhaustion over-whelm him, but the Lama strode away, calling for the young monk: "Jigme, prepare for a journey. We will leave immediately. I hope you've taken good care of that Khampa mule."

"A journey?" the monk said, appearing among the bodhisattvas. His astonishment lit the room like a butter lamp.

"I've been sitting long enough," the Lama said.

With an undignified holler, Jigme rushed from the temple.

Pemba went to the tallest image of the Buddha and unwrapped the kata from his neck. Standing on tiptoe, he just managed to drape it over the figure's open hand.

They reached the city gate at midnight in the midst of a scouring snowstorm. The gate was locked, but the keeper heard their pounding.

"Sonma?" Pemba said. The gatekeeper nodded: "Still alive."

He rushed back to the mule that bore the huddled Lama, led by the bitterly complaining Jigme, and shouted the news to them. When the gate was shut, the wind cut off behind them, he felt his spirits lifting. By the lift of the gatekeeper's lantern, he saw that the Lama slept in the saddle, his lips muttering mantras and the rosary moving through his fingers as he dozed. If he were to die in his sleep, he would be ready with a prayer.

Somehow, word of the Lama's arrival went ahead of them. As they approached Pemba's house, the city's inhabitants appeared along the street, falling prostrate on the cold ground as the mule passed. The door of Pemba's house was open wide, his parents standing to either side, yawning, for they had not slept in days. He waited until the mule had gained the dry lower courtyard, then, leaving his parents to care for the guests, he ran upstairs to the drafty second floor.

Sonma lay stretched out by the fire, her face beaded with sweat. Taktser crouched above her, clutching her hand, his eyes huge and hollow from his vigil.

Pemba sank down beside his brother and their wife and took the hands of each. Taktser whispered, "She's in a fever. She can't stand to be near the fire nor away from it."

Pemba brushed the black hair back from her eyes. Her turquoise beads had been removed. An amber disk was affixed to her forehead, to draw out malign influences. Her eyes were wild and she did not seem to see him at all. He put his hand on her belly and felt an awful stillness.

"Where is he?" Taktser asked. Before Pemba could answer, Jigme rushed into the room, saying, "Here she is. Up here, master!"

The old Lama followed at an effortful pace. He advanced toward the firelight slowly, a folded leather bag under his arm, and knelt down beside Sonma. For a long time he gazed at her and Taktser gazed at him. There was no denying the apparent skill and sagacity of the old Lama as he unfolded his soft leather case and revealed an array of gleaming bone needles.

"I will need boiling water," he said. Pemba's mother hurried to put a pot on the fire, and when it was boiling the Lama dropped in a handful of bitter-smelling powders. He proceeded to bathe and asperge his needles in the infusion, then replaced them in the pouch. All the while, he was chanting in a low voice, his eyes on Sonma.

"As I sat in my cell," he said, "I sometimes could see beyond the rock walls, far out beyond Kricheb, into Tibet itself. I saw a cold blue flame glowing there, a deathly light upon the plains. The Chinese put it there. It turns their millwheels now, where once wind and water did that job. It heats their homes and grinds their grain, so in a sense it nurtures and feeds them with a cold blue fire."

"It is so," Jigme said. "We have sheltered Khampa soldiers after raids into Tibet. They told me many strange things. Far past Lhasa, the Chinese built such a place—a hearth for a new kind of fire. And they've gathered fierce weapons forged in this fire, to which the Khampa muskets are nothing. It frightened me. Do you think such things could come to Kricheb?"

The Lama nodded. "I also dreamed of things that could come to pass. I saw the air filled with trails of fire, like the paths of gunpowder rockets, but glowing that same blue, crisscrossing the air like falling stars—"

Taktser caught Pemba's eye. Pemba nodded to acknowledge that he has told the Lama of the second child, who had died when a star fell.

"—soaring between Tibet and India, falling on lands whose names are like legends: Russia, America. And everywhere they fell, that blue fire spread, and after it came darkness.

"And now here, in this room, I see that fire again. A burning star, a tiny beating heart—a living thing, but a cold thing. I fear as you fear, Jigme, that this is a new demon come to Kricheb."

As he fell silent, every eye in the room lay upon Sonma's belly. Her delirium cleared for a moment, as though clouds were parted by the wind and the stars appeared shining from the black sky. She stared down at her belly and began to scream, "Evil dream! Demon child! Demon!"

The Lama touched her on the forehead and chanted softly until her eyes closed. Still she lay whispering, "Demon . . . demon."

"Your wife is in touch with things far beyond the walls of this old fort," he told Pemba and Taktser. "Perhaps in her pain she has seen more than the Khampas. The woman is the source of creation. I witness these events, but it is through her that they come into the world. I see now that she has been keeping this child back. She fears to give birth to it. With her strong will, she may succeed—but it would kill her."

"What of the father?" Pemba asked. "Who planted this cold blue seed in her womb?"

"The Lamba shook his head. "I cannot say. Perhaps a demon. Perhaps a star that fell, or a vapor that rose from the earth."

"No," Taktser said suddenly, rising. "It was one of us, Pemba or me. If it is a demon, then we fathered it."

He went to the middle of the room, where there stood a pillar that supported the ceiling. Each New Year's the pillar was daubed with an offering of butter, by which the house was thanked for its shelter; with time the butter grew green and slightly furred. It was common practice to paint wounds with the ointment, which had healing properties. All during Sonma's illness she had taken bits of the green substance on her tongue, in order to cure her vitals. But now, as Taktser went to dab her lips with butter, the Lama gestured that he should refrain. The Lama took the daub from Taktser's fingertip and waved it gently under Sonma's nose.

Her brow winkled, she began to whimper. With a hand on her forehead, the Lama passed the moistened finger over the length of her body; all the while, she twitched and groaned.

"She cannot take this butter," the Lama declared. "It is beneficial to many, but some posses a natural aversion. It could cause her to sicken and die."

Taktser looked desolate, as if the Lama had accused him of slowly poisoning her all this while.

"It is not magic but medicine," the Lama said firmly but kindly to him. "You could not expect to know its proper application. Let us wait until dawn, when the sun's rays touch the mountain peaks, and then I shall take her pulse and decide what we must do next."

The Lama closed his eyes and, still sitting, fell asleep. Exhaustion also laid its hand on Pemba; before he realized what had happened, Taktser was nudging him awake. A faint light crept in through the tiny windows, less than the light of the hearth. Jigme gave Pemba a cup of salty tea, with a bit of butter placed on the lip as a sign of respect; his eyes spoke apologies for the manner in which he had spoken the previous afternoon. The two brothers and the young monk remained silent as the Lama shook back his voluminous sleeves and took Sonma's wrists in both hands. For the space of perhaps a hundred heartbeats, he sat as if listening to a distant voice while light slowly filled the room and a sparrow began to twitter. They could hear a prayer flag beating in the wind.

Pemba's parents watched from the far end of the room.

The Lama sat back with a grave expression and unfolded his cloth of bone needles. Pemba wanted to ask what he had learned from her pulse, but this was not the time. From among the dozens of sharp needles, the Lama selected two.

He killed a man, Pemba thought suddenly. Why did he tell me that story? He was glad that he had not shared it with Taktser, who looked so trusting of the old man. It was enough that Pemba thought of it now, when he should have felt faith instead. The Lama asked them to turn away while he worked.

Groping in his chuba as he pulled it closer around him, his finger touched the spiral stone, the shalamar, now warmed by his body's heart. Holding the relic, he began to pray. He wondered how long it had lain in the mountains.

It must be older than the age of the great kinds, now long past. Kricheb had risen and fallen, lost its forest, seen the Buddha come and go. The builders of the fortress had buried themselves in its catacombs. This rock had weathered all of it, curled tightly upon itself, unchanging. It would outlast whatever strange new demons came to the world; it would outlast good and bad alike. Blue fire and black stone. The newest powers and the most ancient.

Behind him, Sonma's breathing quickened; she was gasping now. She moaned. Then she began to breathe more deeply. It took all his will not to turn and look, not to throw the old man aside and pull the needles from his wife's flesh. The Lama had every reason to let the child die. If it were demonic, it would bring great misfortune into the world.

Out of the corner of his eye, he could see the leather case emptying of needles. Only a few remained. The Lama must be applying the points of which he had spoken—the points that saved or killed. That was why he had asked them not to watch. He looked up and saw Jigme staring past him, at Sonma. Why are you allowed to look, young fool, while I must stare at the wall?

Jigme blinked when he saw Pemba looking at him. He smiled and reached out to pat Pemba's hand, nodding.

The old Lama sighed, or had it been Sonma? He looked around, helpless to restrain himself. There she lay, with needles like rays of white light pouring from her, a look of peace on her face. Her eyes were lucid, her breathing easy now.

The Lama snatched out his needles. At last he drew a long spine from her navel. Pemba saw a flash of blue, a ray of cold light shafting up through the ceiling, back to the sky from which it had fallen.

The Lama folded his leather case as Sonma began to gasp. "You may get up now; crouch here, let your husbands squeeze your waist as you bid them." The Lama gestured to the brothers, urging them closer to her, and Pemba found that he was weeping. He threw his arms around his wife's belly, gently, and she gained her feet, crouching by the hearth, her gowns gathered about her waist. He heard the Lama and Jigme and his parents leaving by the stairs. He met Taktser's eyes, clasped his brother's hands, their fingers laced across Sonma's belly. They pushed when she bade them. There was splashing on the blankets and Sonma screamed a last time, her pain transformed to joy as she reached down between her legs. Then both brothers could touch the warm, wet child in that cold room full of the smell of blood and the wail of new life echoing.

Pemba took the Lama and Jigme as far as the city gate, and would have gone farther except that they would not let him. "We will return to baptize the child and give her a secret name," the Lama promised. "Go back to your wife and daughter now."

"What will you name her?" Jigme asked. "Her common name, I mean."

Pemba smiled and drew the black spiral from his pocket. He slipped the warm stone into the young monk's hands, a gift. There were thousands like it in the monastery, but none that meant so much to him.

"Shalamar," he said. ●

CHAND VEDA
by Tanith Lee

"Chand Veda" was purchased by Shawna McCarthy and appeared in the October 1983 issue of IAsfm, *with an illustration by Jim Odbert. Tanith Lee appears less frequently in* IAsfm *than we might wish, but each appearance has been memorable. Here, in one of a sequence of stories with Indian themes, later collected in* Tamastara, Or The Indian Nights, *she shows us that beauty really can be in the eye of the beholder, if you are well met by moonlight . . .*

Tanith Lee is one of the best-known and most prolific of modern fantasists, with well over a dozen books to her credit, including (among many others) The Birth Grave, Drinking Sapphire Wine, Don't Bite The Sun, Night's Master, The Storm Lord, Sung In Shadow, Volkhavaar, *and* Anackire. *Her short story "Elle Est Trois (La Mort)" won a World Fantasy Award in 1984 and her brilliant collection of retold folk tales,* Red As Blood, *was also a finalist that year, in the Best Collection category. Her most recent books are* Night Sorceries *and the massive collection* Dreams Of Dark And Light.

How ill-named she was, he was thinking, in the moments before the train came off the rails. Gita—his 'song.' But she was not like a song, this fat, sullen young bride of his. It had been a terrible affair, the whole wedding. Because of the other girl, the one who had died before he could claim her, he had come to marriage later than most. Perhaps this, and perhaps the contagion of Western skepticism, made him feel ridiculous as he rode in his tinsel headdress on the back of the tall red horse his foolish family had insisted on hiring (wondering all the while if he would fall off, his nervously gripped thighs aching horribly), while the band marched before and everyone else laughed and shouted.

Vikram had seen a photograph of the girl some months ago. He could tell it was a flattering photograph, even though it had not been able, actually, to flatter her very much. She was a lump of flesh, with small furtive eyes and, as he had found out only today, missing a top canine tooth on the left side. That could be fixed, of course. With his fine business, the book shop, on which everyone always congratulated him so vociferously, he could get money to buy Gita a false tooth. (Why then had her well-off family not seen to it?) But what else could he do? Starve her and work her, maybe, so the pounds of flesh melted away. There she had stood in her scarlet and gold bridal finery, and he had dutifully unwrapped her from her veil, wishing his shortsightedness, in that moment, were worse. And to make it more dreadful still, he beheld at once that she, too, thought herself cheated. If Gita was a poor bargain, so he supposed was he. Yes, it was all very well to talk of masculine pride, but a look in a mirror got rid of that. Thin and ugly and blind wed to fat and ugly and toothless. What a pair!

And in that second, as he remembered, as if to compound the nastiness of it all, there was a wrenching and squealing, and a long juddering, during which the world fell over on its side.

When Vikram had opened his eyes, retrieved his glasses and found both lenses to be cracked—yet perforce put them on again—he discovered it was the carriage and not the world which had changed positions. From every side now, within and without the carriage, came a wailing and crying and shouting. Soon, lights were pouring down the track, and through the upside-down window, in the scream of the flares, legs ran about insanely.

"Are you hurt, Gita?" Vikram asked his wife, who was kneeling beside him with a look of gross ferocity.

"No," said Gita. And, as an afterthought, "Are you?"

"Bruised all over, but nothing broken."

She seemed to sneer faintly at this and he could have slapped her. Coupled to the bruising the horse-ride had already given him, the new, minor, all-pervasive and inescapable pain made him feel like weeping.

In a while, a demented official appeared at their upside-down window. After a lot of yelling, Viokram and another man, with some external assistance, succeeded in getting the door open. They, and others, were dragged out. They were not allowed to rescue their hand-baggage, and it was useless to argue. The scene outside was nightmarish, total chaos and confusion. The derailment was comparatively mild of its kind, and few had been hurt, but panic intransigently ruled. Nearby several Moslems writhed on the earth, praying. A goat, which seemed to have been on the train, skipped merrily down the line, butting and bleating.

Vikram stood and watched events through his cracked spectacles. At his side, a dollop of disapproving misery, Gita waited, immobile and witless. People pushed past them. "Well," said Vikram after a time, "shall we walk over there?"

"You are the husband," said Gita. "It is for you to say."

Vikram clenched his fists. He strode, stiffly, up the incline beyond the pushing confusion and the goat, and sat down on a boulder. Gita followed and sat down on another boulder. Beyond the fallen train and the red stream of flares, the night was very black, and far above the stars bloomed bright. Vikram thought of the nights alone, sitting or lying up on the roof of the shop, the stars floating high over the mist of the streetlamps. Waking to find the moon on his face, whiteness soaking through him like water into a sponge. He worked very hard in the book shop. Things were always going wrong. For example, there was the European who came in and stole the glossy paperbacks of temple erotica. One knew he stole them—after he had come and gone two or three of the editions were always missing, and besides he left his cigarash along the lines of the volumes, like a calling card. Or the young assistant who took two hours for a midday meal; always some excuse. Or the books which did not arrive on time, or came in too great

135

quantities. And then there was that account which did not balance. And what was he to do about the electric fan in the ceiling, part of which had flown off and damaged one of the stands. Next time it might decapitate a customer, probably one with influential friends. Could he afford the new fan? Well, he would have to. And then all the expense and the time of this, which he had not wanted, this marriage to a monster. He could not stop himself thinking of the other girl, the one who had died. She had not been pretty, but at least only plain. And he had met her, once, at her father's house, and she had not hated him and they had laughed together. She had had a lovely laugh; he could not help recalling it. It would have filled his life with silver bells. But there. She was dead and he was no catch and they had found him Gita, and here he was with Gita and a wrecked train, his body feeling as if it had been pounded between stones. It was no good looking at the stars, waiting for the moon.

Presently, another official came, closely pursued by a group of frantic people. Over the cries and imprecations, the official told them all they should follow the guard through the forest, to the station. No, they could not go up the line. There was a land-slip piled across it; it was this which had caused the de-railment. Everyone must go around. Yes, yes, they must.

An elderly woman clung to Vikram, sobbing. She was quite uninjured, but the despair of unforeseen, inevitable, mischance was upon her. He patted her. "There, there, my mother. It'll be all right. Look, there is the guard coming now, with his torch. And we will go to the station and they will give us tea, perhaps, free of charge." He glared over the woman's veiled head at Gita. Gita should have been the one to impart comfort. Who did she think she was, some princess? Had she no compassion?

The guard set off into the undergrowth between the tall trees and the tongued bamboos, his life torch flashing, disturbing things. The woman detached herself from Vikram and scuttled after. Everyone followed, chattering or listless. The newlyweds brought up the rear.

Suddenly Gita said angrily, "Wait! My sandal is caught in something."

Vikram stopped and waited. Behind him, Gita panted

and puffed, and the bushes creaked. He did not turn to see. Ahead the flare became smaller. "Hurry *up* Gita."

"How can I hurry? The strap has caught in a root. I can't see what I'm doing." She sounded furious. It was all his fault, of course. "And you might help me."

So he turned and helped, not wanting to touch even her sandal and unable to see her, fortunately, in the darkness. When it was all attended to he straightened, and the light was gone.

"Quickly," he said then, and hurried forward, to fall headlong amid the eager claws of the forest. Scrambling up, scratched and hot with embarrassment that was invisible, while Gita stood like a rock, he muttered, "That way. Over there." And taking her arm, he pulled her after the memory of the wholly-vanished light.

All my life now is to be like this, thought Gita as she stumbled along with the thin ugly man, her lord. *Already he has brought me bad luck. The train has crashed. My sandal is broken. He dislikes me and may refuse to buy me a new pair.* She thought of her father's house, but without nostalgia. Her father and mother had not cared for her, either. It was the pretty daughter who had the attention, the bangles, the silk, the attractive husband. Gita did not blame her family. She did not blame Vikram. Although he was so graceless, bony and pock-marked, his squinting eyes full of reproach, it was a shame he had had to marry someone like herself. *But I am a good cook* she thought defiantly, as a creeper smacked her in the face. *He doesn't know that yet.* Gita's aunts had encouraged her in the domestic skills, while the other sister had been taught everything more casually. After all, if the rice was, for the first months, sticky, the *nan* of an imperfect lightness, this would be forgiven a slender-waisted young wife with huge deer-like eyes. No, Gita did not blame Vikram. She only hated him for hating her, as was quite proper. She had a vague hallucination of their old age together, when she would withhold his favorite dishes (her culinary talent being all she could blackmail him with). Presumably they would have children. She shuddered at the idea of his reluctance or perhaps brutality. And the child, also, as it grew, would probably not like her.

She stopped brooding because Vikram had abruptly

halted.

He stood there, an element of hotter denser substance in the hot black night.

"We're lost," he cried. He sounded in a rage.

Nervous, she could not, nevertheless, resist goading him. "I knew we should be."

"It was your fault, Gita."

Her fault. Naturally.

He waved his arms, and she heard branches crackle and snap.

"Where is the station? Where? Where?" he shouted at the forest. "The guard has disappeared. I can't see anything. What is happening to me?"

It was true, there was no glimmer of light or movement anywhere, and no sound to be heard in any direction.

"Haven't you an electric pocket torch?" asked Gita innocently.

"A pocket torch? I? No, of course not. Did I think when I set out I should be in a train-wreck, abandoned in the jungle?" *But with my bad-fortune,* he thought, *I should have done.*

They stood then for a few minutes, gaping at the blackness to which Gita's eyes at least had somewhat adjusted. It was possible to see shapes, or to imagine they were seen, but not to be certain what they were. At last, Vikram decided. "We must go on." And he marched forward again, only to collide on this occasion with the trunk of a tree. As he scrabbled for his battered glasses in the undergrowth, Gita said, with an air of intolerable wisdom, "It might be better to remain where we are. Surely other people from the train will come by. Or if not, we shall see better in the morning light."

"Morning? Morning? You expect me to spend the night in the jungle?"

"I shall have to do so too."

"I must be in the town tomorrow. I have things to see to. You don't understand the modern world. My business—Already I've wasted so much time—"

"Yes," said Gita.

Something in her voice stayed him, but only for a moment.

"No," he shouted, "I intend to find the station. Come or stay as you please, woman."

As he rampaged forward once more, Gita picked her way after him. He presented a kind of whirling in the darkness, but mainly she located him by the noise he made, thrashing and crashing, and wild cries of pain and frustration, at length ornamented by swearing. Gita attended with interest, but presently even the oaths died. She came upon him suddenly, seated on the ground, nursing a foot all the toes of which seemed to him to have been fractured on a stone. As she loomed over him, he began to make a different noise, unlike all the others. It was a familiar noise, so personally familiar that she did not at once recognize it from another. Slowly, she realized he was crying.

The fool, she thought scornfully. *What does he think there is to cry about?* But she knew, and a wave of loneliness washed over her, terrible loneliness, for she too had shed tears very often, and now she could not help him, was as much the cause of his grief as anything else.

She sat down. She waited, listening to his sobs which, because they shamed him, he tried to quieten. She waited and waited, and listened and listened, and finally she said, "The moment the sun comes up, you'll easily see the way. It won't take long to reach the station. Then someone will take us to the town. They'll be very sorry. They'll be kind. And when we get there, you can rest. We'll send a message to your shop. Let them do without you one day. You work too hard. Let *them* work for a change. I'll make a *thali.* It will be very tasty. And you'll find I won't be a nuisance at all. You can be as free as you want. I shan't fuss. Visit your friends, write your poetry. I understand." She became aware he had stopped weeping and was listening to her. She said, "You'll have noticed, I haven't got a tooth at one side. When I was seven years old a boy from the next house used to run into our courtyard with my brother, and call out at me I was ugly. So one day I took a pan of milk that was curdling and threw it over him. He screeched and yelled, and I was beaten for wasting the milk. But the day after he threw a stone at me and it broke the tooth. So they took me to the dentist's shop and he pulled it out."

In the silence, Vikram gulped. "But that's—dreadful, a

a dreadful thing," he said.

"What did it matter? If I'd been pretty it would have mattered. But if I'd been pretty, none of it would have happened." She hesitated, then said, "You see, I know how I am. But I'm strong. Don't worry about me. I'll be a dutiful wife. In time, we'll get used to each other."

"Oh, Gita," he said.

How strange, he thought, astonished by her dignity, burned by compassion. He could not see her, and all at once, as her dismembered words were murmured in the blackness, he had become aware that her voice was beautiful. Yes, if he had heard her speak, on a telephone, say, never having met her, he would have visualized another woman entirely, a nymph with high, heavy, rounded breasts, serpent waist, dancer's feet, skin smooth as much-caressed marble ... Although Gita's skin *was* soft and smooth, he had noticed it, unconsciously, when he grabbed her arm so roughly. He had a sudden urge to reach out and touch her arm again, gently, investigate the soft smoothness, and if it were true. But he could not make himself.

He signed. He must say something in response to her own brave effort.

"Yes," he said humbly. "It will be all right."

He heard her settle then, and he himself mournfully settled, a tree against his bruised and aching back. If only it *could* be all right, he thought. She was, after all, a decent girl. She had comforted his sorrow instead of mocking him. She had even mentioned his poetic writing with respect. He removed his glasses in order to wipe his eyes. And at that instant, a dim white glow appeared, far over his head. Too ethereal to be anything sent by the railway company, he knew it after a moment for the rising moon. The light swept like a silver blade through the roof of thinner foliage above them. He did not put on his glasses, simply allowing the light to come to him in all its mystery, formless. By his side, Gita did not say anything about the moon.

If only. But if only what? The dream of the moon knew. Soma, binding the earth to the sky by a cord of white fire and divine nectar. If only—Not meaning to, Vikram's glance fell on Gita sitting there passively. Viewed without the glasses, washed in moonlight—yes, that was it. A transformation. The light of the moon, *chand, chandarama,* the silvery, ever-altering one, altering all things—If only he and she might be altered, she for him, and he for her—for she had suffered. By magic, by prayer, by knowledge, by a wish.

He felt himself detached from the flesh, floating in the whiteness.

By his side, Gita thought: *Let him sleep.* She lay back on the tree with him, and forgetting her punishments for his old age, mused, *He is a sad man. Ginger is good for sadness. I will put a little extra in the* thali.

When she woke, it was without haste, but with the sensation of something having touched her eyelids, a fingertip or a frond. There was a lot of light now from the moon, which was directly before her, descending the arch of heaven and shining through the clearing. For it was, after all, a clearing they had stumbled to the edge of. Bushes of flowers were all about them, which she had not noticed before, exuding a delicate sweet scent. The warm moon seemed to bring out their perfume, just as the sun might do by day. Despite the discomfort and catastrophe of the earlier part of the night, Gita felt well, soothed, optimistic. She rose to her knees, and looked round to see if her husband Vikram was still sleeping. Then let out a stifled shriek. For Vikram was no longer there, had vanished. In fact, there was someone, deeply slumbering against the tree. But it was a stranger.

After a few seconds, Gita collected herself. There would be an ordinary explanation, no doubt. While she slept, for example, another lost traveller from the train had come by and Vikram had invited him to join him. Then Vikram himself had had to go off among the trees for the normal reason. Meanwhile the newcomer slept and Gita woke. That was it. She had only to wait a minute or so and her husband would return. "And while she waited, she was at liberty to study the stranger, was she not?

Gita leaned a fraction closer, holding her breath.

The moon described him fully, the long strong length of him, relaxed in his sleep as some graceful animal, some panther out of the *rukh.* He was mature, though still young, his skin of a velvety darkness on the beautiful musician's hands, the arch of the throat, the face, into the hollows and over the plains of which the moon poured so completely. In all her life, Gita had never seen a living man so handsome. Asleep, soulless, he amazed her. But ah, behind the smooth discs of those closed lids, the thick fringes of those lashes, what eyes there must be—It was her desire to behold them, maybe, which caused her inadvertently to nudge against him. So he woke. So she caught a glimpse of his eyes, the eyes she had longed to gaze upon—large and gleaming, and filled by horror, by terror—

Gita sprang to her feet, gasping and humiliated. To wake him was to cause him to look at her. Yes, she was enough to make him recoil, leaning near enough to embrace him, with what emotions, what stupid desire scrawled across her hateful features? It was but too plain. In wretchedness, she longed to obeise herself in apology, but that also would be improper.

"There is no need for alarm," she said. "My husband will return shortly. But I was surprised, and wondered who you were."

The princely man relapsed against the tree again. He breathed hard, staring at her, trembling, she thought, for his thick jet-coloured hair shivered to the momentum. What should she do now? Too late, she greeted him politely. He did not respond. He said hoarsely, "Your husband?"

"Yes, my husband. My Vikram. Didn't you come from the train and meet him, by accident here?"

His mouth, that a fine chisel might have fashioned for a god-being on a temple, was ajar, showing the white teeth. Then his shaking hand came up and set in place on the carven nose, before the wonderful eyes, a pair of cracked and battered spectacles. They did not mar his beauty. Oddly, they enhanced it, a little pinch of the spice of humour, a tiny laughing flaw in his marvel; See, I am not perfect, I am human, too. I may be approached. Oh, one could love him for the silly spectacles perched on his god's face above his hero's body. It seemed he was half-blind, just like Vikram. Gita checked. For not only was he half-blind like her husband, but he had just put on the glasses of her husband. Then with a throb of terror all her own, curiously protective and tigerish, Gita cried at him: "Where is he? What have you done with him—" For surely it was madness that one man might murder another for the use of his broken spectacles, yet this was the forest and who knew what went on her by night— "Oh, Vikram—where is my Vikram?"

The man coughed. He said dully, "I am here."

Gita gave a scream of laughter. But the laughter was brief and left her. Then she sank down again and peered at him, fighting away the urge to cry, at which fight, in her seventeen years, she had become a vertiable champion.

"You? How can you be Vikram?"

"See," he said, holding out his hands to her. She looked and saw rings that she knew. Then she looked again and saw the heroic body clad in Vikram's clothing which somehow fitted it. Then her eyes went back to his face, and the tears came despite herself.

"Oh," she whispered. "What has happened?"

"Don't cry," he said. He seemed to try to touch her, but his hands fell away.

She could not bear it. Some spell or curse had come about, and here she was, the most abject made more abject still. She turned her head and hid herself in a fold of her *sari,* instinctively.

"Gita," he muttered. "Are you Gita?"

Wild anger then in the *sari* fold. "Who else? Who do you think?"

Vikram was not thinking at all. He leaned back on the tree, struggling with great inner turmoil.

At the soft nudge he had woken, the moon across his eyes, and there in the blast of the moonlight was a woman, kneeling close enough that it seemed she had been about to embrace him. Close enough, too, to be easily seen. For an instant he thought it was a dream, but then he knew it could not be, and he was frightened. A poet, he had often read and written of the creatures of the forest, the demons, the nymphs. Her hair was a foaming cloud, her body, traced by silver, flowed and curved, inviting the hands to rest and to journey upon it. Her face had truly the loveliness of something inhuman, an image sculpted from a poreless almond-coloured material that lived, reigned over by two eyes like great black stars.

And then she spoke of her husband. Her husband would

be returning. How would it seem? Somehow Vikram had fallen asleep and woken by this gorgeous one, whose spouse would shortly approach and find them. Compromised, attacked, slain—what else could follow? Then he recollected Gita. And then the gorgeous one began to refer to her husband by Vikram's own name, a coincidence that seemed peculiar. He had put on his glasses, to see if she would look differently, but her splendor was only increased. And then she had shouted in fear, and Vikram had seen that she lacked the upper left canine, just as his Gita did. His fat, ugly Gita. And that Gita, fat ugly Gita, finding the nymph had also lost a tooth just as she had, and the same tooth at that, being kind, had gifted the nymph with her garments before running away.

But now the beautiful, the fantastical one wept and shuddered in Gita's *sari* fold, and he wished only to console her, drinking the tears of her eyes like nectar. Gita? No, this was not Gita. Although she had snarled at him, *Who else?*

He did not dare lay a finger on such excellence. it was the stuff of fantasy and of poetry. And yet—and yet, in those seconds of her gaze, it had seemed to him that she too saw—

Vikram had not forgotten his demented semi-conscious prayer to the moon. It was solely that the memory was preposterous. In the end, however, he took a deep breath of the perfumed night. He fixed the demon-girl with his impaired vision that somehow consistently beheld her clearly, and said, "Gita, look at me. Look at me and tell me what you see." At which she slapped the earth in a fury with one hand, over and over. So he took the hand, to calm it, and sure enough the hand relaxed. "Gita," he said, "I will tell you firstly—when I look at you—you are beautiful, Gita."

It was possible, he knew, she might berate him, might go mad and tear at him. She had been ugly so long, and unloved always. And if, when she looked at him she beheld the complement of what he beheld, looking at her— She did not know, as he did, what he had asked of the moon. Did not know it had been . . . granted?

But there was knowledge, after all. The moon had filled the darkness with it. Presently, she raised her head and her eyes, and out of her glory she gazed at him. And timidly, but hopefully, she said, "I—*also?*"

Vikram laughed. "Also."

He laughed louder and she laughed too, and both their hands met, and their voices went up like a song into the tops of the forest.

In the dawn, as she had said, it was no trouble to find a way through the trees and thickets. The station appeared against the freshly-lit sky, huddled over by the flocks of people who had had to spend the night there.

They walked closely. Vikram and Gita. Sometimes they glanced, shyly aside to each other. The burning arrows of day had had no power of the enduring gift of the moon, and the spell had not faded at sunrise. Each of them stole onward with a supernatural being at their side, tender and accessible, a dream that was also a beloved. And, though they did not yet know, a third person went with them now, who was to be the first of their sons.

The refugees on the platform paid them little heed, the skinny squinting man and his fat ungainly wife. There was nothing remarkable about them, except perhaps the profundity of their intimate silence.

In the eyes of others, then, in the mirrors on their walls, reflective surfaces of all types, they saw the truth, or one truth of two. But in the expression of Vikram when he looked at her, Gita saw the second truth, and he, in her eyes, beheld it also. They were, for each other, the one true mirror.

"Well, it is a good marriage," said the relatives and friends, with some surprise.

The book business was booming the house was a wealthy one. And yes, Vikram had gained some flesh, Gita's cooking, no doubt. Though strangely Gita had lost weight, despite of her childbearing. She would never be a comely woman, even without a gap in her teeth, and yet there was something, her walk, her gestures; not unpleasing. And her happiness was gratifying to those who thought they had aided it. He was a solid proposition, was Vikram, and had added dignity to himself as his fortunes steadied. he no longer squinted, but looked levelly through his spectacles, Authority, yes, Vikram had authority. One could ask his advice. And the poetry had won prizes, of course. Who had inspired some of those passages? Well, best not to worry about that. Gita was happy, and there were plenty of children.

And the children really were a miracle. Like gods and goddesses they stalked the lawns and the rooms, turning to their parents with looks of love one all too rarely noted in these unsettled times. Handsome sons, dark as Krishna, and dark amber daughters, all set with jewels for eyes. It was, the relatives and friends observed privately, something of a curiosity, this. For how could offspring of so much— one must say exceptional—beauty, have grown from such a very beautiless match . . .? ●

THE CALLING OF PAISLEY COLDPONY

by Michael Bishop

"The Calling Of Paisley Coldpony" was purchased by Gardner Dozois and appeared in the January 1988 issue of IAsfm, *with an illustration by Linda Burr. Bishop is one of the most acclaimed and respected writers in SF today, and this story one of a number of memorable stories by Bishop that have appeared in* IAsfm *over the years, since the first year of the magazine's existence. His renowned short-fiction has been gathered in three collections:* Blooded On Arachne, One Winter In Eden, *and* Close Encounters With The Deity. *In 1983, he won the Nebula Award for his novel* No Enemy But Time. *His other novels include* Transfigurations, Stolen Faces, Ancient Days, Catacomb Years, *and* Eyes Of Fire. *His most recent novels are* The Secret Ascension *and* Unicorn Mountain. *Bishop and his family live in Pine Mountain, Georgia.*

Here he offers us a fascinating study of a young Ute Indian girl's strange search for something beyond the life we know . . .

i.

In the Sun Dance lodge, she found that she was one of sixteen ghostly dancers and the only female.

Was this the second or the third day? Or the fourth of one of those controversial four-day dances decreed by Alvin Powers in the late 1970s? No. She'd been a mere child then, and the year after Power's heart attack Sun Dancing with

147

the Wind River Shosones in Wyoming, DeWayne Sky had a vision calling on the Southern Utes to go back to their traditional three-day ceremony.

But the young woman felt sure it wasn't the first day, for on the first day the center pole — the conduit of power from the Holy He-She—supported no buffalo head. Although the sun coming into the Thirst House struck so that she could not really focus on the totem lashed just beneath the crotch of the sacred cottonwood, she could see that *something* was there.

On the second day of the event, the tribal Sun Dance committee had tied it in place—an animal head now so halo-furred that she could give it no clear outline. She was praying to it, as well as to the Holy He-She, to channel water down the Tree of Life into her orphaned body so that she could do miracles. The miracle that she most wanted to do was the restoration of the health and dignity of her tribe. And of herself, too.

Which day is this? she wondered again. How much longer must I dance with these men?

In the path to the center pole next to her own path strutted Larry Cuthair. This was strange. Larry was between his junior and senior years of high school, a grade behind her.

It defied all logic that the Great Spirit had chosen Larry—in too many ways a quasi-Anglicized young man— to dance now. In fact, she would have bet that Larry was a decade or two away from such an honor, if he were going to attain to it at all, and yet he was dancing up to the Tree of Life and falling back from it in the path next to hers. She could smell not only his boyish sweat but also the chalky odor of the white paint smeared all over his belly and chest, his face, neck and arms. The ceremonial skirt he wore, his beaded waistband, and the eagle feathers that he clutched also gleamed white—in eerie contrast to the multicolored garb of the dancers at every other Sun Dance she'd attended.

This, too, was peculiar. But, then, looking around the dance floor of the Thirst House, she saw that all the other dancers—DeWayne Sky, Brevard Mestes, Timothy Willow, *all* of them—had powdered themselves in the same alarming way. Their skirts, ivory. Their waistbands, like bone. Their bare feet, chalk-dusted and ghostly.

The impression that she had was of a room in an insane asylum for spendthrift bakers, men compelled to throw handfuls of flour into the air and then to frolic solemnly in the fallout. But, of course, when she looked, she saw that she (though a woman, and the sort of woman who would pester a Sun Dance chief to accept her into a ceremony once exclusively male) had followed their example. Her own body paint was white. So were her doeskin dress, her sequined apron, her eagle-bone whistle, and every bead on every necklace or bracelet adorning her person. She had joined the crazy bakers in their floury celebration, and this Sun Dance would fail because its purpose was not just to acquire power, but to appease the Old Ones already dead— to guide their spirits to rest in the ghost lands beyond the mountains. Its purpose certainly wasn't to mock the Old Ones by pretending to be an *ini'putc'* oneself.

"Why are we dressed like ghosts?" she cried.

Her cry went unanswered. The noise of the men drumming in the corral's arbor, the gutural chanting of the men and women around the drummers, and the shuffling and shouts of encouragement from the spectators opposite the singers—all these noises kept her from being heard. But maybe that was good. She knew that to talk too much while dancing was considered folly. It cut one off from the trance state triggered by the heat, the drumming, the chanting, the pistoning of legs, the prayerful flailing of arms.

And, she knew, it was this trance state that gave one access to God's Spine, the Tree of Life, the Sacred Rood at the heart of the lodge. For only through the center pole and the totems tied to it could one take the power that every dancer coveted for the sake of the entire Sun Dance community. Maybe it was good that no one had heard her shout. Many of her neighbors already resented DeWayne Sky for letting her—a woman only recently out of high school— dance with the men. They would take great pleasure in telling everyone that she had been guilty of sacrilege, or at least of imperfect seriousness, while dancing, and that her behavior in the corral not only disgraced her and her dead mother, Dolores Arriola, but also destroyed the value of the dance for every Southern Ute. That was the more dreadful result, for all her tribespeople would ostracize her.

But so what? she thought. Ever since Mama D'lo shot herself, I've lived without their help. I don't need them and I don't want their approval. I want the Utes to be strong—to be better than they are—but if they turn their backs on me, so what? It's only what *I've* been doing to *them* since the night Mama spray-painted our walls with her brains. So I'm dancing today—my second day? my third? my fourth?—as a kind of apology for appearing not to wish them well. I *do* wish them well. I just don't want them to smother me with their fretful love.

Again, she shouted, "Why have we all made ourselves look like *ini'putc'?*"

But the shrill piping of eagle-bone whistles and the constant thunder of drums kept everyone from hearing her. Except, she soon learned, Larry Cuthair, who strutted up and rebuked her. Did she want to screw up everything? he growled. The Old Ones would think her questions out of place, disrespectful.

"The way we look is out of place!" she countered, dancing at Larry's side. "The way we look is disrespectful!"

Larry regarded her with something like incredulity. "DeWayne Sky told us to dress and paint ourselves like this—to pretend to be our own ancestors."

We should honor them, Larry, not mock them!"

"But he only instructed us as he did because *your* dreams—the ones you had in the spring—showed us dancing this way. It's all your doing, Paisley."

"Horseshit!" said Paisley Coldpony. She danced away from the center pole, angry at Larry for feeding her such garbage.

All her doing? How?

Yes, the Shoshones at Fort Hall sometimes used white body paint at their Sun Dances, one of which she had attended with D'lo three years ago, but it was idiotic to say that she had influenced Sky to tell every Southern Ute dancer to wear white dress and body paint because of *her* dreams.

What dreams? And why would their Sun Dance chief go along with such a major change solely on her say-so? Some people believed that three or four dancers every year lied about their dream calls, saying that they had had one when they really hadn't, and would-be dancers who went to Sky with a vision requiring novel alterations in the ceremony got looked at askance.

Besides, Paisley told herself, I *had* no dream like that. I had no such dream at all. But if not, what was she doing dancing with these men? They owed their tribe three days without food or water—solely in the hope of gaining the Great Manitou's curing powers, the repose of the dead, and their neighbors' respect. You couldn't dance without being dream-called, but Paisley had no memory of her summons. What was happening here?

Defiantly, she cried, "Why are we mocking our dead?"

An old man on the north side of the lodge shook a willow wand at her. Although Paisley had never known him to dance, he regarded himself as an expert on the ritual. The whites in Ignacio knew him as Herbert Barnes, the Utes as Whirling Goat. He had a face like a dry arroyo bottom and a voice like a sick magpie's.

"Do it right!" he taunted her. "Do it right or get out!"

Dancing toward the Tree of Life, half blinded by the sunlight pouring through its fork, Paisley shrieked her whistle at Whirling Goat, then gestured rudely at him. Another broken rule—but the old sot had provoked her.

"You don't know how!" he called. "You don't belong!"

"Stuff it, goat face," Larry Cuthair said, swerving out of his path toward the spectator section. Barnes retreated a step or two, pushing other onlookers aside, but halted when farther back in the crowd. From there, he croaked again for Paisley's removal—she was fouling the ceremony, turning good medicine to bad.

At that point, the gate keeper and the lodge policeman decided that Barnes was the one "fouling the ceremony" and unceremoniously removed him. Many onlookers applauded.

"Forget him," Larry whispered when next they were shoulder to shoulder on their dance paths. "He's a woman hater."

Whirling Goat confirmed this judgment by breaking free of his escorts at the western door, running back into the Thirst House, and yelling at her, "You foul the dance! You pollute the lodge!" He held his nose in a gesture implying that, against all law and tradition, she had entered the corral while in her cycle.

Many people jeered, but now Paisley couldn't tell if they were jeering Barnes or her. What hurt most was that she was clean, as her people still insisted on defining a woman's cleanliness. And Whirling Goat, a famous toss-pot often as fragrant as a distillery, could not've smelled even Larry's sister Melanie Doe's overpowering styling mousse without having a ball of it stuck directly under his nose. In any case, the gate keeper and the lodge policeman dragged him outside again.

Much aggrieved, Paisley told Larry, "He was lying."

"I know," Larry said. he smiled to show that he didn't mean to denigrate her entire gender, but the smugness of the remark ticked her off as much as had Whirling Goat's old-fashioned bigotry. She moved away from Larry, toward the backbone of the lodge. She tried to make the furry totem on the center pole resolve out of the sun's glare into a recognizable buffalo head.

Meanwhile, it amazed her to see that Tim Willow, a dancer, was wearing reflective sunglasses. His face appeared to consist of two miniature novas and a grimace. Surely, it couldn't be fair to Sun Dance thus disguised, thus protected. Or could it?

ii.

Hours passed. Paisley's thirst increased. Her throat felt the way Barnes's face looked—parched. That was to be expected; it was a *goal* of the dance to empty oneself of moisture so that the purer water of *Sinawef,* the Creator, could flow down the cottonwood into the lodge and finally into one's dried-out body. Thirst was natural, a door to power.

What was *not* natural, Paisley reflected, was the sun's refusal to climb the Colorado sky. It continued to hang where it had hung all morning, forty-five degrees over the eastern horizon, so that its fish-eyed disc blazed down at a slant obscuring the bison-head totem in the Tree of Life. And without eye contact, how could she or anyone else receive the sun power medidated by Buffalo?

As living ghosts, Paisley decided, we've frightened the

sun.

In spite of the sun's motionless fear, time passed. You could tell by watching the spectator section of the lodge. People kept coming in and going out, a turnover that would have distracted her if she hadn't been concentrating on her dancing. But, of course, she *couldn't* concentrate on it—her worry about the whiteness of the dancers and the stuckness of the sun prevented her.

Sidelong, though, she was able to make out the faces of some of the spectators. Two of the people were whites. Although her tribe had a public relations director in Ignacio and publicly encouraged tourism, many Souther Utes had little truck with white visitors at the annual Sun Dance.

Paisley's mother had told her stories about white cultists in the 1960s, drug freaks with more interest in peyotism than the Sun Dance. They had disrupted the event by speaking gibberish at the center pole or by dancing to the point of collapse on the first day. On the first day, no *Ute* would presume to charge the sacred cottonwood, seize it, and fall down in the grip of "vision." But the "Bizarros"— the cultists' own name for themselves—had done such things and worse, thereby defiling the dance.

One of this morning's white spectators looked like a refugee from the 1960s. She wore blue jeans, a T-shirt with Bob Dylan's curly head undulating across her breasts, and a leather hat with a peace-symbol button on the brim. She was pretty, sort of, but Payz could tell that the woman was at least twenty years older than she was—two decades, an entire generation. How did that happen to people? Old Indians, even a sot like Whirling Goat, seemed to have been born old, but old whites—even middle-aged ones—often seemed to have decayed into that state.

Next to the woman stood a man. He was too young, surely to be her husband and too old, Paisley felt, to be her son and too unlike her in appearance, she concluded, to be her brother. What did that leave? Friend? Colleague? Stranger? Whatever the relationship, he was thin—starvation-thin.

He made her think of what an Anglo male with anorexia nervosa would look like if Anglo males were ever to buy in to the grotesque lie that they could be attractive only if their bodies resembled those of famine victims. His eyes, which seemed too big for his head, were sunken in their sockets. Still, he had the kind of face that whites considered handsome—if only it had been less drawn, less pale.

In any case, he *wasn't* a hippie. his blondish hair was short, brushed back from his temples and forehead in a way that looked nostalgically hip. And he was wearing a long-sleeved sailcloth shirt—much too hot for July—with the legend *Coca-Cola* right across its chest.

His female companion lifted her arms, and Paisley saw that she was holding a camera—one of those kind that pop the negative out and develop it right in front of you.

Paisley nearly stopped dancing. Cameras weren't allowed in the Thirst House. People who brought them in were expelled and told not to come back. True, the Shoshones at Fort Hall and Wind River allowed cameras and recording equipment, but the Utes never had, and Paisley couldn't imagine a time when they would. Such things were products of Anglo technology. Although not bad in themselves, they had no place in the sacred corral.

A flash bulb flashed, but the flash was obscured by the sun's pinwheeling brilliance. Paisley thought she heard the camera eject the developing print, but, given the din, that wasn't likely. She *saw* the print, though. The woman in the floppy leather hat passed it to her pale companion, lifted her camera again, and triggered a second flash.

She's taking my picture, Pailey thought half-panicked. But why? I'm nothing to her, and besides, it isn't allowed. Now the emaciated man was holding two prints for his companion, and she was taking a third photo. Her flash exploded impotently in the sunlight.

Someone noted the flash, though. DeWayne Sky, five dancers to Paisley's right, stopped strutting and waved his arms over his head like a man trying to halt traffic on a busy street.

It took a moment, but the Ute men at the drum, seeing their Sun Dance chief's gesture, lifted their sticks. Immediately, all the singers stopped singing.

For the first time since the ordeal had begun—whenever that may have been—Paisley could hear other voices from the camping areas and shade houses around the lodge;

bread frying in skillets, children skylarking, adults playing the hand-and-stick game.

"Seize her," the ghostly-looking Sky commanded the gate keeper and the lodge policeman.

Some of the Ute onlookers near the woman grabbed her arms as if she might try to run, but she stood like a stone. "I'm sorry," she said, embarrassed by the abrupt halting of the dance "Have I done something wrong?"

No one spoke. An Indian man, a visiting Jicarilla Apache, took her camera from her and passed it to another man and so on all the way out of the lodge—as if, Paisley thought, it were a bomb.

"Hey!" the skinny Anglo said, but the Apache who had seized the camera silenced him with a scowl.

"Not allowed," Sky said to everyone and no one. Then the woman was in the custody of the gate keeper and the policeman, who began strong arming her toward the Thirst House door.

Her male friend, although no one had touched him or ordered his eviction, started to follow, but the woman said, "I'm the one who's broken the rules, Bo. You don't have to come with me."

"Not allowed," Sky repeated loudly. He padded across the dusty lodge to look at the man. He pointed his eagle feather-wand. "You can't stay, either," he said.

Why? Paisley wondered, suddenly sympathetic to the visitors. I know that cameras aren't permitted, but what has that poor skinny man done, Chief Sky? Do you deem him guilty because he's here with the woman?

And then she realized that the man—"Bo"—was still holding the developing prints. Ah, of course. It would be a sacrilege to let him depart with them.

Larry Cuthair ambled to the rail of the spectator section and thrust out his hand for the squares of solution-glazed cardboard. The skinny man surrendered them to Larry as if they meant nothing to him. maybe they didn't.

"Now he can stay, can't he?" Paisley said. These words escaped her altogether unexpectedly. She was as embarrassed by them as she would have been if Whirling Goat had been right about her dancing during her period. Every pair of eyes in the Thirst House turned toward her.

"No, he may not," DeWayne Sky said imperiously. "He, too, has trespassed against the Holy He-She—he, too."

"How?" Paisley challenged him.

"It's all right," the white man said. "I'll go with Lib. Just let me by."

No one moved—not the powder-white dancers, not the drummers and singers, not the onlookers. The gatekeeper and the policeman stood motionless at the gate, holding the woman who had brought the dance to a halt by taking photographs. Meanwhile, the stalled sun shone down on this tableau like a huge static flash.

"He's come here for a reason!" Paisley shouted. "He's come to us for healing!"

How do I know that? she wondered. Nevertheless, she did. She had simply intuited that this skinny Anglo had presented himself at the Sun Dance in humility and hope. He was a white, granted, but he was also a sincere candidate for shamanization at the hands of Sky or one of the other newly empowered dancers. So this must be the *last* day of the three-day ceremony. He had come on the third day to keep from having to endure the whole ordeal, an ordeal which he lacked the strength; meanwhile, the woman, his friend, had accompanied him to provide moral support. It was just too bad, that her curiosity—not malice or greed— had led her to carry in the prohibited camera.

"His reasons mean nothing," Sky said. "His crime is bringing moisture into the Thirst House."

"Moisture?" Paisley said. "His hands are empty."

"There," said Sky, pointing the tip of his eagle feather at the man's shirt. "Right there."

Paisley gaped. Sky meant the advertising legend on the young man's jersey—that inescapable soft drink. Even the *name* of the product, because the product was a beverage, was forbidden in the Thirst House. Paisley recalled that once she had seen a fellow Ute expelled because he was wearing a T-shirt advertising a well-known beer. On that occasion, though, the expulsion had seemed okay, for the man had known better. Later, wearing an unmarked shirt, he had returned to a fanfare of catcalls. But this man was a visitor, and his embarrassment would keep him from coming back.

"That's stupid," she said. "Anyone with spit in their mouths would have to leave."

"It's okay," the Anglo said. "I'm going."

DeWayne Sky glared at Paisley. "Spit is a part of who we are. *That*—"gestured to the brand name on his jersey— "is no part of our bodies. It is *no* part of who we are."

You forget, Pailey mused, that there are soft-drink machines at the Ute Pino Nuche restaurant and motel in Ignacio. And you forget that right here on our camp grounds, there are motor homes with refrigerators full of canned drinks.

"What are you sick with?" Paisley asked Bo.

He hesitated a moment before saying, but when he said, everyone looked at him with new eyes—fear-filled eyes. People moved away from him, parting like that sea in the Bible.

"You can't catch it just by standing next to him," the woman in the floppy hat said. "That's not the way it works."

"Take him out," Sky commanded.

Neither the gatekeeper nor the lodge policeman moved.

"I can take myself out," the Anglo said. "Too bad, though—I've been kicked out of places a lot less interesting."

He walked the gauntlet of appalled and fascinated Indians. But as soon as he and the woman had left the Thrist House, ranks closed again. Sky waved for the drummers and singers to resume. Paisley watched the other dancers, including a subdued Larry Cuthair, begin to strut back and forth in their well-trampled paths to the center pole. So she began to jog-dance again, too. The sun still hadn't made any progress in its noonward ascent, and its fiery disk still blurred the animal head tied to the pole.

After a while, Larry strutted up beside Paisley and handed her two developed prints from the white woman's camera. Paisley held them at arm's length, squinting at them as she danced. The images on the slick squares would not resolve any better than would the totem on the center pole. But a fearful uneasiness welled in her—not because the skinny man had a fatal disease—but because Sky had not let him stay. It seemed to her that even though Bo was white, and whites had done little for her people but lash them more tightly to the follies of the past forty years, he owned it to *this* white man to try to heal him.

To Larry's surprise and dismay, Paisley tore up the photographs he had given her. The pieces fluttered to the floor of the Thirst House, where they were quickly ground into the dust by rhythmically shuffling feet.

After that, Paisley lost all consciousness of onlookers—they faded totally from sight. She was a spirit, a powder-white spirit, dancing with other such spirits, and she had the disturbing feeling that she was seeing the event not through her own eyes, but instead through those of the emaciated, dying Anglo.

At last, the sun began to climb. As it did, Paisley, knowing herself on the brink of vision, approached the Tree of Life with more *vigor.* The other dancers recognized how close she was, and Tim Willow began to compete with her, strutting, flailing his arms, making his mirrored lenses pinwheel dizzyingly.

Paisley ignored him. She was dancing faster, driving harder at the pole, urging herself to attack and touch. Only if she *touched* the sacred tree would the waters of the Holy Manitou flow into her, empowering her in ways that might one day benefit them all.

For her final run, she retreated to the backbone of the Thirst House. She lifted her eyes to the glittering eyes of the totem on the center pole. The sun had ceased to blind her, and what she saw hanging where a buffalo head should hang was not Buffalo but . . . something else. Paisley refused to flee. She screamed—not like a frightened woman, but like a warrior—then rushed the pole with such uncompromising fury that all the other ghostly dancers stopped to watch, shrilling their eagle bones.

"Mother!" she cried. "Mother!"

God's Spine staggered her with a jolt of power. She collapsed at its base.

The vacuum left in heaven by this discharge of power sucked her spirit up after it. High above Ignacio, Colorado, she eventually regained consciousness. Her cold body, however, lay far below, a small white effigy in the Thrist House.

How strange, she mused, seeing herself and being seen, dreaming herself and being dreamt.

iii.

Paisley could sense someone kneeling over her cold body, a hand on her brow. It seemed to be the skinny Anglo whom Sky had run out of the Thirst House for wearing a Coca-Cola shirt, just as he had banished that hippie woman for taking pictures.

But when Paisley opened her eyes, reflexively grabbing at this ghost, she found that she was lying on her pallet in her house five miles outside of Ignacio. It wasn't early July, the week of the Sun Dance, but April, and her wood-framed house was cold, just as it had been every night since her mother's suicide.

You've dreamed again, the young woman told herself. Your dream is a call. No one will want you to dance, least of all an old fart like Whirling Goat, and only a bit more a stiff traditionalist like DeWayne Sky, but you've got to face down their opposition. Mama D'lo's an Old One now—it's she who's calling you to dance.

Paisley didn't know the hour, only that it was the middle of a cold weekday night, near Easter. She had school tomorrow, but she couldn't wait until tomorrow to settle this matter. In the empty house, a shell of walls and doors, she dressed as warmly as she could and set off toward Ignacio. The nearby houses of the Willows and the Cuthairs, as ramshackle as chicken coops, brooded by the roadway in the windy dark.

As she walked, carrying her school books so that she would not have to return for them, she pulled her poncho tight and thought about her dream. This was the seventh time she'd had it, or a variation of it, since her mother's suicide. She couldn't ignore the fact that the Old Ones—or, at least, the Old One that D'lo had become—wanted her to dance this July.

That troubled her, for she had planned to leave the reservation the day after her high-school graduation to search for her father. A delay of a month—thirteen years after her parents' divorce—ought not to weigh so heavily on her, but just waiting until the end of school was proving harder than she'd thought. Another month or so would seem an eternity.

Coming into the commercial section of town owned by

Anglo and Chicano business people, she strolled along Main Street past the drugstore, a cafe, the laundromat. The sidewalk was mostly dark and deserted, but as she neared the dim foyer of a bar, two boys—young men, if she wanted to be generous—fell out of the place, staggered toward her grinning, and spread their arms to make it hard for her to get around them without stepping into the street. She knew them as former classmates, moderately well-heeled dropouts with damn little to do.

"Hey, Payz, how 'bout taking a ride with Howell and me?"

"How 'bout *givin'* us a little ride?"

The dreariness of the confrontation, the stupidness of it, made Paisley's dander rise, but she replied only, "Let me by."

"No, missy. Can't do that," Howell said.

"You know us," Frank said. "We're not exactly strangers."

"You're too drunk to drive or ride, either one, Frank."

Frank cursed her roundly, but without viciousness, surprising her by staggering past as if she weren't worth another minute of their valuable time. Tall and burly, he was supporting the gangly, lean Howell in a way that reminded her of a bear trying to push a potted sapling along.

Grateful for their short attention spans, Paisley strolled on toward Pine River, the Pino Nuche motel-restaurant, and the diffuse Ute enclave north of town where DeWayne Sky lived.

But, a moment later, some sort of pointy-nosed sports car with flames pin-striped on its flanks pulled up beside her, Frank at the wheel. Howell, meanwhile, was lolling at the shotgun seat like a manikin stolen from a tall-and-thin men's shop. Frank paced her up Main Street at ten miles per hour, his head half out the window and his mouth slurring a variety of one- or two-syllable activities that he seemed to think she would enjoy sharing with him.

Paisley wasn't amused. She had business in Ignacio. And she was tired of hearing Anglos throw around words like *papoose, squaw, and wampum* as if they were something other than cliches or insults, especially the way Frank was deploying them. She told him to fuck off and declined to speak to him again. At the next cross street, through, Frank blew his horn, turned directly across her path, and dialed up the volume of a song on his tape player whose lyrics were nothing but orgasmic grunts. The pulsing bass of this song put the empty street a-tremble. Even the besotted Howell came around long enough to open his mouth and pop his eardrums.

"Get out of my way!" Paisley shouted. "Move it!"

Frank replied with an elaborate pantomine involving his fingers and tongue. All that she could think to do to show her outrage and contempt was to grab up an official city trash container at the end of the sidewalk and hurl it with all her might at Frank's car. It was a feat that, even as she performed it, astonished her—mostly because the four-sided receptacle, featuring a detachable metal top with a swinging door, had not been emptied recently and weighed at least fifty pounds. When it hit the car, it clattered, rebounded, and scattered debris, some of which spilled through Frank's window along with the dormered lid.

Frank shouted, Howell woke up again, and Paisley recovered the main body of the trash container for another assault. This time, through, she carried it, dripping vile liquids and moist pasteboard, to the front of Frank's car, where she wielded it after the fashion of a battering ram, repeatedly slamming one corner into the nearest headlamp. It took three whacks to shatter the glass, by which time Frank had managed to jettison the trash-can lid. Now he tried to halt her vandalism by running her down. Paisley skipped aside, one-handedly bashing the container into his car again and knocking his rearview mirror off its mount.

A siren began to keen, and they all looked around to see Deputy Marshal Blake Seals come barreling into the intersection in one of Ignacio's two patrol cars.

iv.

Seals introduced her into the middle cell of five in the block at the rear of the marshal's office, and she was relieved to find that none of the others held prisoners. The drunk tank at the end of the damp hall looked exactly like a cave or the entrance to a mine shaft—a concrete grotto. For a time, Seals stood outside her cell, his pock-marked face like a big albino strawberry and his thumbs hooked in the pockets of his windbreaker so that it bellied out in front like a sail. He wasn't a cruel Anglo, just a pompous and partisan one.

"Sorry there's nobody in tonight for you to talk to."

"Couldn't you find any other Indians to arrest?"

"You were making a public disturbance, Miss Coldpony."

"I was the *victim* of a public disturbance. Those turkeys were drunk. Frank tried to run over me."

"The kid was just trying to depart the scene before you turned his Trans Am into scrap metal."

It was a temptation to renew their street argument, but they'd hashed out the details three dozen times already, in the middle of Ignacio, and Seals had sent the "kids"— friends of his—home to bed, promising Frank that the "perpetrator" would spent the rest of this chilly night "incarcerated."

Well, here she was, *incarcerated.* She would have cursed Seals for the fact that the jail stank of disinfectant if not for the linked fact that it would've reeked of something far less bearable if he hadn't earlier bothered to "sanitize" everything. That was one of the questionable bonuses of being deputy of Ignacio—you also got to be custodian.

"Sorry there's only that—" gesturing at the urinal—"if your bladder gets heavy. We don't have many female guests."

"Leave me alone, Deputy."

"I could bring you a bucket."

"Stick your head in it."

He grinned, mysteriously delighted by her retort. "Put my foot in that one, didn't I?" He returned to the office. Paisley sat down on her grungy mattress, which lay askew on what looked like a pig-iron frame. She wouldn't be in for long, though. Her phone call had gone to DeWayne Sky, who, although not overjoyed to be roused at four in the morning, had told her to hang on, he would vouch for her, put up her bail, or whatever. She was welcome to stay the rest of the night with LannaSue and him.

In the drunk tank down the hall, somebody or something coughed, a painfully congested hacking.

"Deputy," Paisley called, "I'm not alone back here."

"That's only Barnes," Seals shouted from the office. "I

forgot about him."

Barnes. Herbert Barnes. Whirling Goat. Seals had shoved him into the cave and forgotten about him. The old man careened out of its bleak dampness, slumped against the bars with his arms hanging through. He was wall-eyed with cheap liquor or bread-filtered hair tonic, and his white hair tufted out from his temples in a way that made him resemble a great horned owl. Usually, reservation police took care of him, but tonight—last night—he had fallen to the efficient ministrations of Blake Seals.

"Hello, Alma." He sounded more weary than drunk. maybe a nap had rubbed the nap off the velvet of his nightly stupor.

"Paisley," Paisley said. "My name is Paisley."

"Your mother called you Alma," the drunk lessoned her. "'Soul' in Spanish."

"I know what it means. But my father named me Paisley, Paisley Coldpony, and that's the name on my birth certificate."

"You lived with your mother longer than your daddy. Your name is Alma Arriola." He pulled some string out of the pocket of his dirty suede coat and, with his hands outside the bars, began making cat's cradles with it. He was remarkably dexterous for so old and alcohol-steeped a brave. Paisley found her irritation with his comments about her name softened a little by the web-weaving of his stubby fingers.

"Jack rabbit," he said, rotating the string figure so that she could see this two-dimensional creature loping across the blackness of the drunk tank.

"Arriola's Spanish name, too," he added pedantically, hacking her off again. Then he dismanteled the airy jack rabbit and began a second latticework figure.

"And Barnes is an Anglo name, Whirling Goat."

Paisley knew that some of her hostility to the old guy was left over from her dream. She resented what he'd said to her in it and was sorry to find him—dare she even think the word?—*polluting* the cell block. (If, given the disinfectant fumes stinging her eyes, further pollution were even possible).

"And this is a goat," he said, holding up the second figure

and whirling it for her benefit. "When I was eight, I rode a goat for three minutes that none of my friends could even catch. My name—it comes from that."

"Which one of your friends had the stopwatch, Herbert?"

But neither this sarcasm nor her rude familiarity would provoke him. He ceased to whirl, and handily collapsed, the goat, only to follow it with several successive string compositions, all of which he was magically weaving for his own amusement. His equanimity put her off. She wanted to puncture it.

"I'm going to dance in the Sun Dance. I've been dream-called."

"What do you think of this one?" he said, holding up a figure that initially made no sense to her. Standing at the bars of her cell, she peered at the crisscrossing strings with real annoyance. Her world-shaking declaration of intent had slipped past him like a coyote squeezing untouched through a hole in a henhouse.

"What is it?" she grudgingly asked.

He coughed, but his preoccupied hands were unable to cover his mouth. "Kar'tajan," he managed.

"What?" The word summoned no resonances for her.

"Kar'tajan," he repeated. "But only the head, Alma— only the head and the horn."

Now Paisley recognized it. It was the head—the head and the horn—of a unicorn. She could not imagine how he had produced it with a single piece of looped string, but he had, and the awkward way that he held his hands to sustain the figure were justified by its fragile elegance. She'd never known that Barnes, *aka* Whirling Goat, had such a talent— or *any* talent, for that matter, beyond making a year-round nuisance of himself and sourly kibitzing every performer at ever important Ute ceremony. But, so soon after the seventh repetition of her dream, the sight of the string figure— *this* string figure—gave her a decided pang. For it, too, seemed part and parcel of her summons.

"Why do you call it a kar'tajan?"

"Because that's it name. That's the name our Holy He-She gave it—before history turned the world inside-out."

"It's a unicorn, Whirling Goat. There's no such animal."

"It's a kar'tajan, Alma. I've seen one."

From the office, Seals shouted, "He saw it drinking over by the Pine with this humongous herd of pink elephants!"

The deputy's words, and then his guffaws, dismantled the mood of balanced wonder and unease that Paisley had been experiencing—in much the way that Barnes's hands collapsed the string figure of the kar'tajan or unicorn. He stuffed the looped string back into his coat pocket and slumped more heavily against the bars.

"Can't you do a buffalo?" Paisley felt strangely tender toward him. She hoped that he wouldn't relapse into the stupor that had probably occasioned his arrest.

"Ain't nothing I can't do with string."

"Do me a buffalo, then."

Barnes coughed, more or less negatively.

Damn you, Blake Seals, Paisley thought. And then, as unbidden as lightening from a high azure sky, a memory bolt illuminating the headless corpse of her mother struck her. She was seeing again the clay-colored feet on the lounger's footrest, the dropped .12-gauge, and the Jackson Pollock brain painting on the walls behind the old chair. She'd just come home from a debate with the kids at Cortez, a debate that her team had won, and there was Mama D'lo, waiting to share the victory with her, messily at ease in the lounger, forever free of motherly obligation. Although maybe not.

"I've been dream-called," Paisley said. Defiantly, she looked at Barnes. "To dance in the Sun Dance."

"Good. Good for you." He hacked into his forearm.

Paisley stared at him. "Didn't you hear me? I've been granted a vision. I'm to dance with the men."

"It's what your mama wants." Barnes shifted against the bars. "She told me. That being so, you should do it."

"Told you? Why would she tell *you*, old man? When?"

"Tonight. A little time past," He indicated the impenetrable blackness behind him. "Pretty funny talk we had."

Seals lumbered into the upper end of the cell block. "Every talk you have while you're swackered is funny, Barnes. Chats with old Chief Ignacio. Arguments with John Wayne. Even a midnight powwow with Jesus."

"Get your butt out of here, Deputy," Paisley said. "Who asked you to horn in?"

Smirking, Seals raised his big hands as if to ward off

physical blows. "Simmer down. I'm going. Just forgot for a minute we was running a hotel here." He backed out, closing the cell-block door behind him.

"You saw her tonight, Mr. Barnes? *Tonight?*"

"Yes. In here. I was on that pissy mattress—" pointing his chin toward it, a shadow in the dark— "and D'lo showed up, maybe from the San Juan Mountains. She stood over me, signing."

"Signing?"

"You know, hand talk."

"But why? To keep Seals from hearing?"

"That didn't matter. He was patrolling." Barnes hunched his shoulders. "Alma, that was her only way to talk. You see?"

Paisly understood. She had seen her mother's *ini'putc* in the Cuthair's stationwagon on the day of her funeral, and the revenant, like the corpse, had had no head. But then the ghost had vanished, leaving Paisley to doubt what she had witnessed.

"What did she say? What did her hand talk mean?"

"Just what you say, Alma. That you must dance this year. That she desires it. That no one should hinder you, girl or no girl."

"It's 'no girl,' Mr. Barnes. It's 'woman.'" She told him as a matter of information, not to scold—for she was ready to forgive the old fart for his bad behavior in her dream.

A moment later, Paisley said, "But why did she visit *you?* Why did she come here to give you that message?"

"I have a reputation," Whirling Goat said proudly.

As a sot, Paisley silently chastised him, but she knew that he meant as an expert on certain ceremonial matters and so refrained from disillusioning him. Let Barnes claim for himself the dubious glory of an *ini'putc'* visitation.

"Also," he said. "Dolores must have foreknown."

"Foreknown what?"

"That you'd be arrested tonight. That it would be good for me to give you my blessing."

"I have your blessing?"

"Of course. I gave it to you already. How many children do I show my string creatures?" He hacked again, magpie croaks.

"Not many," Paisley hazarded.

"Damned straight. Now, though, you're among them."

Talk lapsed. Paisley wondered if her run-in with Frank Winston and Howell Payne had been providential. Yes, it probably had. But she had no time to mull the matter further, for Blake Seals entered the cell block again, this time leading a haggard-appearing DeWayne Sky and announcing loudly that she was "free to go." Her esteemed tribal councilman was vouching for her character.

"What about Mr. Barnes?" Paisley said.

"What about him?" Seals echoed her.

"He's slept it off. He isn't drunk any longer. You should let him out, too."

"It's an hour or two till dawn," Seals protested. "He can get a snootful in five minutes, a sloshing bellyfull in ten."

"Let Mr. Barnes out, too," DeWayne Sky said. He was wearing khaki trousers with a turquoise belt buckle so large that it made Paisley think of a chunk of the Colorado firmanent for which the councilman's family seemed to've been named.

Not liking it much, Seals released the old drunk along with the unrepentant Trans Am basher. In the jail's front office, he called them over to a metal desk to reclaim their belongings. All Paisley had was her school books, but Barnes had a small clutch of items—his wallet, his house key, a few salted peanuts, and some sort of foil-wrapped coin that Sky picked up and turned in the glare of the light bulb as if it were an extraordinary find.

"What the hell are you doing with this, Barnes?"

"He's a Boy Scout," Seals said. "His motto is 'Be Prepared.'"

Sky threw the coin back down on the desk. "Hell, man, you're eighty-something. And nine tenths of the time you're so stinking drunk, your carrot'd have to have chronic droop, anyway."

A rubber? Paisley speculated. Is Barnes, our oldest bachelor, actually carrying a rubber around with him?

"There's the other one tenth," the old man said, neither shamed nor amused by Sky's attack. He stuffed the battered coin into his pocket along with his other pocket fillers and moved to the door as vigorously as he paraded around the camp grounds at the Bear Dance in May and the Sun Dance in July. Those were two weeks out of the year—maybe the only two—that he scrupulously laid off wine, whiskey beer, hair tonic, everything but the old bucks charged with organizing and running the dances. Paisley was proud of him for getting through the door upright, his dignity intact and that silly antique rubber in his pocket.

"What do you want to do?" DeWayne Sky asked her. "Stand here till Marshal Breault comes on duty?"

She didn't and so they left.

v.

The Skys lived in a wood-frame house that, several years ago, they had remodeled in an unusual way. Around it, entirely around it, Sky had had built a conical frame whose summit rose better than forty feet above the original roof. Sky's workmen had stuccoed the frame, windowing it at various places with huge rectangular sheets of Plexiglas to let in the sun. At night, spotlights lit the cone so that you could see it from several blocks away, a garish white tepee rising among the scattered tract houses like an advertisement for a Wild West amusement park.

The cone's huge stucco flap opened to the east, as prescribed for tepees by sacred tradition, but the door to the house inside the frame faced south. Thus, Paisley and her rescuer—once he'd parked his Ford Bronco in the driveway—had to walk an enclosed track between the house and the inside tepee wall to reach the *real* entrance to his living quarters.

Paisley felt decidedly weird following DeWayne Sky around this bizarre corridor, but she remembered that he had erected the fake tepee not just to pretend that he was still living in one, as most whites mockingly accused, but to avail himself of the power to call spirits that round houses—and only round houses—could impart to those living in them. A house with corners, a house with none of the circularity of earth and sky about it, preached DeWayne Sky, cut one off from the spirits and thus robbed one of power.

Although Paisley feared that merely masking a boxy house with a big stucco tepee was not the best way of persuading the gods that you were back in touch with both the earth and the Old Ones, she knew that in the years since erecting his cone, DeWayne Sky's power and influence among the Southern Utes had grown enormously. He'd spent a lot of money on his "folly," but he'd got all of that back, and a great deal more, representing his people at Indian caucuses around the country, presiding as the grand marshal in Frontier Day parades in various towns, and taking part in all five Shoshones-Ute Dances, just like a true shaman. Now, he was chairman of the tribal council and chief of the Sun Dance committee, and who'd have the sand to tell him that his big stucco tepee hadn't gotten him in good with the Great Manitou?

Not me, Paisley thought. Not on a dare.

LannaSue Sky handed her a cup of hot tea, sweetened with honey, and pointed her to a couch covered with a scratchy Navajo blanket. On the knee of her jeans, the tea cup warmed a circle that Paisley couldn't help regarding as a tiny replica of the base of the tepee surrounding them.

When LannaSue returned to bed, Sky paced in front of Paisley in his boots, a stocky man with two tight braids hanging to his waist and a paunch decorated by that sky-blue belt buckle.

"What's the word, Alma? What's going on?

"The word's Paisley," she corrected him.

He waved off the correction with angry impatience. "Tell me stuff I don't know. Tell me important stuff."

"Names are important. Names let us—"

"Okay. If I call you Paisley, you call me Papa Tuqú-payá, got it?" *Tuqú-payá* was the Ute word for sky, one of only a few dozen in her people's tongue that Paisley knew. "Understand?"

"Sure, Papa Tuaú-payá."

"Talk to me, Paisley. But only important stuff."

So she related her Sun Dance dream. Parts, however, she kept to herself, the parts that still frightened or unnerved her.

A lamp in the tiny living room relieved a little of the pre-dawn gloom, but when she looked out its picture window, she saw only the interior wall of the fake tepee. A melancholy claustrophobia rose in her. Nevertheless, she kept talking, and when she was finished, she repeated that tonight's dream had been her seventh in the past five weeks. Therefore her visit to town.

"Women don't dance," Sky declared.

"Women *have* danced, Papa Tuqú-payá. At Fort Hall, they do it all the time. They've done it here, too."

"Twelve years ago, child. Two months later, one of them who'd danced, Theresa Eagle, took sick. The white doctors had no idea with what, but she saw the sacred water bird in the tube connected to her IV bottle and soon thereafter died."

"Mama told me that four other women danced. Nothing like that happened to them."

"No. It happened to other people. Our last Sun Dance chief, the one who let the woman dance—his wife died of a heart attack that year. The aunt of the tribal council's last chairman—she died, too. I could make a list."

"None of that matters, Papa Sky. I'm being dream-called. If I'm not, why am I having this dream again and again?"

LannaSue Sky trundled back into the living room in her robe and sat down by Paisley. "Of course you're being called." She looked at her husband. "Who can sleep with this darling here?"

Sky tossed his braids over his shoulders—apparently, in this context, a gesture of disgust.

"Are you afraid to let Paisley dance? Afraid that, two months later, *your* beloved wife might die?" LannaSue briefly smothered a laugh, then gave up and released it. "Beloved wife, my ass. What he's afraid might die is his beloved *workhorse.*"

"LannaSue—"

"Okay. I'll shut my silly mouth." She patted Paisley's knee, the one without the tea cup, "For a while, anyhow."

The Sun Dance chief started pacing again, trying to recoup some of his pilfered authority. "If I let you dance, your dream says we must all paint ourselves like *ini'putc'*—ghosts."

"I don't know. Is that what it means?"

"I hope not. If we did that, Paisley, it would be like saying the Mauche—we Southern Utes—are dead. Dead people can't ask the Creator to give them power."

170

"They can ask to be resurrected," LannaSue said.

Sky ignored this. "Forget that, for now. Why are there Anglos in your dream—the floppy-hatted woman, the sick man?"

Paisley shrugged. Even now, she could see them clearly—but she was fairly sure she had never met them in life.

"You haven't told me everything," Sky said. "Your dream scared you. It scared you so bad you're afraid to tell it all."

His keenness in this startled Paisley. Some of the Muache said that DeWayne Sky was a fraud—but he had never knowingly violated any ceremonial tradition, and his knowledge of her reaction to her own dream seemed to her a good sign.

"Tell me," he commanded her. "Tell me even what you're afraid to tell."

"Otherwise," LannaSue said, taking the empty tea cup for her, "he won't be able to accept you into the dance."

Grimacing, Sky made a curt be quiet gesture.

"I don't even know that I *want* to dance," Paisley admitted, her mind confusingly aboil again.

"Not your decision," Sky said. "My decision. Tell me so I can decide. If you *don't* tell me, the decision's out of my hands, and it's simple: 'No way, gal. No way.'"

Great, Paisley thought. That would keep me from dancing. And if I don't have to dance, I can leave that much sooner to look for my father. But then it struck her that if she didn't fully divulge the contents of her dream, the dream would continue to recur, and to vary with each recurrence, until it had driven her as crazy as Moonshine Coyote, a woman whose husband and three sons were all in prison and who often sat in a wheelbarrow near Highway 172 drinking cherry Kool-Aid and spitting mouthfuls at passing motorists.

"Come on," Sky said. "You're wasting my time."

"Yeah, you could be sawing logs," LannaSue tweaked him.

"There's three or four things," Paisley said. "The first is those pictures the woman took." Both Skys waited expectantly for her to go on. So she told them that when her dream self had looked at the developed prints handed her

THE CALLING OF PAISLEY COLDPONY

by Larry Cuthair, she found that they showed only the interior of the Thirst house—no dancers, no singers, no drummers, no spectators at all. The people taking part in the event as pseudo-ghosts had become real ghosts when processed by Anglo picture-taking technology.

Which was just another variation, Paisley now realized, on that old cultural-anthropological chestnut about the camera's ability to steal a shy African bushman's, or an innocent Amazonian cannibal's, soul. From what Paisley knew of anthropologists, though, it seemed more likely that it was the people on the *taking*—not the *being taken*—end of the camera who forfeited their souls.

"That frightened you even in your dream," Sky said. "You tore the pictures up. You scattered the pieces."

"Yes."

"What else?"

She told him about the trouble she'd had focusing on the totem on the sacred cottonwood. The brightness of the sun, and the angle at which it shone down, had been the main culprits, but it was also likely that she hadn't *wanted* to see what was in the tree's crotch, knowing that it wasn't Buffalo but . . . something else.

"What?" Sky asked. "What was it?"

LannaSue gripped Paisley's knee, reassuringly squeezed it.

At last, Paisley told them, "My mother's face."

Having confessed this, she could *see* her mother's face again—not blown to smithereens as on the night of the suicide, but as it had been before that. Beaten-looking and imploring. Except that, in the dream, her face had been as large as a bison's head.

"Mama D'lo wants her to dance," LannaSue said. "D'lo's spirit is restless."

"Don't jump to conclusions, woman!"

"She has no son to dance her to rest, DeWayne. If it's to be done, Alma—Paisley here—will have to do it."

Well, that was exactly what Whirling Goat had told her in the jail. It made sense. Mama D'lo's *ini'putc'* had visited Barnes in the drunk tank to ask him to assure her that she was doing exactly right in going to Sky with her seventh dream.

Sky, however, stomped out of the living room into another part of the house. Paisley was perplexed. Maybe Lanna-Sue had so badly provoked him that he was washing his hands of both of them. Women weren't supposed to organize or dance in the Sun Dance, although they could support the men by singing or by bringing willow bundles to them during rest periods—and yet here were two women, his own wife and a teen-age girl, one telling him how to interpret a dream and the other presenting herself to him as a would-be dancer. No wonder the poor old buck was pissed.

But a minute later, Sky was back, holding a red-cedar flute, an instrument that—he said gruffly, sitting down on an ottoman in the middle of the room—he had made himself. Its song would help Paisley make sense of the two shredded photographs.

"How?"

"Shut your eyes. Hear my song. When it stops and I say you're doing something, do it.—LannaSue, turn out that lamp."

LannaSue obeyed, and the room, an hour before dawn, was so dark that Paisley felt better closing her eyes than siting in it trying to find enough light to see by. Sky began to play. The melody was thin, broken, and not terribly pretty. But it altogether took her, snaking in and out of her mind as if seeking a hole to go into and hide. In fact, when the melody stopped, Paisley half believed that it had found this hole.

"A woman dancer in the Thrist House," Sky intoned, "bends down and picks up the pieces of two torn photographs."

That's me, Paisley thought. That's me he's talking about, me he's telling me what to do. And in the darkness of her skull, inside the darkness of a boxy house inside the darkness of a stucco tepee, she saw herself clad all in white, powdered like a ghost, kneeling in the dust to gather up the scraps of treated pasteboard. As she did, Sky began to play again—the same harsh and monotonous, but compelling, tune. He kept playing until the white-clad avatar of Paisley Coldpony kneeling in the Sun Dance lodge of her own mind had picked up every single fragment of paper.

Said Sky then, "The women carries these pieces to the

drum and spreads them out on top of it."

The red-cedar flute crooned again, and Paisley performed in her head what Sky had just attributed to the neurolo-
gical automaton—the day-dream simulation—he called
"the woman." To Paisley, it felt a lot like moving a computer figure through a two dimensional labyrinth on one of the
Apple monitors that they had at school now; the sense of
being two places at once was just that strong, as was her
awareness that she could back out—albeit with a pang of
real loss—at nearly any moment she wanted.

"The woman fits the pieces together—into two pictures.
She takes all the time she needs."

Paisley took all the time she needed.

The flute ceased to croon.

Said Sky, "The woman speaks aloud. She tells everyone
at the Sun Dance what the pictures show."

The obedient self-projection in Paisley's mind stared
down at the puzzle-fit photos on the drumhead. In reassem-
bling them, she had paid their images little heed, but now
she was shocked to find that one was a picture of Samuel
Taylor Coldpony—her father—standing next to the leather
hatted woman who had supposedly *taken* the pictures.
They stood side by side in the corral.

The other photo, meanwhile, was of an emaciated unicorn—or kar'tajan, as Barnes would call it—rearing at the
Tree of Life in the Sun Dance lodge, its front hooves flashing like knives at the totem affixed to it.

Startled, Paisley opened her eyes on the dark.

"She *tells* them," reiterated Sky, "what the pictures
show."

Reluctantly, staring at nothing, Paisley told the Skys
what her dream self had just seen.

Laying the flute aside, her mentor said, "To find your father, Paisley, you must only find that woman."

"What of the sick unicorn?" she blurted. That Barnes
had shown her a string-figure unicorn in the jail seemed not
so much a happy, as a monstrous, coincidence.

"The unicorn and the sick Anglo in your dream," Sky
said, "are different sides of the same coin."

Like the "coin" that Barnes always carries? she wondered. But there was no way to ask Sky such a strange ques-

tion, and she didn't yet know how a young man with AIDS and a kar'tajan with protruding ribs could mirror anything in each other but illness.

No matter. Sky had an explanation: "The parents of the sick young man have turned him away, just as you think your folks have done, Sam by never coming to see you and Mama D'lo by . . ."

LannaSue said, "She knows, DeWayne."

"That's why you saw D'lo's face on the Tree of Life. And why his unicorn is trying to cut up the totem with its hooves."

Suddenly, Paisley could stand no more. "You sound like one of those goddamn BIA psychologists! Like Chief Sigmund Sky of the Muache Shrinks' Association!"

She reached across LannaSue and turned on the lamp. The sudden light made everyone in the room—eyes narrowed, mouths pursed—look constipated.

The Sun Dance chief picked up his red-cedar flute, rose from the ottoman, and stomped off toward his tiny study. At the door, he turned and gave Paisley a bitter look.

"Maybe I do and maybe I don't," he said. "LannaSue, find her something to eat."

vi.

She ate scrambled eggs, to which LannaSue had added diced green pepper and jalapeño cheese. Her hunger surprised her. Ten minutes ago, eating had been the least of her concerns.

LannaSue was nursing a cigarette and a cup of coffee. "What do you want to be when you grow up?"

The question surprised her even more than did the extent of her hunger. "I *am* grown up, LannaSue."

"Okay. What do you want to do?"

"Finish school. Dance in the Sun Dance. Find my father." She couldn't think what else to add.

"You want to be a *po'rat,*" LannaSue told her.

LannaSue Sky's absolute certainty on this score was yet another surprise, and Paisley halted her fork in mid-ascent. "How do you know that? Hell, I don't know that."

The Southern Utes had passed a quarter of a century without a bona fide *po'rat,* or shaman. They had had leaders aplenty, chiefs and organizers and tribal councilmen, but persons with *powa'a*—supernatural authority from the One-Above—well, the Muache had had to import such persons from the Navajos, the Jicarilla Apaches, or even the Shoshones, whose Sun Dance procedures were so lax that they let dancers suck wet towels in the Thrist House and had no ban on photogrpahy so long as the picture-takers were Indian.

Not even DeWayne Sky, tepee or no tepee, qualified as a *po'rat,* although he had striven mightily to help maintain the integrity of the Bear Dance and the Sun Dance. On the other hand, not being a bonafide shaman, he hadn't tried to resurrect the *mawo'gwipani,* or the Round Dance, at which everyone danced to hold white diseases—smallpox, clap, polio—in check. Nor the old wedding rite in which a couple sat together in a smoke-filled tepee to prove their compatibility and faithfulness. nor the ritual of laying a baby's birth cord on an anthill to bless the child with strength and good fortune. Sky's curing powers were beyond the average, but far from impressive in the old way.

For dynamic medicine, a true *po'rat*—a genuine shaman—was required, and Paisley's people not only had no one qualified, they had no candidates. Why LannaSue would suppose that *she* might make a candidate, much less a full-fledged medicine woman, Paisley was unable to guess. No matter how often she claimed to be grown, she knew in her heart that she was still a school girl, whose daddy had never visited her in all the years since his leavetaking and whose Mama D'lo had . . . done what she'd done. And here she was putting away scrambled eggs as if she hadn't eaten at school yesterday and gulping them down like a starved dog.

How can I be a *po'rat?* Paisley wondered. How can this kindly lady see me even as a *would-be* medicine woman?

"DeWayne!" LannaSue called, holding a smoked-down cigarette in front of her. "DeWayne, stop sulking and come here!"

A moment later, Sky propped himself against the doorjamb. "You should've married a poodle, not a man."

"DeWayne, Paisley's dream—it's calling her to be a *po'rat*, a medicine woman, a healer, not only a dancer."

"You've got piñon nuts for brains, LannaSue. If you open your mouth again, they'll rattle onto the floor."

"The sick man in her dream," said LannaSue, undeterred by this warning. Speculatively, she added, "The kar'tajan in the photo she pieced back together to your flute's song."

"What about them?" Sky said.

Paisley was confused again. LannaSue had just said *kar'tajan,* the very word that Barnes had used earlier this morning. Moreover, Sky—despite his put-on disgruntlement—was clearly heeding his wife's words, trying to follow her reasoning.

"The Sun Dance is for earning power to heal with, and the Anglo with the deadly illness in her dream requires healing. So does the kar'tjan in her dream photo—it's angry and sick, too."

Sky was noncommittal. "So?"

"Paisley calls for the man's healing. She wants to help him. But you say he's broken the rules, and you throw him out."

"He *has* broken the rules," Sky retorted, astonishing Paisley by talking about her dream as if it were an event of which he and his wife shared a real memory. "He brought in moisture."

"Only a name on a shirt."

"He brought in moisture, he brought in Anglo advertising, and he brought them with the picture-taking woman."

I only *dreamed* those things, Paisley thought, looking back and forth between the arguing husband and wife. And it was *my* dream. How can they argue about *my* dream?

But another part of her mind declared, Paisley, you dreamed it *seven times.* It's got to be seriously considered, and DeWayne and LannaSue are doing that.

"Fetch the god sheet, DeWayne."

"Christ, woman, that's only to come out at the end of the Sun Dance. Next. you'll be asking me to piss on the sacred fire."

"After asking for the healing of the man you threw out, Paisley had a vision. I think it means she's to become a *po'rat.* Fetch the god sheet. We'll see."

It looked for a minute that Sky might stomp off again, outraged and truculent. Paisley would not've blamed him.

The god sheet, if that somewhat awkward term signified what she thought it did, was a piece of linen that the Sun Dance chief brought forth during the closing ceremonies to impress the Shoshones, Arapahos, Apaches, and Navajos who had come to take part, for only the Muache had anything so impressive to display at dance's end. That Lanna-Sue was asking Sky to get it now, months ahead of time, for no other purpose but to determine her suitability for shamanhood—well, it staggered Paisley. She finished eating, drank the last of her coffee, stared embarrassedly at her hands.

"He's getting it," LannaSue said. "Come on."

They found Sky peeking around his study door into the living room, holding something—the god sheet, Paisley figured—behind it out of sight. "Not a word of this to anyone," he said, "Not a word of this from either of you pathetically shy females to anybody outside this house. Got me?"

"Come on. Bring it out. I'll throw the rug back. You can lay it down right here." LannaSue tapped the floor with her foot.

"Blindfold her," Sky said.

"What? There's nobody here but us, DeWayne."

"Do it. In this, I'll have my way. She has to be blindfolded for the test to work. and turn that damn lamp out again."

Blindfolded? The lamp out? Was she going to get to see the god sheet or not? All the hocus-pocus—which she couldn't relate to the time-honored rituals of either the Bear or the Sun Dance—frightened Paisley. Hell, Lanna-Sue's notion that she had *po'rat* potential frightened her. Before she could say anything, though, LannaSue had tied a clean dish towel around her eyes and further insured her sightlessness by pressing a pair of Sky's sunglasses into place over the towel. Blind man's bluff.

She could still feel, however, and when Sky billowed the sheet out and let it drift down like a provisional carpet, she felt the stirred air slap her like something wet. Moisture, when you were dry, was power, but she wasn't dry, and this whole business—now that she had told her dream and eaten—seemed peculiar. Still, she trusted the Skys, and if they thought this was the way to test her, well, it must be okay.

LannaSue sat her down, helped her remove her shoes and

socks. Then she was standing behind Paisley, her large hands gripping her shoulders. Sky retreated and returned. When his red-cedar flute began to play again (the same painful melody), LannaSue pushed her gently forward, telling her to step lightly on the god sheet.

"Try to make a crossing," she said.

A crossing? Paisley thought. I can make a crossing with my eyes closed—which was a joke almost good enough to laugh aloud at. But when LannaSue released her, all her fragile bravado fell part and she hesitated.

Legend had it that the god sheet—the sacred linen—was an authentic Muache relic. At some point over the past half century, a Ute visionary who had just successfully completed the Sun Dance went walking in the hills near the dance grounds and happened upon the footprints of a stranger. This Indian was wrapped in the sheet that he'd worn into and out of the Thirst House over the three days of the dance, and it occurred to him that these footprints—they were narrow and bare—were Jesus's. The Mormons claimed that the Indians were a lost tribe of Israel, after all, and that, once upon a time, Jesus had appeared in the New World. In any case, the Ute visionary laid his cloaklike sheet atop the strange footprints, and the sheet, according to legend, absorbed them into its fabric so thoroughly that no amount of scrubbing or detergent could lift them out again.

Now, the Sun Dance chief was the keeper of this holy relic, and Paisley stood at its edge, unable to see it, knowing that she must cross it to inherit to . . . well, an apprenticeship that might one day confer upon her divine power.

"Walk, darling," LannaSue Sky encouraged her. "Walk."

Paisley took a step. Sky's flute continued its balky crooning, and the young woman heard the music in the same way that she felt the god sheet—as a spiritual warmth. In fact, although the pine floor was cold and the sheet itself frigid, as she navigated the musty smelling relic, Paisley noticed that the soles of her feet—step by careful step—seemed to absorb more and more warmth, more and more tingly energy, and it was tempting just to dash from one side of the linen to the other.

"The woman in the Thrist House goes slow," Sky said.

"She goes slow and watches what there is to watch."

The flute resumed playing. Paisley overcame the urge to dash. Soon, she found herself observing again her own ghostly automaton in the Sun Dance corral of her mind.

There before her self-projection's eyes, hanging from the holy cotton-wood like Jesus on his Roman cross, was the skinny Anglo in the Coca-Cola shirt. He had been crucified on the center pole, his arms stretched out into unsupportive air and his feet nailed to the Tree of Life with splinters of antelope bone. The gaunt Anglo was saying something, mumbling aloud, but all that Paisley's dream self could make out was the end of his mumble— ". . . forsaken me"— a phrase with the rising intonation of a question.

Whereupon the Anglo faded from her dream self's sight, vanished into the white air of the imaginary Sun Dance lodge, to be replaced on the center pole by another totem altogether—the head not of a buffalo or of her own dead mother, but of a taxidermically prepared specimen of a mythological beast that Paisley knew as a unicorn but Whirling Goat and the Skys as a kar'tajan, as if they all had some ancient knowledge to which she was not yet privy and on which she might never gain a steady grip. All the other dancers rushed this totem. Leaping, then falling entranced, all had visions, while Paisley's dream self watched from her own Sun Dance path, buoyed by the activity but confused by it, too.

Then she saw that the gaunt Anglo, clad now only in an Indian breechclout, stood beyond the Thirst House entrance. He looked at her peculiarly for a moment, then motioned her to foresake the lodge and follow him. Paisley could feel the soles of her feet—her real feet—growing warmer and warmer as she struggled to obey the mysterious Anglo's summons. It was pity that drew her, not quite conviction, and she knew that once she had seen what he required of her, she would return to the Thirst House to apprise herself of the contents of all her fellow dancers' visions.

Suddenly, the pine floor was cold under her feet again.

"You're across!" a woman's voice cried.

Paisley hoped that LannaSue would remove her sunglasses, untie her blindfold, and give her a look at the god sheet, but Sky, she could tell, was gathering up the sheet, hurriedly folding it, and returning it to its hiding place in his study. Only when he had come back from this task did LannaSue turn on the lamp, remove the blindfold, and hug her. Both she and Sky were beaming at her—as if she had just climbed Mount Everest or swum the English Channel. Paisley blinked at them, more confused than ever, her mind a jumble of images—some distilled from dreams and some from all that had happened to her since coming to town.

"I'm taking you as a Sun Dancer," Sky told her.

LannaSue said, "And for training as the new Muache po'rat."

Toying with one of his braids, Sky nodded.

"But why?" Paisley asked them. "What did I do?"

"You walked where the Walking Man walked," Lanna-Sue said. "On the sheet where *his* footprints lie, you put *your* feet."

Paisley looked at her mentor and her mentor's wife. She felt gratitude for their approval of her and of what she had reputedly accomplished, but also skepticism. All she had for evidence that she had done anything very significant was that odd warmth—which still just perceptibly lingered—on the soles of her bare feet. And, of course, the Sky's word that she had walked exactly atop the Walking Man's or Jesus', footprints. It seemed simultaneously a remarkable achievement and a con.

"Great responsibility comes with this honor," Sky said.

Paisley knew. Already, the responsibility had begun to weigh on her. Taking part in the Sun Dance would keep her from leaving to find her father until July, and her apprenticeship as a shaman would require not only her early return but a long sojourn on the Navajo reservation in New Mexico so that a true Navajo shaman could adopt and train her. Life seemed even more complicated than it had after Mama D'lo's suicide.

"It's wonderful," LannaSue said, chucking her under the chin as if she were a baby. "You'll bring us hope again—hope and pride and power."

Paisley slumped to the sofa. She looked through the picture window. The inside of the fake tepee was pinkly agleam, dawnlight filtering through the hard plastic windows set high in its stucco cone. Was it possible that her dreams had led her to such a pass? Her private, impalpable dreams?

LannaSue hunkered in front of her, gripping her knees with her vise-like hands. For a moment, she simply hunkered there—Paisley thought that squatting so must be hard for her, she was by no means a petite woman—but abruptly said.

"Some folks think that dreams aren't real, darling. Some folks think they're nothing but nonsense."

Sky grunted a derisive assent. The derision in it was for the people his wife was talking about, not for his wife. They were in harmony again. Paisley's walk had restored them to it.

"But dreams are of God, and dreams cause real things to happen, and you, a dreamer, are greatly blessed, darling."

"I—" Paisley began.

"Greatly," LannaSue said. She struggled out of her squat and looked at her husband. "When it's time," she said authoritatively, "DeWayne will drive you to school."

vi.

After school, Paisley mooched a ride from Larry Cuthair on his motorcycle. They didn't go home immediately, though, because Larry wanted to buy some notebook paper in Ignacio.

They rode into town together, Larry entered the drugstore, and Paisley sat at the curb on his bike waiting for him to come back. While she was waiting, she looked halfway down the block and caught sight of a man staggering out of the laundromat. It was Herbert Barnes, who'd probably spent most of the day in the washateria with a bottle of cheap booze. He careened along, as if about to fall from the sidewalk into the street. Paisley ran to him and grabbed him by the elbow.

"Whirling Goat, are you okay?"

He cocked a bloodshot eye at her. "Course I am," he croaked, patting the pocket of his coat. "Got me some spirits right here—some dandy Old Crow for a randy old Ute."

"Chief Sky says I'm accepted for the Sun Dance," she said. "He and LannaSue believe I've been dream-called."

"You're pretty?" he said doubtfully.

"Thank you," Paisley said, equally doubtfully.

"You're very pretty?"

"I don't know."

Barnes shifted his weight from one wobbly leg to the other. A look of obscene slyness came into the one eye that he was managing to keep open. "Your mama D'lo told me you oughta take me home with you," he said. "You know, to watch over you."

"Yeah. In hand talk."

"I . . . s-swuh-swear," Barnes half hissed, half coughed.

Up the street, Larry shouted, "Paisley, come on!"

Paisley slipped the five-dollar bill that LannaSue had forced on her that morning into the old fart's coat. He'd only spend it on drink, but there was no way she could reform him in the next ten minutes nor was she about to take him home with her. The money was guilt money, but it was also . . . well, a token of esteem for what he had once been. He believed that he had seen a kar'tajan, and he carried in his pocket a foilwrapped lucky coin—a talisman, both absurd and poignant, of hope.

"Paisley!" Larry Cuthair yelled again.

She kissed the smelly old sot on the cheek and ran back up the sidewalk to climb aboard Larry's motorcycle. ●

GUARDIAN

by Lisa Mason

"Guardian" was purchased by Gardner Dozois, and appeared in the October 1988 issue of IAsfm, with an illustration by Judy Mitchell. She's subsequently made several more sales to us, but this cracklingly-tense story of murder and magic and madness was her first IAsfm story to appear in print.

Lisa Mason is a new young writer who has made sales to Omni, *as well as to* IAsfm. *She lives in Oakland, California, and is at work on her first novel.*

He rams the blade into the crack between the patio door and aluminum jamb. Aluminum's soft; the blade is steel. Don't they know how soft they are, how hard he can be? With a jerk, he bends the metal lip back, twists and twists, and in two seconds, he's forced leeway, made a fulcrum off the jamb itself. Then he slips the blade onto the deadbolt, tip against tip, and with a flick, he flips the lock. Just like that.

He slides the patio door open, slips inside.

No one's home. Well, of course, dude. Old Ray's been watching. Watching these condominiums. Watching the rich asshole condo owners with their cars and their VCR's. "I'm the new owner of Unit hm-hm," they say, smug. Oh yes, the new owner. All full of importance. Ray knows. Ray, who sweeps the parquet and mops the lobby and picks up their cigarette butts and yassirs when they stroll down their plushy-plushy halls. Ray, who drifts around these halls,

184

which are nicer than the lousy little eastside studio he crashes in. Drifts all day, if he wants to, any day. And nobody notices him, of course, nobody notices. He's just the janitor, come to clean, two hundred dollars a week, such a deal.

So he marks their doors with little bits of heavy paper torn off the real estate agent's sales brochure. Folds the tags in half for springiness. Tucks the tags into the door jamb on the hinge side, and waits. Waits and watches, ooh Ray, he watches. They come home from their whitebread jobs, the tag falls out, real subtle, just a bit of paper on the thick tan carpet that Ray vacuums up in the morning. They don't come home; they go skiing at Lake Tahoe or do tennis in Carmel or go wherever rich asshole condo owners go to play; well, Ray, he sees that, too. Sees the little fold of paper, tucked up snug as a bug in the door no one's used. Ray, he knows the tricks. And then, when night falls, when it gets dark . . . .

The bitch has got a VCR, all right, and a Sony Trinitron TV. Silver tea set, Nikon with zoom lens, a tangle of gold chains, diamond earrings, for chrissakes. A goddamned fur coat all silvery fluff, and a Walkman, and a Cuisinart, and a fancy Panasonic phone answering machine blinking with her calls, she's so important . . . .

Ray piles the loot onto her balcony. Hers is one of the back units looking out on the rear lot of the apartment building on Belmont Avenue. He'll drive his van around, scale the flimsy wire fence he's already bent down, shove the stuff in. Then off he'll go to another kind of fence. But before he walks out her front door, cool as can be, just the janitor, after all; before he goes.

He goes back into her bedroom, throws open the mirrored closet door. Jacks the blade through her silky blouses, her bright dresses, slashes slashes, just to do it, rich bitch. Stops off in the kitchen. Her cupboards are filled with china plates, glasses that look like crystal, but not for long. Ray, he just loves the sound of breaking. Next, the refrigerator, some deluxe thing with water and ice dispensers. He sweeps his arms across the shelves, sends food and dishes crashing. God, what a mess, rich bitch. He finds a bottle of wine. Flips the cork, takes a swig, then dumps the rest onto her white wall-to-wall, what phony name do they call that color, ivory or pearl or hummingbird shit. He dumps it, and it's red wine, ooh Ray. He couldn't see through the green glass, couldn't taste anything but sour, but it's red as a baboon's ass, by God, and he laughs as the darkness spills across her hummingbird shit wall-to-wall in a bloody stain.

"So the balance is eight thousand, one hundred and twelve. That includes your first quarter property taxes," says the escrow officer.

Vaughn Kennedy endorses the check. Crazy, but her heart is pounding, her hands are damp. Biggest check she's ever written. She ruefully calculates her account balance. Biggest bite out of her savings she's ever taken. Savings she's built for six years, fifty dollars here, two hundred there. Vacation time spent at home. No car her first three years out of school. Each month, what to do without, what to put off. Reheated spaghetti, reheeled shoes. And all for this, the most important step yet of her adult life: buying her first home.

"Best condominium in the San Francisco Bay area," says the developer's agent, flashing his teeth. "In this market? Just ten percent down. FHA loan at nine percent carries the rest. You've got a good warranty on the unit, too. Congratulations, Vaughn."

"So where's the new place, Vaughn?" asks the escrow officer, checking through the loan documents one more time.

"Right off Lake Merritt in downtown Oakland."

"Oakland," exclaims the escrow officer. "Isn't there a lot of crime?"

"No no no," says the developer's agent. "That's East Oakland you're thinking of. The drug wars. This is the Lake. Northside. Near the Kaiser Center and Piedmont. Lots of lawyers from San Francisco, people from City Hall."

"I see," says the escrow officer doubtfully.

"No, really, it's very nice!" says Vaughn. She feels numb, like she's moving in slow motion, as she hands the check over and signs her name to the Deed of Trust Note. "It is, it's so nice! There's a bird sanctuary and a bandstand where local symphonies play. There's an arts festival every June.

The Grand Avenue shopping district's just down the road, and I can walk to my gallery."

"You own a gallery?" asks the escrow officer, impressed.

"Manage it. The Tamarind, in the Kaiser Mall. We show primitive and naïve pieces, ethnic artifacts, some modern abstracts, antique and modern folk art. Eclectic, but it works. The exhibit for this month just shipped in. A collection from Haiti."

That morning she'd signed the invoice for twenty-two packages express-mailed from the Egg and the Eye in Los Angeles. Slicing through swathes of packing paper and tape, she'd extracted strange riches: bright collages built to three dimensionality with contours of papier-mâché, bizarre twists of boxwood sculpture, a sheaf of painted drawings comprised of crosses, scrolls, glyphs with symmetrical repetitions, eccentric asymmetries.

The drawings were identified with a printed label that read: "Veves: ceremonial drawings that call up spirits in voodoo ritual; circa 1929." A thrill had tickled Vaughn's spine. Voodoo; calling up spirits. Indeed, she'd scoffed, shaking off the tingle of dread. She was a modern thinker, with no use for superstition. Perhaps voodoo was like modern psychotherapy, a manipulation of ritual and emotion to produce archetypal images out of the psyche. Fascinating. But spirits didn't actually materialize.

Still, the power of the veves, their strange shapes, occult designs, had been undeniable. Beautiful, disturbing. Like a secret alphabet setting forth some esoteric truth about the world modern thinkers had forgotten.

"Well, if you don't mind my saying so," says the escrow officer, startling Vaughn out of her reverie. "You should be proud. Buying your own place. Young woman like you are? Single? And black? You don't mind . . . ."

The escrow officer blushes. The developer's agent coughs and looks away.

There was a time, when she was twenty, when Vaughn would have minded. She might even make a joke later with Mrs. Russ Robinson, the cool elegant owner of the Tamarind, about poor white trash like the escrow officer, who gave her junior business school training away with her crude diction and tawdry fashion. Vaughn's master's degree in art history was from Yale.

But Vaughn says instead, laughing, self-assured, "I *am* proud. I'm doing what I always wanted to do. Oh, I could probably make more money as a computer programmer. But I love art; I've always wanted to be around art. And things are going well at the gallery. I have fun." She would gross forty-two five in a salary and commissions this year. It wasn't a fortune, but it wasn't bad either, for thirty-two years old. She'd earned it all herself. She'd worked hard.

"Well, you've got the best floorplan in the best condo complex in the Bay area," says the developer's agent, relieved Vaughn hadn't taken offense at what might have been construed as a racist remark. He gleams with the profit his principal just made and the commission he'll collect. "Low homeowners' dues. Brand-new, quality-constructed, security building. Security garage. The front door has got a telephone intercom and TV monitor; when someone buzzes you, you tune in channel 11, and you can see who's downstairs on your TV."

"I'll take it, I'll take it!" says Vaughn, and they all laugh some more. The developer's agent gathers his copies of the closing documents and takes off. The escrow officer stuffs Vaughn's documents into a huge envelope and shakes her hand goodbye.

"A word to the wise, Ms. Kennedy," says the escrow officer respectfully, trying to make amends. "Security building, TV monitors, all that is fine. But be sure to get yourself a good deadbolt."

Ray leaves the vacuum cleaner running. An ear-splitting bizz-bizz-bizz fills the hall. He looks around. The place is deserted. Nobody's home in the middle of the morning. Well, of course, the rich asshole condo owners are all off to their plushing whitebread nine-to-fives. Middle of the morning is one of the prime times. Everything quiet. Nobody home.

Prime hit time.

Ray leaves the vacuum cleaner standing where the hall veers off to the entry of Unit 208. Places his cart full of mops and brooms and rags and cleanser in front of the angle sloping off 208's door. Extracts the crowbar from the cart.

There's a gap as wide as the Grand Canyon between the door and exterior frame. That asshole developer and his quality construction. What a laugh. Half the front doors in the whole place are hung crooked, gaping around the edges like the mouths of the condo owners who lap up the developer's phony rap.

The crowbar goes in okay. The gap isn't the half of it, though. The front door looks solid, like a vault door. But Ray knows. It isn't solid. These doors are just plywood constructions coated with thin metal skin. Inside, hollow, empty as a pusher's promise. And all he's got to do is peel back the phony face, and a space like a pusher's soul is there. Empty. Nothing but empty.

He works the crowbar in, works it, works it. He makes some racket, but the vacuum cleaner whines and shrieks in the hall. Soon the lips of door and frame are curled back like a snarl, and Ray can see the whole works of the knob's lock. Deadbolt, too. Then it's just a matter of forcing the steel bolts out of their rickety little nests of plywood. He jabs and digs. The locks go click-click!

And he's in. Well, all right, dude. Made it. Into somebody's private place, their sweet little private place, again. He shakes with a quick thrill.

Then he shakes with the cold pain. God *damn*. The Boss of Funktown Gang, biggest gang in the war, just got three successive twenty-year sentences, with no possibility of parole, and the Boss's former lieutenant, that punk Stingray Brown, raised prices on his dope, and Ray didn't have the price last time. He didn't have it, God *damn,* he didn't have it. So he's pissed, and he's hurting with the cold pain. Hurting bad.

Ray creeps into 208's darkened foyer. He knows where to go. One of the amenities the developer offers new owners is a cleaning job by our clean boy Ray. Right when the owner moves in. Ray gets the nails and remnants off the newly laid carpets, scrubs the new tile down, squeaks the new windows clean. And sees everything the new owner has, what's valuable, what's being put where, what's still in boxes. Good old Ray, he sees everything.

The guy in 208 doesn't have much, not nearly enough for what Ray needs. The bastard, the lousy whitebread bastard. The guy has got an aquarium, some fancy little useless thing with lacy looking fish, frilly plants, curliqued coral. Ray heaves the tank up, stinking water splashing all over, and shoves it into the guy's GE microwave. Sets the Temp Control on medium high and flicks the oven on.

"Cable TV's coming out next Tuesday to splice their system onto our rooftop aerial," says the President of the homeowners' association at the monthly homeowners' meeting. "That'll mean we can get cable at a group rate. Maybe nine or ten bucks on your dues, for a thirty-five dollar-a-month service. We're all pretty pleased."

"Arnold?" Vaughn raises her hand. "Cable TV at a group rate is fine and dandy. But I want to know about the break-ins." Her voice trembles, as much with anger as with the growing fear for her home. "All I've heard is rumors. I *demand* to know what's been happening."

Arnold sighs and rubs his jaw. He's got haunted eyes; before he retired from the Oakland police force, his eyes had seen too many bullet-riddled bodies in East Oakland streets. Eight-year-old sentries, twelve-year-old runners, twenty-year-old kingpins turning playgrounds and residential sidewalks into guerrilla fire zones.

"All right," says Arnold. "There've been four break-ins in the past six weeks. Um. Let's just say they got hit bad. Friend of mind at the Hall says there's a ring of pros working the neighborhood over. They come from eastside. They come for goods they can turn over for drug money."

"Oh!" "God, what can we do?" "The bastards!" The homeowners grumble, turn to each other with troubled faces. Most don't really know each other; it's a fifty-unit complex. Behind the false intimacy of the meeting is the tangible chill of just how little they know each other.

"Six weeks!" says Vaughn. "My loan closed two weeks ago. How come the developer didn't tell me about this?"

"Well, honey, what do you think?" says Arnold.

A couple of homeowners titter. "That damn developer, I've called them for three weeks about my bathtub leaking," one fellow says. "Oh yea?" a woman in a three-piece suit chimes in. "I've been waiting a month and a half for the contractor to fix my back windows." "They don't care," announces someone else. "Take the money and run."

"I think I've been given false advertising, that's what I think," says Vaughn, silencing them all. Her sense of having been betrayed almost matches the time Daniel left her. After months of ugly squabbling, and the realization they wanted different things out of life, she and Dan had tried again, had made a commitment to try for the love she thought they both still felt. And then, after a lovely Sunday brunch, and champagne, and lovemaking, her beautiful blond Danny finally said, "It's no use, babe." And he'd left for the Vermont ski slopes he wanted to live by, and she'd left for California.

Betrayal. Vengeance, love-gone-wrong, the evil eye. The dark emotions, most powerful of the loas, the laws of voodoo. Ancient betrayal, as the Dahomeans, the Mina, the Mandingues, the Rada were stripped of rank and land and heritage, were marched into ships owned by slavers. Atrocious betrayal, bound in irons, bound for colonial plantations. Vaughn supposed her disappointments, painful though they were to her, might seem banal in the balance of history. But she learned she shared betrayal with the slave women of the islands who took up the dark arts. She'd tasted betrayal as surely as every mambo whose lover was taken, not by the modern bewitchment of self-absorption, but by a blanching, the subcutaneous white tissue beneath his brown laid bare with a boss's knife. In the secret temple of the oum'phor, the priestesses of voodoo drew veves, summoned the mystères, and cried for vengeance.

In the silence cleared by her anger, Vaughn says, "I was told this was a security building. I've got a good mind to fucking sue the developer *and* the homeowners' association. What do you think of *that*, Arnold?"

"Take it easy, honey."

"Only my mother gets away with calling me honey, mister. Understand?"

"Sorry, Vaughn." Arnold doesn't look contrite.

"That's right, you're sorry. I heard there was vandalism. I heard Steve's angelfish got *microwaved.* I don't think it's *funny,"* she snaps at the couple of homeowners who titter again. "That's not pros, Arnold. That's some crazy. Listen. I've had my cat Sasha for ten years, she's like a child to me.

My insurance can't replace my grandmother's cameo ring or the Wassily chair I had custom covered in peach leather. All right, those are just material things. What about *us*? Look at all the women and children who live here. What's next? Rape? I'm *not* going to take it easy, Arnold. I want some action."

"But I don't know what we can do, dear," says Mrs. Miller, the owner of Unit 507. A small, wizened beauty shop blond, Mrs. Miller has cancer on her lips. In a sad, futile effort to conceal her illness, she holds her fist over her mouth when she talks, so that her voice comes out muffled, barely audible through her carpal bones. The homeowners take a moment to decipher her utterance. "If they're going to get in," Mrs. Miller continues, her logic as futile as her concealment. "They're going to get in."

"No!" Vaughn jumps up, paces before the homeowners. "Pardon me, Mrs. Miller, but that's crap. This place is full of security holes. For example, Arnold," she says, turning her fury back to the president. "The garage is left open. *Open.* All day. Now tell me something. What good is a heavy-duty metal grate if it's left *open?* I demand that the developer close the door."

"Yeah, well, the developer leaves it open so prospective buyers can park their cars," he explains. "The developer has a right to do that, and we all will benefit from full occupancy of the building, and . . ."

"The right! To subject people who've already bought units to an open invitation to your ring of pros? Or worse, to some crazy? I demand that door be closed. I'm warning you, Arnold."

"I'll check it out," he says, voice tight.

"And Vaughnie, how about those fire escape doors on the back patio?" asks Melba, Vaughn's next-door neighbor who lives along with her tiny acorn of a daughter. " 'Member how we got locked out when you were moving in, and we got the door right open with your Visa card?" Melba turns to the group. "We stuck the edge of Vaughnie's card in, and opened 'em up, one-two-three. Thought it was funny at the time," she says morosely.

"That's right, thanks, 'Ba," says Vaughn. "We've got to put some crow-bar-proof plating on the fire doors, on the other exterior doors, too. I demand security measures be taken, Arnold. *Now. Nobody* is getting into *my* home."

"All right, all right." says Arnold, and makes a note. "Close garage. Locks on escapes." He sighs. "I suppose I should mention. For those of you who do have patios or fire escape windows abutting any common area. You should probably look into getting security bars. I just ordered mine."

It's a custom job, with squared-off scrolls, some kind of chink design. Painted camel or putty or French poodle doo to match the tan stucco. Ray, he likes the custom jobs. He likes to see the custom jobs bend before the crowbar, bend like any cheap piece of shit. Ray, he likes to think of all that money and thought and time invested in trying to keep him out. It's enough to make him cry, how they try to keep him out. All that money, thought, and time, and it's not enough, It's never enough.

The bars are tubular steel. Not solid steel. Hollow, all hollow. He can't get over how hollow everything is. Nothing solid, nothing sturdy, nothing ever really like it seems. Nothing ever real, until old Ray gets himself a fix, and then nothing matters. Nothing matters at all, except the next fix.

Not only are the bars cheap tubular steel, the standard for security bars, but the frame is bolted on with four cute little lug bolts at each corner. Shabby shit, rich asshole condo owner. Really shabby. Too expensive for them to get solid steel bolted decently? But then they don't think of that. How come they're supposed to be so smart and so rich, and they don't even think of that? Think they're safe with their poodle doo security bars. Think they're protected. But Ray knows. Ooh Ray, he knows.

He thrusts the crowbar through the bars, angles it off the middle bar, gets the head under the edge of the metal plate that's under the bolt. Jumps his whole weight onto it. *Scree!* Christ, what a commotion. Come on, fucker, give! The bolt jumps a bit out of the stucco, jumps more, then tears loose. The flimsy tubular steel bends back, easy.

Tape goes over the glass where Ray knows a handle waits inside. He makes a quick whisk with the glass cutter. Tools of the trade, dude. Ray removes the circle of glass, slips his hand in, pops the handle, swings the window open. Then squeezes through the gape between dislodged security bars and open window.

He slips into the dark. "Mama!" Stumbles on something small. "Mama! Mama!" Kicks something soft.

A heap of toys: zebras, monkeys, elephants, fur seals, frogs, kitty-cats, tigers, unicorns. A brontosaurus. A stampede of teddy-bears, for chrissakes. And a big, tangly-headed doll with a face like chocolate pudding and big brown eyes who screams, "Mama!"

Lucky kid. Little lucky kid. Little lucky rich kid, with a dozen teddy bears. What did the brat ever do to deserve all this? Just be born?

And it kicks Ray back, all the toys, the dark, carpeted room that smells like popcorn, a miniature bed and chair skirted with lace. Kicks Ray back to when he never had enough. Never had enough, and he was helpless to do anything about it. He was helpless then.

Daddy gone. Mama drinking up the welfare. Cockroaches running through her plate of bacon that she picked at while the social worker, some white lady, Ray remembers, who looked like Santa Claus's wife, looked at them all with horror. And he was helpless to do anything about it. He was just a kid.

Lucky, lucky, fucking lucky. How did B.B. King say it? If it wasn't for bad luck; I wouldn't have no luck. If it wasn't for *real* bad luck; I wouldn't have no luck. At all.

His fury makes him mindless and calm at the same time. Get the glass cutter, dude. Take each toy. Cut its head off. Cut its little head off. Cut and cut and cut.

"I think it's an inside job, Vaughn," says Mrs. Russ Robinson. With meticulous, manicured, creme de cacao fingertips, the owner of the Tamarind takes down the pen and ink whale drawing done for Greenpeace, prepares the gallery's walls for the exciting new Haitian collection.

"Why do you say that, Mrs. R?" Vaughn can hardly keep her eyes open. She can barely get three hours of sleep anymore. She paces through her place, surveying the doors and windows until one A.M. Jolts into wakefulness at four when the garbage collectors bang the dumpsters around. Tosses and turns for the rest of the dawn, starting up at every creak and bump, what was *that?*

"Because it stands to reason," says Mrs. R. With the sigh of one transported by sheer aesthetics, she admires the bas relief of an exuberant village scene.

"Why does it stand to reason?" persists Vaughn. Her head begins to buzz, adrenaline and coffee and fatigue mixing painfully.

Mrs. R. flashes one of her penetrating looks. "First. The robberies always occur when no one's home, no one's around. A couple of them in broad daylight. True?"

"True."

"Second. How could someone from the street know when the occupant isn't home? It isn't always obvious, is it? Not during the day; a thief from the street wouldn't necessarily know who stays home during the day, who's out. Unless you've watched when people come and go; unless you know who owns which car, so when someone's car is gone from the garage, you know they're gone from their unit. All that would take a lot of surveillance, wouldn't it? So someone would have to have access to the complex. Regularly."

"Oh great," says Vaughn. "Do you know how many people have access to the complex, regularly? The newspaper carrier; the garbage collectors; the mail carrier; the contractors; the subcontractors, the electrician; the plumber; the gardeners; the rug layers; the developer's agent; the association management's agent; prospective buyers, people right off the street; not to mention the janitor."

"I wouldn't worry about people off the street, kid. I would worry about those regulars." Mrs. R. adjusts the soaring loop-the-loop of a wooden sculpture on its small dramatic dais, then turns at last to the sheaf of veves, which have become a bit disheveled in their unframed state. "I would watch those regulars. I know cleaning people always get first blame, and nine times out of ten they're good people. But that tenth time, Vaughn. Watch out for that tenth time. The only time I ever had my purse stolen was at Harcourt's in San Francisco, where I was working as a buyer to learn the gallery business. I left the purse on my desk and stepped away for not more than a minute. When I stepped back, it was gone. Some cleaning woman took it. Funny thing, too;

someone found the purse, empty, dumped under a secretary's desk in a building on Montgomery Street. My library card was still in an inside pocket, so the gal looked me up and called me. Well, of course, I found out the same cleaning service worked both buildings."

"Cleaning people." The janitor's face looms before Vaughn. A worn face, with long, deep frown lines from nose to mouth, a troubled gully between the brows, and, underneath the obsequiousness, a dark undercurrent of bitterness. Suddenly it strikes her: *him*. She recalls how she was walking down the hallway to the garage the other day, and she heard angry grumbling, whispered epithets. And then there he was, what's his name, Ray, talking to himself. And he'd looked up, jumped up, shut up, startled, at the sight of her. Looked at her, guilty.

"Oh God, Mrs. R. what am I going to do?" Vaughn starts to cry. "I feel so ripped off by the whole thing."

Mrs. R. puts down the drawings, goes to her. "Vaughn. I want you to get a good alarm system. Wire up your whole place. Will you do that?"

"But those systems are so expensive! Fifteen hundred dollars, Mrs. R. I'm still trying to recover from my down payment."

"I'll advance you your quarterly commissions."

"You just paid me for last quarter. Your accountant will murder you."

"All right. Your mid-quarterly commissions. There's a rich science fiction writer living in the Oakland hills who appreciates esoteric ethnic artifacts. You send him an invitation to the opening. You sell him a veve or two."

"Do you really think we should sell them, Mrs. R.?"

"Do I think ...? Why, of course! They're marvelous, aren't they?" Mrs. R. goes back to the sheaf, lifts a veve. "So provocative. Don't you like them?"

Vaughn runs her finger down the handmade paper, admiring its grainy surface. "I like them very much. I'm moved by them."

"Then why the hesitation?"

"Mrs. R. Do you realize what these are?"

"Veves. Ceremonial drawings."

"That call up the spirits, Mrs. R. The mystères. These

drawings are magical reproductions of astral forces."

"Ah, astral forces. Kid, you've been studying up."

Vaughn admits only that. Not the obsession that has begun to grip her. The ten books on voodoo she's bought at Walden's, the two rare books from the nineteen-twenties she's borrowed from the Alameda Public Library. The candles, the incense, the thick essence oils she's bought at a sorcery shop on Broadway.

"Well sure, Mrs. R.," she says lightly. "My mom said we've got West Indian blood in our family tree. I feel drawn. The black women of Haiti were integral to the preservation of African ritual and lore, the integration of ancient symbols with the Catholicism foisted on the slave population. A Rada tribeswoman named Rose is credited as the mother of voodoo magic. She and priestesses like her, the mambo, preserved their faith, developed it into a unique spirituality, in the face of incredible oppression."

"Interesting, Vaughn. Bring up the history at the opening. But leave this spirit business out, okay?"

"But, Mrs. R.," insists Vaughn. "Don't you see? Is it okay to sell them? I mean, the veve obliges the mystère whose astral energy is depicted to descend to the earthly plane and manifest. The mystère may possess the beholder of the veve, or any inanimate or animate object, or even another person. This is powerful stuff, Mrs. R. Even rational Western observers can't explain some of the events they've witnessed in voodoo ceremonies."

"Look here, kid. Only thing wrong with selling these drawings is that they look like hell unframed," says Mrs. R., deflating Vaughn's feverish enthusiasm at one. "So let's do the framing. Some kind of oriental looking thing, bambooish."

"Bambooish! Mrs. R., please!"

"All right, smart ass. You come up with something. And please promise me, kid. Get yourself an alarm system."

"Promise," says Vaughn. "I'll call Bay Alarm today."

Ray gets the electricity off easy as spit. Meters laid like cockleshells all in a row. And Ray, he can get into the utility room. Well, of course, dude, the janitor's got to have a key to get into the utility room. Little Miss Muff, sat on her tuff, eating her something-or-other, ooh Ray. Along came a spider . . . .

Along comes a spider, rich asshole condo owners. When the electricity is cut, the alarms won't go. Won't buzz, won't call the private security guards, won't call the police, won't alert the neighbors. Won't do shit.

And then Ray. Well, the old spider knows what to do.

Ray cuts off the ju-uice. Ray cuts off the ju-uice. Na-na, na-na-na. Ray cuts off the ju-uice.

Vaughn sifts through the veves, checks each drawing off the catalog, then considers mat and frame styles. The Egg and the Eye had mounted each drawing on a clear, three-by-three foot plexiglass sheet, sandwiched an identical plexiglass sheet over everything, clipped the construction shut, and hung it against black velvet. Okay for exhibition. But Mrs. R. was serious about selling each piece, despite Vaughn's reservations, so she wanted individual mounting. Still wanted, in fact, natural cotton matting and bamboo frame. These Vaughn dismissed as obvious.

So Mrs. R. sent her home for the day with the veves, the exhibition's catalog, a stack of pre-cut mats and frames, and two cans of Spra-Mount. Vaughn needed to be home, after all, for her appointment with the alarm installer in the morning.

But also. There was another reason for her request to stay home for the day. This Vaughn had not mentioned to Mrs. R. Melba had been robbed yesterday. Melba who had an alarm. Wreckage everywhere. Melba's daughter's new puppy's throat cut. A crazy. A fucking crazy. A crazy who could get past Bay Alarm. 'Ba had taken Tricia and fled to her mother's house, intending to call Century 21. "We can never live here again," she told Vaughn.

Vaughn couldn't figure it. In despair, she almost canceled the installation of her own alarm. *If they're going to get in, they're going to get in.* But then the alarm installer enlightened her.

"Got a 'letrical failure yesterday?" he'd asked.

Vaughn thought. No one had announced it, the public utility had left no notice, but, indeed, when she had come home after Melba's robbery, all her digital clocks, in the coffeemaker, the VCR, the clock radio, the stereo, all were blinking at twelve, and she'd reset them without thinking.

"See," said the alarm installer, on hearing about Melba. "Hers is what we call an open system. 'Lectricity goes, the system goes. But we've also got a closed system. A closed system kicks back into its own power source, a battery we install right here by your door. If the power goes, the system not only stays on, it'll call the fire department *and* the police. Automatically."

"Then I want a closed system," Vaughn said.

"Well, miss. That'll be another three hundred and fifty bucks on top of your original estimate."

"I don't care," Vaughn said, secretly despairing over her checkbook.

Now she gazes at the first veve. Like a one-masted sailboat in shape, with curling stern, bow, and rubber. This is the sign of Agwe, mystère of the sea. His colors: blue and green. His realm: all flora and fauna of the sea, fishermen and sailors and boats.

The next looks like a demented Valentine, set with cruciforms and rosettes. Instead of the sender writing, I love you, thought Vaughn, he or she would write, You will love me. This is the veve of Erzulie, the goddess of voodoo. Erzulie loves jewels, cosmetics, pretty dresses. She eats bananas. She can transmute into a serpent. She is loved for her generosity, feared for her jealous rage. Whoever becomes possessed by Erzulie, male or female, is compelled to don a dress and makeup, sway the hips provocatively in erotic dance.

Vaughn chooses a pale gold velum mat for the next veve, the one with maize-colored bulbs like ears of corn set atop the north and south arms of its cross-like configuration. Buttercup flower bursts pose on its horizontal arms, one at what looks like the top of an arrow poised to shoot, two at the arrow's feathers, one again at its notch.

The mat looks great. Then a squared-off white oak frame. Perfect. Clean, geometrical lines and pure color juxtaposed against the bizarre curves and variegated angles of the veve.

Bold, thinks Vaughn. Powerful. What moved some mambo to draw such a thing? The veve grips her more than any other. She thumbs through the catalog, trying to match the design against the tiny, one-inch reproductions of each work. Then there it is.

Sign of Legba, says the catalog. Legba: master of the mystic barrier between reality and the unseen worlds. Chief god of all rituals. *"Legba, ouvri barrie pou nous passer,"* begins the incantation. Opener of the Way. But also a protector. He who opens the mystic barrier to the supplicant shuts the doors of the real world to evil. God of gates and fences and walls.

Guardian of the home.

Vaughn glances at her watch. The afternoon is slipping away. She's got to attend the big opening of the Haitian show tonight. Got to; the rich science fiction writer who collects ethnic curiosities will be there. There's no way she can get out of it. *Mrr?* says Sasha, rubbing a black velvet tail around Vaughn's ankles, glancing up at her with harvest moon eyes. Trusting eyes.

"Our alarm will be on, baby," she tells the cat tearfully. She and Sasha go over and inspect the door for a moment, the wires, the control console, the backup battery. The tiny red light indicating the system is on, staring at them like the eye of a demon. If only she could believe that's enough. After all, the alarm only sounds when the thief's gotten in. And when he's gotten in . . . .

A wild notion strikes her. She takes up the catalog again, takes out a bit of tracing paper. Places the tracing paper over the one-inch reproduction of Legba's design. Carefully draws the design, then cuts out the tiny paper square, places it on the table, stares at it, stares at it. Her hands shake. To dispel her tension, she begins to clap, snap her fingers. As though pulled up by a string, she leaps to her feet, paces. Evening shadows ripple across the room. Wind-driven tree branches click against the window pane, click and clack, like a tapping. Oddly, Sasha hisses, skitters, tail and back puffed, into the bedroom.

And she begin to stomp, she begin to sway, she begin to clap a rhythm, she begin to say: Papa Legba Papa Legba Legba Legba Papa Legba

Ouvri barrie pou nous passer.

Papa Legba Papa Legba Legba Legba Papa Legba

At the doors and the windows and the walls themselves,

let no evil pass.
Let no evil pass.
Papa Legba Papa Legba Legba Legba Papa Legba
Please, Legba, she cry, *guard my home.*

Something's wrong, something's wrong, something's wrong. It's white when it ought to be tan.

Ray jumps up from Unit 211's door, heart thumping. He saw the bitch walk away, some piece of dark meat, in her black leather skirt and white suede jacket, toting a burgundy leather portfolio. He wouldn't mind waiting around for some of that. How he's waited, watched and waited, to get into her place. And he saw her walk away, he saw her walk away, and he knows she lives alone, so her place is empty now. But something's wrong as he peers at the alarm sticker at the bottom of her door.

He checks the carpeting for the bit of tan paper he left in the door hinge this morning. It should have been dislodged by her exit. And there it is on the floor. Well, hey, dude, what is the big deal? She didn't notice. But what's the white fold of paper stuck in the hinge? Like someone's tagging her door too, and didn't notice Ray's marker. Some other thief muscling in on his turf? Shit . . . .

He extracts the white slip of paper. It falls open. Something's wrong, ooh Ray, something's weird. A tiny drawing, for chrissakes, all squiggly and strange. Shock buzzes like a bee dive-bombing his head. Crazy, that he should feel so weird. But what does it mean? In a flash, he gets it: *she knows.*

He goes blank, panicked and blank. Nobody's known, how could anybody know? He's been careful, Ray, he's used all the tricks. He crumples the white slip into spit ball size, shoves it into his pocket, splits. This is not right, dude. This is not the night. Get out.

He goes to the elevator, punches the down button. The door flips right open, like it's been waiting for him. Inside, some old twat with a face like death. "Well, Ray, how are you?" she says, smiling behind the hand she holds over her diseased mouth. It's the old lady in 507. "My my, working so late?" she twaddles. "You should be careful, Ray. There has been a rash of robberies in the building. People are

scared. Some have even suspected you, Ray. You of all
people, someone we should be able to trust. But, Ray, I tell
them. I tell them I know you."

"Thank you, Mrs. Miller." The rich white bitch, she
doesn't know him from diddlysquat. But he keeps his face
straight, he doesn't let on. People suspect? Get out, dude.
Get out of this hellhole.

"Oh yes, I know what you really are, Ray," says
Mrs. Miller. Her crackly, old lady voice sounds suddenly deep and loud, trailing off in a venomous hiss. Ray
glances at her in surprise. She seems much taller than he
recalls. Her pale, wispy hair spews out from her head
in wild, dark dreadlocks. Her face is so shadowed as
to appear deeply tanned, skin nearly as dark as his
own.

"Jesus shit, Mrs. Miller," he says, desperately punching
the garage level button on the elevator's console. "You look
sick."

"I am sick, Ray," she says, issuing a deep, throaty laugh.
She regards him with burning eyes. "I have cancer. I need
money for therapy. Lot's of money. The old man's pension
can't begin to pay for my therapy. I'm desperate. Oh, you're
a junkie, I know, but there's good black market for body
parts."

"Body parts! You're nuts, old bitch!" Ray keeps punching
the down button; the elevator keeps going down down
down. "Jesus! What is this, anyway?"

"Even a junkie's body parts. Your eyes. Your inner ears.
Your kidneys. Your connective tissue. What's left of your
veins. Parts of your stomach. Who knows, even your
thieving junkie's heart."

"Heart? For chrissakes!"

Ray tries to twist away, but the pop-eyed old lady takes
his hand. Her fingers feel like dry tentacles, slithery and
ancient. Her diseased mouth clacks closer.

"I'm stealing you, Ray. Wait'll my fence sees you!" Over
the image of the little old blonde lady flashes a sinewy appa-
rition and, twirling all around it, glimpses of a vast, dark
infinity.

"Stealing me?" chocks Ray. Cold seizes him.

"Body," says the demon. "And soul."

Police sirens wail in the night. Always do, in East
Oakland streets. But this is Lake Merritt, Grand Avenue,
where San Francisco attorneys and people from City Hall
live. At the sound of the wail, Vaughn looks up from the
pleasant excitement of the opening, sighs calmly, pours
more champagne.

She's got protection. ●

HE-WE-AWAIT

by Howard Waldrop

*"He-We-Await" was purchased by Gardner
Dozois, and appeared in the Mid-December 1987 issue of
IAsfm, with a cover by Dennis Potokar and one of Terry
Lee's best interior illustrations. This was Waldrop's first
appearance in IAsfm, but his freewheeling imagination and
strong, shaggy humor soon made him highly popular with
the magazine's readers. Waldrop's stock in trade are bizarre
fictional juxtapositions; here, for instance, he takes us from
the Valley of the Kings, in ancient Egypt, to the concrete
canyons of modern-day Manhattan, in pursuit of a mystery
over 5,000 years old . . . a dark and deadly mystery that may
determine the fate of humanity.*

*Howard Waldrop is widely considered to be one of the
best short-story writers in the business, and his famous
story "The Ugly Chickens" won both the Nebula and the
World Fantasy Awards in 1981. His work has been gathered
in two collections:* Howard Who? *and* All About Strange
Monsters Of The Recent Past: Neat Stories By Howard
Waldrop, *and more collections are in the works. Waldrop
is also the author of the novel* Them Bones, *and, in collaboration with Jake Saunders,* The Texas-Israeli War: 1999.
Another solo novel is coming up. He lives in Austin, Texas.

"In the king-list of Manetho, an Egyptian priest who
wrote in Greek in the Third Century B.C., two names
are missing.

They are Pharaohs, father and son. The father, Sekhemet, by legend reigned one hour less than 100 years. Sekhemetmui, his son, a sickly child born to him in the ninety-first year of his rule, lived less than a year after his father's kingship ended.

I did not say "after his father died". No one knows what happened to Sekhemet. Herodotus, who was initiated by the priest into the Mysteries of Osiris, does not mention either father or son in his list, giving credence to some kind of sacerdotal conspiracy.

A stele, found in an old temple of Sekhmet, had the name of Sekhemet defaced in one of the periods of revision by later kings. The broken and incomplete stele tells of a great project undertaken in his 99th regal year: 10,000 men set out upriver in 600 boats built for the expedition. Then history is quiet.

That a century of human life in this time-and-death haunted land are represented only by carvings on a broken rock is a reminder of all that has been lost to us for want of a teller."

—Sir Joris Ivane
From the Raj to the Pyramids
Chatto and Pickering, 1888

Always, always were the voices and the cool valley wind.

Ninety-seven times he had made the journey down the River to pray to Hapi, his brother-god, for a good flood. Hapi had been kind eighty-six times and had not denied his prayers for the last nine years in a row, since the birth of his last, his crippled son.

Sekhemet, Beloved of Sekhmet, Mighty-Like-The-Sun and Smiter of the Vile and Wretched Foreigner, stood with his retinue on the broad road before his great white house.

Around him was the city he had caused to be built fifty years before, white and yellow in the morning sun. The shadows of the buildings stretched toward the River. Down at the wharf the royal barque was being outfitted for its trip southward up the waters.

Across the Nile were the mastabas of his fathers, and of those before them, cold and grey lumps in the Land of the

Dead on the western bank. Here his ancestors slept, their *kas* prayed for, sacrifices offered them, as just in their sleeps as in their lives.

Sekhemet looked back at the balcony of the great house, where his lastborn Sekhemetmui stood watching him. A strange boy, born so twisted and so late, sired in his hundredth year of life, his ninety-first of kingship. Sekhemet did not understand him or his ways.

"The work on the barque awaits your inspection," whispered his chief scribe to him.

Always, always were the voices, more and more voices the older he became, quieter but more insistent.

His ancestors, who had fought up and down the length of the River, had had an easier time of it: uniting the Bee Kingdom and the Reed Kingdom, bringing the Hawk Kingdom under their sway. They had been men and women of action—war pressed on every side, treachery behind every doorway, quick thinking was needed.

Sekhemet had reigned ninety-seven years. All his wars were won while he was still young. Anyone who could offer him treason had long ago been scattered on the desert winds.

The retinue—Sekhemet, his scribes, guards, bearers, and slaves—began its walk in the city he had built across from the tombs of his fathers. His own mastaba was being constructed in the shadow of his father's. The workmen ferried across the River each morning well after sunup and returned long before dark. No one wanted to be caught on the west bank after nightfall.

So it was that they walked in orderly progress, all eyes of persons they met downcast at sight of them, until they happened by the temple of the protecting god of the city, Sekhmet—she with the hippopotamus-head.

There was a commotion at the temple door—it flew open and the doorkeepers fell back. For, coming out of the courtyard, his garments torn, was the high priest, eyes wild and searching

He shambled toward them.

"Oh Great House!" he yelled. The guards turned toward him, spears at ready. The priest flung himself to the ground, tasting the dirt, his shaven head smeared with ash from the temple fire. "It is revealed to us—wonderful to relate!—a great thing. A few moments ago, a novice, an unlettered boy from the Tenth Nome—but, it is too marvelous!" The priest looked around him, blinking, seeming to regain his composure. He bowed down.

"Oh Great House! Oh Mighty-Like-The-Sun, forgive me! Sekhmet has given a revelation. We come to you this evening in full pomp. Forgive me!" He backed on his knees to the doorway of the temple, bowing and scraping.

Shaken, his heart pounding, like the feet of an army at full run, Sekhemet, Smiter of the Vile and Wretched Foreigner, continued on his way to the royal docks.

After the revelation given by the priests a great flotilla was built. Hundreds of ships were loaded with clothing and tools; provisions of garlic, bread, onions and radishes were laid in, jugs of lily-beer trundled aboard. Work on the mastaba across the water stopped.

The armada was filled with slaves and workmen, artisans, scribes, bureaucrats, and soldiers. The ships set out one gold morning following the royal barge up the River.

Somewhere on the long journey south the flotilla put in, for the royal barque carrying Sekhemet and his son Sekhemetmui came alone to Elephant Island where the Pharaoh made his prayers to Hapi and then returned northward.

Nothing was heard of the expedition for a year. The government was run by dispatches sent from somewhere southward of the city on the River.

At the end of the year the royal barge appeared once more at Elephant Island; again Sekhemet and his son supplicated to Hapi for a good flood with its life-giving *kemi*. Those of the island's temple who viewed Sekhemet said he looked younger and more fit than in years, transfigured, glowing with some secret knowledge.

Then the barque returned northward down the River. It was the last time the old Pharaoh was seen.

Nine months later a small raft came to the dock of the increasingly-troubled royal city. Foreigners impinged on the frontiers, there was rebellion in the Thirteenth Nome, the flood had not been as great as in earlier years and famine threatened the Canopic delta.

On the raft were one priest and the son of the old Pharaoh, Sekhemetmui. He was eleven years old and bore on his stunted breast the tablet of succession.

In a few days he was accoutered with the Double Crown of Red Egypt and White Egypt and became Sekhemetmui "The Glory of Sekhmet is Revealed" and Mighty-Like-The-Sun.

He had been a sickly child. Troubles came in waves, inside his body and out. There was fighting in the streets of the capital. He reigned for less than six months, dying one night of terrible sweats while a great battle raged to the east.

He was put into the hastily-finished mastaba across the River which had been started for his father.

Four hundred years after his death his city was a forgotten ruin and many miles down the River the first of the great pyramids rose up into the blue desert sky.

In the empty temple of Sekhmet there was a stele devoted to the old Pharaoh. On it were carved the signs: "I, Sekhemet, shall live to see the sun rise 5000 years from now; my line shall reign unto the last day of mankind."

**

How it was usually done:

The body of a dead person would be taken to the embalmer-priests by the grieving family, their heads plastered with mud, their bodies covered with dust.

The priest would demonstrate to them, using a small wooden doll, the three methods of embalming from the cheapest to the most expensive. In the case of a Pharaoh it would always be the latter.

Then the family would leave and go into seventy days of mourning.

One of the embalmer-priests would be chosen by lots. He would take a knife of Ethiopian flint and with it cut into the left side of the body just below the ribs. The other priests would scream and wail; the chosen priest would drop the knife and run for his life. The others pursued, throwing stones in an effort to kill him, such was their belief about the desecration of a body, and ran him from The

House of Death.

Then they would return and dig the brains out of the corpse through the nose with a curved iron hook, procuring most of it in this manner. Then they would pump in a solution of strong cedar oil into the brain cavity and plug the nose and throat.

Other priests reached in through the knife-wound and took out the internal organs, placing them in jars with distinctive tops. In the man-headed jar went the stomach and large intestines. Into the dog-headed they put the small intestines; the jackal-headed vessel got the lungs and heart, and into the hawk-headed went the liver and gall bladder. The jars were sealed with bitumen and capped with plaster.

Into the body cavity they stuffed aromatic spices, gums, oils, resins, and flowers, then they sewed the wound closed. They placed the body in a trough of natrum for sixty-nine days, taking it out only to unplug the nose and allow the rest of the brains to run out. They spent the night wrapping the body in linen strips soaked in gum, and placing it in its wooden coffin, which always had eyes painted on it so the soul, or *ka,* of the dead could see.

On the morning of the seventieth day the mummy and jars of organs were given back to the family for burial. For Pharaohs this usually meant a resting place in some tomb or mastaba on the Libyan bank of the Nile, the land of the setting sun and of the dead.

None of this happened to Sekhemet.

When a ruler of Egypt wanted sherbet with his meal next day, word went out to the royal works.

An hour before dawn next morning, several hundred slaves would enter a building divided into hundreds of high-walled roofless cubicles open to the desert air.

The slaves went to the center of the cubicles, from the floor of which rose a pillar six feet tall and a few inches in diameter. At its top was a shallow depression, the rim only a fraction of an inch above the bottom of the concavity. Into this tiny bowl the slave sprinkled a drop of water and smoothed it into a film.

Each slave did this in several rooms, and there were hundreds of them.

The temperature of the desert floor never dropped below 34°F. But a few feet off the ground the air, shielded from any wind by the high thick walls, was colder.

Royal attendants, with a thin spoon made of reed and bearing triple-walled bowls, waited outside the rooms a few moments. Entering them and working quickly, turning their heads to avoid breathing in the pillar's direction, they scraped a fingernail of frost from each pillar-top into the bowls.

Going from room to room, each gathered the ice. The many tiny scrapings were placed in one bowl, covered over, closed and packed in datewood sawdust and carried to Pharaoh's house.

A few moments before it was to be served it was flavored, one or two small portions to the ruler, his wife, his eldest child and one or two highly-favored guests.

These iceworks, three or four acres in extent, were usually found near the palaces.

Early in the twentieth century A.D., an iceworks was discovered far to the south, where no large cities had ever stood. It covered seventy-two acres and contained eleven thousand cubicles, each with the wonder-working silent pillars.

THE HOUSE OF THE *KA*: I

... further into the valley. Perhaps my house will not prove to be safe, will be found out, my resting place defiled, my temple defaced. Surely, though, the priests will not let this happen.

Their hands on me like so many clubs. No pain, just sensation, pressure, as if it were happening to someone else. Things I cannot see.

What if the priests are wrong? Is it possible they tell me these things to put me out of the way? They know my son to be weak: if trouble comes he will not be able to hold the Bee Kingdom and the Reed Kingdom together—the nomarchs of the Delta are too shrewd, as they have always been.

What if they have done these things to be rid of my strength? The thought comes to me now—all their talk, the revelation that I go away from the light to wake to a kingdom my line will rule forever . . .

What madness is this I have done? Guards, to me! Let me up, I say! Take your hands from my divinity!

I cannot move. The cold has seeped through me.

What if the priests do not keep their word? I am lost. My *ka* will be dispersed: I am not dead. They have seduced me, deposed me with only words, words of power and glory I could not resist.

Was ever such a fool on the River Nile?

Now there is no more light, no more feeling. All ebbs, all flows away.

Gods. Sekhmet. Protect me. Thoth, find me not wanting on the scales. Let your baboons weigh me true.

The madness of priests . . .

Outside they came and went, some by design, some because they were lost.

At first they spoke the Old Language, or the black tongue of the south, and the barbaric speech from the northeast. Then they used the long foreign sounds unknown in his time, from far across the salt water, Greek, then the rolling Latin.

Then there were desert languages, and those twisted Latin speech patterns of French and Anglo-Norman, the gutturals of German; Italian and Turkish, then French, English, German again, English, all against the old desert speech.

They brought their gods with them in waves; Shango, Baal, Yahweh, Zeus, Jupiter, Allah and Mohammed, Dieu, God and Jesus, Jesu, Gott again, Allah, Allah, Money.

Twice people tried to get in—once by accident. They were crushed by a four-ton block balanced by pebbles, one of six. The second intrusion was by design, but when they saw the powdered skeletons of the first they turned away, fearing one, two, ten more deadfalls ahead.

Once there was a tremor in the earth and the remaining blocks fell, leaving a clear passage. Once, water fell from a cloud in the sky.

From inside the sounds—voices, earthquakes, rain, deadfall, praises to gods, the sighing of the gentle dusty wind, the slosh and swing of the Nile itself, the groaning of the earth on its axle-tree—were as the long quiet ticks of a slow, sure, well-oiled metronome.

The man ran through the gates of the small town clutching parchment scrolls to him as he stumbled.

Behind him came the drumming of camels' hooves, the clang of their harness bells. The cries of the desert people leaped up behind him.

The running man was old; his head was shaven and his face hairless. He ran by the broken and tumbled buildings that had once housed the Christian desert fathers, deserted for more than two centuries.

He fell. One of the scrolls broke into powdery slivers under his hand. He cried out and pulled the others to him.

He looked over his shoulder. The camels were closer. Black-garbed riders, swords out, bore down on him. Eyes wild, he ran behind the broken legs of a statue of Dionysus, trying to climb the jumbled stones of a small amphitheater. He saw far out to his left the ribbon of the Nile, beyond the date-palm orchards. He yelled in his anguish.

The riders surrounded him, their camels spitting and stamping. One of them dismounted from his knee-walking animal, swinging up his sword. He held out his hand.

Weeping, the old man turned the scrolls over to him.

He had been at Alexandria when they came out of the Northeast in black flowing waves, putting all who resisted their holy war to sword and fire. He saw them capture the city and tear down the idols. He followed them to the Great Library. He had wept when they began carrying out hundreds and thousands of books and scrolls and took them to burn to heat the public baths—enough parchment and papyrus and leather to keep them steaming for six weeks.

He had come as quickly as he could to this town, the site of the old temple, for these scrolls. He was the only one of the Society of He-We-Await who had made it this far. No one had disturbed their resting place. But he had been seen as he left the ruins and the cry had gone up.

"These scrolls," one of the mounted men leaned forward and spoke in a thick language the old man hardly understood. "If they contradict the *Koran,* they are heathen. If they support it, they are superfluous."

The man on the ground opened one, then another, looked at them, puzzled. He handed them up to the one who had spoken.

"They are in the old, old writing," he said. "They are infidel." He handed them back to the swordsman on the ground.

With no trace of emotion, and some effort, the man jumped up and down on them, grinding them to fine shards which sifted away on the breeze.

"We have no time to light a fire," said the mounted leader, "But that will do. Your conversion will come later. First, the books, then the hearts of men."

They turned their camels and sped back toward the wattle-walled village.

Crying, the old man sank down in the mingled dust of writings and bricks, wailing, gnashing his teeth, rubbing his bald head with handfuls of sand.

In the late nineteenth century A.D. artifacts of an especially good quality surfaced on the antiquities market.

The Cairo Museum, responsible for all Egyptian archaeological work, investigated.

They found that a graverobbing family from Deir el Bahrani, near the Valley of the Kings, had made a discovery in the cliffs behind Queen Hatsepshut's tomb about a decade before.

The majority of the tombs which had been uncovered in the Valley had proved empty of goods, the coffins missing their contents.

The graverobbers had found, in a shaft dug into the cliff wall above Deir el Bahrani, a forgotten chapter of history.

There was a marker there, hastily carved, a great quantity of goods from many dynasties, and thirty-six mummies.

The marker told the story—in one of the lawless periods before the XXIst Dynasty, the government fell apart, bandits roamed the towns, foreigners attacked from all sides. The priests could no longer guard the tombs in the Valley of the Kings.

Secretly they entered the mausoleums, took out the royal mummies and brought them to the hidden tunnel, with such of the grave goods as they could carry, and secreted them away, hoping their bodies, and the *kas* of the royal lines, would be safe from marauders.

Of the thirty-six mummies, one—Thutmose the IIIrd—had been broken into three pieces. The others were intact, including those of Ramses the Great; Ahmose; Queen Ahmes, the mother of Hatsepshut; and Thutmose the Ist and IInd. The rest were eventually identified, except one. That of a very young boy about twelve years of age, in wrappings of a much earlier period than the others. He was entered in the catalogue of the Museum, where the mummies were all taken, as "Unknown Boy (I-IIIrd Dynasty?)."

Doctor Tuthmoses looked at the final reports. They were magnetometer scans of the west bank of the Nile, from the Delta, past Aswan to the influx of the Atbara River above the Fifth Cataract, far longer than the extent of the kingdoms of the early dynasties.

All the known tombs were marked; all the new ones found had been checked and proved to be those of later dynasties, of minor officials. The search had gone much further out of the Valley than any burials ever found. Still nothing.

He looked around him at the roomful of books. He was now an old man. There were others devoted to the cause, younger men, but none like him. They were content to sift over the old data again and again, the way it had always been done since the knowledge of the resting place was lost twelve centuries before.

He had devoted fifty years of his life to the quest, through wars, panics, social upheaval, and unrest. He had seen his mentor, Professor Ramra, grown old and weak, and embittered, die, with nothing to show for *his* sixty years of diligent search but more paper, more books, more clutter.

Tuthmoses rang the bell for his secretary, young Mr. Faidul. He came in, thin and dapper in a three-piece suit.

"Faidul," he said. "The time has come to change our methods. Take this down as a record for the Society.

"One: Obtain the best gene splicer possible for a two-day clandestine assignment to be completed on short notice in the near future.

"Two: Send Raimenu and a workaday specialist to Egypt. I want Raimenu to find a woman who wishes to bear a child for a fee of $100,000. Not just any woman. A woman of a family that still worships The Old Way. The specialist is for a mitochondrial check—make sure she's from an African First Mother.

"Three: The first two conditions being met, arrange for a scientific examination of the Deir el Bahrani remains at the Cairo Museum. During this, one of the party is to obtain genetic material from the remains of the "unknown boy," who we know to be the Son of He-We-Await" (Tuthmoses and Faidul bowed their heads).

"Four: The genetic material from Sekhemetmui is to be implanted by the splicer into the egg of the mitochondrial First Mother.

"Five: The child of this operation is to be handed over to the Society and placed in my care to be raised as I see fit.

"End of note."

"So it is written," said Faidul.

"So it shall be done," said Doctor Thuthmoses.

They called him Bobby. He was raised at first by a succession of nurses in an upstairs room which became his world. He was eventually given everything he wanted—toys, games, insects, fish, mammals.

He had large dark eyes, a small head with a high hairline, a short face, an aquiline nose. One of his arms was bent from birth.

What he read and what he saw were censored by Tuthmoses and his staff—everything was tape-delayed and edited. Other children were brought in for him to play with. He was given tutors and teachers.

He grew up self-centered, untroubled, fairly well-adjusted, with a coolness toward the doctor that seemed to be reciprocated.

They were playing one day; Bobby, the teacher-lady and the kids who were brought in after their school let out.

They had been doing some kind of word games, and Deborah the dark-haired girl got up to get something, then had gone over and started talking to Sally Conroe about something. There had been some quiet talk, and then

Deborah did a little dance, humming in a whiny voice:
"Yah-ya-ya-ya-yah yoo yah yoo-yah" and then had sung:
"All the girls in France
Do the hoochie-hoochie dance
And the dance —"
The teacher-lady, at that time a Ms. Allen, stopped her with a sharp command.
Bobby found himself staring at Deborah, whom he did not particularly like.
Then Ms. Allen got them all doing something else, and soon Bobby forgot about it.
Deborah never came back to the after-school group after that day. Bobby didn't particularly care.

One evening he was going through some books—the ones he had with the big black places on some of the pages—and he was looking in the one on music, way over toward the back.
He turned the page. There was a bright gaudy photograph of a music machine.
He read the caption: In the 1940s and 1950s, "jukeboxes" (like the 1953 Wurlitzer 150 pictured here) brought music to the customers of malt shops, cafes and taverns.
The machine had disc recordings inside and a turntable he could see. But it was wide and curved, like a box that ended in a smooth round top. It was bright with neon lights, and the sides had what looked like bubbles of colored water inside.
Bobby stared at the picture and stared at it, as if there were something else there.
He held up his hand slowly toward the photo, moving his fingers closer, staring at the page: His hand curved to grip the picture.
"What do you have there?" asked Dr. Tuthmoses, who had come in to check on him.
"A jukebox," he said, still looking.
Tuthmoses peered over his shoulder a moment.
"Yes. They used to be very popular."
Bobby's hand was still held over the page.
"What's wrong?" asked the doctor.
"It's—like—"

"Well, now everybody has music at home. They don't have to go where jukeboxes used to be. They're anachronisms."

"What are anar- ancho—?"

"Anachronisms. Something that doesn't belong to its time. Something that has outlived its usefulness. One or the other."

"Oh," said Bobby. He put down the book.

Sometimes, late at night, Bobby thought of the word "anachronism." It conjured up for him a vision of a bright orange, yellow, and green jukebox.

The doctor came to Bobby's room one day when he was eleven.

"I've got some tapes we should watch together, Bobby," he said. "You've never seen anything like them. They're about a faraway country, one you've never seen or heard of."

"I don't want to watch the tube," said Bobby. "I'm reading a neat book about American Indians."

"That will have to wait. You should see these."

"I don't want to," said Bobby.

"This is one of the few times you're not going to get your way," said the doctor. He was old and growing irritable. "It's time you saw these."

Then he gave Bobby a mug of hot chocolate.

"I don't want this, either."

"Drink it. I've got mine here. Watch." The old man gulped the thick hot liquid, leaving himself a dark brown mustache.

"Oh, all right," said Bobby, and did likewise.

Then they sat down in front of the television and the doctor put the tape on. It started with flute music. Then there was a cartoon, a black and white Walt Disney, with sounds and a spider inside a bunch of pointed buildings with carvings on the walls.

Bobby watched, not understanding. He found himself yawning. The carvings on the walls, angular people, came alive; strange things were happening on the screen.

Strange things happened inside him, too. He felt lightheaded, like when he had a fever. His stomach was very numb, like the place had been when Dr. Khaffiri the dentist

217

had fixed his tooth last year. He felt listless, like when he was tired and sleepy, only he wasn't. He was wide awake and thinking about all kinds of things.

The black and white cartoon ended and another started —a Gandy Goose and Sourpuss one. They were in army uniforms, in the same place with the skinny curved trees and the pointed big buildings, and Gandy went to sleep and was inside one of them, and stranger things began to happen than even in the first cartoon. Walls moved, boxes opened and things came out, all wrapped—

Things *came out all wrapped.*

There had been a movie after the cartoon and it was ending.

Things came out all *wrapped.*

It had been about the same things, he thought, but it had been like in a dream, like Gandy had, because Bobby wasn't paying attention—he was watching another movie on his half-closed eyelids.

It was like at the hospital only—

Things came out all wrapped.

Only—

Bobby turned toward the Doctor who sat very still, watching him, waiting for something.

Bobby's head was tired but he could not stop, not now.

"I ... I ..."

"Yes?"

"I want to go there."

"I know. We're ready to leave."

"I really want to go there."

"We'll be on the way before you know it."

"I ..."

"Rest now. Sleep"

He did. When he woke up he was in an airplane, miles and miles up, and the air above them and the water below was blue and deep as a Vick's Salve jar, or so it seemed, and he went back to sleep, his head resting on Dr. Tuthmoses' shoulder.

The launch made its way down the brown flood of the Nile. The sun was bright but the air was moderate above the river. There was no feeling of wind, only coolness.

Bobby sat in a chair, watching the river, taking no notice of the other boats they passed, the fellucahs they met. His hands fidgeted on the arms of the deck chair. He would turn from time to time to watch Dr. Tuthmoses. The doctor said nothing; he saw that the wild faraway shine was still in the boy's eyes.

Bobby sat forward. Then he stood. Then he slowly sat back down and slumped in the chair. Tuthmoses, who had his hand up, let it fall again. The launch pilot went back to his fixed stare, whistling a tune to himself.

Another half hour passed in the muddy cool silence.

Bobby shot up so fast Tuthmoses was taken aback.

"Here!" Bobby said, "Put in here!"

Tuthmoses held his hand up, pointed. The pilot turned the wheel and the nose of the craft aimed itself at a large rock outcropping. The old doctor sighed; he had been on an expedition thirty years before which covered this very part of the River and had found nothing. The boat aimed at the western bank, the land of the setting sun and of the dead.

"No, no," said Bobby, jumping up and down, "Not that way. Over there! That way!"

He was pointing toward the eastern bank, the land of day. And of the living.

***

THE HOUSE OF THE *KA:* II

The Light! The light! What place is this?

— is this the room where my soul is weighed? Thoth? My brother-gods?

Heavy. My limbs are heavy. My brain is a lump. Why cannot I think? My dreams are troubled. They are swirling colors.

My son. How he hates the traditions. The things that are done in the name of being god. He shall have to marry his half-niece, many years older than he. I should have had a daughter for him to marry, by his mother also. All his older half-brothers died before him. But his birth killed her.

It is too late to sire a queen. I am old. He was so twisted in his limbs. What pain is that in my knee?

I know you trick me! All of you! These are my last thoughts. You have left me to die; my *ka* to wither away. How did I listen to priests?

What great plan, Sekhmet? To put an old man out of the way?

Where are my eyes? Have they put me in the jars? How do I think? I am going mad mad mad mad mad

My foot itches.

It took two years and the best people and equipment money could buy and a few times they almost weren't enough.

Bobby was still cared for, but left on his own more and more. He found himself sitting for days, wondering what was happening, what had happened, where he had come in, what his purpose was. He knew he was part of some plan, something to do with the trip he barely remembered.

Dark places in the books disappeared, he could have anything he wanted. Books on Egypt were brought to him when he asked. The television now jibed with the *TV Guide.* He watched the news—depressing stuff on wars, plagues, fires, human misery, suffering, death, live and in color.

Sometimes he thought the old way, the days before the trip were better.

Nothing told him *anything* he really wanted to know.

Dr. Tuthmoses, old and subject to palsy, came to him for the first time in months.

"Tomorrow, Bobby," he said. "Tomorrow we will take you up there with us. There will be a ritual. You will need to be there. We will bring you clothes for it. You get to carry things needed in the ceremony. You're an important part of it. I hope you'll like that."

I'm going to get to see him?"

Tuthmoses' eyes widened.

"Yes."

"Doctor?"

"Yes?"

"That time, before we went on the trip. When you showed

me the cartoons and the movie. You also put something in my chocolate, didn't you?"

"Yes, I did, Bobby. It was to help you remember."

"Would you give it to me again?"

"Why?"

"If I'm going to be part of this, I want it to *mean* something. I want to understand."

"Don't you have everything you want?"

"I don't have a place," said Bobby. "I don't understand any of this. I've read the books. They're just words, words about people a long time ago. They were interesting, but they've been gone a long time. What do they have to do with *me*?"

Tuthmoses studied him for a few seconds. "Perhaps it's for the best." He got up shakily and walked to the bookcase jammed with titles by Wallis Budge, Rawlinson, Atkinson, Carter. He picked one up, turned pages. "I'll have the drink brought to you tonight. After you finish it, read this chapter." He held the book out to Bobby, held open with his long thumb to a chapter on ritual. "Then you'll understand."

"I want to," said Bobby.

Tuthmoses opened the door. He turned back. "In a year or so you might be able to leave here, go anywhere, do anything you wish. By then it won't matter what you know or whom you tell. But until then, you have to stay."

"I guess I don't understand."

Tuthmoses' shoulders dropped. "I wish I had been a better guardian, a father to you," said the doctor. "It was not to be. Perhaps, later on if I live, and events do not deter, He-willing, we can learn to be friends. I would like to try."

Bobby stared at him.

"Well, that's the way I feel," said the doctor. "Rest now. Tomorrow is the greatest day."

"Of *my* life?"

"Of all lives," said Tuthmoses. He left.

He was brought into the great long room with the large curtain at the end.

Doctor Tuthmoses, Faidul, and the others were dressed in loose grey robes. Their heads and beards were fresh-shaved.

On the walls were murals, hieroglyphs, evocations to the gods. At one end of the room stood the hippo-headed statue of the god Sekhmet, its thick arms raised in benediction. In front of it was a throne of ivory, facing the curtain.

The room was brightly lit though it was early in the morning. When the door opened and Bobby was ushered in, his dark eyes were blinking. He was dressed in a short kilt, he had bare arms, chest and legs. A white headdress spilled down onto his shoulders.

In his crossed arms were a hook and a flail.

Tuthmoses had told him what the ceremony was; the book and drink the night before told him what it meant.

In the early days, once a year, the chief priest would chase the Pharaoh with a flail around a courseway. As long as the Pharaoh could run, his youth and vigor were renewed by the ceremony.

In later years when the kingdoms were united this was changed. A young man was chosen to run the course before the priest, and his vigor would transfer by magic to the ruler. This was the ceremony of *heb-sed.*

Bobby was the chosen runner.

The course was outlined by bare-chested men, standing four feet in from the walls of the room, holding in their hands bundles of wheat.

Before the throne on a low table were symbols of life and death—four empty canopic jars, their effigy-tops unstoppered, an empty set of scales, an obsidian embalmer's knife, the figure of a baboon.

Another door opened and all in the room, except Bobby and the men holding the wheat along the course, dropped to the ground.

There was the sound of small steps, shuffling feet. Bobby watched the four men bring the shrunken figure in between them.

He was old, old and bent. They had dressed him in another simple kilt. His skin was pitted and wrinkled, stained in patches of light and dark from chemicals.

He doddered forward, eyes looking neither right nor left. His head had been shaven; there were corrugations in his skull like a greenhouse roof. His legs were twisted. One arm was immobile.

They placed him on the throne, then the attendants fell to their faces.

Dr. Tuthmoses stepped forward, bowed.

On the old man's head he placed first the red crown of the Bee Kingdom, then the white crown of the Reed Kingdom. The old man's eyes focused for the first time at the touch of the crown's cloth.

He looked slowly around him.

"*Heb-sed*?" he croaked.

"Yes, *heb-sed*," answered Tuthmoses.

The ancient man leaned back in the throne a little; the edge of his mouth fluttered as if he were trying to smile.

Tuthmoses waved—a priest stepped forward, came to Bobby, took the flail from the hand of his bad arm. Music began to play through hidden speakers, music like in the first of Bobby's dreams while watching the cartoons two years before.

Bobby stepped past the men with the wheat and began to run. The priest's naked feet slapped on the Armstrong tile floor behind him, and the first of the knots on the flail hit him, drawing blood from his shoulder.

He jerked. Faster and faster he ran, brushing by the standing men, and at every third step the flail kissed him with its hot tongue and he yelled.

Some of the wheat covered the floor by the second circuit. On the third Bobby saw spots of blood on the tiles ahead.

They passed the starting point—Bobby kept running. The expected stroke did not come. He looked back over his shoulder. The priest had stopped at the marker, arm still raised. He motioned the boy back and handed him the flail.

Bobby's shoulders twitched as the priest guided him next to Tuthmoses. He was sweating and his chest heaved.

Bobby looked at the old man on the throne—was it only the nearness or did he look less ancient, more human? The music rose in volume, drums, flutes, strings. The old man's eyes grew bright.

"Oh Great House!" said Tuthmoses in the Old Languages, "We wait to do your bidding. Behold," he said, waving his arm, "the sunrise 5000 years later!"

The room lights went out.

The curtain pulled back. Dawn flooded the room twenty-two stories up over Central Park. Great towers rose up on all sides, their windows filled with lights. The ocean was a flat smoky line beyond, and the slim cuticle of the sun's red edge stood up.

The old man stared in wonder.

"I have lived to see it," he said. Then he looked at Bobby. His lip trembled.

"Boy," he said. "Here," he lifted his twisted blotched arms toward him. "My flail, my scepter."

Tuthmoses motioned him forward, indicating that Bobby hand them over.

Bobby stepped up on the dais, watching the shaking in the old man's hands as they closed on the sacred objects, pulling them to his breast.

Bobby stepped backwards, picked up the obsidian knife from the table and jammed it under the ribs of the old man and twisted it.

He made no sound but slid up and over his own knees and spilled forward off the throne onto the floor, the scepter breaking on the chair's arm.

"You were the worst father anyone *ever* had!" yelled Bobby.

There was a gasp of breath all around the room, then the sound of someone working the slide on an automatic pistol. The doctors made a rush toward the bloody old man.

"Stop!" said Bobby, turning toward them, knife in his hand.

They froze. Faidul was aiming a pistol at Bobby's head. Tuthmoses stared at him, eyes wide, breath coming shallowly.

"He has seen the sun rise 5000 years from his time," said Bobby. He dropped the Ethiopian knife back onto the table, knocking over the baboon figurine. "*Now,* his line is ready to reign until the last day of mankind."

He walked to the throne, the barrel of Faidul's pistol following him.

"Only this time," said Bobby, "I'll do it *right.*"

He sat down.

Beginning with Tuthmoses, and one by one, they bowed down before him, prostrating themselves to the floor tiles. Last to go was Faidul, whose hand began to tremble when

Bobby gave him a withering stare.

"What is your first wish, Oh Great House?" asked Tuthmoses from the floor.

"See that my late father is given seventy days' mourning, that his tomb is made ready, that his *ka* be provided for through all eternity."

"Yes, He-We-Await," said Tuthmoses, beginning to tear at his robe and gnash his teeth.

Bobby watched the orb of the sun widen and stand up from the horizon, grow brighter, to bright to stare at.

"Get busy!" he said turning his head away.

So began the last days of mankind. ●

DEATH IS DIFFERENT

by Lisa Goldstein

"Death Is Different" was purchased by Gardner Dozois, and appeared in the September 1988 issue of IAsfm, *with an illustration by George Thompson. Sleek and darkly elegant, as is most of Goldstein's work, it offers us an unsettling look into a very odd sort of afterlife . . .*

A young writer based in Oakland, California, Goldstein is one of the most highly-regarded of that generation of SF writers who began to come to prominence in the late 70s and early 80s. Her first novel, the dark fantasy The Red Magician, *won the National Book Award, and she has subsequently become one of the most critically acclaimed novelists of her day. Her most recent books include* The Dream Years, *and, just released,* A Mask For The General.

She had her passport stamped and went down the narrow corridor to collect her suitcase. It was almost as if they'd been waiting for her, dozens of them, the women dressed in embroidered shawls and long skirts in primary colors, the men in clothes that had been popular in the United States fifty or sixty years ago.

"Taxi? Taxi to hotel?"

"Change money? Yes? Change money?"

"Jewels, silver, jewels—"

"Special for you—"

"Cards, very holy—"

Monica brushed past them. One very young man, shorter even than she was, grabbed hold of the jacket she had folded over her arm. "Anything, *mem*," he said. She turned to look at him. His eyes were wide and earnest. "Anything, I will do anything for you. You do not even have to pay me."

She laughed. He drew back, looking hurt, but his hand still held her jacket. "All right," she said. They were nearly to the wide glass doors leading out into the street. The airport was hot and dry, but the heat coming from the open glass doors was worse. It was almost evening. "Find me a newspaper," she said.

He stood a moment. The others had dropped back, as if the young man had staked a claim on her. "A—a newspaper?" he said. He was wearing a gold earring, a five-pointed star, in one ear.

"Yeah," she said. Had she ever known the Lurqazi word for newspaper? She looked in her purse for her dictionary and realized she must have packed it in her luggage. She could only stand there and repeat helplessly, "A newspaper. You know."

"Yes. A newspaper." His eyes lit up, and he pulled her by her jacket outside into the street.

"Wait—" she said. "My luggage—"

"A newspaper," the young man said. "Yes," He led her to an old man squatting by the road, a pile of newspapers in front of him. At least she supposed they were newspapers. They were written in Lurqazi, a language which used the Roman alphabet but which, she had been told, had no connection with any Indo-European tongue.

"I meant—is there an English newspaper?" she asked.

"English," he said. He looked defeated.

"All right," she said. "How much?" she asked the man.

The old man seemed to come alive. "Just one, *mem*," he said. "Just one," His teeth were stained red.

She gave him a one (she had changed some money at the San Francisco airport), and, as an afterthought, gave the young man a one too. She picked up a paper and turned to the young man. "Could you come back in there with me while I pick up my suitcase?" she said. "I think the horde will descend if you don't."

He looked at her as if he didn't understand what she'd said, but he followed her inside anyway and waited until she got her suitcase. Then he went back outside with her.

227

She stood a long time watching the cabs—every make and year of car was standing out at the curb, it seemed, including a car she recognized from Czechoslovakia and a horse-drawn carriage—until he guided her toward a late model Volkswagen Rabbit. She had a moment of panic when she thought he was going to get in the car with her, but he just said something to the driver and waved goodbye. The driver, she noticed, was wearing the same five-pointed star earring.

As they drove to the hotel she felt the familiar travel euphoria, a loosening of the fear of new places she had felt on the plane. She had done it. She was in another place, a place she had never been, ready for new sights and adventures. Nothing untoward had happened to her yet. She was a seasoned traveler.

She looked out of the car and was startled for a moment to see auto lights flying halfway into the air, buildings standing on nothing. Then she realized she was looking at a reflection in the car's window. She bent closer to the window, put her hands around her eyes, but she could see nothing real outside, only the flying lights, the phantom buildings.

At the air-conditioned hotel she kicked off her shoes, took out her dictionary and opened the newspaper. She had studied a little Lurqazi before she'd left the States, but most of the words in the paper were unfamiliar, literary words like "burnished" and "celestial." She took out a pen and started writing above the lines. After a long time she was pretty sure that the right margins of the columns in the paper were ragged not because of some flaw in the printing process but because she was reading poetry. The old man had sold her poetry.

She laughed and began to unpack, turning on the radio. For a wonder someone was speaking English. She stopped and listened as the announcer said, " . . . fighting continues in the hills with victory claimed by both sides. In the United States the president pledged support today against what he called Russian-backed guerrillas. The Soviet Union had no comment.

"The weather continues hot—"

Something flat and white stuck out from under the shoes

in her suitcase, a piece of paper. She pulled it out. "Dear Monica," she read, "I know this is part of your job but don't forget your husband who's waiting for you at home. I know you want to have adventures, but please *be careful.* See you in two weeks. I love you. I miss you already, and you haven't even gone yet. Love, Jeremy."

***

The dinner where she'd met Jeremy had been for six couples. On Jeremy's other side was a small blond woman. On her other side was a conspicuously empty chair. She must have looked unhappy, because Jeremy introduced himself and asked, in a voice that sounded genuinely worried, if she was all right.

"I'm fine," she said brightly. She looked at the empty chair on the other side of her as if it were a person and then turned back to Jeremy. "He said he might be a little late. He does deep sea salvaging." And then she burst into tears.

That had been embarrassing enough, but somehow, after he had offered her his napkin and she'd refused it and used hers instead, she found herself telling him the long sad chronology of her love life. The man she was dating had promised to come, she said, but you could never count on him to be anywhere. And the one before that had smuggled drugs, and the one before that had taken her to some kind of religious commune where you weren't allowed to use electricity and could only bathe once a week, and the one before that had said he was a revolutionary . . . . His open face was friendly, his green eyes looked concerned. She thought the blond woman on his other side was very lucky. But she could never go out with him, even if the blond woman wasn't there. He was too . . . safe.

"It sounds to me," he said when she was done (and she realized guiltily that she had talked for nearly half an hour; he must have been bored out of his mind), "that you like going out with men who have adventures."

"You mean," she said slowly, watching the thought surface as she said it, "that I don't think women can have adventures too?"

The next day she applied to journalism school.

She didn't see him until nearly a year later, at the house of the couple who had invited them both to dinner. This time only the two of them were invited. The set-up was a little too obvious to ignore, but she decided she didn't mind. "What have you been doing?" he asked between courses.

"Going to journalism school," she said.

He seemed delighted. "Have you been thinking of the conversation we had last year?" he asked. "I've thought about it a lot."

"What conversation?"

"Don't you remember?" he asked. "At the dinner last year. About women having adventures. You didn't seem to think they could."

"No," she said. "I'm sorry. I don't remember."

He didn't press it, but she became annoyed with him anyway. Imagine him thinking that a conversation with him was responsible for her going to journalism school. And now that she was looking at him she realized that he was going bald, that his bald spot had widened quite a bit since she'd seen him last. Still, when he asked for her phone number at the end of the evening she gave it to him. What the hell.

It was months later that he confessed he had asked their mutual friends to invite them both to dinner. But it was only after they were married she admitted that he might have been right, that she might have enrolled in school because of him.

For a while, since he didn't seem to mind, since he neither praised nor blamed, she told him about her old lovers. The stories became a kind of exorcism for her. The men had all been poor (except, for a brief time, the drug smuggler, until his habit exceeded his supply), they had all been interesting, they had all been crazy or nearly so. Once he mixed up the revolutionary who had stolen her stereo with the would-be writer who had also stolen her stereo, and they'd laughed about it for days. After that the chorus line of old lovers had faded, grown less insistent, and had finally disappeared altogether. And that was when she knew something she had not been certain of before. She had been right to marry Jeremy.

The radio was playing what sounded like an old English folk song. She turned it off, read and reread the short letter until she memorized it, and went to sleep.

LISA GOLDSTEIN

The young man was on the sidewalk when she stepped out of the hotel the next morning. "What can I do for you today, *mem?*" he asked. "Anything."

She laughed, but she wondered what he wanted, why he had followed her. She felt uneasy. "I don't—I don't really need anything right now," she said. "Thanks."

"Anything," he said. He was earnest but not pleading. "What would you desire most if you could have anything at all? Sincerely."

"Anything," she said. You mean, besides wanting Jeremy here with me right now, she thought. Should she confide in him? It would get rid of him, anyway. "I want," she said slowly, "to talk to the head of the Communist party."

"It will be done," he said. She almost laughed, but could not bear to damage his fragile dignity. "I will see you tomorrow with your appointment," he said, and walked away.

She watched him go, then opened her guidebook and began to look through it. A travel magazine had commissioned her to do a piece on the largest city in Amaz, the ruins, the beaches, the marketplace, the famous park designed by Antonio Gaudí. How was the country holding up under the attack by the guerrillas, under the loss of the income from tourists which was its major source of revenue? "Don't go out of the city," the magazine editor had said. "Be careful. I don't want you to get killed doing this." Five hours later, when she'd told him about the assignment, Jeremy had repeated the editor's warning almost word for word.

But she had other ideas. As long as the magazine was paying her travel expenses she might as well look around a bit. And if she could find out if the Russians were arming the guerrillas or not, well, that would be a major scoop, wouldn't it? No one had seen the head of the Communist party for months. There were rumors that he was dead, that he was with the guerrillas in the hills, that the party itself was about to be outlawed and that he had fled to Moscow. She laughed. Wouldn't it be funny if the young man could get her an interview?

She began to walk, stopping every so often to take notes or snap a picture. The morning was humid, a portent of the heat to come. Her blouse clung to her back. She passed fish stalls, beggars, a building of white marble big as a city block

231

she supposed was a church, a used car lot, a section of the city gutted by fire. On the street, traffic had come to a standstill, and the smells of exhaust and asphalt mingled with that of fish and cinnamon. Cars honked furiously, as though that would get them moving again. The sidewalk had filled with people moving with a leisured grace. Silver bracelets and rings flashed in the sunlight. Once she came face to face with a man carrying a monkey on his shoulder, but he was gone before she could take his picture.

She took a wrong turn somewhere and asked a few people in Lurqazi where the Gaudí Park was. No one, it seemed, had ever heard of it, but everyone wanted to talk to her, a long stream of Lurqazi she could not understand. She smiled and moved on, and looked at the map in the guidebook. Most of the streets, she read, were renamed, so the guidebook had rather unimaginatively called them Street 1, Street 2, and so on. After a long time of walking she found the park and sat gratefully on a bench.

The benches were wavy instead of straight, made of a mosaic of broken tile and topped with grotesque and fanciful figures. The park looked a little like Gaudí's Guell Park in Barcelona, but with harsher colors, more adapted, she thought, to this country. She was trying to turn the thought into a caption for a photograph, and at the same time wondering about the structure on the other side of the park—was it a house? a sculpture of flame made of orange tile and brass?—when a small dirty boy sat on the bench next to her.

"Cards?" he asked. "Buy a pack of cards?" He took a few torn and bent cards from his pocket and spread them out in the space between the two of them.

"No thanks," she said absently.

"Very good buy," he said, tapping one of the cards. It showed a man with a square, neatly trimmed beard framing a dark face. His eyes, large with beautiful lashes, seemed to stare at her from the card. He looked a little like Cumaq, the head of the Communist party. No, she thought. You have Cumaq on the brain. "Very good," the boy said insistently.

"No," she said. "Thanks."

"I can tell time by the sun," the boy said suddenly. He

bent his head way back, further than necessary, she thought, to see the sun, and said gravely, "It is one o'clock."

She laughed and look at her watch. It was 11:30. "Well, if it's that late," she said, "I have to go." She got up and started over to the other side of the park.

"I can get more cards!" the boy said, calling after her. "Newer. Better!"

She got back to the hotel late in the evening. The overseas operator was busy and she went down to the hotel restaurant for dinner. Back in her room she began to write. "Why Antonio Gaudí accepted the old silver baron's commission in 1910 no one really knows, but the result—"

The phone rang. It was Jeremy. "I love you," they told each other, raising their voices above the wailing of a bad connection. "I miss you."

"Be careful," Jeremy said. The phone howled.

"I am," she said.

The young man was waiting for her outside the hotel the next morning. "I did it," he said. "All arranged." He pronounced "arranged" with three syllables.

"You did what?" she asked.

"The interview," he said. "It is all arranged. For tomorrow."

"Interview?"

"The one you asked for," he said gravely. "With Cumaq. The head of the Communist party."

"You arranged it?" she said. "An interview?"

"Yes," he said. Was he starting to sound impatient? "You asked me to and I did it. Here." He held out a piece of paper with something written on it. "For tomorrow. Ten o'clock."

She took the paper and read the ten or twelve lines of directions on it, what they had in this crazy place instead of addresses, she supposed. She didn't know whether to laugh or to throw her arms around him and hug him. Could this slight young man really have gotten her an interview with the man everyone had been trying to find for the past six months? Or was it a hoax? Some kind of trap? She knew one thing: nothing was going to keep her from following the directions the next morning. "Thank you," she said finally.

He stood as if waiting for more. She opened her purse and

gave him a five. He nodded and walked away.

But that night, listening to the English news in her hotel room, she realized that there would be no interview, the next day or ever. "Government troops killed Communist party head Cumaq and fifteen other people, alleged to be Communist party members, in fighting in the Old Quarter yesterday," the announcer said. "Acting on an anonymous tip the troops surrounded a building in the Old Quarter late last night. Everyone inside the building was killed, according to a government spokesman."

She threw her pen across the room in frustration. So that was it. No doubt the young man had heard about Cumaq's death this morning on the Lurqazi broadcasts (But were there Lurqazi broadcasts? She had never heard one.) and had seen the opportunity to make some money off her. She thought of his earnest young face and began to get angry. So far he had sold her a sheet of poetry she couldn't read and some completely useless information. If she saw him again tomorrow she would tell him to get lost.

But he wasn't in front of the hotel the next day. She went off to the Colonial House, built in layers of Spanish, English, and Dutch architecture, one layer for each foreign occupation. The place had been given four stars by the guidebook, but now it was nearly empty. As she walked through the cool white stucco rooms, her feet clattering on the polished wooden floors, as she snapped pictures and took notes, she thought about the piece of paper, still in her purse, that he had given her. Should she follow the directions anyway and see where they led her? Probably they were as useless as everything else the young man had given her, they would lead her into a maze that would take her to the fish stalls or back to her hotel. But time was running out. Just ten more days, ten days until she had to go back, and she was no closer to the secret of the rebels. Maybe she should follow the directions after all.

She got back to the hotel late in the afternoon, hot and tired and hungry. The young man was standing in the marble portico. She tried to brush past him but he stopped her. "Why were you not at the interview this morning?" he asked.

She looked at him in disbelief. "The interview?" she said.

"The man's dead. How the hell could I have interviewed him? I mean, I know you don't read the papers—hell, you probably don't ever have newspapers, just that poetry crap—but don't you at least listen to the radio? They got him last night."

He drew himself up. He looked offended, mortally wounded, and at the same time faintly comic. She saw for the first time that he was trying to grow a mustache. "We," he said, gesturing grandly, "are a nation of poets. That is why we read poetry instead of newspaper. For news we—"

"You read poetry?" she said. All her anger was spilling out now; the slightest word from him could infuriate her. How dare he make a fool of her? "I'd like to see that. There's ninety percent illiteracy in this country, did you know that?"

"Those who can read read the poems to us," he said. "And then we make up new poems. In our villages, late at night, after the planting has been done. We have no television. Television makes you lazy and stupid. I would have invited you to my village, to hear the poems. But no longer. You have not followed my directions."

"I didn't follow your directions because the man was dead," she said. "Can't you understand that? Can't you get that through your head? Dead. There wouldn't have been much of an interview."

He was looking offended again. "Death is different in this country," he said.

"Oh, I see," she said. "You don't have television and you don't have death. That's very clever. Someday you should tell me just how you—"

"He will be there again tomorrow," the young man said, and walked away.

She felt faintly ridiculous, but she followed the directions he had given her the next day. She turned left at the statue, right at the building gutted by fire, left again at the large intersection. Maybe what the young man had been trying to tell her was that Cumaq was still alive, that he had somehow survived the shooting in the Old Quarter. But every major radio station, including those with Communist leanings, had reported Cumaq's death. Well, maybe the Communists wanted everyone to think he was dead. But then why were they giving her this interview?

The directions brought her to an old, sagging three-story building. The map in the guidebook had lost her three turns back: according to the guidebook the street she was standing on didn't exist. But as near as she could tell she was nowhere near the Old Quarter. She shrugged and started up the wooden steps to the building. A board creaked ominously beneath her.

She knocked on the door, knocked again when no one came. The door opened. She was not at all surprised to see the young man from the airport. Here's where he beats me up and takes my traveler's checks, she thought, but he motioned her in with broad gestures, grinning widely.

"Ah, come in, come in," he said. "It is important to be in the right place, no? Not in the wrong place."

She couldn't think of any answer to this and shrugged instead. "Where is he?" she asked, stepping inside and trying to adjust her eyes to the dim light.

"He is here," he said. "Right in front of you."

Now she could see another man in a chair, and two men standing close behind him. She took a few steps forward. The man in the chair looked like all the pictures of Cumaq she had ever seen, the neat beard, the long eyelashes. Her heart started to beat faster and she ignored the peeling paint and spiderwebs on the walls, the boarded-over windows, the plaster missing from the ceiling. She would get her scoop after all, and it was better than she ever thought it would be.

The young man introduced her to Cumaq in Lurqazi. "How did you survive the shooting in the Old Quarter?" she asked the man in the chair.

Cumaq turned his head toward her. He was wearing the same earring as the young man and the taxi driver at the airport, a gold five-pointed star. "He does not speak English," the young man said. "I will translate." He said something to Cumaq and Cumaq answered him.

"He says," the young man said, "that he did not survive. That he came back from the dead to be with us."

"But how?" she asked. Her frustration returned. The young man could be making up anything, anything at all. The man in the chair had no wounds that she could see.

Could he be an imposter, not Cumaq after all? "What do you mean by coming back from the dead? I thought you people were Marxists. I thought you didn't believe in life after death, things like that."

"We are mystical Marxists," the young man translated.

This was ridiculous. Suddenly she remembered her first travel assignment, covering the centenary of Karl Marx's death. She had gone to Marx's grave in Highgate Cemetery in London and taken the pictures of the solemn group of Chinese standing around the grave. A week later she had gone back, and the Chinese group—the same people? different people? the same uniforms, anyway—was still there. Now she imagined the group standing back, horrified, as a sound came from the tomb, the sound of Marx turning in his grave. "What on earth is a mystical Marxist?"

The man in the chair said two words. "Magicians," the young man said. "Wizards."

She was not getting anywhere following this line of questioning. "Are the Russians giving you arms?" she asked. "Can you at least tell me that?"

"What is necessary comes to us," the young man said after Cumaq had finished.

That sounded so much like something the young man would have said on his own that she couldn't believe he was translating Cumaq faithfully. "But what is necessary comes . . . from the Russians?"she asked. She waited for the young man to translate.

Cumaq shrugged.

She sighed. "Can I take a picture?" she asked. "Show the world you're still alive?"

"No," the young man said. "No pictures."

An hour later she was still not sure if she had a story. Cumaq—if it really was Cumaq—spoke for most of that time, mixing Marxist rhetoric about the poor downtrodden masses with a vague, almost fatalistic belief that the world was working on his side. "You see," he said, "it is as Marx said. Our victory is inevitable. And our astrologers say the same thing." She wondered what they made of him in Moscow, if he had ever been to Moscow.

"You must go now," the young man said. "He has been on a long journey. He must rest now."

"How about some proof?" she asked. "Some proof that he isn't dead?"

"He spoke to you," the young man said. "That is proof enough, surely."

"No one will believe me," she said. "I can't sell this story anywhere without proof. A picture, or—"

"No," the young man said. "You must leave now."

She sighed and left.

The next day she rented a car and drove to the beaches, took pictures of the white sand, the tropical blue water, the palm trees. The huge airconditioned hotels facing the water were nearly empty, standing like monuments to a forgotten dynasty. In one the elevators didn't run. In another the large plate-glass window in the lobby had been broken and never replaced.

She stayed at one of the hotels and took the car the next day to the ruins of Marmaz. Even here the tourists had stayed away. Only a few were walking through the echoing marble halls, sticking close together like the stunned survivors of a disaster. A man who spoke excellent English was leading a disheartened-looking group of Americans on a tour.

She and the tour finished at the same place, the central chamber with its cracked and empty pool made of white marble. "Tour, miss?" the guide asked her. "The next one starts in half an hour."

"No, thank you," she said. They stood together looking at the pool. "Your English is very good," she said finally.

He laughed. "That's because I'm American," he said. "My name's Charles."

She turned to him in surprise. "How on earth did you end up here?" she asked.

"It's a long story," he said.

"Well, can you tell me—?" she asked.

"Probably not," he said. They both laughed. Ghosts of their laughter came back to them from the marble pool.

"How do people get news around here?" she said. "I mean, the only broadcasts I can find on the radio are foreign, the United States and China, mostly, and what I thought was a newspaper turns out to be poetry, I think . . . ."

He nodded. "Yeah, they're big on poetry here," he said. "They get their news from the cards."

"The—cards?"

"Sure," he said. "Haven't you had half a dozen people try to sell you a deck of cards since you got here? Used to sell them myself for a while. That's their newspaper. And—other things."

She was silent a moment, thinking about the boy who had tried to sell her the deck of cards, the card with Cumaq's picture, the boy shouting after her that he could get newer cards. "So that's it," she said. "It doesn't seem very, well, accurate."

"Not a lot out here is accurate," Charles said. "Sometimes I think accuracy is something invented by the Americans."

"Well, what about—" she hesitated. How much could she tell him without him thinking she was crazy? "Well, someone, a native, told me that death is different in this country. What do you think he meant?"

"Just what he said, I guess," he said. "Lots of things are different here. It's hard to—to pin things down. You have to learn to stop looking for rational explanations."

"I guess I'll never make it here, then," she said. "I'm a journalist. We're always looking for rational explanations."

"Yeah, I know," he said. "It's a hard habit to break."

She did a short interview with him—"How has the shortage of tourists affected your job as a guide to the ruins?"—and then she drove back to the city.

In the next few days she tried to find the shabby three-story building again. It seemed to her that the city was shifting, moving landmarks, growing statues and fountains, swallowing parks and churches. The building had vanished. She showed a taxi driver her directions, and they ended up lost in the city's maze for over two hours.

She went back to the airport, but the young man was gone and no one seemed to remember who he was. The old man who had sold poetry was gone too.

And finally her time in the city was up. She packed her suitcase, read the note from Jeremy one more time, and took her plane back to San Francisco. She tried to read on the plane but thoughts of Jeremy kept intruding. She would see him in three hours, two hours, one hour . . . .

He wasn't at the airport to meet her. For an instant she worried, and then she laughed. He was always so concerned about her safety, so protective. Now that it was her turn to be worried she would show him. She would take a taxi home and wait calmly for him to get back. No doubt there was a logical explanation.

The apartment was dark when she let herself in, and she could see the red light blinking on their answering machine. Six blinks, six calls. For the first time she felt fear catch at her. Where was he?

"Hello, Mrs. Schwartz," the first caller said, an unfamiliar voice. She felt annoyance start to overlay her fear. She had never taken Jeremy's name. Who was this guy that he didn't know that? "This is Dr. Escobar, at the country hospital. Please give me a call. I'm afraid it's urgent."

The doctor again, asking her to call back. Then Jeremy's brother—"Hey, Jer, where the hell are you? You're late for the game." Then a familiar-sounding voice that she realized with horror was hers. But she had tried to call Jeremy *last night*. Hadn't he been home since then? Then the would-be writer—she fast-forwarded over him—and another strange voice. "Mrs. Schwartz? This is Sergeant Pierce. Your next-door neighbor tells me you're away for two weeks. Please call me at the police station when you get back."

With shaking fingers she pressed the buttons on the phone for the police station. Sergeant Pierce wasn't in, and after a long wait they told her. Jeremy had died in a car accident.

She felt nothing. She had known the moment she found herself calling the police and not the hospital.

She called a taxi. She picked up her suitcase and went outside. The minutes passed like glaciers, but finally she saw the lights of a car swing in toward the curb. She ran to the taxi and got in. "To the airport, please," she said.

At the airport she ran to the Cathay Pacific counter. "One ticket to—" Damn. She had forgotten the name of the country. She fumbled through her purse, looking for her passport. "To Amaz, please."

"To where?" the woman behind the counter said.

"Amaz. Here." She showed her the stamp in the book.
"I never heard of it," the woman said.

"I just got back this evening," Monica said. "On Cathay
Pacific. Amaz. In the Far East. Do you want to see my
ticket?"

The woman had backed away a little and Monica realized
she had been shouting. "I'm sorry," the woman said.
"Here's a list of places we fly. See? Amaz is not one of them.
Are you sure it's in the Far East?"

"Of course I'm sure," Monica said. "I just got back this
evening. I told you—"

"I'm sorry," the woman said again. She turned to the next
person in line. "Can I help you?"

Monica moved away. She sat on a wooden bench in the
center of the echoing terminal and watched people get in
line, check their gate number, run for their planes. She was
too late. The magic didn't work this far away. It had been
stupid, anyway, an idea born out of desperation and something the crazy American had said at the ruins. She would
have to face reality, have to face the fact that Jeremy—

A woman walked past her. She was wearing a gold five-
pointed earring in one ear. Monica stood up quickly and
followed her. The woman turned a corner and walked past
a few ticket windows, her heels clicking unnaturally loudly
on the marble floor, and got in line at Mexicana Airlines.
Monica stood behind her. The glass windows behind them
were dark, and the lights of the cars and buses shone
through the windows like strange pearls. "One ticket for
Amaz, please," the woman said, and Monica watched with
renewed hope as the clerk issued her a ticket. Amaz had apparently moved to Latin America. Monica could not bring
herself to see anything very strange in that. "One ticket to
Amaz, please," she said to the clerk, her voice shaking.

The plane left almost immediately. She was very tired.
She leaned back in her seat and tried to sleep. Two sentences looped through her mind, like fragments of a forgotten song. "Death is different in this country." And, "You
have to learn to stop looking for rational explanations." She
tried not to hope too much.

She must have slept, because the next thing she knew
the stewardess was shaking her awake. "We've landed,"

she said.

Monica picked up her suitcase and followed the others out of the plane. The landing field was almost pitch dark, but the heat of the day persisted. She went inside the terminal and had her passport stamped, and then followed the crowd down the narrow corridor.

Jeremy came up to her out of the crowd. She dropped her suitcase and ran to him, put her arms around him, held on to him as if her life depended on it. ●

CLOSE ENCOUNTERS WITH THE DEITY

by *Michael Bishop*

Here's another story by Michael Bishop, whose "The Calling of Paisley Coldpony" appears elsewhere in this anthology. This one was purchased by Gardner Dozois and appeared in the March 1986 issue of IAsfm, *with a striking illustration by Gary Freeman. In it, he takes us to the ends of the universe, and beyond, to witness the strange apotheosis of a man who sets out in search of the Ultimate Mystery . . .*

Everything was set in order ere anything was made.
　　　　　　　　　　　　　　—Juliana of Norwich

So maybe the end is in sight for theoretical physicists if not for theoretical physics.
　　　　　　　　　　　　　　—Stephen Hawking

I

They place the deformed Demetrio Urraza in an iridium-alloy voyager, wish him godspeed, and shoot him through space toward the bright southern-hemisphere star Alpha Piscis Austrini, better known as Fomalhaut.

Urraza is a Chilean theoretical physicist and cosmologist. He is also a devout Catholic of New Reformist upbringing. In his fragile-looking but sturdy ship (funded by a global confederation of astronomy and physics institutes), Urraza will observe part of the multibillion-year process of planetary genesis around the sun whose Arabic name means The Fish's Mouth.

The honor—not to say the folly—of this expedition has come to Urraza for his role in formulating a Grand Unified Theory of the four major forces that structure the physical universe. To date, his equations have resisted every experimental trial to disprove or modify their import; and his reputation worldwide puts him in a gallery of indisputably great physicists including, of course, his immediate predecessors Einstein and Hawking.

Urraza, like Hawking, has had to overcome a physical handicap to do his work. As a result of his mother's daily exposure to radioactive wastes secretly and illegally dumped near Taital, his birthplace, Urraza came from the womb missing part of his small intestine. More important, his body also lacked every extremity but his head, a leg, and one malshaped foot. (His leg and foot the young Demetrio learned to use as most other human beings use their arms and hands.) Had a priest not taken the crippled infant to a doctor in Antofagasta, better than a hundred miles away, and had the doctor not willingly become the child's benefactor, Demetrio Urraza would have died within the week.

Today Urraza enjoys pointing out that his surviving to become a physicist involved a chain of events as unlikely as the fine tuning of a universe in which thinking observers might eventually arise. He is an anomaly, he cheerfully admits, adding that of course life itself is an anomaly.

In a sense, Urraza has won a lottery sponsored by the world's scientific community.

The winning ticket consisted of his publication, less than two decades ago, of the Grand Unified Theory bearing his name, i.e., Urraza's GUT: (In English, this is an ugly—perhaps deplorable—pun that Urraza finds as delightful as humanity's questing sentience in a seemingly disinterested cosmos.) The prize for drawing the winning ticket, now that Demetrio Urraza's GUT has encompassed the centuries-old hunger of theoretical physicists for The Answer, is a one-way trip to Fomalhaut, 22.5 light-years from Earth.

Why Fomalhaut? many have wondered.

Because, eighteen years before the publication of the GUT that most of Urraza's peers agree has put an end to theoretical physics, astronomers detected around Fomalhaut a planetary disk suggesting that the star is sorting out a solar system similar to the one that became our own. Further, although this process—beginning with the creation of the protosun at the system's heart—may take as long as five billion years, Fomalhaut has already advanced beyond the stage at which a blast of flare gas or of scouring ultraviolet has blown the dust in its inner disk out into the transsolar void. In other words, this star is already well on the road to planetary creation and hence—if one has faith—to the oozy birth and chance-directed uncoiling of life.

Conceivably, Earth will have have died before Urraza completes his observations of the process, for, waking for week-long periods between dozens of millennia of self-preserving slumber, he will survive several hundred million years. Humanity, during this time, will either perish utterly or escape its inevitable local holocaust by removing to other parts of the galaxy. Maybe Urraza's fellow human beings, arriving later, will find his voyager and resurrect him to life on a utopian Terra Nueva orbiting Fomalhaut . . . .

II

"This is suicide," Talita Bedoya, the man's New Reformist priest, told him an hour before the workers at the lunar launch station put him in his ship's life-support casket. Father Bedoya was trying, as she had all along, to prevent his departure.

"Nonsense," Urraza replied. "I find suicide—in my own case, at least—as sinful as you do."

"But, Demetrio, you'll never be coming back."

"Pardon me, Father," Urraza said, touching the woman's sleeve with his articulate foot, "but maybe I see myself effecting my own salvation by returning to the stuff out of which the Holy Spirit summoned the entire cosmos."

"Is it suicide to seek salvation? The reverse, Father, exactly the reverse. No one can sidestep death, but I go to Fomalhaut to see and record, not to surrender and die. For God's sake, then, relent and give me your blessing."

"Demetrio, it's simply not in me to do as you wish."

"Then shrive me. Surely, this is the last time I'll be able to oblige myself of the services of a human confessor."

Father Bedoya prepared herself and then reluctantly heard the physicist's confessions. As he had done on several past occasions, he confessed to the sins of detraction, pride, lust, and now that he was setting forth on a voyage requiring him to take most of his nutrients through his veins or in tablet form, gluttony. The night before, he had gorged on genetically synthesized lobster, lamb, and turkey, to the point of deliberately vomiting and beginning again. Although on launch morning, in Talita Bedoya's presence, he did not feel nauseated, he *was* ashamed of himself. Theory is not the only passion of Demetrio Urraza.

III

Outward into the interstellar ocean, the vessel that this man has christened *La Misericordia de la Noche* glides. Urraza, in his control-casket-cum-pivoting-cryonic-berth, has donned the ship with such happy self-extinguishment that he feels himself to be wearing it like a skin. He wakes and sleeps on the outward leg of his trip almost as he would in his modest home near Santiago. He spends a good deal of time plotting quasar-prediction formulae, sending radio messages Earthwards, and listening to the music that he has brought along.

As a whimsical way of connecting to an earlier era of space exploration, Urraza has insisted that *Misericordia* carry duplicates of the recordings hurtled outward aboard the Voyager probes in 1977. Already, then, he has worked on his equations to the sounds of a mariache band; an erupting volcano; Bach's second "Brandenberg Concerto"; traffic noises; a greeting spoken in Amoy ("Friends of space, how are you all? Have you eaten yet? Come visit us if you have time"); frog-and-cricket cacophonies; Chuck Berry's "Johnny B. Goode"; the sweet whisper and suck of a human kiss; and the soulful Cavatina of Beethoven's late string quartet, Opus 130. He has also played grand opera, the eclecticulture mooings of his own day, and some of the eerie Inca Indian flute tunes taught to him by the doctor who saved his life.

Video stimulation—although he could summon almost any image that a connoisseur of either beauty or ugliness could want—the physicist receives only rarely. Such images interfere with his mental picture-making. If ever he chooses to look up from the work at hand, he pivots his control casket to a position giving him an awesome view of the heavens. And feels, despite the tinny voices of his human siblings droning at him over the laser link, like the only human being alive in the cosmos.

"This star-flecked darkness is an unbounded fishbowl, and I'm an insignificant cricket dangling in it for bait."

When listening to music, receiving and sending messages, and plotting equations ceases to amuse him, Urraza reads. For long, self-lost periods, his reading takes him deep into the devotional prose of Saint Augustine, Bernard of Clairvaux, Francis of Assisi, the unnamed English monk who wrote *The Cloud of Unknowing,* Juliana of Norwich, Thomas à Kempis, Francis de Sales, Brother Lawrence, Francois Fénelon, and others. Speculative theology interests him far less than meditative works that feed the hungering faith that he already possesses. Hence, when he swivels his computer screen to call up reading matter, he nearly always prefers the committed ancient and medieval writers to the besieged, grasping-at-straws, and apologetic moderns.

Bait? He, Demetrio Urraza? To catch what?

God, perhaps. For the line in Juliana of Norwich's *Revelations of Divine Love* that Urraza finds himself inwardly rehearsing again and again is *"I saw God in a point."* The implied physics of the woman's claim, asserted not with braggadocio but with awe-stricken humility, enormously pleases *Misericordia's* pilot.

He is grateful to Father Bedoya for advising him to include Mother Julian's little book in his vessel's computer library.

"I saw God in a point."
"The things that He will keep secret, mightily and wisely, He hideth them for love."
"The beholding of Him—this is an high unperceivable prayer."

And so on, insight after insight, until Urraza realizes that the fourteenth-century recluse who penned these thoughts was on a voyage of discovery as devout as his own aboard *La Misericorida de la Noche.* At the same time, however, he understands that this analogy between a medieval female visionary in her anchorage cell and a twenty-first century physicist flying solo to Fomalhaut would befuddle most of his contemporaries. They respect him for the work he has done, but regard the traditional belief system that has sustained him in this work with, at best, smug or uncomprehending tolerance. "Urraza's quirk," they like to call it.

In his life-support casket, the anchorite from Taital smiles in anticipation of the final Gnostic redemption of his malformed body in a universe-ending return to Pure Spirit.

And gleefully mouths, *"I saw God in a point."*

IV

Eighteen months into his journey, El Sol a glimmering diamond to the rear, Urraza activates the equipment that will ease him into cryonic sleep and then maintain him in this state until his voyager has reached its destination a quarter-light-year above the swarming planetary disk of Alpha Piscis Austrini. Hibernation, he terms this condition, for the weather between suns is an uncompromising everlasting winter that only rarely clicks on the wheeling furnace of star formation. Now I lay me down to sleep.

And hears a voice say, *"Thou shalt see thyself that all manner of things shall be well."*

His ship accelerates. Its drive is a laser-pulse engine. With this revolutionary motive force, it makes its jaunt to Fomalhaut in eighty-nine Earth-standard years.

All but a fraction of this time Urraza spends iced in his casket, dreaming cold dreams and praying to the remotest quasars with the glacier edge of consciousness. His every bad dream is a wintermare, but all shall be well, and all manner of things shall be well . . . .

Misericordia calls Urraza from slumber. Groggily, he awakens, disoriented not only by his trip of 22.5 light-years but also by the icy trash piled up at the front of his brain. Recordings and video displays brief him to his whereabouts and purposes, and he rolls in his casket to look "down" with eye and computer-enhanced imaging equipment at the solar system spread out "beneath" him like an immense gauzy target in the void.

Complicating matters is the fact that Fomalhaut, a young white star, has a small partner of spectral type K a few billion miles beyond it. A dark abyss separates this star from the outer edge of the gauzy disk lumbering about The Fish's Mouth. The *size* of this chasm leads the physicist to suppose—as he supposed even before embarking on his journey—that the emerging planetary system is not likely to be significantly perturbed by the yellow companion.

Indeed, the nebulous target spirals around Fomalhaut encourage him to think that in another four hundred million years or so a planet near the star's cooling bull's-eye may acquire an atmosphere, water, lightning-freed carbon and nitrogen compounds, amino acids, enzyme hints, and— most gracious surprise of all surprises—the molecules responsible for life on Earth. To the creatures arising on this world (should they ever look up), the yellow companion will be nothing more than another good-sized light in the sky.

Mother of God, Urraza murmurs. And after many readings eases himself once more into cryonic sleep.

V

Spiraling down, he recollects reading Juliana of Norwich almost a century ago, an illusory time span that seems but "yesterday." Like the anchoress, Urraza never married. Some, looking upon the crippled body that he refused to "improve" with modern prosthetics, thought him physically unsuited to marriage—but the truth is that the siren song of the flesh has always tormented Urraza. At university, he abused himself, whored, and even played the Casanova with women who would have loved him in a higher way, had only he permitted them to.

Eventually, though, he heard a call more powerful than this carnal siren song and resolved to devote himself to the priesthood of theoretical physics, the fellowship of cosmologists. Ever since, he has redirected the energy of sexual desire into the pursuit of incorporeal satisfactions deriving from either his science or his faith. Like Juliana, like the reformed Augustine, like his confessor Talita Bedoya, he has chosen celibacy as the best means of . . . well, of seeing God in a point. Had I married, he thinks, I would not be out here now, for what wife would release her husband to the infidelity of a one-way trip to another star?

And yet he knows that he could never have oned his soul—to use Juliana's terminology—with the cosmos (as he feels that he is now doing) had he remained on Earth, his major accomplishments in physics behind him and nothing ahead but refinements best left to men and women younger and more intellectually elastic than he. A superannuated genius, he knows, is as sad as a faded beauty or an uninhabitable ruin.

But faith may buoy him yet. And when he wakes again, he finds that *Misericordia*'s displays are showing him a time-lapse sequence concentrating two-thousand years of planet-forming activity into a week's worth of kaleidoscopic images. Rocks collide with boulders, orbiting Gilbraltars tailgate whirling Diamondheads and Sugarloafs, the Black Hills bash into the Rockies, the Urals and the Alps play demolition derby with a thousand wheeling Himalayas, and Fomalhaut itself foams and spits, storms and simmers.

Urraza video-records, catalogues, collates, cross-files, prays, and wonders in passing if his species has died out or maybe built a postindustrial Garden of Eden on Earth. Because radio broadcasts from Earth mysteriously ended during his long recent sleep, he has no way either of knowing or of discovering the fate of his species over the past two millennia, but he trusts that extinction, if it actually occurred, was not self-inflicted. It has been a shaky article of faith with him, ever since graduate school in Boston, that his own kind would come to its senses before any irreversible catastrophe befell it—*"All manner of things shall be well"*—but that belief was, has been, and remains harder to sustain than the conviction that "Everything was set in order ere anything was made." Hence, not only the loneliness of being light-years from home preys on Urraza, but also the loneliness of fearing that, even if he and his ship were physically able to retrace their journey, no real home would exist to go back to.

Now I lay me . . .

The chill descends. Urraza winters again in his life-support casket, a corpse laid out for viewing by invisible mourners. His dreams spiral like the coalescing promontories and jagged clifflets of Fomalhaut's protoplanetary disk.

Meanwhile, his dreams are indistinguishable from the actions of the Formalhaut system or the undergirding strength of his faith. They assure him that he will live again.

VI

Another two thousand years go by. Because only the dreaming Urraza is there to count them, they pass in a midge's span. Not long after the pilot has resurrected again, he becomes aware of a stunning interstellar phenomenon five or so light-years beyond the Fomalhaut system. Streams of distorted light flicker palely on one of the voyager's displays, a sprinkle of lambency pattering against his vision. Excited, Urraza understands that he has "sighted" a black hole utterly invisible to astronomers on Earth.

He pivots to figure out how long it will take the laser-pulse engine to carry *Misericordia* from its anchorage above the Fomalhaut system to the singularity. Twenty years, tops. Well, he can do that—making a jest of the matter—in his sleep. Indeed, for a chance to explore such an anomalous heavenly wonder, he would sleep until Doomsday. Fomalhaut and the planets taking shape from its accretion disk be damned; he now intends to visit the black hole—a tiny anomaly with only five or six solar masses—lurking like a hidden trapdoor into nowhere.

All his life has pointed toward this exploration, this visit, and so Urraza programs into the voyager the coordinates that will take him there. Then he drifts off into yet another wintermare, to dream away the years whose passage must finally strand him at the hungry mouth of the singularity. He also programs *Misericordia* to wake him before disaster overwhelms the voyager.

Twenty years later, it does. However, as Urraza's ship rushes toward the maw of this dark sink, every navigational aid in the coal-black skies is bent, blurred, and refracted out of true by the vacuuming forces at the event horizon of the hole.

How could this have occurred? Urraza wonders. He has awakened to close to the singularity, and now he appears doomed to hurtle down to oblivion. He can do nothing to reverse, slow, or abort his fall; and as he approaches the ebony O-gape of the hole, he watches a vast spinning tiara of stars pirouette across the scalp of its event horizon. He sees a mirage of twisted starlight rather than the stars themselves, for the lens of this rotating gravity tunnel has warped and refocused their images into a daunting crown.

Still, some stellar material is actually accompanying him on his fall into the hole. He fully expects *Misericorida* to shudder, shimmy, and, yes, soundlessly collide with spinning chunks of this forced downward migration. Here, several million years too soon, in the prime of his extraterrestrial life, Demetrio Urraza is going to die. Or perhaps, transcend himself.

VII

The gape of the singularity—the mouth of a fish bigger than the primal carp theorized by ancient cosmologists—lifts higher and higher. The maw looms. Swiveling his screens into place, Urraza begins to do math. This is the ecstasy toward which he has directed his life and work; the formulae marching in jaunty ranks across the display terminals, summarizing, predicting, describing, seem to him not only the abstract hieroglyphics of his science but also the priestly polynomials of his faith in the First Mover behind Creation.

In a period of bodily sickness, Juliana of Norwich saw sixteen visions of the suffering Christ, but Urraza sees the Holy Spirit—from Whom all else has issued—in *Misericordia*'s endless descent into the pit. Down the gravity well, downward to revelation. In fact, the physicist realizes that this specific black hole is not only every other black hole that has ever, or will ever, exist but also the original singularity out of which everything that was made was first made. Neither time nor space has meaning herewhen, but Urraza nevertheless understands that, like a hologram, the interior of this gravity sink reproduces and contains the interior of every other . . . .

And so he plummets toward the Point that exploded, the Mind that made it explode, and the meaning that everlastingly abides in the fateful coincidence of the two.

The metal skin of *La Misericordia de la Noche* has long since integrated fully with his own. Urraza, thus perfectly clothed, tumbles into the naked singularity that has seized him. He falls forever through an anomalous medium no longer possessing dimension or duration.

He is being swallowed, but, in an eviternal flash of insight, he knows that he has *always* been "being swallowed." What is happening to him "now" was mandated, arranged, and predestined, with his own enthusiastic complicity, from the "beginning." The light whirling down this gravity maelstrom with him illuminates him inwardly, and by it he "sees" that he has no body to stymie or bedevil him further, and that "now" it is solely his own discrete mind that hurtles beginningwards.

The heretical Christian gnostics believed that each human being has a divine spark, imprisoned in flesh, whose principle yearning is to reunite with the Godhead from which earthly incarnation has estranged it. Urraza wonders—he has "always" wondered—if his disembodied consciousness is going home in a way that *Misericordia,* even with plenty of fuel and time illimitable, could never have managed. He is Adam, All-Man, and he is Jesus Christ, the Godhead, suffering blissfully, and sempiternally, this new passion of being forever torn apart and sucked downward to union.

"If I might suffer more, I would suffer more," Urraza calmly quotes the words of the Savior as He vouchsafed them to Juliana in one of her bloody visions. And his widening mind—his changing consciousness—quotes this squib not from any leftover biological bent for masochism but rather from all the kinds of love anciently signaled by *agape, caritas,* and, given the ecstasy of his passion, even *eros.*

Light falls in upon Urraza. Although this weird herewhen lacks either dimension or duration, the man gets smaller and smaller even as his mind grows larger and more powerful. As his body collapses into a fiery point, his consciousness inflates, acquires spin, and, at one with the Immemorially Cyclical Intention of the Holy Spirit, begins to radiate . . . .

Beyond the event horizon of the black hole that has gobbled Urraza, the universe—by other measures of process than those at work inside this fantastic all-encompassing hole—has long since fallen back on itself. However, some of this fresh radiant energy, a collaboration between God and the representative transhuman mind of Demetrio Urraza, at last escapes the gravity sink compacting all time and matter into the urproton of re-Creation.

And Urraza, subsumed by the Increate, hears their huge bodiless voice command, "Let there be light. Again." ●

—for the students at Clarion '85

NOMANS LAND
by Lucius Shepard

"Nomans Land" was purchased by Gardner Dozois and appeared in the October 1988 issue of IAsfm, *with a series of grisly illustrations by Laura Lakey. It was the most recent in a long string of Shepard stories—more than a dozen sales to* IAsfm *since his debut sale here in 1984—that have made him one of the mainstays of the magazine, as well as one of the most popular new writers to enter SF in a decade or more. Shepard won the John W. Campbell Award in 1985 as the years' Best New Writers, and no year has since gone by without him adorning the final ballot for one major award or another, and often for several. In 1987, he won the Nebula Award for his landmark novella "R & R"—an* IAsfm *story—and in 1988 he picked up a World Fantasy Award for his monumental short-story collection* The Jaguar Hunter. *His first novel was the acclaimed* Green Eyes; *his second the bestselling* Life During Wartime; *he is at work on two more. And we have several more Shepard stories in inventory at* IAsfm. *Born in Lynchberg, Virginia, he now lives somewhere in the wilds of Nantucket.*

Here he explodes a darkness heavy with ancient evil and timeless mystery, a darkness that just might contain the world itself . . .

1

Four miles due south of the Gay Head Lighthouse on Martha's Vineyard lies Nomans Land, an island measuring one mile wide and a mile and a half in length, rising from sand dunes tufted with rank grasses and beach rose on its eastern shore to a cliff of clay and various other sedimentary materials some thirty feet high that faces west toward the Massachusetts coast. Prior to 1940, the island was the site of several small farms, but during World War II, when German submarines began to be sighted along the coastline, the government confiscated the land, removed the inhabitants and erected large concrete bunkers on the beaches from which military observers scanned the sea by day and night for enemy periscopes and conning towers. Following the war, the island was ruled off-limits to civilians and utilized as a target area for bombers and fighters stationed at Otis Air Force Base, a practice that continues, albeit sporadically, to this very day; on winter nights when the din of the tourist season has passed, it is possible to hear the rocket bursts as far away as the island of Nantucket some twenty-five miles to the east. Yet in spite of this, thousands upon thousands of gulls and terns and a lesser number of old squaw ducks—often seen flying in peppery strings against the sunsets—have chosen the island for their nesting place, and as a result it has been designated a National Wildlife Preserve. It may seem peculiar that a wildlife preserve should be subjected to bombing runs and rocket fire; however, the point has been made— and to many conservationists it is a point well taken—that these intermittent attacks do less harm to the avian populace than would the influx of human beings (no matter how high-minded their intentions) that would occur should the island's restricted military status be voided. And so Nomans Land remains isolate, its silence broken only by wind and surf, the mewing of gulls, the occasional barking of seals at sport on the beaches, and the inconsequential noises of the moles and other rodents that tunnel through its soil. All except the newest bomb craters have been filled in with grass and sand, but walking is a difficult chore because much of the land is dimpled rather like the surface of an enormous golf ball, and it is easy to make a misstep. Scrub pine covers most of the island, hiding all but the tallest ribs of the splintered farm buildings, and the sight of these ruins in conjunction with the lonely cries of the birds, the evidences of war and warlike activity, gives the place

an air of desolation wholly in concert with its name. And
as to that name ... could there be some profound significance to the running together of the words "no" and "man,"
to the lack of an apostrophe implying possession? Or is this
merely due to the carelessness of a clerk or a mapmaker?
And even if it is such, does the inadvertency of the nomen-
clature reflect an unconscious knowledge of uncommon
process or event? There are no evil rumors associated with
the island, no legends, no sailors' lies about strange lights
or wild musics issuing from that forlorn shore. But a lack
of legend and rumor in these legended waters, where every
minor shoal is the subject of a dozen supernatural tales,
seems in itself reason for suspicion, for wonderment; and
perhaps a more compelling reason yet for suspicion lies in
the fact that despite the island's curious past, despite the
penchant among New Englanders for collecting and tran-
scribing local histories, not one has come forward to ask the
many questions that might well be asked concerning
Nomans Land, and no human voice exists to give the answers tongue.

2

On the night of October 16, 198-, during the worst storm
of the season, the fishing trawler *Preciosilla,* with its engines dead and wheelhouse afire, was swept through the
Muskeget Channel between Martha's Vineyard and Nantucket, then westward in heavy seas toward Nomans Land.
Four of the ten-man crew had been lost in the explosion that
had ripped apart the engines, and three more had been
washed overboard. As the vessel drew near Nomans Land,
the survivors caught sight of the island silhouetted in a
lightning stroke against churning clouds, and, knowing that
the *Preciosilla* could not long stay afloat, they committed
their souls to God and their bodies to the sea in an attempt
to reach solid ground. One of the three, Pedro Arenal, a
Portuguese man of New Bedford, was carried by the tidal
rip past the island and never seen again. However, the remaining two, Odiberto "Bert" Cisneros, age forty-six, also
Portuguese, and the ship's cook, Jack Tyrell, an Irishman
just entering his thirtieth year, reached shore within fifty
feet of one another and took shelter in the lee of a concrete

bunker, where they sat shivering, too cold and shaken to think, stunned by the thunderous concussions, gazing out at the toiling darkness, at detonations of lightning that illuminated waves peaking higher than circus tents and plumed with phosphorescent sprays.

It was Tyrell, a thin, black-haired man with a sly cast to his sharp features, who had the urge to move inside the bunker, feeling the cold more intensely than Cisneros, who was the better insulated of the pair, being muscular and bandy-legged, with the beginnings of a pop belly, a seamed, swarthy face, and—at the moment—a terrified grimace punctuated by two gold canines. He gave no sign of hearing Tyrell's shouts, and at last Tyrell came to his feet, staggering with the wind, his hair flying, and took hold of Cisneros under his arms. Cisneros let himself be hauled erect, but when he realized that Tyrell was trying to wrestling him inside the bunker, he tore loose from the Irishman's grasp and went stumbling farther down the slope of the dune. To his eyes the bunker, with its pale cement bulk and black slit mouth, had the look of an immense jawbone from which the demented howling of the wind was issuing, and he wanted no part of it. A powerful gust buffeted him, driving him backward, his eyes rolling up toward the sky in time to spot a flash of amber radiance and the sweep of the beam from the Gay Head light crossing the bottoms of the racing clouds. Though he had sailed those waters for twenty years, in his panic he had no recollection of the lighthouse, and the blade of light seemed a portent from hell. He dropped to his knees in the mucky sand and crossed himself, deeper into fear than ever before, shreds of prayers running through his head like tattered distress flags.

Tyrell was tempted to leave him. He had no great love for the Portuguese, none whatsoever for Cisneros, who had twice menaced him with a knife aboard the *Preciosilla*. But their ordeal had welded something of a bond between them, and besides, Cisneros' fear acted to shore Tyrell up. "Damn your ass!" he shouted, fighting through the wind to Cisneros' side. "You stupid piece of shit! Do you want to freeze . . . is that it?" Once again he grappled with Cisneros, hauled him up and began dragging him toward the bunker.

His brush with prayer had left Cisneros resigned to fate. What did it matter how he died, whether blown into the sea or crushed in the jaws of the bunker? At the last moment, as Tyrell pushed him in over the cement lip and into the black maw, his fatalistic resolve eroded and he tried to break free; but strength had drained from his limbs and he toppled in onto the floor. Tyrell crawled in after him, and they huddled together close to the wall. Lightning flashes strobed the interior of the bunker, revealing pocked walls streaked with whitish bird droppings, matted with cobwebs, and more cobwebs spanned the angles of the corners, billowing and tearing loose in the wind. Cisneros shut his eyes, preferring blindness to flickering glimpses of what seemed to him redolent of dungeons and torture chambers. He began to mutter the Stations of the Cross, repeating those consoling words until they had insulated him against the fierce battering of the storm, and before long, shrinking like a child from a confrontation with his fears, he sank into a deep sleep.

Tyrell, too, was afraid, but his fear derived not from the storm or the island, but from the past few hours aboard the *Preciosilla*. He stared into the darkness, seeing there the faces of the dead, the burning wheelhouse pitching like a great mad window inset into the darkness, with the blackened, shriveling figure of the captain erect amid the flames, still clutching the wheel, and the mate, his eyes slits of reflected fire, throwing up his arms like a benighted Christian to welcome the huge talon of ebony water that had plucked him up and borne him down to Hell . . . . Tyrell shook his head, trying to clear it of those nightmarish images. Peeled away his slicker and rubbed at a cramp in his thigh. A shudder passed through his chest and limbs, seeming to liberate all the dammed-up weakness inside him, and he leaned back, resting his head against the wall, feeling distant from the storm, from all that had gone before.

What a bloody mess! he thought.

Still and all, he'd been in worse spots. He was a survivor, and he had survivor's luck. Take the time he, Joe McIlrane, and Pepper Swayze had been trapped by the Brits at Pepper's house, with only one rifle and a hail of bullets shattering vases and pictures on the wall. And then prison. God, hadn't that been a stroke of fortune, to be stuck in the same cell as the best damn break-out artist in the IRA? And the same luck had been working for him in fleeing Ireland, making it to the States and the sweet life, with a nice girl and a clean bed and plenty of time for mucking around and having a few beers in the evening. Of course sooner or later he'd be bound to take up the struggle again. He couldn't be letting others have all the glory of driving the goddamn Brits back to their gloomy little bloat of a kingdom . . . . A violent burst of lightning split open the black moil of the storm, burning afterimages of the bunker walls on Tyrell's eyes, and he let out a squawk.

"Jesus!" he said to the sky. "Are you wanting to kill me?"

Thunder grumbled, the sea boomed.

"Well, fuck you, then."

He tried to force his thoughts back to Ireland, but found that his memories—that was how he related to the lies he'd told so often, as fond, brave memories, inhabiting them with more frequency than he did his actual past—he found that they had ceased to be a comfort. He wondered how much longer the storm would last. Probably no less than a day. Afterward he'd build a fire on the north shore, big enough so they'd notice the smoke at Gay Head. It was for certain *he'd* have to do whatever was necessary, because Cisneros wasn't going to be any help. The bastard had been all nails and sharp edges with a deck beneath him, but just tip him over, give him a shake, and he wasn't worth spit. Well, old Bert was a fortunate soul this night, for he had as companion the Scourge of Belfast, one Jack Tyrell, who never yet had been known to let a brother-in-arms fall untended by the way.

"Easy there, old son," he said, patting Cisneros' shoulder. "I'm ever with you, don't you know."

Bert Cisneros moaned, the world cracked and dazzled, and Jack Tyrell, who once had laughed in the face of the firing squad of dreams, laughed now, believing there was no terror in the entire universe that could withstand the arsenal of his imagination.

3

Cisneros did not so much sleep as fall down the staircase

of his forty-six years, tumbling slowly head over heels, bumping and rolling across the landings, taking long enough at each to register its consequential evils. The man he'd knifed when they'd put into Nantucket during a nor'easter; the friends he'd cheated; the women he'd beaten. He saw his wife, her face purpled and lumped with bruises, tear-stained, clutching the little gold cross that hung from her neck, and for the first time he felt shame. It was a foul dark slant of a life, an inch of time fractioned by violent stupidities, energized by an ego convinced—despite all the evidence against—of its mental superiority, and looking at it in this wan light, he had a sense of relief on passing the final landing and plummeting back to where he had begun, lying curled like a dark pearl in the mouth of a giant oyster, not asleep, but somnolent. He could see the whole island, see it from alternating perspectives and through a lens of perception that transformed each sight into a strange jeweled design upon a black ground: birds with ruby eyes tucked in among the dune grass, which showed as waving silvery cilia, and ghostly pale clouds eddying above, and the shattered timbers of an old ruin edged with an unholy shimmering of green fire amid the winded pines, and jade blue waves marbled with an iridescent circuitry of foam that broke over a cliff to the west, and the wind a whirling gray-green fog. He wondered how he could be lying in the bunker and yet appear to be hovering above different quarters of the island, and then he noticed the thousands of golden wires extending from his body, each connected to some point on the island. It was through these wires, he realized, that his senses were being channeled, allowing him to overlook the place, to inspect every detail. He heard a voice . . . no, two voices. One was muffled, agitated, calling him back to the darkness of life, and he resisted it, listening instead to the second voice, which was soft—more a musical sonority than actual speech—and transmitted a feeling of tranquility and power similar to that he'd experienced as a child when kneeling in church: a feeling he associated with God. He didn't believe that the god speaking to him was the god of his childhood, but he was gratified that his prayers had reached someone's ears, and since to his mind one god was much like another, he had no moral problem with the transference of faith. And when his thoughts began to change, becoming oddly angular and literate, full of grim resolve, when he began to think of himself not as Bert Cisneros but as Quentin Borchard, to see himself as a tall pale man with hawkish features and deep-set eyes shaded by tufted eyebrows, dressed in his Sunday suit of black broadcloth, he did not question this, knowing that God's ways were not his to understand, and surrendered to those thoughts . . .

. . . and found himself walking in a high blue day with mackerel clouds far out to sea, planting each step firmly, squarely, as if intending to leave a clear track. When he reached the edge of the western cliff he took a stand in the knee-deep grass, leaned forward and peered down at the cliff face. With its fissured gray surface, it had the look of an ancient decaying forehead rising from the sea, grooved by harrowing thoughts. The cauldron of waves at its base seemed to pull at him, to lodge a knot of their chill tonnage in his stomach, and he straightened, fixed his eyes on the sunstruck sea, on cobalt swells flowing away to the horizon. He thought it peculiar that he had no pain. It had been the pain gnawing at his intestines that had brought him to this point, and now, as if his decision had proved a cure, he felt calm, translucent, free of affliction. If it had been only that, only pain, he would have seen it to the end; but he could no longer stomach the sight of his illness etching new lines on Martha's face, disfiguring her as hideously as the sea had disfigured the cliff. This was the best way, the moral way. She would never believe him a suicide; she would assume that he had been walking by the cliff, suffered a spasm and lost his footing. She'd have the money from the land, and she was still pretty enough to find a new husband, a new father for the children. Blessedly they were too young to feel the true sting of grief. Oh, they would weep and think of him in Heaven. But time would heal those wounds, and all that he could do for them now was to hasten their healing by dying swiftly. And that would not be as difficult as he'd thought. He was dead already, killed by the force of his commitment. Standing there, he felt walled off from the past, from life, and he thought he could feel the entire island at his back. The cove on the eastern shore where urchins clung to the rocks of a tide pool; the beachvine fettering the north slope, its complex shadows trembling in the breeze; a vole peeking from its tunnel, its black eyes starred like Indian sapphires; the white spiders—unique to the island—that annoyed him with their incessant biting, but wove webs of unsurpassed intricacy among the pines; the terns wheeling and wheeling above the deep. He felt them all summed up in a unity of tension, as if they were a power that stood beside him, joining him in what must be done. He was not a religious man. His pragmatic nature had not allowed him to accept the existence of a hereafter, and he could not accept that possibility now. However, he believed that if there was a god it would be—like the island—an isolate thing capable of absorbing the lesser quantities that came within its sphere, assimilating winds that had touched the tops of Balinese temples and tides that swept past the shores of Tenerife. In a sense the island *had* been his god, the object of his devotion, his labors and hopes, and he felt closer to it now than ever before. He loved the old place, and perhaps that, not some mystical abstraction, was the definition of a god: something labored over and nourished, a thing that through long process of devotion became indistinguishable from its devotee. It seemed his thoughts were being orchestrated by the crashing of the waves and the screams of the gulls into a kind of music, a flight of logic and poetry, and he realized that he had stepped forward, that he was falling. He had an instant of fear, but the shock of impact, the stinging cold of the water, numbed his fear, and he went pinwheeling down in blue-green light, icy light, icy dark, slowly, slowly, into a dream of a storm, into a secret place where others shared the dream, and no man lives, and truth was form, and form was chaos, and chaos was ordered anew.

4

Morning, and the storm held over Nomans Land. Slate-gray waves piled onto the beach, eroding the beach; the clouds blackened and lowered, and the wind flattened the dune grass, keening across the island, driving slants of rain into the mouth of the bunker, stinging Tyrell awake. All his muscles ached, and there was grit in his mouth. He groaned, rubbed a cramp from his thigh, scratched an inflamed spot on his wrist and noticed Cisneros still curled up asleep, his neck and head turtled beneath his slicker, several cobwebs spanning between his legs and the wall. Tyrell hawked, spat, and said, "Hey, Bert! Rise and shine, you filthy spic!"

Cisneros didn't move.

Tyrell reached out, gave his shoulder a nudge, and Cisneros mumbled, but remained asleep.

"Worthless bastard," said Tyrell. "I'm better off without you, anyway. Plucking at your damned rosary and complaining to the saints like an old woman! To hell with you!"

He sucked at the scummy coating on his teeth, glancing around at the bunker. Cobwebs everywhere fettering the pale yellow stone, with dozens of white spiders creeping along the skeins, some suspended like tiny stars on single threads. He felt itchy movement on his calf, let out a squawk and crushed a spider that had climbed up under his jeans. He staggered to his feet, his flesh crawling, and began stamping on spiders that tried to scuttle away into the dark corners. When he was certain that the floor was clear, he stood shivering, hugging himself against the cold and keeping an eye cocked for any spider that might lower from the ceiling.

"Cisneros," he said shakily. "Wake up."

The sleeping man appeared to shudder.

"You want these dancey little fuckers traipsing all over you?" he said, cheered by the sound of his voice. "Fine then, Bert. That's just fine with me, old son. For myself, I've fucking had it. My stomach's empty as a country church on Tuesday midnight, and I'm going to find me an oyster or a dead bird or some damn thing to fill it." He climbed half-out of the bunker mouth, sat perched on the lip turning up the collar of his slicker. "Can I bring back something for you, Bert? No? Well, maybe you'll feel differently after you nap. I'll be checking in on you. Sleep tight, now."

He swung his legs over the lip, sank to his ankles in the sand, then slogged up the face of the dune, stumbling, crawling on all fours to the crest. He got to his feet again, struck full by the wind and the slashing rain, and stared out across a broken ground: tufts of pale green grass sprouting from bowl-shaped depressions, some of them twenty feet wide, and beyond, where the land flattened out, stands of Japanese pine through which he could make out a fresh crater about a hundred feet off. Rising above the pines, near the center of the island, were spears of darkwood, obviously ruins. He started toward them, and something big and dirty white in color flew up from the grass, screeching, its wings flurrying at him, black beak punching the air in front of his face; he shrieked, threw up his arms, swung his fists, fell and went rolling down the dune.

He came to his knees at the bottom of the dune and looked around for the tern. It was nowhere in sight. He must, he realized, have come too near its nest, and he wondered if there were any eggs. Last resort, he thought. Last fucking resort. For one thing, raw eggs were low on his list, and for another, he wasn't eager to tangle with the tern again. He stood, brushed clots of wet sand from his jeans, and set off for the ruins, picking his way among the overgrown craters. The air in the pines was shaded to a greenish gloom, with raindrops beaded like translucent pearls on the tips of the needles; the ground was less broken, but cobwebs were everywhere—the webs of white spiders like those that had infested the bunker. He tore them away, clearing a path, and after a few minutes' walk emerged from the sparse cover into a large clearing centered by the ruins. From the spacing of the standing timbers, the shingles lying amidst the other wreckage, he decided that they must have been part of a barn. And that mass of shattered boards to the right, smashed flat as if by a gigantic fist, that had likely been the main house. He walked over to the ruins, prodded the wreckage with his toe. Glistening dark planks with white brocades of mold, weeds poking up between their overlaps; shredded pieces of tin. He'd been hoping he might find an old store of canned food, but it was apparent there was nothing left that would do him any good.

The clouds frayed overhead, rips of ashen sky showing through for an instant, the rain diminishing; but then they closed in again, lowering, thick slabs of blackish gray like fleshy dead leaves matted together, and the wind gusted in a mournful rush, bending the pines all to one side, then letting them snap back to upright, like a line of tattered green dancers. Tyrell turned, unsure of what course to follow, wondering if he could knock off one of the birds with a stone, and could have sworn he saw someone standing at the edge of the clearing. Someone slender, wearing a hooded black slicker. His heart stuttered, he took a backward step. Then he understood that what he must have seen had been no more than a roughly human shape formed by an artful combination of shadows and the actions of the wind and the textures of discolored needles in a niche between two of the pines. However, a moment later he heard movement, and this time he caught a glimpse of a figure slipping behind a pine truck.

"Is that you, Bert!" he called anxiously, and when there was no response, he called again. "Who's there?"

The rain picked up, spattering off the splintered planks at his feet, blurring his view of the pines, seeming to measure the passage of seconds with the oscillating hiss of drops seething in the pine boughs.

"Hey!" Tyrell shouted. "Hey, who the hell are you?"

Again there was no response, and, unnerved, imagining the presence of some madman or worse, he was about to head back to the bunker, when the figure moved out into the clearing and came toward him with a faltering step. A woman. Strands of whitish blond hair plastered to her forehead. In her late twenties, or maybe a bit younger. She had Nordic features, glacial blue eyes, a strong chin and mouth—a face that while not beautiful had a kind of imposing sensuality. She stopped a foot away, regarding him with a look that was both hopeful and cautious, and made an incompleted gesture with her hand that made him think she had wanted to touch him. "You're from the boat," she said.

"How do you know that?" asked Tyrell, taken aback.

"I saw it burning last night." She brushed stray hairs beneath the hood of the slicker; a raindrop slid down her cheek to her chin. "I tried to get down to the beach last night, but the storm was too fierce. I lost my way. This morning I went to the bunker. I knew if anyone had survived they'd take shelter there." She wiped her face with the back of her hand. "Your friend's still asleep."

"Is he now? Well, he had a hard night." Tyrell blinked at a drop that had trickled into the corner of his right eye. "My name's Jack Tyrell."

"Astrid." She pronounced the name tentatively as if

hesitant about identifying herself.

"And what are you doing here?"

"I was . . . studying. The spiders . . . the white ones. You must have seen them. I'm an entomologist."

"Bugs, is it?"

"Yes, I . . . I was supposed to be picked up, but the storm . . . the boat couldn't get out. My friends . . . they'll be here once it lets up."

Tyrell could understand her timidity—a woman alone in this godforsaken place; but he sensed that her hesitancy was the product of something more than a simple fear of assault, that she was in the grip of some profound uncertainty.

"Maybe," he suggested, "we should go back to the bunker. Get out of the rain."

"No," she said, glancing behind her, to the side, then fixing Tyrell with a wide-eyed stare. "No, I've got a place. It's . . . closer. And there's food if you're hungry."

"God, yes! I'd be eternally grateful for anything you can spare." He flashed her his most winning smile, but it didn't brighten her; she kept darting glances in all directions as if to reassure herself that everything was as usual. He noticed the swell of her breasts beneath the slicker, the flare of her hips, and felt a pang of desire that—with a dose of Catholic guilt, chiding himself for such lustful thoughts— he put from mind. Besides, he told himself, her friends would be coming. Now, if she wanted to get friendly . . . well, that was another story.

"There's no reason to be frightened," he said. "I won't harm you. Now Bert . . . that's my mate. He's a different matter. Beats his wife, he does. And carries a knife." He laughed. "And in spite of that, in spite of being ignorant as sin, the sod thinks he's a bloody genius. Yeah, you best watch yourself with him about. He's a menace even to himself. But I'll keep him in line, never you worry."

Her expression flowed between confusion and astonishment, and then those emotions resolved into a mournful laugh. "Oh, I'm not worried," she said. "I know there's nothing to fear."

5

Cisneros slept on, slipping from dream to dream, dreams

that would have amazed him with their bizarre materials
under any other circumstance, but which he had come to
recognize as part of an intricate and consequential process
that was most natural in its incidence, the underpinnings
of creation itself. All life, he understood, was a dream. This
was something his mother had told him when he was a child,
and he had accepted it as a child's truth, the idea that one's
days were but a fleeting image upon the mirrored pool of
God's imagination; he doubted that his mother had seen it
as other than a pleasant fairy tale. Now he realized that it
was the ultimate truth. Life and dreams were, indeed, one
and the same, and he had been fortunate enough by virtue
of fatigue and terror to dive deeply enough beneath the
surface of sleep so as to reach the source of dreams, the
place from which life derived its impulse and meaning.

Millions upon millions of lives, of dreams, flowed to him
along the golden skeins that held him fast, but with a connoisseur's selectivity he chose to inhabit only those who had
been involved in some way with the island: Indians, farm-
ers, soldiers, civilian observers, and those who, like him, had
come there by chance. He dreamed he was a boy playing
atop the cliff, dropping stones into the boil of water at its
base, lying on his back, the grasses tickling his nose, and
watching clouds so big and white and fat, they looked like
famous souls. Then a young woman came with a man from
Gay Head to take him as her first lover, and he lingered in
that dream, deriving prurient delight from her tremulous-
ness, her pain and pleasure. Then a mad submarine com-
mander who had been stranded by his crew and thought
his craft was gilded with baroque ornamentation like something out of Jules Verne, that it was armed with crystalline
torpedoes containing drugs and music, and believed he had
sailed in secret waters wherein he and the crew visited lost
continents and sported with sea-green women and were
borne to ecstasies of sensibility by the verses of rhapsodies
with beards of kelp and black pearls beneath their tongues.

These dreams were more complicated than the others in
aspect and particularly in their use in playing the game of
the world. Compared to the rest, they were like rooks and
bishops in relation to pawns . . . for an instant he didn't understand where he had gotten that image. He had never

played chess, had no familiarity with the pieces or the moves. But then he realized that, informed by the dreams, he was becoming a new man. All the evil compulsions of his former life were falling away like an old skin; his petty lusts and avarice, all the intemperate qualities of his nature were gradually being subsumed by a contemplative, sensitive character whose parameters were dictated by the contagious sweetness of more civilized souls, and he began to see that there was purpose to this change, that not by accident had he been led to Nomans Land. He was to provide a new turn in the affairs of God, to implement a new conceit. This knowledge dispelled the remnants of his fear, and he gave himself over utterly to the usages of the dreams, eager now to learn not only what deeds he must perform, but at whose agency he was to perform them. He felt he was dwindling, growing insubstantial, becoming merely another dream, and rather than allowing this to unman him, he experienced an intoxicating joy in the act of surrender, in the sense of unity that pervaded him, in the understanding that despite all his human frailty and faults, his sense of destiny and special purpose was soon to be fulfilled, that his sins had been forgiven and he had been chosen to know the lineaments of his God.

6

Set back from the ruins of the old farm, half-hidden in the grayish green shade of the pines, was a small shack with a tin roof . . . probably a tool shed that somehow had survived the years of rockets and foul weather. Its weathered boards were black with dampness, and the roof was half rust. Astrid had done a good job in making a home of the place. A large hotplate—battery-operated; with two burners—and a hurricane lamp were set on a rickety table, and beside them was a litter of scientific equipment: microscope, test tubes, and so forth. The floor had been covered with a carpet of dry grasses, and a supply of canned food was stacked along one wall; the gaps in the boards had been sealed with mud, and a sleeping bag was spread in the corner, with a couple of blankets folded atop it. After a few minutes, with the lamp giving off an unsteady orange glow and the hotplate heating the little space, warming cans of stew, the shack had taken on a cheery air; the sounds of the wind and rain seemed distant and unimportant. Only the cobwebs spanning the rafters struck a contrary note, and when Tyrell, thinking they might be too high for Astrid to reach, asked if she wanted him to beat them down, she said in a dispirited voice that there wasn't any point.

"They'll just come back by morning." She handed him a scorched can of stew, cautioning him to grip it with a rag because it was hot. "They're all over . . . millions of them."

"Yeah, some of 'em were busy making a nest out of ol' Bert." He sat down with his back to the wall, cradling the stew. Watched her sit opposite him. She had taken off the slicker, and proved to be wearing jeans and a heavy white wool sweater. A bit on the skinny side, he thought; but not bad. She caught him staring at her, and he tapped his spoon on the can. "This is good."

She said nothing, continuing to stare, tension in her face.

"Is anything wrong?" he asked.

She gave a start as if her mind had been elsewhere, shrugged, and said, "No."

"Must be something," he said. "You look like a little noise would put you through the roof."

She laughed nervously. "It must be the storm."

"Sure," he said in an arch tone. "That must be it."

She ducked her eyes, stirred her stew.

"Aren't you hungry?" he asked, and had another bite.

"Not very." She glanced up sharply, appeared about to say something else, but kept silent.

He spooned in more stew, chewed. "Tell me about yourself. Where are you from?"

"Woods Hole," she said listlessly.

"Never been there. I'm from New Bedford myself. And before that I was living in Belfast."

He had expected her to make some response, but she just kept on picking at the stew.

"I had to get out of there," he said. "Trouble with the Brits, y'know."

Silence.

"I was with the IRA," he added weakly, his mood hovering between anger at her disinterest and concern that she might not believe him. He decided on hostility. "Am I boring you?"

"In a way," she said. "In other ways . . . no."

"Oh, is that right?" He set down the can. "Perhaps you should enlighten me as to how it is I'm boring you so I can avoid it in the future."

"It's not important," she said.

"Maybe not," he said. "But I've got a notion you're thinking badly of me."

"What if I am?"

"I'd prefer you didn't, that's all. Is it you're swallowing all the bloody Brit propaganda about the IRA? Because if that's it . . ."

"Stop," she said. "Just stop."

"Because if that's it," he went on, "I'm here to tell you it's nothing . . ."

"I don't want to hear it!" Her voice shrilled. "Everything's enough of a lie as it is without you adding to it!"

"Listen to me, now!"

"No," she said. "You listen! You were born in Belfast, but you never had anything to do with the IRA. Three years ago you emigrated to work at your cousin's restaurant in New Bedford, and you've done nothing more notable since than get a local girl pregnant."

For a moment he sat stunned, unable to voice a denial. "How," he said, "how could you know that. I'm never seen you before."

Her chin was trembling. "I've a gift," she said, and gave a despairing laugh.

"You mean you're psychic . . . something like that?"

She nodded.

He caught her wrist, angry, afraid, not wanting her to know his secrets; but she wrenched free and stared at the place where he had held her as if expecting to see a bruise. She looked up at him, and he thought he detected a new fervor in her eyes; he took it for disgust with his lies, and wanted—for a reason he couldn't quite fathom—to repair the damage.

"I'm sorry," he said, wanting to confess everything, to explain that self-deception had sustained him against the guilt he felt on fleeing Belfast. "You see, I was . . . My uncle

was in the IRA. I never felt right that I didn't follow him.
The family . . . he was all they ever talked about. My bloody
uncle Donald. Famous and in jail. But I couldn't take after
Donald. I was afraid . . . that was part of it. But mostly I
just never understood how it was you lifted a gun and killed
a man. I mean, God, I hated the Brits. But I never could
understand how it was you killed. You know what I'm
telling you?"

She said nothing, but he could feel the pressure of her
cold blue eyes.

"Are you listening to me?" he said. "Goddamn it, I'm
talking to you. Are you listening?"

"I am."

"I'm a coward," he said. "I'm not ashamed of it, really.
I was worried what other people might think of me. Donald
was so goddamn famous . . . I didn't want to suffer by comparison, and that's why I've lied. But I'm quite satisfied being a coward. There's nothing wrong with it. If there were
more of us cowards, the world would be a better place." He
held her eyes, trying to read her opinion. "Well?"

"We're all of us frail." She said this with such wistfulness,
he had the idea that she was not likely to judge him, that
nothing he had done for bad or good was of any consequence
to her. And that made him uncomfortable. Without the armor of lies, the motivation and structures of guilt to direct
his conversation, he couldn't think of anything to say. He
picked at a shred of beef with his fork.

"Do you want some more?" she asked.

"Not just yet."

Rain hissed against the shack, a gust of wind shuddered
the boards, and thunder grumbled in the distance. "I should
see about Bert," he said glumly. "He'll be hungry, too."

Astrid put a hand on his arm. "Stay a while longer," she
said. "Just a little while. I've been here alone for so long."

"How long have you been here?"

"Seems like years," she said distractedly.

Tyrell leaned back against the wall, the warmth in his
belly making him feel expansive against his will. "I suppose
Bert can wait for a bit." He gestured at the cobwebbed ceiling. "Why don't you tell me about your tiny friends here?"

Her face froze.

"You said you were studying them, didn't you?"

"That's right," she said, a catch in her voice.

"So . . . what's their story."

She said something he couldn't hear.

"What's that?"

"They're poisonous." she said.

"Poisonous?" He sat up straight, feeling the inflamed spots on his arms and legs. "Shit, I must have half-a-dozen bites! What should I do?"

"Don't worry," she said. "The poison acts quickly. There'll be some hallucinations, probably. But if you've been bitten and you're still alive, then you're immune." She laughed palely. "Like me."

He remember Cisneros. "I've got to get Bert! They were all over him. I . . ." Something in her face stopped him, and a chill point materialized between his shoulderblades, expanded and fanned out across his back. "You were down at the bunker. You said he was sleeping."

"You'd been through so much," she said. "I didn't want to . . . I don't know. Maybe I should have told you. I was confused. I've been here so long with just the birds and spiders . . ." Her chin trembled, and her eyes glistened.

"What happened to him?"

"Your friend wasn't immune."

"What are you saying . . . he's dead?"

"Yes."

"Jesus." Tyrell glanced up to the ceiling, to the star-shaped white spiders crawling along their webs. He remembered talking to Cisneros that morning, nudging him, and the man already half a corpse. Filled with loathing, he jumped to his feet, grabbed a stick from the table top and began swatting at the webs.

"Don't . . . please!" Astrid caught him from behind, got a hand on the stick and wrestled for control of it. She looked terrified, wide-eyed, a nerve twitching in her cheek, and more than her struggles, it was the sight of her face that made him quit.

"What's the matter?" He pushed her away, swung the stick at the webs. "You like the little bastards, is that it?"

"No, it's not that. It's . . ."

He took her by the shoulders, gave her a shake. "Will you

do me a favor? Tell me what it is with you? One second you act like I'm the last man in the world and you've a great inner need for my company, and the next it's like you've heard the beating of leathery wings and the howling of wolves." He shook her again. "There's something not right here. I want you to tell me what's going on."

"Nothing," she said. "Nothing."

"Damn it!" He slapped her. "Tell me!"

"Nothing! Nothing!"

He slapped her a second time.

"It's the truth!" She began to laugh, half to cry, building to hysteria. "Absolutely nothing! I swear it!"

Ashamed of himself, he helped her to sit and put his arm around her, comforting her with muttered assurances. Maybe it *was* loneliness that had gotten to her . . . that and the morbid nature of her studies. She'd probably been stranded here a week or so, and knowing what he did now, he doubted he'd be able to take more than a week on Nomans Land without showing a few cracks. She signed, collapsed against him, nestling beneath his arm, and he was astonished at how settled and solid that little show of trust made him feel. He couldn't recall having felt this way for a very long time—perhaps he never had—and he wondered if it was the fact that he'd been forced into honesty, into confession, that had cleared away the rubble and granted him such a unimpeded view of himself and the world. It seemed that in giving up his defenses, his lies, he had also given up guilt and fear; and now, sitting here with his arm around a strange woman in a strange place, as vulnerable as he had ever been to the assaults of chance, he felt capable of making real choices, ones determined by logic and the heart's desire, and not reactions to something dread, something he wished to forget. His fear, too, had fled, and he could see that fear for him had not been specific, not merely concern for his own life in the political moil of sad Belfast; he had been frightened of everything, of every choice and possibility. And he realized that not only had his fear been based upon falsity, but that everything he had loved as well—women, country, and all—had been emblems of that fear, objects upon which he could pin the flag of his lies and the affectation of morality. Staring at the grain of the

274

weathered boards, as intricate and sharp as printed circuitry, he thought he could see the path ahead. How he would give up his illusory notions of heroism. Find a mild, strong life. Become an ordinary hero. Sacrificing for family, for friends. That was the best you could do. The world was too strong a spell for any single man or idea to break. No matter how passionate your outcry, how forceful your blood and intent, it went on and on in its wicked, convulsed web, spinning nightmares and tragedies. That was the lesson to be learned of Belfast, of all the wild boys and their warring heat. Surrender. Look within yourself for worlds to conquer and principles to overthrow.

He noticed that Astrid's breathing had grown deep and regular, and thinking she was asleep, he started to lower her to a prone position, intending to cover her with a blanket and then rub out the cramp that was developing in his arm. Her eyelids fluttered open, and she tightened her grip around his waist.

"Don't go," she whispered.

"You're asleep," he said.

"No, I'm not . . . I'm just resting."

"Well,"—he chuckled—"maybe you better do your resting in the sleeping bag."

"All right."

She got to her feet sluggishly, went to the sleeping bag and then, her eyes downcast, kicked off her shoes and skinned out of her jeans. That caught him by surprise. He watched her work the jeans past her hips, step out of them with the delicate awkward poise of a crane. Her legs were long and lovely, pale, pale white, and he could see the honey-colored thatch of her pubic hair through the opaque crotch of her panties. His mouth was dry. He looked away, looked back as, instead of getting inside the sleeping bag, she lay down atop it, covering herself with a blanket. Her hips bridged up beneath the blanket, her hands pushed at her thighs, and he knew she was removing her panties. She turned onto her side, facing him. In the shadowy corner her eyes were large and full of lights.

"Come be with me," she said.

The storm slammed a wall of wind against the shack, rain drummed on the roof, and although Tyrell felt in the grasp of a curious morality, put off by Astrid's invitation, because they were strangers and this should not be happening, the fury of the storm moved him to stand. He went over to the table, extinguished the hurricane lamp. The cherry red concentric circles of the hotplate's heating coils floated on the darkness like bizarre haloes. He stripped off his clothing and, shivering, squirmed in beneath the blanket, turning to her as he did. She had pushed her sweater up around her neck, and her breasts rolled and flattened against his chest, warming him. In the dim effusion of light from the hotplate her features were rapt, her eyes half-lidded. He wanted to ask her a question, to understand why this was happening, to make certain that it was nothing low, nothing small, but rather something clean and strong, something to suit the tenor of his cleansed sensibilities; but as she pressed close to him, he knew that it was good. He thought he could feel the whiteness of her limbs staining him, and when he sank into her, he felt the movement as a sweet gravity in his belly, the kind of sensation that comes when you take a tight curve in a fast car and settle back into the straightaway with the whole world pushing you deep into the plush tension of the machine.

"It's been so long," she whispered, holding him immobile, her hands locked around his back. "So long."

He wasn't sure of exactly what she meant, but it seemed true for him as well, it seemed forever since he had felt this perfect immersion, and he hooked his fingers into the plump meat of her hips, grinding her against him, easing deeper, dredging up a soft cry from her throat, and, without understanding anything at all, said, "I know, I know."

Tyrell waked to find the storm unabated. Pine branches scraped the outside of the walls, and the wind was a constant mournful pour off the sea. Dim reddish light fanned up from the hotplate, seeming to diffuse into a granular dust near the ceiling, like powdered rust on black enamel. He was disoriented by the oscillating pitch of the wind, the incessant seething of the rain, and to ground himself in waking he turned to Astrid, letting his left arm fall across her waist. She didn't stir. He peered at her, his eyes adjusting to the darkness, and when he made out her face, his heart was stalled by what he saw. Empty sockets; desiccated strings of tendon cabled across the bare cheekbone; the teeth gaped and the jawbone visible between tatters of yellow skin; hanks of pale hair attached to a parchment scalp. The stink of the grave cloyed in his nostrils; he could feel her clamminess beneath his arm. He let out a shriek, rolled off the sleeping bag and only the dry grasses covering the floorboards, and crouched there, panting, resisting the impulse to give in to fear, trying to persuade himself that he hadn't really seen it.

"Astrid?" he said.

Not a sound.

He fumbled for his jeans, struggled into them. Called her name louder. Nothing. His skin pebbled with gooseflesh. He pulled on his sweater, slipped his feet into wet shoes.

"Astrid!" he said. "Wake up!"

He wanted to kneel beside her, to take a closer look and make sure of what he'd seen, but couldn't work up the courage. He backed away. The corner of the table jabbed his thigh; the hurricane lamp swayed, nearly toppled. He caught it, fumbled on the table for a match. His hands were shaking so badly, he wasted three matches trying to light the lamp, and when the light grew steady, it took all his willpower to look toward the corner and the sleeping bag. He shrieked again and staggered against the door, unable to catch his breath, transfixed by the sight of that horrid deathshead poking from beneath the blanket, sightless eyes focused on a white spider dangling on a single thread just above the face. Then the strand snapped. The spider dropped into one of the empty eye sockets, and for the briefest of instants the eye appeared to twinkle.

Tyrell's control broke. Screaming, he clawed the door open and ran full tilt through the pines, wet branches whipping his face and chest. He burst out into the clearing, stopped beside the wreckage of the main house. Rain slanted hard into his face, soaked the wool of his sweater. He wiped his eyes, started toward the beach, the bunkers, then pulled up, remembering that Cisneros was dead, not knowing in which direction safety lay. The winded pines bent their dark green tips, lightning made a vivid white crack in the massy leaden clouds of the eastern sky, and from the beach came the cannonading of the surf. Suddenly terrified that Astrid had followed him, he wheeled about. Someone was coming toward him from the pines. But it wasn't Astrid. It was Cisneros. Dressed in jeans and a wool hat and a slicker glistening with rain. Smiling.

Tyrell's thoughts were in chaos. He retreated from Cisneros, but as he did he realized that everything Astrid—ghost or whatever she was—had told him must have been a lie. Cisneros wasn't dead. Obviously not. But he couldn't quite believe that, and he continued to retreat, calling out to Cisneros.

"Bert!" he shouted above the wind. "Where you been, Bert?"

"Hello, Jack! What's the problem man?"

"Bert?" Tyrell was still uncertain who and what it was that confronted him. "I left you in the bunker. I was coming back, but I wanted to let you sleep."

"I had a real good sleep," said Cisneros, closing on him. "Nice dreams. What you been doing?"

"Trying to find some food."

"Find any?"

Tyrell's answer died stillborn. His stomach was full—no doubt about that. And if Astrid was a ghost, how could that be? He wiped his eyes clear of rain again, thoroughly befuddled. Cisneros had stopped a few feet away, his image blurred by the rain driving into Tyrell's face.

"You look fucked up, man," said Cisneros. "There's no reason be fucked up. This is a good place."

Tyrell spat out a sardonic laugh. "Oh, right!"

"You having a bad time, man?" Cisneros chuckled. "Just take it easy. Relax. God is here."

"God?" A chill began to map Tyrell's spine; his scrotum tightened, and he blinked away the raindrops, trying to bring Cisneros into clear focus. He felt at the center of a grayish green confusion, a medium without form, without border, the only real think in a vast unreality. "What do you mean . . . 'God'?"

"I'm not talking 'bout Jesus," said Cisneros with another sly chuckle. "Oh no! I'm not talking 'bout Jesus."

"Well what *are* you talking about?"

"It's interesting," said Cisneros. "I wonder if the idea of

God was based on a premonition of what exists here. It's possible, you know. It's obvious there are some outstanding similarities between the laws of karma, certain Christian tenets, and the true process of the—" he sniffed, amused "—the divine."

Cisneros' unnatural fluency and abstract self-absorption disconcerted Tyrell; he'd always been one to put on airs, but because he had nothing intelligent to say, the effect had been ludicrous. Now the effect was a little scary.

The rain intensified, and Cisneros wavered like a mirage. Something was dangling from his hand, swinging back and forth, and peering through the rain. Tyrell saw that it was an eight-pointed star that had been crudely carved from a piece of seashell, holed, and strung on a length of twine.

"What's that?" Tyrell asked.

"Just something I made . . . while I was waiting for you." Cisneros flipped the star high, grabbed it in his fist. "Things have changed for me, Jack. I'm not the man I used to be."

"None of us are," said Tyrell, trying to make light of it and taking a backward step.

"That's true," said Cisneros. "More than that. It's the only truth."

Tyrell noticed for the first time that the rain didn't seem to bother Cisneros: it was trickling into his eyes, yet he never even blinked. He wanted to run, but he didn't know if there was a secure place to hide, and neither did he know what he would be hiding from.

"Tell me about God, Bert," he said, deciding against fear, hoping that this Cisneros' behavior was merely derangement resulting from exposure and fatigue.

"You really want that, Jack? You don't look like the kind of man who cares too much 'bout God. But—" he twirled his little star on its string "—if you want to hear, you come to the right place. 'Cause I'm the man's going to tell everybody 'bout God . . . soon as I get off this island, that's what I'm going to do. Going to preach the truth 'bout the God that is and the world that isn't." His smile seemed the product of absolute serenity. "You understand?"

"Not hardly," said Tyrell, "Explain it to me."

"This world," said Cisneros, waving at the pines, "it's nothing but a dream." He giggled. "Thing is, nobody knows who's doing the dreaming. Nobody 'cept me."

"And who's that?"

"And when I tell everybody." Cisneros went on, ignoring the question, "when I tell 'em nothing's all there is, that anything they do is all right, 'cause there's nothing for anybody to hurt, it's all a dream ... then there's going to be chaos. Maybe it'll be blood and sex and madness. A beautiful chaos of dreams. But maybe it'll be the beginning of a new and glorious possibility. I believe that might just be the case."

Tyrell kept up his bold front. "Is that so, Bert?"

"You don't believe me, do you?"

"Nobody's going to believe you ... an illiterate little Portugee. They'll laugh your ass back to New Bedford."

"Want me to prove it, Jack? They've taught me how to do quite a few tricks. I'm sure I can find one that'll impress you."

"I'd love it. Go ahead ... show me your stuff."

"It'll be my pleasure." Cisneros' smile broadened, displaying his gold teeth; his dark, seamed face looked to have an impish, stylized evil, its detail lost in the streaming rain. Then the face began to pale. "Dreams, Jack. That's all there is. Dreams like me, like you. Like your girlfriend back in the shack."

Tyrell started to ask how he had known about Astrid, but alarm stifled his curiosity, held him motionless and cold. Cisneros was fading, growing vague and indistinct, becoming a ghost in the rain; but his voice remained clear.

"You remember this, Jack, when you think you know something. You know nothing, man. Nothing. You're smoke, you're haze on the water, you're not even real as the dew. And what you feel and what you know is even less than that. Think of yourself as a spark flying up against the darkness, visible for a moment, then gone. But not gone forever, Jack. Gone forever, that's for real things, things that live and die. You're in the wind, a pattern, a shape that what's real calls back now and again to play with, to make new dreams, to amuse itself. You're part of a game, a play."

Cisneros had almost completely disappeared; all that remained of him was a roughly human shape hollowed from the rain, an indistinct opacity against the backdrop of the pines.

"Dreams," came Cisneros' voice, a sonorous whisper rising above the keening of the wind. "Sometimes they're beautiful, Jack. Beautiful and slow and serene."

More lightning in the east, accompanied by a savage crack of thunder.

"But sometimes they're nightmares."

7

How, Cisneros thought, could he have sunk to the depths that he had in his former life? How could he have been such a posturing bully, a tormentor of women and the weak? He supposed that—like most of his friends—he had been enslaved by tradition, by the spiritual and physical meanness of life among the Portuguese of New Bedford. It was for certain that his father's constant abuse of his mother had informed his own behavior, and he had not been able to rise above those origins. Well, now he had been given a chance for redemption ... more, his lifelong desire for knowledge and the skills with which to employ it had been satisfied, and he planned to take full advantage of the opportunity. And in the process of spreading the truth he would make up all the bad times to his wife and children, to everyone whom he had wronged. He, unlike Tyrell, had untapped potential; he was capable of change. He knew how foolish it was to take pride in himself considering his ephemeral nature; but although he was merely a creation, an illusion, that was no excuse to ignore the decencies or to deny his potential. Even if Tyrell were able to accept the way things were, which Cisneros doubted, he would never be able to maintain his humanity; he was not strong, not resilient. It was a pity, but Cisneros had no time to spare on pity. He had a world to teach, to enlighten, and Tyrell's fate was not his concern. Later he'd have another try at talking with him. But for now there was so much to learn, so much to understand. He let himself fade into the dream and the deep places beneath it, where he communed with the trillion forms of the Creator.

8

It was almost twilight, the storm still raging, before Tyrell screwed up the courage to approach the bunker. He was soaked to the skin, his sweater a foul-smelling matte of drenched wool, and he was shaking with cold; yet he stood at the side of the bunker for quite some time, leery of knowing what lay within. Huge slate-colored waves marbled with foam piled in from the sea, crashing explosively on the eroded beach, driving a thin tide to the bunker's lip, then retreating, leaving a slope of tawny sand cut by deep channels; the wind flattened the grass at the crest of the dunes. But despite the ferocity of the elements, Tyrell sensed that the worst of the weather was past, that by morning the sea would be calm and the sky clear and any fire set upon the beach would be noticed by the keeper of the Gay Head lighthouse. One more night, then, and he would be safe. But that one night loomed endlessly before him, and he realized that—if from nothing else—he was in peril from the terrors of his mind. That, he thought now, must be the cause of all he had seen and felt. The trauma of the fire aboard the *Preciosilla,* of the swim to shore . . . these things must have unhinged him in some way, because he was not about to believe in what he had seen. And in order to quell his fears, he had to look inside the bunker, to begin ordering his mind, firming it against the solitude of the night to come.

Finally, steeling himself, he made his way down the slope, sinking to mid-calf with every step in the wet sand. He paused at the corner of the bunker, drawing strength from the power of the sea, filling his chest with its power, its briny smell; then he slogged around the corner and peered in over the lip. He felt relief on seeing Cisneros lying curled up in the shadow of the lip, still wearing his black slicker and jeans, his face turned to the wall.

"Bert!" he shouted. "Wake up!"

Cisneros didn't move; cobwebs bridged between his body and the bunker wall, and more cobwebs formed a linkage between his ankles, his knees. No spiders in sight . . . not on his body, anyway. And not as many as there had been on the fouled walls and ceiling.

"Come on, Bert," he said, with a real wealth of anxiety and pleading in his voice. "Get the fuck up!"

Maybe he *was* dead, Tyrell thought. And what did that say about Astrid? He'd half-talked himself into believing that she hadn't been real. He shouted again, and again there was no response. He drew a breath, held it, leaned in over the lip and poked Cisneros with a forefinger.

The finger sank knuckle-deep into Cisneros' shoulder, and Tyrell felt ticklish movement along its length.

He cried out in shock, fell back. Cisneros' body appeared to ripple, to shift, and as Tyrell watched, it began to break apart, the realistic-looking slicker, the jeans, the seam of swarthy skin visible between the ragged black hair and the slicker's collar, all of this dissolving into a myriad separate white shapes, thousands and thousands of spiders spilling, crawling over one another, proving that the body had been composed of nothing but tiny arachnid forms, a boiling nest of little horrors, a tide of them that scuttled across the floor and fumed toward him over the edge of the lip.

Tyrell screamed and screamed, scrambling away from the bunker, falling, wriggling on his back, then crawling toward the sea, right to the verge, into cold water. He sat up, staring at the bunker. The spiders had not followed him; they were poised on the lip, all in a row, riding one another, a fringe of them several inches thick, and he had the idea that they were watching him, amused by his panic. He got to his feet, gasping, choking on fear, and there was an explosion at his back. He turned just in time to be knocked flat by an enormous breaker that dragged him over the coarse sand of the slope. He scrambled up, coughing up salt water. The mass of spiders was still perched on the lip, still watching him. He started to his right. Stopped. Went to his left. Stopped. A sob loosened in his chest, his eyes filled.

"Oh, Jesus God," he said, singing it out above the pitch of the wind. "Please don't do this!"

A lesser wave broke at his back, sending a flow of chill water to rushing about his knees.

"Please," he said. "I don't want this anymore."

He wished there was someone who would answer, someone to whom he could appeal this thoroughly unfair circumstance. That, he thought, would be his best hope. There was nowhere to run, nowhere to hide. But at last, having no other option, he began to run, giving the bunker a wide berth, pumping his knees, mounting the dune and cresting it, picking his way nimbly through the overgrown craters, through the pines. He came to feel light in running, as if each step might lift him high above the island, even above the storm, and seizing upon this comforting irrationality among all the terrifying irrationalities that ruled over Nomans Land, he thought he might be able to run forever or until he dropped or until something even more irrational happened, something that through terror or pain would free him once and for all from the fear that for so long had ruled over him.

Night, a toiling darkness illuminated by strokes of red lightning that spread down the darkness like cracks in a black and fragile shell, and a flickering orange light was shining beneath the ill-fitting door of Astrid's shack. Tyrell stood in the pines, hugging himself for warmth, his teeth chattering, chilled to the bone. Hallucinations, she'd said. Maybe that had been responsible for all that had happened. Hallucinations brought on by the spiders' venom. If her version of things were accurate—hallucinations. Bert dead—the he had nothing to fear inside the shack. He wanted badly to believe her, because then he could get warm. Warmth seemed the most important quality in all the world, and he realized he was going to have to give it priority very soon or else he was not going to survive. He kept edging nearer to the shack, stopping, listening, hoping to pick up some sign of occupancy and from that sign to gauge the nature of the occupant. But the only sounds were the pissing of the rain in the pine boughs, the moaning of the wind, and the occasional concussion from the sky.

Tyrell crept to the side of the door, peered in through a gap in the boards, but could make out nothing apart from blurred orange light. He could feel the warmth inside, steaming out at him, and its allure drew him to pull the door open. The shack was empty. After a moment's hesitation he ducked inside, closed the door behind him. He stripped off his clothing, wrapped himself in one of the blankets and stood by the hotplate, warming his hands over the coils, standing there until his shaking had stopped. Then he sat down on the sleeping bag, covered himself with a second blanket, and stared blankly at the ceiling, where dozens of white spiders patrolled the intricate strands of their webs. He felt weak in every joint, every extremity, too weak to consider doing anything about the spiders, and he became mesmerized by their delicate movements; there seemed to be patterns involved in their shifting, at the heart of which was the maintenance of a structure, a constant process of adjustment, of equalization. He laughed at himself, *Christ, he was really losing it!* He settled back against the wall, let his eyes close, the light of the hurricane lamp acquired a dim yellowish-orange value through his lids, like the color of a summer sunset, a clean, sweet color, and it seemed he was falling into it, drifting away on a calm breeze that carried him beyond this storm, beyond all storms.

He came awake to find Astrid looking down at him, shrugging out of her slicker. He sat up, tension cabling the muscles in his neck and shoulders, waiting for her to change back into a corpse. But no change occurred. She ran her hands along the sides of her head, pulling the damp heft of her hair into a sleek ponytail.

"I was worried about you," she said. "I didn't know where you'd gone."

He had trouble mustering speech. "I . . . uh . . ." He swallowed. "It was those hallucinations you talked about. I woke up and I saw something that frightened me."

"What did you see?" She kneeled beside him, and he had to restrain himself from scrambling away.

He told her what he'd seen in the shack, in the bunker; once he had finished he laughed nervously and said, "When you said there could be hallucinations, I didn't think you had anything that bad in mind."

She plucked at a wisp of grass, her features cast in a somber expression. "I have to tell you the truth," she said. "I don't suppose it's very important whether or not you believe me. Or maybe it is . . . maybe it's important in some way I don't understand. But I do have to tell you."

He felt something bad coming; a sour cold heaviness seemed to be collecting in his gut, and the weakness in his limbs grew more profound.

"I came here in the summer of 1964," she said. "I . . ." She broke off, reacting to his horrified stare. "I'm not a ghost . . . not in the way you think. Not any more than you are."

"What the hell's that mean?"

"Just listen," she said. "It's going to be very hard for you to believe this, and you won't have a chance of understanding unless you listen carefully and hear me out. All right?"

He nodded, too frightened to move, to do other than listen.

"I came here in '64," she continued. "To study the spiders. I'd heard about them from a botanist who'd spent some time on the island, and I'd seen a specimen. That was enough to convince me that we were dealing with an entirely new sub-species and not just a variant. Their poison, in particular, fascinated me. It incorporated an incredibly complex DNA . . . Do you know what that is? DNA?"

"I've a fair idea," he said.

"Okay," She put her hand to her brow, pinched the bridge of her nose, a gesture—it seem to Tyrell—of weariness. "God, there's so much to tell!"

This sign of weakness on her part boosted his confidence. "Go ahead. We've got all night."

"At least that," she said; she drew a breath, let it sigh out. "Aside from the DNA, I found what appeared to be fragments of human RNA in the poison." She looked at him questioningly.

"Something to do with memory, storing memory or something . . . is that right?"

"Near enough."

Wind curled in beneath the door to rustle the dry grasses carpeting the floor; the flame of the hurricane lamp flickered, brightened, and a tide of orange light momentarily eroded the edge of the shadows on the walls. The rain had let up to a drizzle, and the thunder had quit altogether; the storm, Tyrell realized, was nearing its end. For some reason this made his anxious. He was not feeling very well. He kept wishing for something solid, some edifice of thought, to hang onto; but there was nothing within reach, and this caused him even more anxiety. He tried to focus on Astrid's words.

"Anyway," she went on, "after a week or so I ran up against some pretty frightening questions. The poison, I'd discovered, was unbelievably potent. I figured that death would follow within seconds of a bite. Yet I'd been bitten many times and I was still alive. And I couldn't understand how the spiders had been isolated on the island. Surely, I thought, they must have been carried off on the boats that had landed here over the years ever since the Indians occupied the land. And if that had been the case, given their hardiness, their breeding capacity, there wouldn't be too many people left alive. Without a sophisticated technology, there was no way an antidote could have been produced. The poison was extremely complex." Another sigh. "Then I began having dreams."

Tyrell remembered Cisneros, his ravings. "What kind of dreams?"

"They weren't dreams, they were experiences of other lives. Men, women, children. All from different era, some of them Indian lives from pre-colonial times. None earlier than that. It wasn't that I was watching them. I was inside their heads, living their days and nights. And it was from these dreams that I began to understand the truth, that the spiders *had* been transported off-island . . . a long, long time ago. They'd been carried to the mainland, back to Europe on the colonial vessels and then gradually had spread to Asia, Africa. Everywhere. By my estimate their population had come to span the world by the mid-nineteenth century. I very much doubt that humanity survived into the twentieth. Of course what I know of human history belies that . . . that's part of their fabrication. But in reality that last hundred years or so of mankind must have been awful. People dying and dying. The population shrinking to a mere handful of souls who hadn't been bitten."

It took him a long moment to absorb what she had said. "Now wait a minute! We're living proof of . . ."

"No, we're not," she said. "We've not alive. We never were." He tried to interrupt, but she talked over him. "I don't fully understand it. Or perhaps I do. I can't be sure. It's difficult to explain things in human terms, because though the spiders with their poison have managed to ensure a kind of human survival, I have no idea of their motivations . . . or if they even have motivations. This may all be just reflex on their part. Or maybe it's that they've become a unity, intelligent in a way, because of a symbiotic use of our genetic material. A group mind or something of the sort. Maybe the best analogy would be to say . . . Have you heard about the concept of people's personalities being translated into computer software? That's similar to what the spiders have done. Transformed our genetic material into a biological analogue of software." She blew out a sharp breath between her pursed lips. "Sometimes it seems to me that it's all a game to them, a pageant, this continuation of the history of a dead race. The way they appear to attach special significance to this island, and the human creations involved, like you and me, it's as if they develop a fondness for them. They bring them back over and over, and occasionally they'll let them live—" she laughed "—happily. As if they were celebrating us, thanking us for what we've done for them by dying, by giving them a new level of consciousness." She took his hand. "Do you remember asking me why it was that one moment I'd be looking at you with longing, and the next I'd be frightened? It's because I think they mean for us to live happily for a while, and I want it so much, I don't want to lose the chance. Maybe it's only a dream, an illusion. But it feels so good, so strong, to be even this much alive compared to what I've been . . . almost nothing, a flicker of consciousness subsumed into a hive of dreams."

He pulled his hand away from her. "You're fucking crazy!"

"I know that's how it sounds . . . "

"No it doesn't *sound* crazy. It *is* crazy!" He drew up his knees, shifted deeper into the corner; the lamplight fell across his toes, and when he pulled them back into shadow he felt much more secure. "You sit here and tell me that we're the figments of the imagination of a bunch of goddamn spiders, and that they've been carrying out the evolution of human history in this fantasy kingdom they've created . . ."

"Yes, I . . ."

"And you expect me to swallow *that*? Jesus Christ, woman!"

"I'd think," she said stiffly, "that of all people you'd be able to comprehend it . . . what with your living in a fantasy of your own all these years."

"When it comes to fantasy, lady, I can't hold a candle to you."

"It's not so alien as it seems," she said. "Philosophers

have been ... "

He snorted in contempt.

" ... saying more or less the same thing for centuries. Think about it. Didn't your friend say what I have? Didn't he?"

His shock at her knowing what Cisneros had said must have showed on his face, because she laughed.

"How could I have known that?" she said. "Unless his truth had been communicated to me through dreams." Again she took his hand. "You'll understand sooner or later. It's always hard for those of us who're brought to the island to accept. It's like waking up to find you're dreaming. But eventually you become sensitized to what they intend, what their patterns are, their tendencies."

Tyrell shook free of her, his mind whirling. Was everything he'd seen and felt since his arrival a hallucination? That couldn't be right. The hallucination theory, that was *hers* ... no, she'd denied that one when she'd tried to convince him about the spiders. So maybe it *was* right. Maybe all this had been a fever dream, maybe he was laying passed out in the bunker, or maybe even back in his berth aboard the *Preciosilla* ... His thoughts went skittering off into the corners of his brain, hiding like spiders in the convolutions, and he sat empty and unknowing, bewildered by the infinity of confusions accessible to him. Astrid said something, but he refused to listen, certain that whatever she would tell him would only offer more confusion. He could hear his thoughts ticking in secret, little bombs waiting to explode. His heart was ticking, too. The entire world was running on the same pulse, building and building to an explosive moment. He closed his eyes, and the light seemed to be growing brighter, more solid, to pry beneath his lids with thin glowing orange talons.

"Jack! Look at me!"

Oh, no! He remembered what had happened the last time he'd had a look at her.

"Are you all right, Jack?"

Let me be, damn you!

She was very near, her breath warm on his cheek and he couldn't resist taking a peek. That close to him, her face was a touch distorted; but it *was* her face. Strong Scandinavian features framed by hair like white gold. She looked beautiful in her concern, and he didn't trust that. Not one bit.

"Don't leave me, Jack," she said. "You have to understand . . . they've given us a chance to live, for more of a life than anyone else can have. But you have to accept things, you can't go against them. They'll simply . . . stop you. Do you understand?"

"Yes . . . yes, I understand."

He couldn't take his eyes off her, waiting for the smooth skin and icy eyes and white teeth to give way to corruption and poked bone.

"Do you remember earlier?" she asked. "Making love?"

"Uh-huh."

"Make love to me now. I want to feel that way again."

Her face drew closer yet, and he knew what the plan was now. They would wait until he was kissing her to make the change, and he would find himself kissing death, his tongue probing into a joyless void of rotted gums and broken teeth. Revolted, he shoved her hard, sending her back against the table. Her head struck the corner, cutting short her scream, and she fell on her side. He sat there, breathing rapidly, expecting her to get up. Then he noticed the blood miring the back of her pale blond head.

"Astrid!"

He threw off the blankets, crawled over to her, searched for a pulse.

She was dead.

Well, he thought, that proved she was wrong. You had to be alive in order to die.

Didn't you?

He was repelled by his insensitivity, by how casually he could accept the death of this woman with whom he had made love only hours before.

But maybe they *hadn't* made love, maybe . . .

He scrambled to his feet. Time to stop this shit, stop this ridiculous metaphysical merry-go-round. He'd killed a woman. She'd been a lunatic, but he was liable for the act, and he'd damn well better cover his tracks. He struggled into his wet clothes, trying to think; but his thoughts were muddy, circulating with sluggish inefficiency. Then in pull-

ing on his trousers he lurched into the table and nearly over-
turned the lamp. He grabbed it by the handle, held it above
the table a moment. A mad little thought cracked in his
head. Kill two birds with one stone, he would. He wedged
his feet into his shoes, avoiding looking at the body. But
as he shrugged on his slicker, his eyes fell upon it and emotion tightened his chest. A tear leaked down onto his cheek.

"Aw, Jesus!" he said. I didn't mean to."

As if Jesus were listening.

He made promises to God. *Lord,* he said to himself, *get
me out of this. I swear I'll live a clean life. I'll go back to
Ireland, I'll take a stand for God and country.*

And then he chastised himself for his weakness. He'd
done the deed, and he'd have to face up to the consequences.

*Damn! Did every fucking thing you decided about your
life, your morality, sound as feckless and as unattached to
reality as the things he was trying to decide?*

He backed to the door, pushed it open and held the lamp
high. Astrid's body receded into shadow; only her feet were
in the light. He said a prayer for her, for himself. Then he
dashed down the lamp, and as the grass upon the floor burst
into flames, he sprinted out into the darkness.

Within seconds, the entire shack was ablaze, flames snap-
ping, shooting into the starless sky, high and bright enough
that they would surely be seen by the keeper at Gay Head.
Tyrell had become so accustomed to the violence of the
storm that the relative calmness of the night felt unnatural,
inimical. He glanced behind him, expecting some threat to
show itself; but there were only the pines, the faintly stirring dark. When he turned back to the shack, however, the
threat he had feared materialized.

It was a spectacular sight, the flames leaping, wisping
into thin smoke and sparks that shot out into eloquent
curves over the pinetops, and the shack itself a skeleton
with molten knots of fire peeping between the boards ...
so spectacular, in fact, that at first Tyrell didn't notice
movement inside the building. And when he did notice it,
something dark and spindly twisting and rippling behind
a wall of flame, he thought it merely some internal structure
being eaten by the fire. But then that something came to-

ward the door, paused in the doorway, a black streaming figure with fiery hair and stick-thin limbs, reminding him of the captain in the burning wheelhouse of the *Preciosilla*. But he knew this was not the captain. The figure stood for a few seconds without moving; then, with the slow precision of a signalman, it began to wave its arm back and forth, back and forth, each repetition of the gesture charging Tyrell with the voltage of fear. He would have liked to bellow, to scream, to roar, anything to release the tension inside him; but he was enervated, on the verge of collapse, and he managed only a muted squawk. The muscles of his jaw trembled, and his heart seemed to have tripled its rhythm, less beating than quivering in the hollow of his chest.

He was too frightened to turn his back on the burning figure, and he retreated slowly, carefully, feeling behind him, brushing aside clumps of wet needles, dragging his feet so he wouldn't stumble and pitch over into one of the craters. Only after he had put a hundred yards between himself and the shack, its fierce reddish orange glow, like that of a miniature sun fallen from the heavens, casting the pine trunks in stark silhouette . . . only then did he run, breaking free of the pines, climbing to the crest of the dune overlooking the bunker, and there sinking to his knees. Neither exhausted nor out of breath, of strength, but rather totally confused, seeing no point in further flight. He sat cross-legged, watching the amber sweep of the Gay Head light across the bottom of pale scudding clouds, feeling empty, hollow, barely registering the gentle touch of the wind on his face, watching the pitch and roil of the sea, which was still heavy and running high.

"Hello, Jack," said a man's voice to his right.

Nothing could shock Tyrell anymore. He felt a prickle of cold traipse along his neck like the tip-toeing of a spider, but nothing more. He turned his head a quarter of an arc and saw a man standing some ten or twelve feet away. A most unusual man, a man who in outline displayed the short, bandy-legged form of Bert Cisneros, complete to the shape of the wool hat atop his head, but whose substance was the blue darkness of the night sky beset with a sprinkling of white many-pointed stars.

"That you, Bert?" ask Tyrell.

"More or less," said Cisneros. "You know how it is."

"No, I don't Bert. Maybe that's my problem. I don't have a fucking clue about how it is."

"I tried to tell you." Cisneros flung out a starry arm, gesturing inland. "And so did she."

The stars in his body were moving, shifting into strange alignments, like living constellations. It was troubling to see, and Tyrell lowered his eyes to the sand.

"Was that the truth, then?" he asked.

"The truth." Cisneros laughed. "No matter how illusory a species we are, every man's still his own truth. I've heard you say much the same thing, Jack."

"Did I, now? I wonder what I meant by it."

"You'll understand soon enough."

An immense slow wave lifted from the dark, towering over the beach, and came crashing down, its vast tonnage exploding into splinters of white spray. The smell of brine was strong.

"So what's to happen now?" asked Tyrell.

"For you?"

"Yeah, for me."

"I'm afraid you're just not cut out for the next part," said Cisneros. "It sometimes happens that the created prove unsuitable. Not even the creators are infallible."

Tyrell sniffed. "I was ever a disappointment to my mother, too." He was silent a moment, tracing a line in the sand with his forefinger. "I'd like to believe that Astrid's alive somehow . . . that either what you're saying's true, or else that I'm round my fucking twist and none of this is happening."

"Don't worry about it," said Cisneros. "Nothing I tell you is going to be a solid assurance one way or the other. It's not in your nature to accept that from me. But you've done nothing to be ashamed of . . . not really."

"From all you're telling me, Bert, can I assume that given your version of reality is accurate, we still have a bit of free will left to us."

"If you want to call it that. Things are little different from how you always thought they were. The only salient difference is that instead of an unknown mystical creator, there's a knowable, explicable one. Of course in the beginning—"

Cisneros shrugged "—who can say?"

Tyrell glanced at him, then away. "Even if you are an hallucination, you're still an asshole. I never could figure how an ignorant git like yourself could think he knew *anything*. But maybe you do know something now. Whatever, you *are* a changed man, Bert. And I'm not talking about the suit of special effects. Quite erudite, you are. They must have something important in mind for you."

"It's as I told you," said Cisneros. "As I've shown you. I am to instruct with words and miracles. To invest the play with a new spirit. Who knows what the result may be?"

"You sound pretty much in control, Bert. You sure about that? You sure the fucking spiders haven't got something nasty in mind for you? I mean, how come an asshole like you, a real punk . . . how come you get to win the world?"

"God works in mysterious ways."

A broken laugh guttered out between Tyrell's teeth. "I wish I could buy all this crap."

"So do I, Jack. So do I." Cisneros sidled off a couple of feet. "I'm going to leave you now. Things are at an end here, and I can't help you. Perhaps someday we'll meet again. You never know."

"I suppose I should be hoping for that eventually," said Tyrell without taking his eyes from the patch of sand before him. "But tell you truth. I don't hope for it very much."

When he looked up after a minute or so, Cisneros was gone. But he was not alone. Horribly burned, her face melted and blackened, her eyes like shattered opaque crystals, breasts smeared into shapeless masses, bone showing through the crispy meat of her right leg, Astrid was standing where Cisneros had been. Tyrell's gorge rose, his fear returned. But nonetheless he remained sitting on the dunetop. "Go away, damn you," he said.

He heard a horrid wheezing and recognized it for the sound of air passing in and out of charred lungs; the breeze rustled frays of burned skin on her arms. He buried his face in his hands. "Oh, God!" he said. "Just let me be for a little while, all right? Just let me be."

A throaty husk of a noise, speech trying to issue from her throat.

"Ahh!" He pushed himself erect, tripped, rolled down the

face of the dune. He got to one knee, gazed back up to the crest. For a moment he thought she had vanished, but then the Gay Head light flashed across her, etching an image into Tyrell's mind: a female thing with black crusted thighs, her flesh displaying shiny fracture lines like overlapping slabs of anthracite, blind eyes, and bits of papery skin fluttering like hanks of hair from her skull in the fitful wind. The image wouldn't fit inside his head. It kept expanding, forcing out thoughts, until there was no room for anything else, and still it continued to expand, driving a hoarse cry out of his chest, sending him staggering toward the edge of the shore.

He couldn't see Astrid, but he felt the push of her vision, and to escape that he waded out into the water, going waist-deep, breasting into a crawl that took him flush into a breaking wave. He dived underwater into the heart of the wave, felt it billow above him, and surfaced in a trough so deep that he could not locate the shore. The water was terribly cold, but after a few seconds his flesh grew numb, and this lack of sensation inspired him. He stroked away from the island, realizing that this way led to death, but no longer caring, no longer willing to suffer the obscenities that sprouted from the darkness of Nomans Land. Another wave lifted above him, and again he dived into its heart, surfacing far beyond it. All around, the sea was peaking into enormous waves whose flowing slopes carried him high, then sent him hurtling into pitch-black valleys. He tried to swim, but it was futile. The weight of his soaked clothing was dragging him under, and his feeble strokes were merely exertion, serving no purpose. Fear overwhelmed him. A cry formed in his throat. But as he went slipping into yet another valley, the momentum of that rushing decline dissipated the cry and he felt exhilarated, like a child on a carnival ride. He went under, came up choking, flailing, spitting salt water. The tilting side of a swell bore him under a second time. He beat his way to the surface, thrusting his head into the air, knowing that he was drowning, that the cold had robbed him of strength, regretting now his decision to flee the island, regretting everything, his lost opportunities, his failures, the loss of fleeting moments of happiness, so few by comparison to the long periods of doldrums that had dominated his life. But as he sank for a last time, a white nail driving itself into the black flesh of the sea at the core of his panic and regret was a profound satisfaction, the knowledge that he was dying, *really* dying, that madness had afflicted him and nothing of what he had undergone on the island had the least reality. That he was a man and not a pale imagined thing. He had a moment of bitterness amidst his fear. What had he done to deserve this? He was no worse than most, no more a coward or charlatan. He didn't think these things as much as he experienced them in a bleak current of emotion, and once that current had exhausted itself, he accepted—along with the unfairness of life—the cold embrace of the sea and sank twisting into the depths, his arms floating up with the grace of a slow dancer, his lungs filling, his mind growing as black and serene as the water surrounding him, dwindling to a point of ebony stillness that seemed to hang in a suspension, a peaceful place between dread and the object of dread in which he perceived the pure thing of his soul, his essential things, touched them, found them strong and unafraid, and then, this necessary business done, he went without reservation about the small and final business of dying.

9

Two nights after being rescued by the Coast Guard from Nomans Land, Bert Cisneros sat at a round table in the Atlantic Cafe on Nantucket, where just that afternoon he had been interviewed by members of a review board assembled by the Maritime Union and by the owners of the *Preciosilla.* He was accompanied by two friends from New Bedford, sailors who were in aspect and temperament much like his former self and were from the fishing vessel *Cariño,* which had put into port during the storm and was undergoing engine repairs. One of these men, Jose Nascimento, after listening to the relation of Cisneros' adventures, asked if this was the story he had told the investigative board.

"No," said Cisneros. "The time wasn't right then to begin the process of illumination."

His companions exchanged looks of concern; they had never heard their friend speak in this manner.

"But now," Cisneros went on, "now the time has come." His gaze swept over the dark, monkeylike faces of his companions. "You don't believe anything I've said, do you?"

"Hey, Bert," said Nascimento. "You been through some rough shit, man."

"That's right," said the second man, Arcoles Gil. "You be well pretty soon. Just take it easy, have another beer."

"Don't you notice a difference in me?" Cisneros asked.

"Well," said Gil, "you talkin' funny, that's for sure."

"It's not just my way of speaking that's changed," said Cisneros. "I've changed totally. When I think back to the man I was, the things I did, particularly to women . . ."

"You gotta hit a woman sometimes, man," said Nascimento. "Shit, Bert. You know that. Sometimes they put you in a position where you ain't got no choice . . . where if you don't hit 'em, they cut off your balls."

Cisneros felt sad for Nasacimento. Looking at his friend was like looking into a mirror that reflected his own foulness, his own brutal stupidity. It would be easy now, given his new perspective, to try and put his old life behind him, to hide his past away and neglect his friends in the interests of complacency and contentment. But Bert Cisneros was a man of honor. It was his duty, his trust, to bring enlightenment to men like Nascimento. To all men.

"When I think back," he said, "despite the fact that I realize my entire life is a beautifully articulated fantasy, I'm sick to my stomach." He paused, thoughtfully rubbing the little eight-pointed star he had brought from the island with the tips of his fingers. "I often wonder if the violent dream the spiders have made of the twentieth century is an accurate reflection of what would have occurred had humanity survived . . . if through some biochemical genius they've managed to predict the twists and turns that would have resulted from human greed and lust. I don't suppose the answer's important any longer. Now that I've been called to inform the world of its insubstantial nature, perhaps things will be returned to a kind of normalcy. Perhaps we'll be able to regain control of our destiny . . . no matter how illusory it is. After all, who can judge the potentials of an illusion? But I really believe they want something good for us."

The men's faces displayed emotions ranging from pity to alarm, and Cisneros laughed. "Come, my friends," he said, getting to his feet. "I'll prove it to you." They remained seated. "Come! I'll prove it in a way you won't be able to deny. I'll show you what the world really looks like. Come on!"

Grudgingly, they followed him through the crowd at the bar to the door of the cafe, and then along the sidewalk until they came to the main street of the town. Buildings of brick and wood frame, cobblestones, a few cars moving, pedestrians looking into hotly lit shop windows. Graceful old trees leaning in over the rooftops.

"What do you see?" Cisneros asked.

Gil and Nascimento once again exchanged concerned glances.

"The street," said Gil with a puzzled expression.

"No," said Cisneros. "You see a dream. I'll show you the *street.*"

He concentrated his will, and within seconds the scene before him rippled, wavered, like something melting in the rain, and in its place, lit by a bone-white full moon, was a ruin. Sad fragments of another time, another dream. The broken shells of a handful of weathered gray houses fettered in ivy, their windows shattered, half-hidden by brush and oak and hawthorne; the cobblestones were thick with moss. Mice scampered in the complex skeins of shadow beneath the boughs. Something long and yellowish brown protruded from a pile of leaves—a human bone. They were probably all around, he realized, the bones of the spiders' last victims. And spanning between limbs of trees, the cross-pieces of windows, everywhere, were veils of cobwebs tenanted by white spiders. After the bustle of the street of dreams, the emptiness of reality was harrowing. The age and solitude of the place made Cisneros feel old, as if the weight of years was a kind of contagion.

"There . . . you see," said Cisneros, turning to his friends.

But they, along with the shops and the cars and the pedestrians, had vanished.

Cisneros was startled but not afraid. Perhaps, he thought, he had misunderstood the discretion of his control; perhaps it was impossible to reveal the totality of the actual without eliminating all observers. Of course, he told himself. That must be it. He tried to reinhabit the world of the dream, but—and this did frighten him—he could not remember how it was done. The knowledge of how to manipulate the materials of the unreal had seemed innate, as uncomplicated and natural a process as breathing, and yet now . . . he ran a little ways forward into the center of the deserted street, panicked, slipping on the damp mossy stones. He tried again, focusing all his will on the act of return, clenching his fists, squeezing his eyes shut. But when he opened them he discovered that nothing had changed. He could sense the forms and tensions of the dream just beyond his range, just out of reach, tantalizing, unattainable. They had tricked him, the spiders had been playing with him, weaving another duplicitous web of his deepest needs and desires. He whirled around, expecting to see some vast trap closing on him; but there were only the shattered buildings, the trees, the desolation, and he realized that the trap had already been sprung. They had raised him high and left him in a place where wit and knowledge had no audience, no meaning, and thus were a torment.

The ruins appeared to be closing down around him, the network of shadows shrinking to encage him. The bone-knob moon with its scatter of ashy markings looked to have lowered and been caught in the fork of two oak limbs, pinning him in place with its strong light. Rustles and skitterings from within the abandoned houses. Something tickled his cheek; he brushed at it, and a spider came away on his hand, perched like an ornate ring on the middle joint of his forefinger. With a shout, he knocked it off. The sound of his fear was swallowed by the silence.

Despair heavied him, and he dropped to his knees, wanting to call upon God, but understanding now the futility of prayer, full of useless comprehensions. Why had they done this? He had believed in them, in the possibility of repentance. He would have entertained them, given new complexity to an old, old game, and they had betrayed him. Or perhaps they had not, perhaps fate was a matter of chemistry. That could be it, he thought. What if all personality and fate were the resolution of biochemical laws that the spiders enacted in their dream of the human world? Perhaps they had merely allowed him to act out the essential directives of his personality? More useless insight. He clasped his hands behind his head, trying to hold in his fear, to stop thought, and yet thinking, thinking, always thinking, imagining now that the last men living in these ruins, in other ruins all over the world, must have felt this same desolation and bewilderment, bereft of love and the possibility of salvation, of the least good thing. He tracked his gaze across the ruins of Nantucket Town, taking in the gaunt oaks and their skeletal shadows, the blind windows, the husks of old grog shops and apothecaries, and feeling in the depths of his soul the hopelessness of his circumstance, he let out a terrified wail, a white plume of a cry that seemed to go up and up, arcing out over the emptiness, carrying with it all the fears and cares and heart of the single, solitary inhabitant of that endless country of failed dreams and broken lives known as Nomans Land.

●

In addition to his role as editor at Isaac Asimov's Science Fiction Magazine *(for which he won the 1988 Hugo Award for Best Professional Editor), Gardner Dozois is an award-winning author: he received Nebula Awards two years in a row, for "The Peacemaker" (1983) and "The Morning Child"(1984). He is also a celebrated anthologist, whose* Best of the Year *collections are generally considered the standard against which all others are judged. He lives in Philadelphia with his wife, his son, and his two cats.*